THE THREE LOVES OF
SEBASTIAN COOPER

ZOË FOLBIGG

Boldwood

First published in Great Britain in 2022 by Boldwood Books Ltd.

Copyright © Zoë Folbigg, 2022

Cover Design by Alice Moore Design

Cover Photography: Shutterstock

A CIP catalogue record for this book is available from the British Library.

Paperback ISBN 978-1-80426-937-4

Large Print ISBN 978-1-80426-933-6

Hardback ISBN 978-1-80426-932-9

Ebook ISBN 978-1-80426-930-5

Kindle ISBN 978-1-80426-931-2

Audio CD ISBN 978-1-80426-938-1

MP3 CD ISBN 978-1-80426-935-0

Digital audio download ISBN 978-1-80426-929-9

Boldwood Books Ltd
23 Bowerdean Street
London SW6 3TN
www.boldwoodbooks.com

For my dad

PART I

1

JUNE 2019, NORTHILL, OXFORDSHIRE

Don't look, don't look...

Clair Cooper kept her eyeline down, towards the carpentry and carpet at the base of the pale stone plinth, framed by a mushroom-coloured curtain with a neat pelmet at the top: twee frills and folds in calming, muted shades that did nothing to reflect the character, the vibrancy, of the man approaching in the coffin on the shoulders of broken giants.

It reminded Clair of a nightmare she used to have when she was a child: a monster she mustn't make eye contact with, or she'd die. The monster had broken into her home and was on the rampage, and Clair and her younger sisters had to hide behind a table. And not open their eyes. Clair would feel that compulsion to do it in her dream; daring to rise and see what the beast looked like, knowing that if she made eye contact, she would never wake up.

Don't look, don't look.

But she always woke, just in time, crying out for her parents and sisters in a raging hot sweat. This was a nightmare Clair couldn't wake from, but she kept her gaze fixed firmly to the join of the plinth and the floor. She couldn't die today, the kids would have no one.

He's coming.

She stared into space, noticing the swirls in the stone at the base of the plinth, trying to filter out the sounds of the coffin's approach; the howls of a wailing woman across the aisle; the gentle tones of Coldplay's 'Yellow'.

The casket creaked faintly against the sound of footsteps, music and cries. Clair had helped Seb's parents choose a coffin made of bamboo lattice and rope. She'd never had the discussion with Seb before: 'What sort of coffin do you want?' Why would she? But she'd decided, along with his parents Martin and Tina, Penelope and Peter, that Seb wouldn't have wanted anything stuffy or heavy. He wouldn't want to leave a negative impact on the planet. So they'd chosen the greenest option the funeral director had. It sounded a bit flimsy now, with Seb approaching in it.

As Clair kept her eyes fixed down, limiting her window to the world, she pulled in her daughter, Millie, under her right arm, and kissed her long hair. Millie curled into her mother, trying to fold teenage limbs and tuck herself inside Clair's armpit, but she was almost as tall as her mother. Under Clair's left arm, her hand resting on his right leg, her son, Jasper, clutched his camera, scrolling through holiday photos on the screen of his digital SLR.

Clair had encouraged Jasper to look at the photos on the screens on the walls on either side of the pleated curtain – a tactful slideshow of an exuberant man with piercing blue eyes, a strong nose, and a broad, mischievous smile – to bring Jasper out of his bubble, help the reality sink in. But he didn't like looking at his dad as a baby; his dad in a cowboy outfit; his dad's graduation photo; his dad on his wedding day – even though he liked how happy his dad and his mum looked. Jasper couldn't remember much about his parents being together.

He didn't like the photos on the big screen because he didn't recognise the man everyone else in the chapel was looking at, tilting their heads to one side as they clutched tissues. Jasper preferred to look down at his own camera roll. *His* dad: playful and cross-eyed as he sucked on a milkshake at the 11th Street Diner in Miami. *His* dad from behind, in shorts, a pale lilac T-shirt and Converse, outside The Carlyle as he walked towards its white deco façade. *His* dad, arm wrapped around Millie, both smiling at the camera as they stopped on the boardwalk to take a picture. It was the last photo Jasper had of his father. It was taken only four weeks ago.

Jasper, feeling the comfort of his mother's hand on his leg, leaned into his grandma on his left and scrolled through the camera roll again. He, too, could hear the coffin approaching. He tried to ignore it. Tried to find another tiny detail in a photo he might have missed. Zooming in, zooming out. Checking every idiosyncrasy of his dad's face. The wholehearted, infectious smile surrounded by sunlit stubble. His brown ruffled hair. The bright blue irises, encircled with black hoops that made his eyes look all the more brighter. His tanned nose and reliable shoulders Jasper wanted to hug and hide in.

No offence to Grandma Guilbert.

Jasper didn't realise his dad was handsome until after he died. There was a lot of detail a nine-year-old noticed: the bony contours of a stygimoloch dinosaur's skull; the lines and circles of an old computer motherboard; the options on the screen of a digital SLR. And there was a lot they didn't.

As the whimpers became more breathless and the wave of cries rolled forward through the crematorium, Clair turned left, then right, to kiss each child's head, then returned her gaze defiantly down. She felt her sisters behind her squeeze a shoulder each;

recognised the quiet cry and coughs of her mother and father next to them.

Don't look, don't look.

In her small window to the world, Clair saw smart shoes edge into sight, doing an awkward dance as the six men who filled them did their best to not drop the casket. It was the most important job of their lives.

Don't drop him.

The feet shuffled, arched, bent, until the bamboo casket, shaped like a sarcophagus and topped with white roses, snap-dragons and stocks, was placed on the stone plinth, and the foot-steps retreated.

Six ashen pallbearers, relieved that that part was over, grateful that a woman in the congregation's cries were taking the focus off them. Still shocked that the life of their most vibrant of comrades had been extinguished.

Clair looked at the anguished dance of a variation of black shoes: Jake's were obviously the Burberry brogues; Uncle Roger's were definitely the shabbiest. Seb's dad, Martin, his shoes must have been the most polished: slightly creased along the toe but shiny as a new penny. Anyway, Clair could tell which shoes were Martin's from the way they turned in. Even his feet looked sad.

Don't look, don't look... you might die.

Did they put shoes on his body?

Don't look, don't look.

Which suit did they use?

Don't look, don't look.

Did Penelope put his wedding ring on him or did she keep it for the kids?

Cries rose as Chris Martin sang about skin and bones.

I hope she didn't have any say in what Seb's wearing.

Clair felt a silent roar of protectiveness and pulled Millie and

Jasper in closer still, as they huddled, shell-shocked and heartbroken.

Jasper finally looked up, away from his camera, and saw the sarcophagus.

'No!' he whispered, a stealthy cry slipping out involuntarily as he looked at the casket.

Eight rows back, Jasper's best friend Arthur shook with his own silent cries, hoping his shared grief would take some of the pain away for his friend.

Millie looked at the coffin fleetingly. The lure of knowing her dad was there, maybe she could see him one last time, made her eyes dart for just a second. The burst of flowers she had chosen with Clair looked beautiful, and Millie started to shake.

'It's OK, darling,' Clair whispered, squeezing Millie in, knowing that it wasn't. Inhaling her children's scents; trying to pull their anguish out of them and into her with each inward breath. She looked up to the pitched roof of the chapel to release her pained breath and exhaled.

Why did I let you go?

* * *

'Please be seated,' said the sympathetic vicar with a greying bob, although Clair and the kids hadn't been able to get out of their chairs.

As the murmuration of mourners lowered onto their seats, Clair glanced back over her shoulder, at a sea of people who had stuck to traditional black, even though they had said to come in anything; colour was what Seb would have wanted. The family, friends, colleagues and cousins who had got there early enough to get a seat; the acquaintances and school parents Seb had befriended over the years, standing at the back, stunned. People were bursting out of the doors of the crematorium beyond a portico, clutching their orders of service and shaking with stifled tears.

Clair's fiancé, Dave, leaned forward from his seat next to Clair's youngest sister, squeezing her shoulder and letting her know he was here for her too. She gave a short smile to let him know she appreciated it as she leaned forward to glance across the aisle, still avoiding looking at the casket.

Don't look, don't look.

On the other side of the aisle Clair saw Uncle Roger and Aunty Dora, sitting next to Seb's father, Martin – a man who had inspired and disappointed Seb in such immense ways – who, pallbearing duty done, lowered into his seat next to his wife and their daughter.

Clair leaned forward a little more, to see if that most anguished of cries, the one that was ensuring it was the loudest, was coming from Seb's half-sister, but she could only see Jake, tall, and imposing, at the end of the line. Seb's best friend and he of the Burberry brogues, repositioning himself in his seat next to his wife, Christine. Jake gave Clair a gentle, heartbroken nod and Clair gave an even smaller one.

And then Clair saw her. A few rows behind Seb's dad. Cheekbones hollow, eyes empty. The woman her husband had left her for.

Clair looked back quickly, to her safe spot, the join of the plinth and the floor, as she waited for Reverend Jane's eulogy to begin. She thought about a boy no one could take away from her – the cheeky boy in biology, almost flirting with the flustered teacher with those eyes; the opportunistic boy sliding his arm around her neck in the dark of the cinema; a vinyl record tucked inside his bomber jacket, waiting to give it to her when the lights came up.

2

CLAIR

October 1994, Guernsey

'"Baby I Love Your Way"? Cool!'

Seb's khaki bomber jacket offset his late summer tan as they came out of the Beau Séjour Leisure Centre, which doubled up as a cinema and a theatre. They had just watched *The Lion King* – a compromise after Seb had wanted to see *Speed* and Clair *Four Weddings and a Funeral*. But *The Lion King* was the only film showing today and they were relieved they both fancied it. Clair had sobbed into Seb's arm as Simba scrambled around for his father, embarrassed she might have left some snot on his shoulder; but he stroked her long ponytail, and wondered whether now might be the time to lean in for a kiss.

No, he thought. *Too opportunistic.*

Even for a fifteen-year-old boy with raging hormones, Seb was good at reading a room.

I'll have a much better chance when I give her the record.

As they came out of the 'Beausie' and walked the cobblestones of the compact capital towards St Peter Port's yachts, motor boats, clippers and ferries on the picturesque harbour, eyes adjusting to the daylight, Seb straightened the vinyl he'd squirrelled away inside his jacket in the cinema – the twelve-inch record had been jabbing at his ribs for two hours – before they stopped on the water's edge so he could give it to Clair. The cover was slightly crumpled in all four corners, so he smoothed it out as he presented it to her proudly.

'What's it for though?' Clair asked in surprise. Her tone came across as curt, even when she was mush inside. It was why people always thought she was more serious than she was.

'It's for you.' Seb grinned.

'That's very sweet of you!'

Clair didn't tell Seb that her dad, Adrian's record player was broken – years of abuse at the hands of Clair and her sisters, Elizabeth and Rachel, playing the *Annie* soundtrack over and over while doing a routine to 'You're Never Fully Dressed Without a Smile'; or divvying up the roles on the *Grease* soundtrack (Clair was always Frenchie; Elizabeth was Rizzo on account of having dark hair and Rachel was Sandy on account of being blonde – three sisters with three different hair colours).

Seb didn't need to know any of that, and it didn't matter. This record was the first love token Clair had ever received and she was going to put it up on her wall like artwork, not play it. She looked at Seb and sighed. She was desperate for him to kiss her, and she rose a little on the balls of her feet. The autumn sky was already darkening – St Peter Port's tall narrow buildings in shades of white, cream, peach and pink were dulled by the looming grey sky. But that didn't matter either. In Clair's heart, a sunbeam broke through and was illuminating just the two of them, in a bubble by the lapping water against the harbour walls.

Clair had warm brown eyes and mid-brown hair that was golden at the tips for all the outdoors activities she and her sisters spent the summer doing: surfing, canoeing, sailing, lacrosse. Winters too. Her cheeks were always flushed pink in summer; red in winter, and her small waist, full bottom and strong legs gave her a sporty, wholesome quality in her jeans, long-sleeved tops and gilets. She'd ditched her comfy walking shoes today though in favour of Elizabeth's brown ankle boots, fleece lined to keep her feet warm. Clair always had cold feet.

Her eyes were pretty but not heart-stopping; her cheeks were flushed but not defined; her mouth was full but not jaw-dropping. Everything about Clair was neatly proportioned and symmetrical: giving her a kindness and neutrality that made her a confidante to everyone. Any prettier and the Mean Girls would have seen her as a threat; any more wholesome and the nerds would have thought she was one of their own. Clair Armitage's warm eyes and clipped tones made her a friendly and no-nonsense ally to everyone.

And boys fancied her. Not the way they fancied Kayleen Hartley (big tits) or Megan Bell (insanely flirty). But in an under-the-radar way. Sebastian Cooper, who Clair sat next to in French, biology, and was on the mixed lacrosse team with, seemed to fancy her. She hadn't realised it until Seb asked her one day in French if she wanted to go to '*un surprise party*' – he joked, in his best French accent – at his house, and suddenly his cocky smile and cheeky eyes went all serious.

* * *

Seb lived in the Forest region of Guernsey, on the south of the island, in a modern glass-box house facing France. His dad, Martin, designed the home in the early eighties, but spent much of his time away from it; travelling with work as an architect, or on the mainland, in the Oxford office he had started with his best friend, Roger, the Curtis of Curtis + Cooper.

Seb's mother, Penelope, was an artist, who loved capturing the bleak days over the Channel the best, painting moody seascapes of the space between her garden and Brittany, which she sold in St Peter Port's small shops and galleries. For someone whose paintings were so grey and foreboding, she had a glorious sense of serenity and calm that befitted her willowy beauty.

'Oh, Sebastian, look at the stars!' she would gush at the night sky.

'Darling, would you like some winter tea?' her soft voice would call if Seb had a cold.

'You can stay at home, just for today...' she would say with a knowing smile, when Seb was pretending to be sick.

His mother would see through all of Seb's charades but still mopped his brow, tended to him, got him soup and kept a peaceful house while Seb read under a blanket on the sofa as Penelope painted in the top-floor studio. The quiet was just disquieting enough for a lively and sociable boy like Seb to want to go back to school the next day. He adored watching his mother paint, but he loved to be around people and the rabble of his friends, Jake, Leo and Woody, even more.

Penelope was warm and welcoming to any friend Seb brought home. He had always assumed it was because he was an only child; that his mum had to go the extra mile to have young voices in the house. Actually, it was that she had a lovely and welcoming heart. She liked her space but she liked other people to enjoy it too. You were always looked after in Penelope's Guilbert Cooper's house. She'd tidy your shoes in a pair by the front door and would brandish a jug of lemonade and a tray of pastries or cookies when boys were playing basketball on the driveway, or on the Amstrad and GameBoy in Seb's room. Penelope would breeze past, offering goods, her short blonde hair dressed in a wrap of a silk scarf that flowed down her back.

* * *

The first time Clair went to Seb's house was for his mother's fortieth birthday party. Martin had organised a surprise and all their island friends came, plus Uncle Roger and his wife, Dora, from the mainland. Roger wasn't really an uncle but he was Seb's father's best friend and business partner – and he had been around for all of Seb's life. He taught Seb to play pool; advised Seb on GCSE options; they spent holidays together. Roger and Dora's daughters, Emily and Zara, were slightly older than Seb, and he referred to them as his English cousins. They were handy when it came to Seb's sex education: they had first told him about periods, kissing, and how a penis actually slotted into a vagina (and not through the belly button as Seb thought). Zara even let Seb try kissing on her, and rated him as good when the flustered twelve-year-old came up for air.

Martin told Seb he could invite five friends to his mother's fortieth birthday party, so he chose his best mates, Jake, Leo and Woody, plus Clair Armitage and her friend Lucia Pereira, who Jake fancied. Seb was doubly pleased when Clair said yes. He was a people pleaser, so he was even happier for Jake, who'd been obsessing about Lucia – who had glossy black hair, broad shoulders and long brown legs – for months, than he was for himself.

The party felt elegant and grown-up to the teens, who ate blinis and mixed bad cocktails at the drinks station. All the grown-ups looked super old, apart from Penelope, who was the youngest in their social circle, having had Seb at twenty-five.

At 10 p.m., Martin gave a heartfelt speech about his beloved 'Penny From Heaven' and everything she had achieved: what an amazing, loving, patient mother she was; what an exceptional oil painter; how her soft voice and calm demeanour could disarm his worst of moods. How their finest creation was their son, Sebastian, who they both adored. Martin was never shy to get emotional after a few brandies and tell people how much he loved them. Everyone said, 'Ahhh,' and looked around the room for Seb – standing at the front of a large circle in their large living room. Clair noticed how handsome his bashful face was; how his eyes sparkled and his cheeks had flushed pink. He ruffled the back of his hair and looked embarrassed, but inside he was bursting with pride. His mum *was* awesome. He agreed with everything his dad said – and he said it so charmingly and confidently, he felt his dad was pretty awesome too; his parents were enviably united. He felt secure. Seb stole a glance at Clair along the line from him, who was smiling for him, and he half wished his other friends weren't there. Leo and Woody were being goons, and Jake and Lucia must have sneaked off to the garden.

'To Penelope!' Martin cheered, as he commanded everyone to raise their champagne flutes and follow him out to the driveway, where a blue Lotus Elan sat with a large silver bow on it.

'There are no motorways on Guernsey!' Roger guffawed.

'Darling!' exclaimed Penelope.

'Cooool!' Seb's friends gasped – except for Jake and Lucia, who had just been making out on the boot of it and had to scram to the bushes.

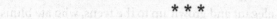

* * *

A week after Penelope's party, Seb had asked Clair to the cinema, on their own. No big family do and people to have to explain. No jibes from Leo and Woody trying to be funny. Just him, Clair, and a twelve-inch of 'Baby I Love Your Way' by Big Mountain between them.

'Thank you,' she said, crisply, liquid brown eyes burning into his bright ones. Hoping her perfunctory tone wouldn't put him off. 'I love it!'

As the song spun in her head, Clair rose a little higher, onto her fleece-warm tiptoes, closed her eyes, and kissed Sebastian Cooper for the very first time.

3

JUNE 2019, NORTHILL, OXFORDSHIRE

She's seen me. Back here.

Desiree Cruz-Campbell didn't miss much with her wide, astute eyes. She had seen Clair's lightning-quick glance – along the front row, back to her and then forward in a flash, as fast as she had registered her. Checking to see who was wailing.

It's not me crying like that.

Checking to see that Desiree was there, in her place. Fourth row back. Away from the kids. She picked a thread of cotton off her lap with her free hand, from her impeccable black leather pencil skirt, and dropped it to the floor.

I so want to talk to them.

The kids Desiree also loved and her heart broke for. The kids she missed terribly. She missed taking Millie shopping, for footless tights and Frappuccinos. She missed talking to her about what was coming up at Sadler's Wells, or, better still, taking her there to see a show. She missed baking with Jasper, even though she wasn't much of a baker and didn't have a sweet tooth; and Jasper's quiet demeanour meant Desiree wasn't sure if he was having fun or not. But she had dug out the scales on the weekends Seb had the kids, so she could bond with him. Baking suited Jasper. The science and mechanics. The silence and precision. And she, Seb and the kids all enjoyed the ritual of sitting down on a Saturday afternoon with a cup of tea and a slice of whatever. Rum cake was her happiest baking memory. She had called Granny for the recipe, and Jasper pretended to be drunk half an hour after polishing it off. It was the most playful Desiree had ever seen him.

I did that. I made him smile.

From her angle now, on the right-hand side of the aisle, four rows back, she couldn't see Jasper's face but she pictured the grief in his small, polite features. She saw Clair's protective arm around Millie, shielding her.

She felt a twitch of the hand she was holding.

'Are you OK, Granny?' Desiree whispered gently, to the shrunken woman sitting next to her, with the lined brown face and huge round glasses, as she squeezed her hand back, released it, and repositioned them both so they were enveloped in a huge shawl. 'Are you cold? Would you like an order of service?'

It was a warm day in early summer, but Granny was often cold and the crematorium must have been air-conditioned with so many people in it.

The stowaway with shrunken bones and a colourful hat with three felt flowers on it took the order of service gratefully from her granddaughter but didn't say a word. She didn't open it for now. Instead, she clutched it in her tiny gloved hand to take home and read later. Desiree's grandmother, Violeta, liked to collect funeral orders of service – and at eighty-nine, she had a lot of them in her bureau. But this was the most harrowing funeral she had been to – after burying her beloved Wilfred ten years ago. But this felt like the most unjust. Sadness coiled around her slowing heart, wringing it and choking it, even though her wrinkled face looked serene and unmoved.

Violeta had wanted to come to pay her respects, despite the mission to get her there; despite the concerns of Desiree's parents, who themselves had wanted to come but were flying back from holiday and couldn't make it. They were half relieved Desiree wouldn't be alone, even though she would have lots of friends there.

'OK, well, be careful, Desi love, and get her home safe...' her mother had said from a sunlounger in Tulum.

'I will, Mum. Promise.'

Desiree had left her flat in Clapham at 7 a.m. to drive to Portsmouth, pick up her granny from her old people's home on the seafront, and drive them to Oxfordshire to make it in time for the funeral at 1 p.m. Violeta had adored Seb since Desiree first brought him to visit her on Spice Island. He was charming, friendly – she was mesmerised by the brightness of his eyes and he loved her wicked sense of humour. Seb had listened intently to stories of Violeta's youth in the Caribbean – she talked as if she had been a swashbuckling pirate, swigging rum and swinging from ship to ship. In truth she had.

The tiny woman, whose sparkling brown eyes had disappeared under the myriad folds of her eyelids, gave a gentle nod and a bewildered smile that couldn't convey she was trying to soak up Desiree's pain. So they sat, united under the shawl – listening to the music come to an end.

Desiree looked to the front again, to the backs of Millie's and Jasper's heads, willing the kids to turn around so she could see their faces. Tell them how loved they were. How happy they had made their father in his last days.

She looked to the bamboo casket and wondered what Seb looked like: she knew all of his sleeping faces but not his dead one, but the thought nearly winded her so she clutched Granny's hand again. She pondered the craziness of the past few weeks. How hard it had been to try to visit him in the chapel of rest – the obstacles and barriers put in place in order that she would give up.

It's just as well.

Seb was such an *alive* man. Despite the frustrations and phone calls from her office in Shoreditch to the funeral parlour in Northill, she'd dropped her usual determination and conceded that perhaps it was for the best. She would rather remember him at his most vibrant. She would rather remember his haunting words, when they last spoke.

She thought back to the conversation she had mulled over a thousand times; she thought about the final time she saw him. She had made him drink a floral cocktail before she hurried to her meeting and he went to catch his flight. She'd looked at him over their small table and thought, even after all that time, how handsome he was. Piercing, flirtatious eyes as blue as the sea off the cliffs of Negril, encircled in a hoop of black. She had contemplated a million times what those eyes might look like, on a child with brown skin like hers. It was a fantasy she hadn't dared articulate. And now it would never happen.

As they drank cocktails in a hotel bar overlooking the Thames, Seb gave off a sense of *liveliness*. There was a chaos and an optimism in him that went against the sadness of their circumstances. She thought about a confession; secrets they both held back, how they didn't matter now. She thought about their final kiss as she got up and left. His eyes looking back at her, as intrigued as they were the day they met.

I wish I could go back.

As the music came to an end, Reverend Jane stepped up to the lectern of the chapel and smiled.

It's too late.

4

CLAIR

May 1997, Guernsey

'Quick, Clair! It's Leo!'

Woody burst into Clair and Seb's huddle on the dance floor, pulling them apart and breaking up their kiss as they moved slowly, like a mirrorball in gentle rotation to 'Wonderwall'.

'Jesus Christ!' Clair snapped, angry from the shock of Woody having made them jump. 'What's he done now?' she groaned.

Seb pulled back and smiled as he ran his fingers through his hair, rolling his eyes as if to say, *What is it this time?*

'He's puking purple *all* over the breakfast room! It's the whitest fucking room in the hotel!'

'All the rooms are white, Woody,' Seb deadpanned.

'The breakfast room was only painted yesterday! My dad is going to go *mental*!'

Woody grabbed Clair by the hand and led her out, her black and red Chinese-style dress hugging her tiny waist and big hips, followed by Seb in a tux and a *don't mind me* look. They weaved from the main dining room, which had been converted into a ballroom/disco, along the corridor to the conservatory where breakfast was to be served in the sunshine. Except the sun didn't shine through the fronds of the palm trees outside it at 1 a.m. The breakfast room was stark and dark. It smelled of fresh paint and vomit.

Woody's parents had bought a wreck of a building on the nearby island of Herm, razed it, and built a pristine hotel not far from the small docking jetty, painting it all white and foolishly agreeing to let Woody hold his eighteenth birthday/end-of-exams party there the weekend before the hotel was due to open.

All their friends and most of their year-group had taken the catamaran at sunset from St Peter Port, their finery getting creased and flecked with saltwater splashes.

Clair had captained her family's weatherworn Bénéteau sailboat, taking Seb, Jake, Lucia, Leo and his girlfriend, Elise, who went to another school but seemed cool, with her. On the journey over, standing at the back of the boat with her hand on the wheel, Clair had looked over the heads of their friends on board, ahead to Seb at the front, sitting on the bow in his new suit, legs dangling as he watched the sun set beyond the silhouette of the hotel ahead; at the pale sandy beaches that skirted the island. The puffins, gannets and storm petrels had already tucked themselves up for the day, and Clair, satin dress accessorised with a life jacket, had looked at Seb's thoughtful face and wondered what he was thinking.

I love him so much.

Clair felt like the luckiest girl in the world. To have fallen in love with Sebastian Cooper; to have lost her virginity and had wonderful, meaningful sex with him. To have finished her A levels and be privileged enough to sail with her friends, the people she adored most in the world after her parents and sisters, to an idyllic island for one last hurrah. Clair had felt so lucky in that moment, she almost hadn't wanted to reach Herm.

'Bloody hell, Leo! What are you doing?' Clair gasped at the boy curled in a ball on the floor. Woody, wearing a checked suit and a busy bow tie to distract from his enormous ears, was almost tearing his hair out. 'Right, help me get him on his side,' Clair commanded, as she and Seb rolled Leo, retching and heaving purple liquid that smelled of onions, aspartame and bile, all over one side of the hexagonal-shaped conservatory room.

'Mind that wall, MIND THAT WALL!' Woody shouted, skinny arms and legs flailing all over the place.

'Urgh!' Seb winced, trying not to inhale the smell, while Clair positioned Leo – away from her dress – to face the skirting board.

'You fucking puke on that wall and—'

'Get a grip, Woody!' Clair scolded. 'Seb, get me some towels from the restaurant toilet. Woody – do you have a bucket?'

Woody looked blank while he tried to think.

'Does anyone know where Elise is?' Clair asked. Leo groaned.

Jake was up in the super-deluxe suite, christening it with Carrie Woodrow, his third shag since Lucia had dumped him when he was sixteen – which Lucia put down to his wandering eye, but actually it was because she fancied girls like Carrie Woodrow more than she fancied Jake. She just hadn't told anyone yet.

Revellers were stopping to revel in Leo and his misfortune. You could always rely on Leo to take things too far, so people stepped over him with a Nelson-Muntz-style 'Haaa haaa!' as they stumbled through the breakfast room on their way to the ballroom, the reception, the back garden and the pool, where head boy, Damian Congreve, was dive-bombing in his tails.

Clair stroked the bone around Leo's sweaty eye sockets, soothing and calming him into a restful foetal pose.

'Elise...' Leo mumbled as his seasick head started to relax a little.

Clair kept her hand on his brow as she looked out of the window panels.

'I'm not sure people should be in the pool, Woody...' she said in a schoolmarm tone, nodding to the splashes rising into view beyond the glass.

'They fucking shouldn't!' he said, through gawkish lips. 'It cost £800 to have it cleaned yesterday! I'm going to have to pay if it needs cleaning again!'

Woody froze, looking like Shaggy from *Scooby-Doo* in a suit, not knowing which fire to fight first.

'Worse still is if someone drowns, Woody,' Clair admonished. 'Go and tell them to get out of the pool. Seb and I can sort Leo...'

As if on cue, Seb came rushing back in with all the hand towels he could carry from the basket in the restaurant toilets – all white of course – and helped Clair use them to mop Leo's brow, his face, and the purple sick on the floor.

'The drugs... *don't*... work...' Leo said labouredly between the retches, which were now dry.

'Drugs?' Clair scowled. 'Jesus, Seb, what's he taken?'

Seb put his hands up as if to say, *I don't know.*

'Snakebite and black, the pussy.' Jake laughed as he walked through the swing doors fresh from the bedroom, Carrie giggling conspiratorially under his arm. 'Want one?' He held up a pint glass to Seb that looked a shade similar to the sick on the floor. Clair saw the twinkle in Seb's eye, the spark of a challenge.

'Don't you dare!' she snapped. 'I am not cleaning up after you too!'

'It's sunstroke...' protested Leo, now crying again in a ball. 'Elise!'

Despite the chaos. Despite knowing she would be scrabbling

around to find an empty bed or sofa on which to sleep with Seb, despite the fact that she knew she would be mucking in and cleaning up an entire hotel in the morning before sailing home, Clair didn't want the night to end. She loved her friends, even the stupid ones. She loved the Channel Islands and the idyll of her life there. She loved Sebastian Cooper. And she knew that when they all went off to university, to York and Oxford and Warwick and Birmingham – to opposite sides of London in her and Seb's cases – they would probably all drift apart. The odds weren't exactly in their favour.

5

JUNE 2019, NORTHILL, OXFORDSHIRE

Who are all these people? Why are they looking at me?

Glancing fleetingly over her shoulder, Noemie Morel saw the burn of two hundred pairs of eyes boring into her skull, or that was what it felt like in the hot front row of the chapel. Her turquoise vest and floaty colour-block skirt – no black for this bohemian woman – encouraged a trickle of sweat to run down the base of her spine, as she hugged her ribs and rocked back and forth. She tried to regulate her breaths with the jingle-jangle chiming of the chains on her wrists and ankles, moving as she moved.

'Doucement, ma chérie... doucement...' her mother said next to her in a low command. *'Respire comme au yoga...'*

The involuntary wails came and went as Noemie gazed at the casket, placed on the plinth in front of her. If she put her hand out she might be able to touch him. Instead, she hugged herself and kept rocking, sometimes looking frantically left and right along the row.

All these people!

People she didn't really know, apart from Seb's father, Martin, and her own mother, Camille, both in the limits of her blurred peripheral vision. Aside from Millie and Jasper, she didn't recognise anyone on the other side of the aisle, the hordes of people behind. She looked down the other end of the row, further along her side, and saw Jake and his wife, Christine, by the window. She hadn't even registered Jake was one of the pallbearers as Martin had sat down next to her; she hadn't realised Christine was sitting alone at the end of the row as she waited for her husband.

He was nice to me.

Noemie had met Jake, Christine and their baby, Axel, once, a couple of months ago, at a BBQ at their house in the Cotswolds over Easter weekend. Jake had been nice: Noemie had liked how tall, warm and handsome he was as he welcomed them with open arms and popped open bottle after bottle of red. But she hadn't liked the way Christine hugged her baby protectively; the way she clearly didn't want to hear Noemie's parenting advice; the way she spoke in her *American accent*; the way she gave Noemie polite smiles and said sweetly that she was figuring it all out, *one day at a time*, shutting Noemie down.

'What does she know, Seb?' Noemie had said in the car on the way back to Northill. 'She's had one baby, I've had four! She thinks she knows better than me?'

Noemie hadn't liked Christine at all.

Miss 'igh and mighty, Noemie thought as she looked along the row and Christine returned a sympathetic smile, her glittering brown eyes filled with tears. Something about Christine's glossy hair and polished make-up, in her tight dress and high heels, made Noemie assume she was an ally of Desiree. Which further added to her mistrust.

At least they didn't bring their ugly kid. If they bring their baby and I can't bring mine...

Noemie's erratic breaths sped up at the thought of her kids not being in their rightful place around her, and she started to hyper-ventilate a little more. She put her palms on her temples.

'*Doucement, Noa... doucement...*'

'It's OK,' mouthed Jake, from against the window as he leaned forward.

Noemie looked at him, sitting in a sharp suit with his arm around his wife, handsome face ashen from the burden of carrying his dead best friend on his shoulders, of the tribute he was preparing to deliver. He met Noemie's eyes and tried to calm her with a nod. So her cries wouldn't further traumatise Millie and Jasper; so the congregation would be able to hear what Reverend Jane was about to say. Noemie looked back through her tears, her mouth open in distress.

He look at me funny. He thinks this is my fault.

Noemie's breathing started to race again.

'*Doucement, ma chérie... doucement...*'

Noemie's stout mother, with silver hair and high cheekbones, tucked a strand of beachy blonde hair behind her daughter's ear as she tried to regulate her cries.

'*Doucement, Noemie... tout ira bien...*'

Noemie tried to ignore Jake and Christine bringing her down. She focused on Martin to her left. He had a presence about him she'd found attractive when she had first met him on Christmas Eve. A presence that made her wonder what kind of a lover he was. He had the same bright eyes as Seb, the same charming smile, only Martin was more ruggedly handsome, more craggy and tanned. His forehead lined with deep creases, made even deeper by grief.

Noemie had sought comfort in Martin's face since Seb died: since he had flown out to help her. Martin had held her when there was no one else to, while he and Jake got down to the practicalities of paperwork and repatriation. He hadn't questioned Noemie too much. He'd let her speak when she was ready. His harrowed face was comforting; although she was so heavily sedated it was all a blur. She couldn't even remember what she had told him.

She looked down at her skirt. Tiered blocks of turquoise, fuchsia and cream. Her mother's hands on her knee. Seb's father's right leg pressing up against her left. She pondered Jake's nod. It wasn't all kindness.

He's shutting me up!

And with that she burst into a loud, curdling cry that even made Reverend Jane look taken aback.

They think I did this!

6

CLAIR

July 1997, London

It was a strange feeling to walk around your father's home, not knowing which kitchen cupboards housed the glasses or how to unlock the little balcony door that looked out onto the Thames. But after Seb and Clair dropped their backpacks onto the bed of the spare room one Tuesday lunchtime in early July, they excitedly looked around the Limehouse flat; opening windows onto the Marina and exploring cupboards to get a gauge of what food they needed to buy.

The flat was like many in the riverside complex in a wharf off Narrow Street: newly built apartments bought by City boys who liked to look at the view of Canary Wharf, to appreciate how much money they made working there. Men who favoured black pleather sofas and enjoyed the trappings of champagne socialism; unwittingly bankrolling murders in Central America through the cocaine they snorted at dinner parties where the food was Fair Trade and organic.

Flat 212 didn't belong to a City boy though – it was the London pied-à-terre of Martin Cooper and a handy base from which Seb and Clair could visit their prospective universities.

If they got the results they needed, Clair would be going to study nursing at Middlesex University, part of the Project 2000 initiative to get more people into the profession; Seb was hoping to get the grades to go to The Bartlett, UCL's prestigious architectural school on Gower Street – for seven years of study so he could follow in his father's footsteps.

Since as long as he could remember, Seb had loved to build. Play-Doh, Duplo, Lego, Meccano. He had wanted to do his school work experience with his dad and Roger at the Curtis + Cooper office in Oxford, but Martin was out of the country that week, and fixed him up with a friend in St Peter Port. After that week Seb loved it even more. He loved drawing, imagining, creating – and when his dad was in Oxford, or London, or *away*, Seb would sit in his study on the top floor of the glass house on the hill overlooking the Channel, and imagine his dad's desk was his own, as his mother painted.

Martin's desk, with its pens, tracing paper and scale rule, looked out towards Jersey; Penelope's view on the other side of the top floor faced the Breton coastline. As a boy, Seb loved to roam between the two workspaces, between the different worlds his parents created: his father's lines of physics, precision and building blocks; his mother's more whimsical strokes.

Seb decided from a young age that he wanted to be an architect like his father. Not only did he love building, but he liked the relia-bility of it, the safety of his dad's hands and sketches. The process. His mum might sell a painting a month; she might sell ten. Seb liked nice things enough to know he wanted a regular, solid income.

Following a career in architecture showed dedication and creativity, two attributes Seb admired in Martin, even though he was often away and he missed him terribly. He knew his father was working on some amazing structure, whether it was a leisure centre in Banbury, a hotel in the Canaries or a housing project in Addis Ababa.

Martin had trained with Roger, and set up the practice with him in Roger's hometown of Oxford in the mid 1980s. He'd commuted from Guernsey to Oxford on a fortnightly rotation – staying in the granny annexe of Roger and Dora's home, or using it as a base for trips, until Dora's parents moved into the annexe in the 1990s, and Martin bought the flat in Limehouse. He believed east London was a great investment: it was getting a makeover with millennium money and it was close to City Airport, connecting him to Guernsey, and a driveable distance to the Curtis + Cooper office on Cowley Road in Oxford. Plus it was a convenient base for Martin, Penelope and Seb to stay for weekend trips to the mainland or ahead of big family holidays out of Gatwick. It was super handy for Seb and his friends when they had been checking out universities.

'It's all a bit... tidy,' Clair noted, looking at the clear surfaces and sparse décor.

'Yeah, he has a cleaner.' Seb nodded, without thinking too much about it.

It wasn't so much that, Clair thought. More the generic artwork that looked as if it had been sold with the apartment in the show-home phase. 'I didn't realise your dad was so anal.'

'You've seen how tidy his corner of the top floor is!' Seb laughed, comparing an architect's space to that of a painter. 'And he's not been here lately – Lanzarote is taking up so much of his time.'

Seb had hoped to overlap with his dad for a few hours in London, but he was working on a luxe sports resort in the Canary Islands. A large consolation was that he and Clair could romp around the flat as freely as they fancied, so he pulled her in for a kiss then went to put on some music.

Seb opened a console cupboard to look for the hi-fi he remembered his dad using last time they had all stayed there. He must have been fifteen or sixteen and they'd been to a family friend's big Greek wedding, first at the Orthodox Church on Moscow Road, and then to a party at Hampton Court Palace. As they'd got back to the apartment on Limehouse Marina, Martin had put on his best of Burt Bacharach CD and held Penelope in a small turning circle as they'd danced to 'What the World Needs Now Is Love' by Jackie DeShannon. Penelope was almost as tall as Martin in heels and they made a handsome couple. It had made Seb grimace and go to bed in the room they'd just dumped their rucksacks in, but he had fallen into a contented slumber, happy in the knowledge his parents adored each other.

He flipped through the stack of CDs and stopped at *The Very Best Of Marvin Gaye*.

'That'll do.' He laughed.

'You sure he's away now?' Clair asked, seeing the twinkle in Seb's eye.

'Definitely...' Seb said, pulling Clair into him and squeezing her bottom. She flushed red – her tight jeans and puffed gilet were too hot for summer in the city.

'Well...'

It would be nice to play house for a few days. Imagine what it might be like to live together. They hadn't had much space with

Clair's younger sisters always around at home, and Penelope always painting in the lookout room on the top floor.

They kissed in the middle of the living room to the opening notes of 'I Heard It Through the Grapevine', the vamping bassline tempered with a tambourine, as Seb untucked Clair's top from her jeans waist.

'Not now,' she said, with a schoolmarm edge, before pulling away. 'Later.'

Clair had a way of levelling Seb. She was good at keeping him in check: when he was about to drink snakebite and black with his mates; when he was ordering a frivolous takeaway despite his mum having left them dinner in the oven; when he was speeding around the island in the sports car his mum never drove. Clair's sensible wholesomeness was the perfect counter to Seb's recklessness. She knew how to help him along the right path, and right now, the right path was the marina walkway to the nearest Tesco Metro to get supplies.

'Let's get some pasta and sauce, eh? Maybe walk along the river?'

'OK,' Seb conceded, his rumbling tummy countering his urge to take their clothes off. He kissed Clair's straight nose. She paused and kissed him back. He really was very sexy and she was very excited to be alone with him in London. His hands started to roam again.

'Stoppit, we need food.' She laughed as she pulled back and threw her bag across her body. 'Oh, hang on,' she said, pivoting from the living room to the kitchen, to see what essentials were there. 'There's no point buying pasta if there are already bags of it.'

She opened a few cupboards and slammed them shut on seeing crockery, salt and condiments. There was a half-full packet of pasta bows. Some Cadbury's Animal biscuits. A weathered ketchup bottle. A few tins of tuna.

'Jesus, I thought your dad was more sophisticated than that!' Clair laughed as she opened another cupboard.

'They're probably all mine. And massively out of date.' Seb picked up the Animals biscuits to see if he should try them.

'Cookbooks!' Clair said with a guffaw. 'I didn't think your dad was the Ken Hom type...'

'He isn't. But he buys them all for my mum so she can make fancy dinners and he name-drop chefs...' Seb rolled his eyes affectionately.

Bluebird, Ken Hom, Rick Stein, the Quaglino's cookbook. Seb pulled out the colourful spine of the Quaglino's one.

'He's definitely not going to make lamb ravioli with these Tesco pasta bows,' Clair said, looking over Seb's shoulder as he flicked through with a bemused half-smile. A page opened with a postcard slotted inside it, which fell to the floor at his feet.

On the front it said 'Redstone Lake' under a photo of a silver-haired man on waterskis with 'WISH YOU WERE HERE' in an arc over the man's head. It looked as if it was taken in the 1950s and was quite camp. On the back was a Canadian stamp and a familiarly incomprehensible script. 'Oh, it's from Uncle Roger...'

Roger was famous for his hieroglyphic scrawl, so much so that Seb didn't think to try to decipher the card, but the address caught his eye.

Marty and Tina Cooper.

'Tina?'

Clair leaned over his shoulder as he crouched on the kitchen floor.

Seb tried to think of an affectionate nickname Roger might have for his mother. He'd only ever heard him call her Penelope Pitstop, or Penny From Heaven, but that was more to echo Martin when he'd had a few brandies. Nothing to do with Tina. It didn't make any sense. He didn't remember Roger ever calling his mother Tina.

Then he looked at the address.

Hope Cottage
The Baldons
Oxfordshire

From Seb's silence Clair could tell he was discombobulated.

'Did your parents ever live in Oxfordshire, maybe when your dad and Roger were setting up...?'

Seb turned the postcard over a few times.

'No. He stayed with them at times, but that's not Roger's address.'

Seb stood up and squinted to look at the postmark. 'It says 1995. Two years ago.'

'Well, it must be someone with the same name and they crossed paths. Although it says Marty, not Martin.'

'He sometimes calls Dad Marty. And why would Roger send another man called Marty Cooper a postcard from his holiday?'

'Are you sure that's Roger?'

Seb read out the postcard, slowly, as he translated the scrawls.

'"You really... ought... to take a holiday you... bloody... martyr! Roger, Dora & the girls."'

'That's Roger!'

'Well, that doesn't even make sense. We go on holidays...' Seb said slightly defensively.

'Maybe it was intended for another friend – another Martin – and he got the last names mixed up.'

'Then why would it have ended up in this flat, if it wasn't for my dad?'

'Maybe it's a name/address mix-up. Remember last Christmas, Francesca Smith stopped speaking to Emma Palin because Emma accidentally mixed up the Christmas cards with the envelopes?'

Seb scowled. Clair wittered.

'She had said in Lily Simpson's card "Happy Christmas to my best friend in the whole world"... but put it in Francesca's envelope, and Francesca went ballistic. That's what will have happened. Your mum and dad would have got some equally offensive postcard destined for whoever lives in Oxfordshire – probably addressed to Bill and Penelope or something and he's muddled up the names. He was probably drunk writing them, knowing Roger.'

'But my dad *did* get this postcard... this is all so weird.'

'Come on, let's go, I'm getting hungry.'

* * *

On their walk to Tesco Metro, on their trip along St Katharine Docks, where Seb convinced Clair to forget about the pasta and sauce and eat at Pizza Express instead, he had a sick feeling about Roger's postcard. It didn't make sense. But he couldn't work out what *did* make sense. Less so after three bottles of Peroni. Back at the flat Clair got out the *Jerry Maguire* VHS she'd rented and packed – she said the cinema in Leicester Square was silly money – and they watched it. Seb didn't even try to have sex with her, he just sat stewing about the postcard, now propped up on the kitchen worktop.

When Clair had fallen asleep, Seb went back to the kitchen and picked it up again. The joy of the image. A catalogue man with silver hair and a taut chest, waving at the camera as if the photographer were a mistress. Its sunshine, vitality and cheekiness irked Seb. So he walked over to the phone on the kitchen wall and dialled Directory Enquiries.

'What name, please?'

'Cooper.'

'And the address?'

'Hope Cottage, The Baldons.'

'Hope Cottage, The what?'

'Baldons.'

'Can you spell that, please?'

Seb peered at the card.

'B-a-l-d-o-n-s, I think.'

'Hope Cottage, The Baldons... Oxon?'

'Yes, that's it!'

'I'm sorry, that number's ex-directory.'

* * *

The next morning, Seb told Clair he wasn't going to Gower Street to do the tour of the architectural faculty at UCL. He was going to Oxford instead.

'What? To the office? Your dad's away!'

Clair knew Seb could be impulsive – his eyes had a steely determination behind their brightness – but this seemed mad.

'Seb, you've not slept all night, you're not thinking straight.'

'I am, I have to go...'

'Because of a postcard? You'll miss so much! You might even blow your chance of a place.'

'No, I won't, it's not an interview. I've got the offer, I just have to get the grades.'

Clair's kind brown eyes implored him, and Seb softened a little. 'I'll jump on tomorrow's tour. They probably won't even notice. Shepherding one less person one day and one more the next. I'll just say I was sick today, or my flight was cancelled and I got over a day late. No one will give a shit.'

The university was running tours, over the Wednesday and Thursday, but Clair had hoped to go with Seb to see his uni before looking at hers in Edmonton on the Thursday.

Seb was always more cavalier than Clair, and it irritated her.

'I give a shit. If you do your tour tomorrow, we can't see each other's unis.'

Seb shrugged.

'Doesn't matter, does it?'

Clair looked hurt.

'Our offers aren't dependent on each other,' Seb snapped, although as he said it he knew it was too sharp. 'Sorry,' he conceded.

'Seb? What's wrong?'

'Are you coming or not?'

* * *

Two tubes, a train and a taxi ride later, they pulled up at the address on the postcard and Seb looked from it to the words above the door. Hope Cottage in a clean white font cutely curved over a dove-grey door. A rampant lilac rose was pegged back so it didn't collapse under the weight of its bountiful blooms. A white picket fence set a neat boundary to an English country garden framing a symmetrical chocolate-box home.

'Here you go, mate,' said the taxi driver chirpily.

Seb looked through the open window hesitantly,

'What are you going to do?' Clair asked, touching Seb's arm.

'What do you mean?'

'Well, we're here at three in the afternoon. What are you wanting to do, or expecting to say? "I think I've got your postcard, how about a cup of tea and some cake?" What if no one's in? We wait? Post it through the door? We should keep the taxi...' Clair looked around, to the village green, a little pub, the road up ahead with a tree-canopy tunnel back to the A road. They shouldn't let the taxi go. It had already cost £20 from Oxford station – they didn't want to be stranded in the middle of nowhere.

Seb shook out of a daydream-like state.

'Wait here, then.'

'Huh?'

'Won't be a second, mate,' Seb said to the cabbie.

He opened the car door.

'Wait!'

Clair slid along the seat and climbed out behind him.

'Please don't go anywhere!' she said to the driver, pressing her palms together.

The driver chuckled.

'You ain't paid me yet, love, I'm not going anywhere!'

Clair nodded, honest eyes reassuring him.

Seb opened the gate to the cottage and walked up the path. The lilac rose bounced a little in the summer breeze as he knocked on a black circular door handle with a solid *rat a tat tat*.

'Mother!' came an instant bellow from behind the front door. A girl's voice.

A muffled indistinguishable call came from beyond that.

'I can't!' the girl hollered, a petulant-sounding prima donna. 'I'm not the fucking butler!'

Seb and Clair looked at each other and almost laughed, before a thunder of footsteps indicated the door was about to be opened somewhat begrudgingly.

They were surprised when a dumpy-looking pre-teen in a peach-coloured satin dress opened the door. Her Shirley Temple ringlets jarred with her surly face.

'Oh,' Seb said. Surprised at the sight in front of him. The girl's haughty face and arched eyebrows didn't match her childlike attire and sloped shoulders.

'Yes?' she said, disparagingly. Her face was entitled and incredulous; her chin wobbled against the bow at the neck of her dress.

'Oh, er, yes...' said Seb, clutching the postcard in his left hand. 'I'm looking for a Marty or Tina Cooper...' Seb wondered why this girl wasn't mentioned on the postcard.

It must have been a mix-up. Maybe Roger really is drinking too much.

'Well, who do you want? Martin or Tina?'

Seb and Clair heard a woman call out from up the plush carpeted stairs. The décor behind the girl looked as chintzy and as twee as her dress.

'Who is it, darling?' called a warbling, wobbling voice.

The girl frowned at Seb and Clair as she looked them up and down and went to open her mouth but it was clamped shut in puzzlement.

'If it's the car I'm not ready!' the woman upstairs – Tina, they presumed – called.

'Oh, it doesn't matter,' Seb said apologetically, realising how ridiculously he'd been acting for the past twenty-four hours. 'It's just Marty Cooper... I have a postcard that was meant for him, and it's just he has exactly the same name as my—'

Seb's jaw dropped open as his dad came walking down the hallway, white dress shirt open at the neck and a black bow tie loose in his hand.

'Sebastian!' the man gasped, as if he'd seen a ghost.

'Dad!'

'What?' Clair looked aghast.

'Daddy? DADDY!' The girl was repeating it, increasing in anger and volume every time as her father – Seb's father – stood speechless, an end of a tie in each hand, getting all dressed up for an afternoon event that had just been ruined.

Seb turned on his heel and walked down the garden path, back to the taxi, before he might throw up.

Clair, torn between needing answers from Martin and running to the car, gave her boyfriend's dad a look of disgust.

'Seb!' Martin called in despair.

'Seb!' Clair shouted. 'Wait!'

'Daddy, what IS going on?' asked the girl in the peach dress, like a headteacher about to tell off her charge, while her stressed mother called nervously from the bedroom.

'I'll be another ten minutes! The car wasn't booked until three-thirty!'

* * *

Seb said nothing until they got out of the taxi at Oxford station and he vomited into a bin and shouted 'FUCK!' afterwards. He didn't speak again until well after Reading, but Clair kept her legs touching his under the table between them, holding him together with the inside of her calves.

'I fucking knew it, Clair, I knew it...'

'What? How could you know?'

'Not that! But I fucking knew something was rotten. I knew it! The minute I saw that card. And Roger...'

Seb looked out of the train window, eyes narrowing and hateful, on the graffitied walls of bleak city outskirts as he whizzed backwards. Peripheries of the capital as the train made its way to Paddington.

Clair took Seb's hand on the table between them and cupped it in hers.

'This is in-sane! But I'm sure there's an explanation...'

'What – my dad has an identical long-lost twin?' Seb shot. 'Also called Martin.'

Clair looked despairing.

'Call your mum when we get back to the flat – see if she's OK and whether she knows where your dad is...'

'I want to go home.'

'But the tours. The tutors. We need to meet them.'

'You can – how can I?'

Clair looked firmer now. Her curtness coming back to the fore.

'There will be an explanation, whether it's one you like or not – but don't throw away UCL and four years – seven years – a career, because of something there might be a simple explanation for.'

'There is no simple explanation.'

Clair winced.

'Let's go and have a look tomorrow. I'll go to Edmonton; you go to UCL. Sort out our futures before throwing them away over what could be a total miscommunication and confusion that can be explained away.'

'There's no confusion, Clair. That man was my dad. That awful girl was calling him Daddy. I have a fucking sister. At *least* one!' Seb looked up and down the carriage to see which way the loo was. He felt as if he might be sick again. 'Shit!'

'It does sound bad,' Clair admitted. 'But let's get back to the flat, call your mum and reconvene.'

'I'm not staying there,' Seb said flatly. The evening sun bounced off the silver spinning turbine vents on the roofs outside Paddington. 'He'll probably be there when we get back.'

The rush-hour traffic on the roads and rails beyond the train window was starting to build as the train slowed through west London.

'Well, what on earth are we going to do?'

* * *

'We only have a deluxe king, I'm afraid...' the woman in the neat waistcoat said without much remorse as she looked at the tatty backpack at Seb's feet. Expecting him to turn around and end whatever joke it was he was playing on his girlfriend.

'OK,' Seb said neutrally. 'For two nights, yes?'

'Yes, that'll be £479 for tonight and £600 for tomorrow. It's a weekend rate on a Thursday...'

Seb looked passive; Clair frowned.

'And would you like breakfast with that? In the Palm Court.'

'Does that price not include breakfast?' Clair scowled at the concierge.

'Yes, whatever – put it all on this,' Seb said, handing the woman his credit card. The one attached to his dad's bank account. The one saved for emergencies.

'Seb...' Clair pleaded behind gritted teeth.

The woman took the card, looked at it and said, 'Very well.'

'Seb, if the card needs authorisation—'

'Then my dad will grant it,' he replied icily.

I dare him not to.

'You can call him, if you like – he has a mobile phone – he'll authorise it.'

The woman ignored Seb's offer and went out the back to process the payment. Seb hoped his dad wouldn't be informed that he was using his credit card to check into The Ritz, only because he didn't want his dad to know where he was, so he could come and find him. He had no qualms about the *fuck you* on next month's credit card statement. For now, he just wanted to get through the next forty-eight hours and get the Aurigny back to Guernsey. To his mum. His home. His A level results.

'All perfect!' the woman said as she came out of the back room.

Seb nodded and placed the credit card back in his wallet.

'Emmanuel here will help you with your bags and show you to your room.'

Clair looked at Seb, wide-eyed, and for the first time that day, Seb cracked a half-smile.

7

JUNE 2019, NORTHILL, OXFORDSHIRE

Penelope Guilbert stroked her grandson's hair as she listened to the vicar begin her address. She examined the texture and swirls of the mid-brown shades and observed it was the same colour, probably the same length, as Seb's at that age, in the late eighties. She pulled him in and kissed his crown again. Her beautiful prince was gone.

It shouldn't happen this way around.

Penelope had wanted Seb's body flown back to Guernsey, to be buried on the island where he had been born. She had wanted Reverend Roden to deliver the sermon and for him to have a religious funeral, with all the grace and elegance of their parish church, not a modern new-build crematorium with a visiting vicar and a hastily planted rose garden. She had wanted the wake to take place at the glass house he had grown up in, the summer sky sparkling overhead. Not in the pub they were booked into later, as pretty as the orchard garden was.

Reverend Jane had been nice though, her warmth and compassion had won Penelope over, and she had ceded to Clair's and Martin's wishes that the service happen in Northill; that his cremation and wake would take place there too; that her grandchildren would be close to their father's memorial plaque in time.

She had apologised for making a fuss.

'I'm sorry, Clair, I wasn't thinking,' she'd said despairingly, over dinner a few nights ago.

'Don't be sorry. It's hard for any of us to think,' Clair replied. 'No parent should lose a child.'

'And no children their age should lose a father.'

In the two weeks since Seb's body had arrived back in Britain, Penelope, her husband, Peter, Martin, Tina, Clair and their best man Jake had met; looked at order of service styles; discussed music and caskets; drunk tea and cake and sat in disbelief. At night, Penelope and Peter would return to their Premier Inn hotel room in Northill town centre and Penelope would sob herself to sleep, drained, raw and numb, before putting her face on again the next morning and thinking it was an odd thing to do: to wear mascara when your son had died.

Penelope hadn't met Noemie but she had heard her in the background on Martin's mobile and she could hear her now across the aisle. She had seen her, coming out of the funeral home one afternoon as Penelope was going in. A young woman with beachy hair and flip-flops, and large oversized sunglasses. But it was only after she had gone, when the funeral director had mentioned someone had just been in with Seb, that Penelope realised the woman must have been *her*.

The planning had been surprisingly harmonious given their rare familial circumstances. Penelope let Martin, Clair and Jake take on most of the tasks as she and Peter listened on; and Clair's fiancé Dave made sure everyone was looked after, the kids had what they needed; liaising with school, Clair's parents and sisters, and ordering takeaways.

Martin's phone kept ringing with interjections and suggestions from Noemie: ideas for songs; thoughts that had crossed her mind; ramblings about their final days. But most of the conversations went around in circles caused by Valium, wine and grief; and it gave the group peace of mind to know Noemie's mother was staying with her and managing her medication.

No mother should lose a child.

* * *

'My darling...' she whispered into Jasper's hair as Reverend Jane said a few words about housekeeping and fire exits. Given that most of the fire exits were blocked by mourners, she stressed the importance of it with an understanding eye. As light and airy as it was, the modern magnolia chapel building wasn't big enough for the enormity of Seb's personality. For the love all the mourners had for him, in all their different ways.

Penelope didn't take it in as Reverend Jane said she would over-look the fact they were exceeding fire regulations; thank you for coming; that they were there to celebrate the life of Sebastian William Martin Cooper. She could only feel the warmth of her husband Peter's hand on her leg. She could only smell the scent of Jasper's shampoo.

I only wanted one child and now he's gone.

Penelope closed her eyes so she could hear the sound of the sea lapping on the shores of the island Seb grew up on. So she could picture him playing around the lush green terraces of their garden on the hill, strewn with buttercups and daisies, overlooking the Channel below. So she could picture Seb running along clifftops of lilac sand crocuses and bright pink sea thrifts and pimpernels; to the cornfields around the Martello tower. So she could take away

the anguish that had swept over his once-happy resting face as he'd
stood in the kitchen and confronted her with the biggest heartache
of his life.

8

CLAIR

July 1997, Guernsey

'You knew?'

Seb sat on the kitchen stool, heels together and toes out as his feet perched on the bar halfway down it. His back slumped and his eyes bloodshot and bewildered. He rubbed them to see if this whole mess might disappear, but there was no clarity beyond the heel of his hand. 'All this time... you knew?'

His mother nodded.

'Oh, darling...'

'Is he even my dad?'

'Of course he is!'

Penelope looked horrified. She wanted to cross the kitchen and go to Seb, to envelop him, but she suspected he might shake her off.

Clair leaned on the island, the golden ends of her summer-kissed ponytail flowing down the back of her gilet as she hugged her mug of hot chocolate on an evening that had turned blowy. Penelope made the best hot chocolate: creamy Channel Island milk mixed with organic cocoa powder and grated with cacao nibs she got at the health food shop in St Peter Port; with a dash of cinnamon.

Seb's drink was going cold next to him.

'Your father's love for you is unwavering and unquestionable.'

'How do I know that? I don't even know who he is!'

'You do! You just don't know that... that part of his life.'

Clair wanted to ask how this all happened, but she knew it wasn't her place.

'Are there more kids?'

'Not that I'm aware...' Penelope half laughed, then remembered how her son's heart ached. 'No,' she said seriously now. 'It's just her.'

'What's her name?'

'Sara-Jayne. They call her SJ. She's twelve.'

'So, what, Dad had an affair and got some woman pregnant?'

'Well, unfortunately, she's not some woman. Tina *is* his wife.'

'But *you're* his—'

Penelope shook her head apologetically.

'Oh, darling...'

Seb's mouth hung open, his face a shade of puce.

'You know your father was married before I met him, right?'

Seb nodded. He didn't ever really think about his father's first marriage. It was so insignificant. He had married someone called Carole too young and it had barely lasted. They didn't even have kids before they split up and she moved to New Zealand.

'Why do you think it ended with Carole? Why do you think she moved to New Zealand? To start her life again in her mid-twenties?'

'I dunno.' Seb shrugged on his stool.

'She was heartbroken, Seb. Your father and I were having an affair.'

Clair looked a bit embarrassed by all this.

Seb was totally puzzled.

'I was the other woman.'

'What?'

Clair looked at the space between Penelope and Seb, somewhere near the stove, and wondered if she should offer to go home. But Seb had said he wanted her there.

'We met through the Arts Society and just... you know... fell in love...'

She looked to Clair for solidarity.

'Sometimes good people do bad things...' she said breezily, looking only slightly guilty. 'Carole was desperate to become a mother but your dad and I, we wanted to be together, we saw a future together. We very quickly had the son she wanted – we had you!'

'You had me out of wedlock?'

Seb had never been troubled by tradition, but suddenly sounded quite stuffy.

Penelope winced, as if that wasn't the half of it.

'To Carole... I was Tina.'

'I just thought the Carole thing... I thought it was a mistake, Dad got married too young; that she left him to see the world.'

'Well, it sort of was a mistake, but it was a messy one. She was heartbroken and angry, and she made it very difficult for your father to divorce. So much so, that he and I didn't ever get round to getting married.'

Seb's mouth hung open now.

'You've never been...? But what about...?' He couldn't get the words out as he looked around the large open-plan living space beyond the kitchen, to the sideboards over by the sofas. And only then did he realise that the array of photos he knew so well, the familiar pictures of a happy and glamorous couple: not one of them was a wedding photo. Yet any one of them could have been. Penelope and Martin Cooper had always looked like newly-weds to their son.

'How could I not know my parents weren't married?'

'What does it matter?'

Seb pushed his hair back and almost fell off his stool.

'What does it matter? What does it matter? Jesus, Mum!'

'Seb...' Clair pleaded for calm.

'Everything was a lie! I was born into a lie, you and Dad nurtured a lie, then you told a whole set of new lies. Why didn't you get married?'

'Oh, darling, being married wouldn't have made any difference – sadly a leopard doesn't change its spots.'

'Is that why you didn't have more children? Because he left?'

Even as Seb said it he knew it didn't make sense. He thought of the showy gestures; the slow dances; the adoring glances between his parents.

'He didn't leave – we just didn't bother to separate. We still love each other.'

'What? This is mental.'

Seb slumped his head between his hands and looked down at the dark blue denim of his legs; the burgundy N of the New Balance on his feet zigging and zagging in his brain.

'Oh, Seb...' Clair put her empty mug down and walked over to him and rubbed his back.

'Anyway, I didn't want more children! I didn't think I could love anyone as much as I loved you.' She looked at him proudly. 'You are everything, Seb.'

Clair looked at Seb's face, relieved to see comfort flash across it.

'So when he took a mistress on the mainland – she was their

bloody receptionist – and he had to tell me she was pregnant, well... it was awful. He had done to me what we had done to Carole. I suppose it was my just deserts.'

Clair gave Penny a sad and sympathetic smile as she continued.

'But part of me – a teeny tiny part of me – enjoyed some relief. I didn't feel pressured to have more children. I know your father wanted a sibling for you.'

'Weird way to go about it!' snapped Seb.

'Well, it wasn't deliberate, your father didn't plan it...'

Clair listened, quiet and supportive, while Seb looked up and heard his mother out.

'And – well – because our lives here are so...'

Clair thought she were going to say *proper*.

'So... content. Why upset the applecart?'

Seb half laughed. Most of his life had been a lie but his mother seemed to think it was idyllic.

'He spends half his time over there. There's very little crossover.'

The room was quiet but for the summer wind whipping up on the cliffs.

'Do *they* know about Seb?' Clair asked carefully. Penelope nodded.

'Tina does. She knew Martin had a family when she started working for Curtis + Cooper. She knew about us over here. But, well...' She shrugged thoughtfully. 'You know what your father is like, he probably charmed her. Said he was going through a messy divorce. Probably failed to tell her that the divorce wasn't from me.'

Seb shook his head.

'It's not her fault. And at least it wasn't a flash in the pan, eh?'

'What?' Seb scowled.

'Well, they got married when Tina fell pregnant. Your father and Carole were freshly divorced by then, and Tina's parents are very Christian apparently.'

'What?'

'Wow,' Clair said, not meaning to. She couldn't imagine how much that must have hurt Penelope; she looked at Seb and hoped he would never do something like that to her.

'Marriage meant more to Tina than it did to me...' she said casually. 'I had to be accepting anyway, or perhaps lose your father in our daily lives, to her and to the mainland.'

Seb looked at his mother, confused. Had she been complicit or was she a doormat?

He rubbed his eyes and let out a huge sigh.

'Does the girl know?'

'Oh, I doubt it. I don't take much interest in her, to be honest. She sounds ghastly to me, and the demands she makes. But your father must love her...'

Seb remembered the homely scene – a family getting ready for some summer party or event. A bow tie in his hand. A stranger calling his dad 'Daddy'. He thought he was going to puke again.

'He loves you more,' Penelope said with a wicked sparkle in her eye. 'You'll always be his number one.'

Seb shot his mother a hateful look, which cut his heart because, as angry as he was, this must have been awful for her too.

'Were you *ever* going to tell me?'

Penelope sighed.

'We knew it was coming, with you going to London to study... but not like this, darling. Not like this.'

Seb shook his head again when he remembered how hot his face had felt and the despair in his heart on the doorstep of Hope Cottage. How could his parents have done that to him? To live a lie then let him find out by accident.

What the fuck?

He threw his arms up in despair.

'I'm so, so sorry...' Penelope said, looking at her son intently.

Seb slid off the stool, grabbed his jacket, and walked towards the door.

'Seb!' called Clair, looking to Penelope nervously, to check if she should go after him. Penelope nodded, and Clair went running out.

* * *

Seb ran – down the lane past their neighbours', turning into a cornfield high with husks. He ran through the gold towards rectangles of green on the other side of it, to the lush field where a Martello tower stood guard, once keeping watch on Napoleon's army but now a pretty cylindrical ruin, where the grasses grew long and swayed in the balmy scirocco.

When his legs couldn't keep up with the adrenaline pumping his heart, Seb slumped into the grass, looking out to sea. Far enough from home but not too far that Clair couldn't find him.

'Seb!'

He propped an elbow on each knee as he listened to the sound of his fast breath bouncing against the wind, then picked a strand of thick green grass, twisting it around his forefinger, stopping the blood from flowing to the tip.

'Seb!' Clair caught up, out of breath and worried, and slumped down next to him, the grass almost up to her pink cheeks.

'Try not to be angry with your mum, it's not her fault.'

'Are you joking?' he scorned, looking to Clair then feeling bad, so he softened his shoulders a bit and looked out to sea. 'She's lied to me all my fucking life.'

Clair looked at Seb's face in profile.

'Well, actually, she hasn't...'

Seb flashed Clair another look. 'If the affair only started when you were, what, five? Six?' Clair's matter-of-factness was usually a tonic, a happy counter to Seb's fanciful frivolousness. But not now.

'For fuck's sake, they pretended they were married!'

Clair looped her left arm around his right and leaned into his side.

'But did they?'

Seb looked at Clair with disdain. Whose side was she on?

'Did they ever pretend? Or did it just never come up?'

Seb softened, shaking his head in the basin of his arms. Under the looming watch of the tower they looked out to sea for a few minutes, boats, oystercatchers, wheatears and a Montagu's harrier, carrying on regardless as if Seb's world hadn't stopped turning. The sun was lowering on the horizon, bringing a calm over the swaying grasses.

He spoke thoughtfully. 'I assumed my mum kept her maiden name for work.'

Clair nodded.

'"Penelope Guilbert Fine Arts" – it says on her cards. I never knew my parents weren't actually married.'

Clair stroked his arm with her free hand.

'They weren't honest with me! How can I believe anything either of them say, ever again? Especially that fucking lying cheating...'

The thought of Martin with his arms around a daughter; the thought of all the times he was told his dad was away with work, or working out of the flat in Limehouse, but really he was living in a cosy cottage, being a dad to someone else. The thought of the man he adored and admired, the person who made him want to study for seven years to be an architect *just like him* made his head drop again and he let out a gentle sob.

Seb hadn't been able to cry in London – he had been too angry and closed off. But suddenly, as he stared out to the choppy sea, the tears started to tumble.

'My whole life is a lie.'

'Oh, Seb!'

'I thought I was an only child. I thought I had a dad. But he's someone else's dad. I don't know him.'

Clair entwined both her arms around Seb's arm now and kissed his right cheek. 'Well... your half-sister, or whatever she is, doesn't really know him either, does she?'

He shrugged.

'Seb, this is awful, but actually it doesn't change anything. He loves you, he's *your* dad. He could have left your mum and you, cut loose from the island, but clearly he didn't want to. He wouldn't! He's so excited about you spending more time in England with him, he's been buzzing about you going to The Bartlett. I see the proud look in his eyes whenever he talks about you or sees you!'

'Well, I don't want to see him. I don't want to see that awful SJ. And fucking "Tina"? If my dad thinks I'm going to be cool about this like Mum... he's fucking wrong. I can't, Clair, I just can't...'

As Seb broke again and stifled his sobs on the knee of his jeans, Clair held him tight. It was the first time she had seen him cry. As she rubbed his back and arms and peppered his neck with kisses, she knew she would be there for him, whatever life threw at him.

9

JUNE 2019, NORTHILL, OXFORDSHIRE

Clair... Noemie not Naomi... Shit, who was the middle one? Clair... D-D-D-D... I could definitely write a book about this.

Reverend Jane hadn't met The Middle One – in fact she'd only met Clair, but Clair had explained Seb's unusual situation – his parents' and his own – and Reverend Jane had heard Noemie's anguished voice in the background of her calls to Martin during meetings over the past two weeks.

It was obvious who Noemie was – the broken woman with the messy blonde hair in the front row fitted the voice of the crying woman on the phone – but Jane couldn't for the life of her work out who the middle one was. Nor could she remember her name. And she really ought to acknowledge them all, privately at least.

Clair... Noemie... D-D-D-Debbie?

Jane considered the curvy woman with red lipstick sitting next to Seb's father, until she saw her lean forwards, reach out, and put a sturdy, conciliatory hand on Noemie's arm on the other side of him.

Ahhh, the half-sister.

Jane had decided before the service that whatever the whisperings were, or whatever the family thought about each other, she was going to bend over backwards to make every woman feel valued and supported. The mothers, the wives and the lovers. They would all be grieving. But she just couldn't place the middle one or remember her bloody name as she began her introduction, did the housekeeping stuff and welcomed everyone who had travelled near and far to get to Northill today.

Clair... Noemie...

As if the Lord himself were jogging her memory, she saw the sad eyes of a beautiful woman halfway back; staring at her, dimples in her cheeks even though she wasn't smiling. She wore a black blazer over a cream blouse and a wrap that had fallen off one shoulder.

Desiree. That's it.

She hadn't met Desiree but she knew she was a significant part of Sebastian's life; Penelope had told her as much and been keen to involve her in the ceremony, but said it was awkward.

Jane was good with awkward. Jane had met lots of blended and complicated families during all the births, marriages and deaths she'd been party to cementing and celebrating, but none like this family where the father had lived a double life and had a secret child; where the young man who died too soon had left three women utterly broken-hearted. As she'd talked to Martin and Tina, Penelope and Peter, and Clair and Dave at Clair's home and the vicarage, the story had unfolded of a family like no other.

I really could write a book about this.

From their meetings Reverend Jane could see Tina adored Martin with quiet reverence; she could see how a young tennis player like Peter would fall in love with an older woman like Penelope. She could see why Clair would mourn a man so powerfully despite being about to marry another.

She had heard the stories of how Sebastian Cooper lived and

how he died. And through listening, to the words spoken and the blanks unfilled, she pieced together the portrait of a man she wished she had known too. A man it was going to be hard to eulogise, he sounded so enchanting.

Just don't get their names wrong.

Clair.

Desiree.

Noemie, not Naomi.

10

CLAIR

October 1999, London

'I'm thinking about transferring courses.'

Seb and Clair were lying in bed, staring at what looked like a brown urine circle on the ceiling, when he dropped the bombshell. Clair glanced at him, pulling the duvet up around her for security.

'What? You've just started your third year! You're over halfway through.'

'I'm only halfway through Part One.'

'But I don't understand!'

Seb rolled onto his side so he was facing Clair, their cheeks flushed from morning sex. He'd thought she'd be OK about it if he told her now, but the furrow of her usually straight brow made him realise he needed to be more candid.

'I'm struggling.'

It was harder for him to admit than he realised, so he rolled back and looked up at the ceiling of her Edmonton bedsit. Shades of brown and yellow sat off centre, like an ill-placed rosette, clouding their post-orgasmic euphoria. They had contemplated the stain on the ceiling many times before: had someone in the flat above peed that badly, ten or twenty years ago, that it seeped through carpet, floorboard, joist and plasterboard? Or had it risen, from where the former tenant had sat, chain smoking their life away in the bleak room Clair called home? The bedsit certainly had the linger of stale smoke in the atmosphere.

'Struggling? With what?'

'With this.'

Clair looked downhearted.

'With London, I mean. My course...'

'But you're at The Bartlett, Seb! It's amazing. You wouldn't have got there and passed two years if you *weren't* brilliant!'

'You have to get 66 per cent to pass. I got 66 per cent exactly.'

'So you passed!'

'It's so competitive, I'm treading water. I'm bottom of the class.'

'You are not!'

'OK, second bottom maybe. I've never felt settled.'

Clair sat up and propped the pillow behind her back, still clutching the thin duvet to her chest. She looked astonished. How could she have not known Seb was so miserable? For two years.

'So what course will you transfer to? What will you study?'

'Still architecture.' He looked sheepish, as if he was holding something back. 'Just not in London.'

'What?'

'I'm not good enough. I'll be lucky to pass the third year. I won't get the plush placements.'

Clair pondered it. Seb was always so confident, she'd never heard this defeatist talk.

'Well, you've always got Curtis + Cooper to fall back on for the placement. Don't leave because of that!'

'Well, actually, that's what I was thinking...' Seb was trying to make it sound as though it weren't already decided. 'About transferring to Oxford Brookes...'

'What?'

'Finish my Part One there, do the Part One placement with Dad and Rog. Apparently I can transfer all my credits.'

'You've been speaking to your dad about this?'

'Yeah.'

'Oh.'

* * *

Seb and his father must have been rebuilding a relationship faster than Clair realised. They had broken the ice with a nervy lunch at the cottage in The Baldons a year ago – Martin had been desperate for it to happen for months with invitations Seb wasn't ready to accept. When it did happen, he welcomed them with open arms and Tina pulled out all the stops to make it as lovely as possible, cooking up a Sunday lunch feast, her nervous birdlike face twitching on turbo as she served roast chicken with honey-glazed carrots and parmesan-encrusted parsnips. But the tension was high, not helped by Sara-Jayne throwing a tantrum when she wasn't getting the numbers to buy her favourite streets in Monopoly. Her handsome big brother was coming for lunch and she had been excited about it, but ended up in tears when the dice weren't rolling in her favour.

Martin placated his daughter when he landed on Mayfair, bought it, and swapped it with SJ for Pentonville Road.

'Light blue for a dark blue, princess?' he assuaged.

Seb was almost sick in his mouth.

And when Seb later bought Park Lane because he was a

mischievous bugger, SJ called him a bastard, 'In the true meaning of the word.'

Tina gasped and Clair looked affronted, although Seb laughed it off. SJ was so riled that Martin quickly called time on the game – and suggested they walk to the village pub to get some air.

'Blue for a blue princess?' Clair had parroted scathingly on the train home. 'What kind of a thirteen-year-old cries over Monopoly?'

* * *

It wasn't that Clair didn't want Seb to have a healthy relationship with his dad – she had hated to see him so heartbroken over the betrayal and he hadn't been himself that first year in London. She had encouraged him to accept the lunch invitations from Martin and Tina after his parents had finally called it a day; she had encouraged lunches since, even though Tina's flapping and SJ's rudeness stressed her out. Clair too had missed Martin's charm and wit in Seb's life – in *their* lives. She had been about the same age as SJ was at that lunch when she'd first met Martin – but she didn't like the idea of Seb and his dad having plotted this move behind her back.

'Would Oxford Brookes take you?'

'Apparently...' Seb said hopefully. Hoping mostly not to upset Clair. This wasn't an indictment on their relationship.

'Where will you live? Not with your dad, Tina and SJ surely?'

'God, no! I can get student digs in the town. There are lots of students in Oxford...' he said with a wry smile. Clair lightly hit Seb's naked chest, then stroked the light smattering of hair on it.

'Or I can live with Jake, if one of his housemates move out.'

'Oh god!' Clair tried not to groan, imagining what *that* kind of house share might look like and not liking it one bit.

They lay silently.

Clair never said, 'What about me?' because she always put other people first. But she was thinking it, and she couldn't hold her fears in.

'Jesus, Seb...' she said sadly as her eyes started to fill up. Seb hated it when Clair cried. The symmetrical beauty of her face crumpled and she pulled the duvet up over it.

'How can you be so... cavalier?'

'I'm not!'

He pulled the cover back off her face so he could see her, reassure her.

'Yes, you are. This is what you do! Whether we're ordering a takeaway or you're going to uni. You change on a whim without a word of warning.'

Seb shook his head.

'This doesn't change anything!'

She ignored what he said, thinking *it had better not*. Dreading the thought of him and Jake, out partying together at uni. Spoiled handsome boys from Guernsey who could get off with any girl they wanted.

'Look at this shithole I'm living in!' Clair snapped. 'You have a plush riverfront flat in Limehouse you do anything to avoid. You spend most of your time in The Norfolk Arms or here... I don't think you realise how lucky you are!'

'I know, I'm a dick...'

'You're not a dick.'

'I just don't feel happy here. And when you're unhappy, isn't it best to change something?'

'But isn't this just you being impulsive? Have you actually thought it through?'

'I've thought about it for two years. I scraped my exams in May.

I got a bollocking from my tutor. I'm always being told I could do better...'

He talked so much about the course, Clair wondered if this was more about his dad than university. Or worse, her.

'Well, it sounds like you've already decided. You, your dad and Roger.'

'The course there is good too, Clair. Oxford is cool, man.'

Clair scrunched her nose up at him. 'Cool "man"?'

'The home of Radiohead! Ride! Supergrass! The buildings, the vibe!'

'But mostly your dad.'

Seb looked embarrassed and nodded.

Clair hoped it was about his dad. She already felt deeply inadequate, that she wasn't enough. She'd always felt it: in biology, when he and Jake were the class clowns and three steps ahead of the teacher; at parties when he was off mixing drinks he would later throw up. In London, when he would go to The Norfolk Arms or any of the Bloomsbury pubs on his own, happily without her. She knew she had to run to be able to stand still with Seb, but she didn't want it to keep happening; she was growing too, almost twenty-one and close to qualifying next summer. She'd done her placements on surgical wards, medical wards, orthopaedics and A & E; she'd traversed from North Middlesex hospital to the Whittington a thousand times and done community and mental health placements. She wanted to become a theatre nurse and was looking forward to her next placement at UCL Hospital on Euston Road. Near The Bartlett round the corner on Gower Street, which seemed a bit futile now.

'When you finish, you should move over too. If you want to. I'm sure they have hospitals in Oxford.' Seb laughed again, relieved his plan was all out in the open. Clair couldn't help but feel some comfort at his suggestion – perhaps she *could* keep up with him.

'Where do all Inspector Morse's case victims end up, eh? The hospitals in Oxford must be full of them!' He laughed.

'You idiot,' she said, rolling her eyes, pushing the duvet off them both and getting up, under the brown and yellow cloud above them.

11

JUNE 2019, NORTHILL, OXFORDSHIRE

A man with a shiny bald pate and a neat goatee stood up holding cue cards and a sad face. As he walked the few paces from his seat to the lectern at the front, those he passed saw his indecipherable writing on the cards he clutched. Hieroglyphics in their eyeline; notes and revelations, except no one could read Roger's writing without some serious code-breaking, so his words, his memory prompts, were safe.

He stepped up, stopped and paused, rubbing the beard that framed a parched mouth.

'Thank you, Reverend,' he said, formally.

Martin had asked Roger if he would say some words about Seb before Martin read a poem: he was too cut up to do the eulogy himself, and Roger had known Seb since the day he was born, so said it would be an honour.

He cleared his throat and arranged the cards on the wooden shelf in front of him, taking time and using the precision only an architect could, to lay out five A6 rectangles. He so wanted to do the boy justice.

'On behalf of Clair, Millie and Jasper; Penelope and Peter;

Martin, Tina and Sara-Jayne – and myself, Dora, Emily and Zara – I'd like to say a few words about Sebastian.'

Clair took a deep breath and exhaled it into the air above her head. Martin looked at the space between his shoes and listened intently; he knew if he looked up at his friend, he would burst into tears.

Roger paused. Caught his breath and started at the beginning, and the magical, Seb-like way Sebastian Cooper came into the world, like a gift-wrapped mystery.

* * *

'Now, I was a big know-it-all about being a dad, because we'd recently been blessed with our beautiful daughters, Emily and Zara...' Roger looked to Dora and his girls, huddled together and smiling nervously back at him for encouragement. 'And as the months of Penelope's pregnancy passed, my stories of gory births and sleep-deprived nights only grew exponentially...'

Penelope rolled her eyes and smiled. She hadn't seen Roger for years; but his face offered comfort now.

'I told Martin how bloody it all was; how long and boring labour is; how he might just want to go to the pub instead...' There was a small chuckle in the congregation.

'But, of course, Martin's baby wasn't going to be born in any normal way. His son's birth wasn't going to be standard. Nothing about Sebastian was standard. And when he was born he arrived "en caul" as they called it. A veiled baby. Still in the unbroken amniotic sac, like a perfect parcel, wrapped in a bubble.'

Gentle gasps of wonder and groans of sadness rolled through the mourners as friends who didn't know this marvelled at such a miracle; as those who did thought of Seb as a sleeping baby, his face under a veil of membrane; his sleeping face now in the box in front of them.

What did it look like?

How damaged was he?

Does his face still look handsome in there?

Roger continued.

'Martin being Martin, well... I didn't believe it when he rocked up at our holiday house that night – we were staying on the island for a few months; we even thought about setting up the practice there, but I digress... Martin, he had cigars and whisky in hand. I thought it was one of his exaggerations; one of his tall tales, if you will. I looked to Dora but even she hadn't heard of it. We didn't have the Internet then, so I couldn't check whether Martin was embellishing, not as easily as I can now anyway, if he's telling me it's thirty degrees in Marbella in December, or exaggerating his golf scores.'

A ripple of nervous laughter waved through the gatherers now. Penelope leaned forward and looked across the aisle, down the line at Martin, but couldn't see his face for SJ in front of him, who from the look on her face clearly didn't like this anecdote about her father's life *before*.

'But now I can search it up. And reading about *en caul* births ahead of today I now know just how rare it was. One in eighty thousand births apparently. In some cultures, babies born *en caul* are revered as magical, as gifted. And that was Sebastian all right. Although he was one in a million...'

Small stifled sniffles crept through the congregation, punctuated by Noemie's cries, which became louder again. She felt horrified that not only had she never heard of an *en caul* birth – even though she had birthed four babies *and* it sounded French – she didn't know this was how Seb had come into the world. They hadn't had time to discover all the things she had wanted to. She hadn't been able to think much about anything, other than the way in which he left it.

'And that was Sebastian's way,' Roger continued, after he composed himself. 'He was never going to be ordinary... he was a trouper, an energy giver, an inspiration – and a hero, in life and in death...' Roger glanced at Jasper, whose eyes burned back at him.

Roger looked back at his cue cards and talked about the joy Seb brought his parents: when he was riding through the glass house on a wooden horse on wheels; his obsessions with Evel Knievel and *The A-Team*; with his love of building: net boxes, sandcastles, Lego, Meccano – then the buildings and hotels that were to become his legacy. He talked about Seb's sense of fun, how he always had a twinkle in his eye. Yet he had the pathos and empathy of a wiser man, carrying the weight of the world on those strong shoulders of his.

'Architecture is the marriage of art and science, and Seb's wisdom and his intelligence made him a wonderful architect; he was able to balance patience and passion with determination and drive. Qualities he had in abundance.'

Roger didn't mention the family estrangement in case mourners didn't know about it – now wasn't the time for big reveals, and it didn't matter anyway – so he skipped the late teens and spoke enthusiastically about what a pleasure it had been to have Seb in the office of Curtis + Cooper in Oxford. How he breathed fresh air into the studio and put brilliant ideas and energy into every project he worked on, in his work placements as an architectural assistant and as a fully qualified architect; how he was the safest pair of hands to take over the business when Roger, and, more recently, Martin, decided to retire.

The Curtis + Cooper staff, who had all waved him off on holiday last month, wept.

Roger spoke about Seb's pride in his own children, Millie and

Jasper, and said that Jake would talk more about that, before ending with a poem.

'I'll finish by reading a poem by William Wordsworth that Martin had hoped to read...' Roger looked to his friend, gently shaking his head at the floor. 'But I will do him the honour.' He cleared his throat.

> *'My heart leaps up when I behold*
> *A rainbow in the sky:*
> *So was it when my life began;*
> *So is it now I am a man;*
> *So be it when I shall grow old,*
> *Or let me die!*
> *The Child is father of the Man;*
> *And I could wish my days to be*
> *Bound each to each by natural piety.'*

12

CLAIR

Christmas 2002, Guernsey

'It's so cold!' Clair hollered, on the back of Seb's moped, as her mittened gloves held onto his stomach. Actually, it was his mother's moped he'd borrowed for the afternoon so they could zip around the island, catching up with friends and family, although Clair regretted them not borrowing a parent's car.

Penelope had swapped the Lotus Elan for a small Renault Clio and a Vespa and paid Martin back the difference when they split up. The return of the car money was a token gesture because there was no way she was parting with the house. She loved its views, its peace and her top-floor studio. Plus Seb had had enough upheaval that fateful summer he went to university, she wasn't going to upend him and move. It had become a sanctuary for both of them.

With Seb studying on the mainland and Martin having less reason to return to Guernsey, Penelope cut him loose the New Year after the summer Seb found out. She still loved Martin terribly, and at first he was horrified at the thought of losing her, but those lonely evenings when she thought about Martin with his other family, now it was just her on the island, felt too painful. She knew it was finally time to be everything to someone.

When word got out that Penelope was single, most of Guernsey's divorcees and charlatans started showing interest in buying one of her pieces but Penelope liked the look of her tennis coach, Peter, the most, who was fifteen years younger than her and had once been semi-professional. Seb liked Peter, even though he was only ten years older than him, but he was called Peter Parker, which Seb found funny. And his mother certainly looked at him as if he were a superhero: he adored her and was clearly a safe pair of hands. Peter gave his mother an effervescence he'd never noticed before.

Seb knew he'd have to tell his dad about Peter, and he knew he wouldn't like it. But Martin did well to veil his heartache, as the frequency of family dinners at Hope Cottage increased, and he'd hear more about Penelope and Peter. It hurt him like a stab in the chest, although he knew it was for the best. Penelope deserved the best: to be happy. To have someone who was 'all in'. Plus it eased his guilt and made life less complicated to have only one wife; one household; especially for a man in his fifties.

* * *

'What are you doing?' Clair shouted over the gentle hum of the engine, as Seb pulled into a grassy lane in the island's only land-locked county and turned off the ignition. In the distance the airport landing strip drew a line between where they had stopped and Seb's house on the other side of it. Clair had been hoping to get back to it, they were staying at Seb's tonight. 'What are you doing? I'm freezing!' she repeated.

They'd been to see Clair's parents and sisters for lunch up in Vale in the north, then stopped at Jake's for glühwein with his German parents in St Peter Port.

'Bear with me...' Seb said, as he swung his leg around and got off the moped. 'Come on!' He held out a gloved hand.

* * *

For the six Christmases since Seb and Clair had left the island to go to university, they had always come back to the Channel Islands, alternating between Clair's parents, and Penelope and Peter, who had since moved in. The first Christmas after the family bombshell was tense: Seb, Penelope and Martin sat around a silent dinner table overlooking the grey seascape. Everything about the joyful Christmases of his childhood seeming like a lie.

Over turkey and trimmings, Seb asked his dad what his other family thought about him never being there on Christmas Day. Martin wrongly thought it might be a salve for Seb to know that he and Tina had lied to SJ in favour of him.

'We just say Daddy always has to work abroad over Christmas, so she's never known otherwise. We celebrate it before I go or after I get back.'

But it didn't make Seb feel any better. It cut him up that his dad was dad to someone else; he couldn't bear to look at his father's treacherous face. It even made him feel slightly sorry for SJ.

For six gruelling months, Martin had tried to make everything right and keep up the charade of two separate families, but when the tinsel was packed away that January and Penelope had her own epiphany, Seb knew which parent he would be prioritising in the holidays.

They hadn't considered Christmas in The Baldons yet, although Tina had said they were always welcome at Hope

Cottage. But they had their own house now. Clair had got a job as a graduate theatre nurse at the John Radcliffe Hospital in Oxford, Seb had finished his BA and was doing his Part Two back in the university studio at Oxford Brookes, working at Curtis + Cooper for his placement.

The terraced student rental off Cowley Road had been handy for Seb to get to the office and Clair to the hospital, but the rent was sky-high and they couldn't live like students for ever, even if Seb was technically still a student.

They had recently bought a 1930s Art Deco fixer-upper in Northill, a small market town in the Oxfordshire countryside, two towns away from Martin, Tina and SJ. Given the dining room – with its 1970s wallpaper, threadbare brown carpet and broken Arts and Crafts fireplace – was in no fit state to host a first Christmas yet, and given they lived so close to his dad and his other family, it was the perfect excuse to go back to Guernsey again. Besides, SJ hadn't got any more gracious playing board games now she was seventeen, and they all had to turn a blind eye to her cheating.

'Can't we go home?' Clair groaned. She tucked her cold hands into her puffa jacket pockets. 'Your mum will be getting worried.'

It was dusk, and Penelope didn't like Seb using the moped in the dark. Let alone in winter.

'It's fine, we're twenty-three, not thirteen!' Seb protested with his disarming smile. 'Let's go up to the chapel, it's best in this light...'

'OK.' Clair shrugged. She did always soften at the suggestion of a ramble, a walk, a challenge. It was why she'd joined the climbing, hiking and ultimate Frisbee clubs at Middlesex University, and the rowing club since joining Seb in Oxford.

They walked along the small green valley of Les Vauxbelets and up the steps to The Little Chapel, built by a French friar in the 1900s, in homage to a basilica in Lourdes. As they looked up, their hands in their pockets, it was illuminated like the gingerbread Christmas house on Penelope's dining table. Except this structure sparkled as you neared it, decorated in a patchwork of broken china, seashells and pebbles.

'So pretty!' Clair said as they walked up the steps.

'That's a sight to warm you up, huh?' Seb said proudly. Clair looked at him with a cautious pause. She loved his positivity; his sense of fun.

'God, I don't think I've been here since school!' Clair said, wondering why she hadn't.

Seb always loved the chapel. To him it was the next step up from Lego in his architecture journey. The patience that the monk had put into building it – three times over three decades, since he had destroyed it the first time – much like Seb with his early structures, because it wasn't quite right. The second time it was demolished after an embarrassing incident when the rotund Bishop of Portsmouth couldn't get through the doorway on a visit to the island in 1923. The third was deemed good enough to decorate in china, glass, buttons and mother of pearl. Seb loved the notion of Brother Déodat getting his building perfect; of the love, care and time that went into the small structure. How tiny turrets and a miniature spire could look so majestic.

'Well, let's go inside, then...' Seb said, excitedly.

Clair hadn't seen him so happy and relaxed at Christmas in a long time so they skipped up the stairs, their tummies full of Linda Armitage's famous *bûche de Noël*.

There weren't many stairs, and at the top Seb stopped and took Clair's hand.

'Wow!' she gasped, looking at the tealights refracting the light inside. Buttons and china sparkled. She examined some fragments up close. Part of a butterfly on a plate; the eye of a tiger on another; pale cream porcelain with delicate bluebells. Clair read something from a shard. 'Author and poet... year in exile... the divide...' she said, marvelling at what it might have said; pondering if the other pieces of the same china were elsewhere within these walls.

Her eyes widened as she looked up at the low ceiling. Her brown hair still tinged blonde at the ends, despite midwinter. Warm chestnut eyes glowing in the candlelight.

'I wonder who comes up here to light it at night.'

Seb smiled to himself and pulled her in.

'Err... That would have been me.'

'What?'

'Well, today anyway.'

'Pardon me?'

'And Jake.'

'Jake? Is this where you two went off?'

As it dawned on Clair, Seb dropped to one knee, wincing slightly at the zealousness with which his patella hit the stone floor. His smile huge and his blue eyes sparkling in the candlelight.

'Oh god!' Clair admonished, trying to sound as happy as she felt. She softened and stroked his chin as he gazed up at her. 'Are you OK?' she asked, nervously.

'I'm more than OK.'

Clair stifled a laugh. Seb Cooper was always full of surprises, but this one she had just cottoned onto.

'Clair. Clair...' he said, with a twinkle and a beam. 'Will you marry me?'

13

JUNE 2019, NORTHILL, OXFORDSHIRE

'Me, is it?' Jake said, looking up at Reverend Jane for confirmation. She nodded earnestly, as Jake stood from his chair at the end of the line and straightened his jacket by its solitary fastened button. Christine looked up at him adoringly and gave his free hand a squeeze.

'You got this,' she whispered to him and he gave a grateful nod without looking at her.

Jake Koch was the CTO of a tech start-up and regularly gave 'all-hands' meetings to staff, had dinner with dot.com billionaires, led agile meet-ups to young techies and gave TED talks, without giving them a second thought. This was the hardest gig of his life.

The last time he had done a speech about Seb was when he was best man at his wedding to Clair back in Guernsey fifteen years ago. Then it had been resplendent with anecdotes about drunken mishaps and stories from their youth. Given Seb had married young and Jake met Christine a decade later, Jake followed a path of travel, misadventure, and business risks that all paid off. He had only become a dad eighteen months ago; Seb had been a dad for fourteen years. But despite their different trajectories, Jake always gravitated back to his best friend from school; the friend he shared bottles of Thunderbird and Mad Dog 20/20 with at island parties; the friend he suggested should transfer to join him at Oxford Brookes if he was so miserable in London; the friend who had designed his Cotswolds house for him, for free, because that was the kind of mate Seb was.

Jake was taller, darker, brown-eyed and even more handsome than Seb. They'd made a devilishly disarming double act, picking up right where they left off every time they caught up: whether it was university holidays back in Guernsey; drinks in Oxford, curries in Brick Lane or family lunches in Northill and the Cotswolds. They'd always had an ability to know what the other was thinking. Jake knew if Seb were able to see the room right now he would be scratching his head, half laughing, and saying, 'What the fuck?'

With long strides Jake got to the lectern as if he were in a hurry, before clearing his throat. Reverend Jane handed him a bottle of water.

'Is it gin?' he quipped sadly to the smiling reverend, who gave an apologetic no, before looking up and addressing Millie and Jasper for the entire duration of his eulogy.

'You two kids are the coolest,' he said, after sipping from the bottle and rubbing his temples. 'I mean, I knew you were cool from the minute you were born and Seb called me to say he was a dad for the first time, and then again with you, Jasper. I remember it clear as day. He called with you, Millie, he was outside the John Radcliffe; I was in Greece with... an old friend...' He looked at Christine with mock guilt, who was encouraging, her watery eyes filled with love. 'And he sounded so happy and relieved that you had been born safe and well that I could see the fucking sparkle in those pretty eyes of his, even over the phone... shit, excuse my language.'

There were laughs dotted between the cries in the room as Jake cleared his throat again.

'And you were a text, Jasper, because I remember it on my old Nokia. "A SON!!!!!" he texted. No emojis, because we didn't have such things in the old days. But I'm sure if he had he would have used the cute baby emoji – 'cause you were proper cute, and a pink heart because he was a contrary bugger. Probably the pink heart with the bow on it because he's always seen you as a gift.

'But then, getting to know your brilliant personalities over the years, seeing the pride in your dad's face as he watched you showing me one of your backflip things, Millie, or telling me how bloody clever you are. And you, Jasper, how you could recite shit he had long forgotten, it just made him so proud. Watching him watching you was just...' Jake shook his head '... heart-swelling. Even then.'

He paused, hands gripping either side of the lectern, head dropped between his shoulders.

'Now I'm a dad...' he said soberly. 'I know how it really feels. How much he loved you. How he would have done anything for you.'

Noemie let out a gut-punch of a cry, which startled Jake, and he looked at her for a second, before getting back to the kids. This was going to be about the kids.

'I don't want to get all *Lion King* on you, but his spirit, that love, it's in you. Have confidence in that. His smart brain and beautiful heart and soul and courage, that's in you kids, so you will never walk a step without him – without your brilliant dad – on your shoulder.'

There was a pause again, and nearly everyone in the building was fighting the urge to crumple into a heap, Reverend Jane included, as Jake gathered himself.

'Jasper, you've got a really cool stepdad coming, but if you need anyone to go on a photo walk with, or to go fishing and have a chat with, call me. Millie – I'm shit at tennis and I don't understand the gymnastics scoring system, but any time you want to thrash someone, or for a muppet to cheer you on at some competition, I will be roaring for you, on behalf of me and on behalf of your dad. And I will roar the loudest, I promise.' He loosened the knot of the noose around his neck, as if clearing his throat to roar now.

Millie looked back and choked.

'Never forget that I am always here for you. I know it's not me you want and life sucks, and I'm really sorry about that. But genuinely...' His head slumped, and a silence washed over the chapel. 'You have so much promise, so much life ahead of you. This will shape you but it won't ruin you. You are so full of his love. He loved you more than anything in the world – and nothing will ever take that away.'

14

CLAIR

May 2004, Guernsey

'If I can just ask for your attention, for one last speech...'

Everyone on the terrace of the clifftop restaurant was surprised when the groom's father spoke into the microphone. Clair's dad, Adrian, a statistician with a domed head, had already given a muted yet loving tribute to his eldest daughter; and the guests were still wiping their tears after Jake's hilarious retelling of an encounter between Seb and a seventy-two-year-old flamenco dancer on his stag do in Seville. People looked at each other in surprise when Martin Cooper stood up from his bow-backed chair, opposite his son on the round table in the middle of the sun-dappled terrace, and took the microphone from Jake as he sat back down.

* * *

* * *

It had been a frou-frou and familiar Guernsey affair. After the church ceremony in Clair's parish of Vale, the wedding party had migrated to the clifftop venue where the couple posed among the floral arches and fig trees in the gardens before sitting down to eat Guernsey crab, herb-crusted lamb and rhubarb crumble. Clair wasn't a girly girl but she'd gone all-out (under pressure from her sisters) and worn a strapless ivory dress with a sweetheart neckline and a whole lotta tulle from the waist down. She had five brides-maids: her sisters, Elizabeth and Rachel, her best island friends, Lucia and Elise. Plus Seb's half-sister SJ, who was now nineteen but still carried the clumsy look of a young and sullen teen. All five of them wore midnight-blue dresses of varying designs to suit each of their shapes. Seb looked dashing in a midnight-blue suit that brought out his eyes with a pale peony buttonhole to complement Clair's bouquet. Jake was a solid best man, sharp and spot-on with his speech, and Leo and Woody were slightly flustered groomsmen, all three doing their best to fend off the advances of SJ, the drunker she became on Archers and lemonade.

During the photos in the gardens, SJ had a tantrum about being stood between Elise, an elfin pixie with cropped white-blonde hair, and Lucia, an Amazonian goddess with the broad bronze shoulders of an Olympic swimmer. But Clair's middle sister, Elizabeth, who was on a graduate programme at the Foreign Office and had been party to an SJ tantrum when they were wedding-dress shopping, dealt with it deftly and diplomatically, sand-wiching her between Rachel and Clair, which seemed to appease her as she puffed out her shoulders next to the bride.

* * *

Now the sun was setting, the festoon lights on the terrace were lit but not yet glowing, and tables of guests who had been getting more and more raucous chinked forks against glasses to ask for peace while Martin Cooper, father of the groom, stood, with a sage subduedness that made all the guests go quiet.

Tina nervously stroked Martin's arm in encouragement. Penelope and Peter exchanged an intrigued look. Clair squeezed Seb's leg.

'As most of you who love Sebastian know, his family has grown in somewhat "unusual" circumstances...'

'Yay!' came one mistimed holler, from a university friend of Seb and Jake at the back. A nervous murmur of a laugh floated among the guests; SJ shot the blushing perpetrator a dagger from her table with the bridesmaids and their partners.

Seb took a deep breath.

Please, Dad...

'It's been a hard and enlightening journey, for all of us. And as I stand here, on the occasion of Sebastian's wedding day...'

Please.

'...to Clair, who we all adore...'

Adrian and Linda looked proud and hopeful as Martin continued.

'I can't pass on saying a few words myself. Adding to what Adrian and Jake have said about this happy union. But I speak for me and Penelope, Tina and Peter, when we say how happy we are on this day...' He looked down at his place setting to catch his breath while everyone clapped. Then the mood shifted again as he ruffled his neat temples.

'But I speak for me when I say how proud I am, as a father, of the man Sebastian has grown into. Of what a fine fully qualified architect – and now fully qualified husband – he has become.' There were more cheers from the wedding guests. 'Some of you might not know this yet, but, if I may...' Martin looked at Seb, to seek his permission; he nodded back. 'Yesterday, Sebastian was offered a job at a prestigious studio in London. Rennie + Byrd. If you haven't heard of them you'll have seen their fancy hotels in fancy travel magazines.' He rolled his eyes to a loud applause. 'And while Roger and I certainly can't keep up with that, and while we're devastated to lose him, his sense of humour and the unparalleled enthusiasm he brings to our office – and a few hearts are breaking today, Clair, I have to say—' the uni lads gave a rowdy cheer while Clair looked at her friends and sisters on the bridesmaids' table in despair '—we see him sail off with pride. Because there can be no prouder father on this planet right now than I am of you, Seb.'

The rowdiness petered out as hearts softened in the late afternoon sunshine and Martin wiped a tear with his thumb.

'So, if I may, I'd just like to read this short poem by William Wordsworth...'

15

JUNE 2019, NORTHILL, OXFORDSHIRE

I am a shell of a man.

Martin sat with SJ to his left and Noemie to his right, the waxing and waning noise of her sobs loudest to him, although he was the most tolerant of them, so it was probably just as well. He had held onto her in Florida; he had coaxed her out of bed and got her to eat a few meagre French fries from the room-service menu at the apartment complex, while they sat at the large dining table in a kitchen that had barely been used.

He had encouraged her children to use the pool and had given the lifeguard $200 to make sure they were furnished with snacks and juices they barely touched. He had held her tight and told her that her mother was on her way.

Noise. There was so much noise out there.

Noemie's sobs. Jake's frustrated appeals. The sound of the children splashing in the pool. He had paperwork and forms to fill at the county coroner's office and the British consulate. Medical bills to pay, even though Seb had arrived at the hospital deceased. He had to wait on hold, sometimes for hours, to insurance companies back in the UK, only for them to tell him, 'Sorry, sir, we don't think he's covered for that, I'll get my manager to call you back...'

Martin had to repeatedly answer questions about whether the death was unnatural or violent; whether arrests had been made or charges brought.

Clair had flown out with him and Jake, and took Millie and Jasper straight back to the UK, which left a no man's land of waiting for Camille to arrive and take over with Noemie and her grandchildren. Jake said they weren't there to do that, but Martin had felt obliged.

After Camille arrived, Martin and Jake were free to sort out the business that needed sorting. Ask questions. Speak to lawyers and sheriffs. Fill in more forms. Every evening, they would get dinner, sitting shattered in a restaurant surrounded by holidaymakers, looking at their phones or taking calls from Clair, Penelope and Tina, with no appetite for the food in front of them; and just wonder how the hell it had all gone wrong.

I want to hug her.

Martin stared at his feet, even though he wanted to look down the line.

I need to hold her.

He thought about his son in the box. He thought about how he had marvelled at Penelope when she lay holding their newborn, after his miracle birth. He thought about how radiant and proud she looked. He thought about the lie that broke his son's heart and wondered if he had died in peace about it; whether he had truly forgiven him. He thought about all the years he had wanted to go back, to Guernsey, to be a family again. But Seb and Penelope were a team; they were fine without him. It was as if the relief of his secret not being a secret any more solidified their life without him. They didn't need him.

I have to hold her. I have to see her now.

As if sensing his torment, Tina leaned forward, putting her small hand across their daughter's wide lap, and touched Martin's knee with her fingertips.

16

CLAIR

November 2004, London

'So what did you think of Seb's office?' Clair twirled spaghetti enthusiastically on her fork in an Italian restaurant on Marylebone High Street.

'It was very impressive,' Martin contemplated, taking a bounteous sip from a large vessel of red wine and pursing his lips to savour the flavour. 'A wonderful workspace for a wonderful team, I'm sure.' Martin looked sideways at his son next to him.

Two hours earlier, Martin had stood with his hands in his pockets, appraising the large open space of the middle of the Rennie + Byrd office in Shoreditch; its capacious centre with glass-walled offices of frosted glass panels shooting off each wall and corner – for the more senior architects, although Sebastian was starting in the middle bank of more recently qualified Part Twos and Part One assistants.

Martin had been in London for meetings with clients; to meet estate agents about selling the Limehouse flat; and he had wanted to call in on Seb at work, so he could see his son in situ at his new workplace. When Seb told him Clair was in London too, on a course at St Thomas' Hospital, Martin said he'd swing by late afternoon and take them both out to dinner.

Meals in the lively market town of Northill, or at the cottage in The Baldons, were pleasant enough, but Martin liked to break free for an evening – that much hadn't changed.

'Jill was definitely flirting with him...' Seb winced as he slid his knife into a succulent veal steak. 'I've not seen her flustered before.'

Jill was the Rennie from Rennie + Byrd – a Scottish powerhouse in a pocket size. She and her husband, Terence, had taken New York by storm in the nineties, overhauling the Meatpacking District from butcher carcasses and grime to edgy art galleries, sleek boutiques and restaurants that looked like European cafes Picasso and Stein might have drunk in. When they were tired of New York, they set their sights on London, returning to the city they had met and trained in.

'Who can blame her? A handsome dog like me,' Martin said, with a twinkle in his eye. But he was right. In his mid-fifties, Martin still had the dashing charm that had won over Carole at school, Penelope on the St Peter Port social circuit, and Tina at the Curtis + Cooper office in Oxford. Tina still had the look of a stressed-out hummingbird, eyelids blinking ferociously, heart pulsing a thousand beats per minute whenever a woman put her arm on Martin's shoulder and flirted with him – so he liked to go out without her every now and again.

Seb laughed to himself, desperate to tell his dad something, but he hung onto it.

'How was your course, Clair?'

'Oh, super. It was in robotics, led by reps. All interesting tech I will struggle to get my head around, no doubt. It was quite tiring.'

She paused, drank some water, then carried on.

'My sister, you know, Elizabeth? She works at the Foreign Office, which was just around the corner! So we went to Pret for lunch and... well, it's been a busy day.' She looked at Seb, who was tucking into his dinner. So she carried on.

'Nice to have a break from the JR, to be honest. Sounds really nerdy but I love learning new things; trying to imagine what nursing will look like as time goes on; as I move up the grades... All pretty *tiring* though, you know, taking so much in...' Clair gave Seb a loaded stare as he looked up.

'No, I think it sounds really interesting. You are brave. I don't know how you do what you do without being squeamish. I can't even have a blood test without feeling nauseous. Although robotics sounds more pleasant than some of the courses you've been on. That bowel one didn't sound very—'

'Well, I've not been so brave of late...' Clair nodded pointedly at Seb, to finally take his cue.

'Yeah, Dad,' Seb said, clearing his throat. 'Actually, we've got some news.'

Seb put down his knife and fork; he was beaming like an excited child.

'Oh, yes! Is the kitchen all in?'

'Yeah... yeah, the worktops arrived. It looks great.'

'Was that oven OK?' He looked at Clair, and she tried not to seethe internally.

'Works like a dream!' Seb answered quickly. 'We can stop getting takeaways from Aziz...'

'Oh, good – yes I think you made the right choice with the wood over the Corian. You have to oil it regularly, but it wears beautifully.' Martin took another sip of wine.

Seb and Clair had been renovating their 1930s Art Deco house on Priory Green for two years and no one was keener on talking construction quality, kitchen/diner extensions and fixtures and fittings than Martin. He loved the aesthetics as much as the build.

Seb had marvelled how the chocolate-box cottage in The Baldons was so different from the glass box in Guernsey, but his dad had been equally house-proud and passionate about both. And he'd been even more enthusiastic about Seb and Clair's renovation, which made Seb realise that his dad was passionate about buildings in every form. Or perhaps his enthusiasm was due to his relief that Seb and Clair had laid down roots near him when he thought he had blown everything.

Last week the kitchen had finally gone in and the renovations from tired 1930s relic to modern, light, family home were almost complete. Which was just as well.

'Yes, the kitchen's great – it's more Clair... she's, er, struggling at work—'

Clair rolled her eyes at Seb for making a mess of it all.

'Why? What's happened?'

'Oh, no, no – just with her feeling so sick and all.'

Seb had wanted to make the announcement special. He was going to become a father – surely this was a pivotal life moment, breaking the news to the one man who would know how he felt. Except he wasn't getting it.

'Oh god, has norovirus been going round the JR? There's been a terrible outbreak in Tina's mum's care home...'

'No, Dad—'

'I'm pregnant,' Clair interjected, matter-of-factly.

Martin almost spilt his wine.

'Good god. That was quick. Well—'

Clair nodded.

'It was lucky,' she said.

'Due in the spring,' Seb confirmed proudly.

Martin coughed a little on the last of his crab linguini as his eyes welled up, and turned to Seb, who was beaming.

'Does your mother know?'

'We told her a couple of weeks ago; she and Peter were over. Wanted to tell you in person, but didn't get the chance—'

Martin wasn't worried about timelines or hierarchies. He was just happy at the thought of how happy Penelope must be; how happy he was. His ribcage expanded, his chest puffed out to enable his swelling heart to grow. Seb and Clair waited for him to gather himself.

'I thought I couldn't possibly be more proud of you earlier, at the office,' Martin said, formally. 'But – well, Sebastian, you continue to amaze me. Clair. Sorry!' He stood up, took her hand and kissed her on both cheeks over the table. Clair stood, a little flustered, and blushed. 'Congratulations, how wonderful. You are going to make the most fantastic parents, I know it.'

Clair gave a shy smile and looked over at Seb, whose eyes were also filling up. They had got there in the end.

'Sod it, let's get champers!' ordered Martin, dropping his napkin to his lap and looking around for their waiter. 'One tiny drop won't hurt, eh? And we'll get a taxi back. No schlepping through Paddington for you, my dear. The driver can drop you in Northill on my way through.' Martin's cheeks flushed with mirth. It had all been OK. 'My son.' He grinned. 'A father!'

17

JUNE 2019, NORTHILL, OXFORDSHIRE

Would it be bad to write a post about funeral dating?

SJ pursed her lips and wiped the corners of her mouth with a swollen ring finger to clear the cracks of Ruby Woo she knew would be gathering there.

Shame Jake's off the market, I would have loved to finally bang him.

She was getting sweaty in her faux-fur stole, which she wore because she liked how glamorous it looked, while also being sombre, in a muted shade of cream that offset her black dress and fake pearls perfectly. SJ hadn't stopped to think how hot she might get in faux fur on a midsummer's day; only that she wanted to look stylish. Style didn't have to go out of the window just because you were mourning, did it?

I bet there are hot guys back there. Seb had loads of hot friends.

SJ thought about the upside of when her world came crashing in when she was twelve and her mother and father sat her down on the sofa and explained that the boy at the front door a few weeks ago was her half-brother. That Daddy used to be with someone else; that he had a family he had walked away from.

Because he loves you so much, Tina had assured.

As she looked at her heartbroken father's thigh next to her, she thought about his treachery.

I bet they expected a full-on tantrum.

But the girl with tonged Shirley Temple hair and a thousand shiny party dresses hadn't really cared. Nothing had existed before she existed, had it? As long as he wasn't going to take her daddy away from her.

'No, darling,' explained Tina, blinking furiously. 'You're his number one.'

Tina knew as she said it that Martin wouldn't like it, but this was damage control on the day they had dreaded for much of their daughter's life.

SJ contemplated it.

'Well, can I have a pony?'

Martin and Tina were so relieved they said yes.

Her parents had failed to mention when, exactly, Martin had walked away from his first (second) union; or that he hadn't actually walked away, Penelope had pushed him, but he hadn't told Tina the whole truth about that either. And SJ hadn't stopped to put two and two together and ask why they only told her *after* the boy had turned up at their front door, looking so *angry*. Perhaps she just didn't want to know.

Woody's probably back there. Woody's always game.

SJ had grown accepting of the handsome half-brother – especially when her teen friends started seeing photos of him on the fireplace and a few of them had serious crushes. He was good currency when, at fourteen, she pretended to her friends that she had lost her virginity to one of his; and then when she actually did lose her virginity at fifteen, she lied and said she had shagged one of Seb's hot uni mates, not Robert Bush behind the McDonald's in Headington.

Now she was thirty-four and still hankering.

It would make a great blog post.

'Three Little Birds' by Bob Marley was playing as the committal started to loom and Noemie's wailing was starting to get on SJ's tits.

I used to fucking like this song.

SJ had tried to like her – Noemie was a welcome relief after Desiree, who was a bit too competent and composed for SJ's liking. Noemie had a wildness that made SJ feel delightfully on edge. Plus Desiree had split Seb's family up and pulled him away from her niece and nephew, because it was all her fault, *the bony bitch*. So SJ tried really hard to like Noemie, to spite Desiree more than anything. However, she couldn't help noticing the book – *her* book, *The Superlatively Single Girl's Guide To Dating*, the book she had gifted Noemie on Christmas Eve – was left on the shelf at Seb's house last week, still sitting on the unkempt paper and ribbon she had torn from it. It must have been untouched for six months.

Ungrateful cow.

Now she had even more to answer for, except no one could get much sense out of her. And while Bob Marley sang about everything being all right she was *fucking wailing* like a child, which, really, was a bit tacky, all things considered.

SJ wiped the corners of her thin lips again and contemplated her next move. Woody would be back there for sure and her book sales hadn't been great. Maybe it was best to give up the *Superlatively Single* blog, find a husband and start a family. The bloggers with babies were doing so well and getting so much engagement, perhaps Woody was her ticket. He owned a hotel in the Lake District. That could be pretty Instagrammable.

It worked for Mummy, giving up her little typing job when she got knocked up with me.

SJ flicked her wavy bob at the thought of her entry to the world, how nicely she decorated it. How many followers she had.

It would be the ultimate tribute to Seb, wouldn't it? One out one in, and all that...

SJ glanced back over her shoulder, beyond Desiree, to the men standing at the back. The architect types. Seb's dad friends he had made in Northill. The school mates from the drab island she'd once visited for the wedding.

Ahhh, there he is.

Woody stood out at the back for his string-bean height, hands in his pockets and scruffy hair tucked behind big jug ears. She had first fucked him at that wedding – the night after she'd fucked the porter at the hotel they were staying in; then again one time Woody was staying in Northill and SJ engineered a visit to join a group of them on a walk – taking a detour via a rapeseed field where they came out with yellow buds in their hair and oil marks all over their clothes. Then at Seb's thirtieth – Woody mounted SJ as she clung to the hatchback of a Vauxhall Vectra in the pub car park while everyone sang 'HAPPY BIRTHDAY TO YOUUUUU' in the small barn.

Wow, it must have been ten years.

He caught her eye and looked sadder than she had ever seen him. She gave him a brief smile and looked back to the front.

He'll be game. He'll be my babyfather. If only those ears weren't so bloody big.

18

CLAIR

April 2005, Northill, Oxfordshire

Clair opened the front door of their Art Deco delight to see SJ on the doorstep looking shell-shocked. Shell-shocked in a way that looked as if SJ might be acting shell-shocked in a Mexican *telenovela*. Her wavy bob bounced in the breeze around her chin and her eyes darted dramatically side to side as she hugged the long parka around her middle.

'Oh, I thought you were in Nottingham!' Clair said, puzzled. She'd only just got home from her shift, kicked off her shoes and put on her slippers. This was her quiet time.

'Well, clearly not...' SJ said sardonically, sucking a large intake of breath through her teeth. 'I had to come home,' she said with a gasp; her red lipstick doing little to lift the beige pallor that matched the beige oversized scarf around her neck.

Clair hadn't had a chance to shower away the smells of saline, hand sanitiser and flimsy cheese sandwiches (she'd forgotten her packed lunch today and had to go to the canteen) that permeated her hair, hands and skin after a shift. She hadn't even had a cup of tea, so she felt caught on the back foot, half regretting opening the door, which she felt bad about.

'Are you OK?' she asked.

SJ shook her head dramatically.

'Well, excuse the state of me,' Clair apologised. 'I wasn't expecting—'

'Expecting. That's about right.' SJ gulped, walking past Clair and charging through the hallway.

'Come in,' Clair said to herself, as SJ flounced into the kitchen/diner at the back of the house and slumped on the sofa by the patio doors.

'Are you OK? Would you like a cup of tea?'

Clair heaved and cupped her belly with her right arm as she hung her fleece on the back of the kitchen door with her left, before smoothing down her long ponytail. After the wedding, Clair had her long hair cut into a practical bob, but all her pregnancy hormones were making it grow back again. Wisps of golden-brown baby hair flourished around her hairline.

'I need something stronger, but tea will have to do, I suppose.'

Clair nodded, perplexed, but put the kettle on while SJ lay back, put her feet up, closed her eyes, and put her hand to her brow.

'When did you get home? Are Martin and Tina OK?' Clair asked as she took a tea caddy down from the shelf.

SJ put her hand up as if to say *too many questions*, so Clair stopped asking them.

'Seb's away, if you wanted to catch him.'

'Oh, right,' SJ answered through closed eyes, uninterested. Clair continued the chitter chatter in her matter-of-fact tone, although she *really* wanted a shower.

'Antwerp. His first overseas project. Well, he's assisting...' Clair looked over at SJ, to see if she was as excited for Seb as she was, as she took the milk out of the fridge.

Her statue-like face said nothing.

'Are you OK? Do you need some painkillers or something?'

SJ opened her eyes, readjusting them to the light of the late spring afternoon, unravelled her scarf from around her broad neck, and sat up.

'I'm think I'm pregnant.'

Clair's mouth fell open as a silence burned through the noise of the gas on the hob.

'Pardon me?'

SJ's eyes filled up and she swept her big gaze out towards the garden, as if she were auditioning for a role and giving it some emotion, some welly.

SJ nodded.

'Yuh.'

This was the thing with SJ, she was so dramatic in every encounter, Clair could never tell what was real and what was theatre.

'Christ! How far gone are you?'

'Well, it can't be long, I've only missed one period.'

'Have you done a test? They're very reliable now...'

'No, I haven't!' she snapped defensively.

Clair took a deep breath, widened her eyes and got on with the tea. She had been looking forward to putting her feet up, putting a pizza in the oven and watching *The Apprentice* – a guilty pleasure Seb didn't like. She wasn't banking on coaching SJ through another drama.

'Sorry – my head is just scrambled,' she said, a thick hand on each cheek as she stared into the mid-distance of the lawn outside.

Clair felt bad for her in case she was pregnant. SJ was absolutely not ready to have kids.

'That's OK. You've got a lot to process.' Clair stopped to look at her, eyes full of concern. 'Earl Grey?'

SJ shot her a look.

'Do you have Rooibos?'

'No.'

'OK, Earl Grey will do.'

Clair busied herself making the tea and getting the oven on, and decided not to ask anything unless SJ volunteered it, which she did, a few minutes later.

'I've been schtupping my drama and performance lecturer,' she confided. 'We slipped up.'

'Oh.'

SJ nodded enthusiastically, as if she were a teenager bragging to friends.

'Yeah – our in-depth explorations of Shakespeare, Marlowe and Johnson resulted in in-depth explorations of my vagina...' She sighed. 'He can't get enough of me.'

Clair tried not to wince.

'Oh dear. Is that right? Should lecturers be sleeping with students?'

'Not the married ones,' SJ said, raising an overgroomed eyebrow.

'Oh, SJ. What are you going to do?'

She was only twenty, about to finish her second year of English at Nottingham with her life ahead of her. Clair thought of Martin and Tina's faces. How devastated they would be. If she *were* pregnant. A niggle in the back of her mind couldn't help wondering. SJ often suffered scares that turned out to be nothing: the suspected coeliac disease, the undiagnosed dyslexia, the dramatic pre-wedding weight-loss worry, when the bridesmaids' dressmaker said the fit was still perfect.

'I just don't know!' she said, taking the tea and hugging the mug.

'Look, do you want me to nip to Sainsbury's, get you a test?'

Clair felt a kick in her tight stomach – she was thirty-four weeks pregnant and SJ hadn't even asked how she was.

'If you'd be a darling,' SJ said, her eyes wide as she sipped her tea and rubbed her own stomach, rounded by beer and university life. She lay back on the sofa and put her shoes up on one end.

'It's cramping so much, maybe this is the embryo embedding...' she said as she leaned back and put her hand to her brow again.

Clair looked at SJ, reclining with the haughty curves of a Beryl Cook subject, as she closed her eyes again.

'I'll be back in a bit, then,' Clair said efficiently.

'Oh, can you get me a *Marie Claire* and maybe a Chocolate Orange too, please? You're a star.'

19

JUNE 2019, NORTHILL, OXFORDSHIRE

Think happy thoughts, think happy thoughts...

Millie sat between her mum and Aunty Dora, trying not to think about her dad's lifeless body in the box in front of them. The trauma of a holiday at the Most Magical Place on Earth. How scared she was to be left alone with Noemie, whose wails she could hear now.

You have to hold it together, for Jaspy and for Mum. For Grandma Guilbert and Peter. Grandad and Tina.

Happy thoughts.

Millie thought of how her dad roared and punched the air when she completed her first back handspring and layout step-out on a balance beam with no wobbles – and only went and won the regional competition. As she arced her body and the world around her blurred, her dad's face was the one constant in the auditorium, anchoring her with every flip and turn.

She thought about how her dad always claimed she was named after Millicent Fawcett and called her a pioneer in everything she did, leading the way for her younger brother.

She thought about the scents of citrus fruits and saltwater as they ambled along the boardwalk at the back of Miami Beach. She thought about the exhibition their dad had taken them to at the Wolfsonian on Washington Avenue. Wandering around the cool, air-conditioned gallery with her father's reassuring palm on the small of her back – letting her know that he was looking at the same picture.

Think happy thoughts, think happy thoughts.

She thought about her father's huge presence, his own citrus smell – of bergamot, orange and amber, although she didn't know that was what the concoction was – but never wanted to forget it because smell was something that you couldn't get from a photo.

She thought about the way he winked at her. The way he always championed her. The way he was always with her, even though he didn't always live with her. On holidays by the sea; learning to ride a bike on the green; hiking hills and mountains – even when she claimed to hate going on a long walk – walking side by side with her father offered Millie a comfort she couldn't put her finger on.

Even during the less happy times, when she was angry at him. During the trips between two homes and the awkward doorstep drop-offs, her dad's sad face saying goodbye always made her feel guilty. How could she be angry at someone she loved so much?

Don't think about the sad things, don't think about her. *Think happy thoughts, think happy thoughts.*

Millie thought about that night in the hotel room, when it was just the three of them. They had watched *Black Panther* and fallen asleep, huddled together in the same bed, exhausted and relieved to have got away.

If I'd known what was to come, I would have stayed awake all night. Hugged him the whole time. Begged him not to go back.

She thought about the smell of suncream, the ice-cream hut, the adoration as he looked at her and said goodbye. The wink, the way he said '*Love you*' as if it weren't the last time.

That was the trouble. Every happy thought she had was tarnished. They all led to the box in front of her.

20

CLAIR

May 2005, Oxford

'Oh, my goodness, she's a beauty!'

Seb sat on the hard, plastic chair at Clair's bedside, his proud mother standing on the other side of the hospital bed, holding a swaddled newborn in her arms. Penelope's cool blonde hair was now mostly silver, and the thin silk scarf tied around it brushed her granddaughter's cheek as she gently swayed. The baby twitched and settled, tiny lips puckering in her sleep.

'I've never changed a girl's nappy, you know,' Penelope confessed. 'I'll be learning with you.'

Clair smiled. Her mother-in-law always had a soothing, singsong grace that was very different from Clair's sparing way with words, but it never caused them to clash. The way Penelope rocked gently and spoke softly and supportively helped reassure Clair while her lower half burned and seared. Penelope had always been so supportive and encouraging of their relationship, and now Clair had given her the most wonderful gift of a grandchild. The smile was pale but content – she was exhausted, shattered, proud after a marathon labour, as she gazed up at her sleeping baby in her grandmother's arms.

Seb had been to and from Antwerp twice more in the last month of Clair's pregnancy, the excitement and nerves increasing each time he went. But Clair went beyond her due date – seven agonising days watching *Bargain Hunt* and *Doctors* while she waited for her waters to break, which they did on a walk among the blue-bells in the woods.

Three agonising days later, a 6 lb 11 oz girl was dragged out by a ventouse vacuum, giving her skull a conical sensibility, which you couldn't notice under the yellow bonnet Penelope had knitted.

Clair's nurse and doctor friends kept passing by, from Theatre to the maternity unit on level seven at the John Radcliffe – via the hospital shop to pick up Milk Tray, tulips, and a copy of *Hello!* magazine.

'Mum, sit down,' Seb insisted, getting up out of his chair.

'No, darling, you must be worn out too. Anyway, I like bobbing from side to side when I'm holding a baby. They like the movement...'

Penelope mused how long it had been since she last held a newborn – it must have been at least twenty-five years, but even in her fifties her own reflex to sway had come right back.

'Do you have a name?' she asked Clair.

'Seb likes Lilly, after a German architect...'

'Lilly Reich.'

'But there is already a Lily in our NCT group, she was a few weeks early. Seb doesn't think it matters but I'm not so sure... They got there first.'

'How about Millie?' Penelope suggested. 'That's a pretty name. My mother's middle name was Millicent.'

'Really?' asked Seb, surprised. He'd never known Sabine Guilbert's middle name was Millicent.

Clair tried it out for size.

'Millicent. Millie... Millie Cooper. I love it!'

She looked at Seb, who rubbed his eyes and nodded a me too.

'There you go!' The proud grandmother smiled. 'Millie... middle name?'

Colour was starting to come back to Clair's cheeks.

'Rose, we both loved Rose for a middle name, didn't we?' She looked to Seb, who smiled dreamily.

'Well, that's that, then!' said Penelope. 'Welcome to the world, Millie Rose Cooper.' And with an enchanted smile, she kissed her granddaughter on the nose and handed her back to Clair.

21

JUNE 2019, NORTHILL, OXFORDSHIRE

Who are these people? What is this music?

Noemie's mum wafted a fan under her chin, hoping that the oppressive drone of these moribund English songs would stop because they were making her feel so stifled, so helpless.

My daughter is in pieces, this music, it does not help!

Camille Morel had liked Seb when she first met him at Christmas. Camille was over to stay from Paris, delivering presents to her daughter and grandchildren, when Seb knocked on the front door and Noemie announced she was going out.

'Ahh, I didn't know Noa had a boyfriend!' Camille said as she ushered him into the kitchen of the ex-council house Noemie had artfully strewn with upcycled lampshades and leopard print.

Camille was pretty miffed with her daughter for casually mentioning she was going out when she had only just stepped off the Eurostar, but was placated by Seb's handsome face and all-encompassing smile. Seb had a way of disarming older women with that smile.

'You look like very nice...' she said with a grand appraisal.

'*Parles-tu français aussi?*' Camille asked, with a noble twinkle in her eye.

'*Non, je suis désolé...*' Seb said awkwardly.

'Ahhh, Rosbif, he try!' Camille shrugged with a laugh, as Noemie walked into the kitchen and inserted an earring before smoothing down her mussy hair. Camille sent them out with a smile while also notching it up as something to be bitter and resentful with Noemie about when the handsome man wasn't around.

* * *

Camille didn't imagine, during that fleeting meeting at Christmas, that in just five months she would be flying out to America to help clear up the mess of what had happened. To bring her sedated daughter and shell-shocked grandchildren home. That a few weeks later, she would be sitting in a memorial chapel in England, full of strangers, listening to stories about someone her daughter seemed to love, but hadn't told her much about. She hadn't ever told her mother much about anything.

Camille leaned forward and looked along the line, across to *les gens de l'île* Noemie had told her about. To the ex-wife. The children.

Why are those kids here but not my grandchildren?

She squeezed Noemie's leg again, and noticed Martin's solid hand on the other side of her, resting on the crease of his trouser, tanned from a life spent mostly abroad since he'd retired. A ring on his right hand that looked like an heirloom. She fanned herself further and let out a sigh that actually sounded like *ooh la la*.

At least he doesn't think she killed him. Dashing man.

22

CLAIR

* * *

April 2009, Northill, Oxfordshire

'Come on! It's your party too!'

In the small barn in the pub garden of The Blue Bell in Northill, a shattered and sweaty Seb was airlifted onto Jake's and Leo's shoulders as a circle of friends stood around them singing a rousing rendition of 'Happy birthday to you'. His shirt damp from beer flying and dancing, he called Clair over from the periphery of the circle to the middle, knowing hell would have to freeze over before she climbed on anyone's shoulders or attempted a human pyramid.

'Come on!' he shouted, beckoning her over with a wave and a smile.

Clair shook her head in defiance, grateful that everyone was looking at Seb, as per usual.

Clair already turned thirty in January – Seb had taken her for afternoon tea in Paris with a night at a boutique hotel near the Sorbonne. Clair spent most of the trip feeling anxious about having left Millie with Martin and Tina for a day and a night. Not because she didn't trust Martin and Tina – they were loving and doting grandparents – but it all felt a little frivolous and self-indulgent, and she worried what people might think. She much preferred other people to be the centre of attention, and, conveniently, Seb always loved it, so she had set about planning a party for his thirtieth birthday in April and booked the barn.

But after almost four exhausting years mothering a daughter who had still not mastered the art of night-time sleeping; and working three and a half gruelling days a week in Theatre – on bowel surgeries, hysterectomies and laparoscopies – Clair realised she couldn't plan a big surprise party on her own. She didn't have the energy to sort the invitations, the food and the music. That was stuff Seb tended to get excited about; it felt counterintuitive trying to do it without him. So one February night, on the sofa in her slippers and PJs, Clair confessed what she was planning, but handed over choosing the buffet, the playlist and designing a Snapfish evite to Seb.

Now April had arrived, Seb was hoisted on the shoulders of his friends, shattered himself, but savouring the moment of being thrust in the air while 'Happy Birthday' segued into 'Mr Brightside'.

'It's Clair's thirtieth too!' Seb shouted, to a roar of claps, cheers and whistles as the party was amping up a notch.

Now they were thirty the purple vomit and messy unfulfilling sex was a thing of the past (Woody and SJ's moment against the back of a Vauxhall Vectra aside). Most of Seb and Clair's island schoolfriends had also moved to the mainland to start their careers: Leo was a hedge-fund manager – not the most popular guy right now – and lived in one of those marina flats near Martin's old Limehouse pad. He was still trying to hook up with Elise, who now worked in publishing, and also lived in London. Woody had followed his parents into hospitality and ran a hotel in the Lake District that the guys went to visit for Leo's thirtieth last autumn – and Woody found it lonelier than he let on. Lucia had competed in three Olympics since school, swimming for Team GB in Sydney, Athens and Beijing, but had recently retired and taken a job with Swim England. She was now in a relationship with Carrie from school – they had recently reconnected on social media and Carrie had moved to Loughborough to be with Lucia.

Jake was the exception to the group and lived overseas for now. Social media also favoured his fortunes and he had a job at Facebook in Palo Alto, California, but was back for the Easter holidays. By all accounts (well, his Facebook account) Jake had a nice life riding bikes around San Francisco, drinking a lot of red wine in vineyards on the weekends, and was dating a new tech wonder woman every week, which helped soothe his ego when he saw Lucia turn up with Carrie.

The Guernsey pals mingled with Northill friends – mostly fellow parents they'd met through Millie at nurseries, playgroups and in the park – all as tired and as wiped out as Clair and Seb. Clair's nurse friends from the John Radcliffe and Seb's workmates from Rennie + Byrd also came, although Jill and Terence hadn't made it out to the sticks (but they did send a nice Fortnum & Mason hamper).

Those revellers who had children were just about managing to stand up. Those who hadn't were celebrating the fact it didn't matter how drunk they got tonight; they were loving the flurry of thirtieth birthdays this year.

Penelope and Peter were over from Guernsey for Seb's birthday, so they had happily offered to babysit Millie and stay home, but Martin and Tina chatted with Seb's workmates – Federico, Fatima and Mei-Xin, who were all 'marvellous people', as Martin kept saying, the drunker he got.

As 'Mr Brightside' reached its crescendo, SJ stumbled back in. Her pregnancy scare at uni had been just that and the test had been negative, which was just as well as she was carving out a career in blogging, a new world that was opening up to English grads who had no idea what they wanted to do for a living. Her dating blog – tales of alleyway encounters and sex-toy reviews – was getting traction she didn't mind her parents knowing about. A baby wouldn't have fitted in with all that. One blogger friend said she would soon be able to monetise her masturbation, if she played her cards right.

'Oh! Did I miss the cake?' she shrieked as Seb and his friends danced to The Killers, Kings Of Leon and Kasabian.

By midnight Clair almost fell asleep on Seb's shoulder as they slow-danced to 'True' and she noticed ketchup on the shoulder of her wrap dress.

'Thanks for my "surprise" party,' Seb slurred. He kissed Clair's lips clumsily, lids drooped, his forehead almost slumping onto hers. Clair kissed him back briefly and pulled away. She was glad he'd had a good night but she was stone-cold sober and didn't have much patience for Seb in his drunk state. She wanted to though. It was his thirtieth birthday and she loved him terribly. She rested her cheek on his solid shoulder.

'I'm glad we did it, even if it wasn't a surprise.'

'So am I,' Seb said, drunken eyes smiling. 'It's been wicked.'

Clair pulled back with characteristic abruption.

'I do have one surprise for you though,' she stated, matter-of-factly, as they revolved slowly with the last of the local friends –

everyone else had left to get back for babysitters or catch their last train home.

'What is it?' Seb asked, leaning back, his heavy lids jarring with his playful pupils.

'I'm pregnant.'

23

JUNE 2019, NORTHILL, OXFORDSHIRE

I thought I was being drowned.

As the enriching, slanting strings of 'Bitter Sweet Symphony' struck up and violins flooded the chapel, a cooling crosswind roused papers and notes and orders of service from one side of the chapel's open doors to an emergency exit Reverend Jane had just opened on the other, to let some air in.

She obviously wasn't aware of the crosswind, this wasn't her usual patch, up at the new crematorium. Jane usually held funerals at her church in the town centre. She gave another apologetic smile she was so good at, and picked up a couple of papers from the feet of the people sitting in the front row.

The wind whispered at Jasper's short, unkempt hair, his double crown swirling in the breeze as he looked at the roll on his camera, sitting neatly on his lap.

A hand was forcing me under.

He didn't have any pictures from That Day. The timeline of Jasper's photographs ended during the car journey back from Miami. He had tried to take a photo of a pelican flying alongside them over a bridge on the highway. It glided, just above the eyeline of the car so Seb, Millie and he all had to lower their heads a little to see the majesty of its beak, its serene body, like a fighter jet bringing them safely in to land. That was what it felt like to Jasper, that the pelican was offering them protection.

The photo was mostly a blurred one, of the back of his dad's seat and a tiny bit of his hair, but he could just see the pelican's tail feathers and pink, tucked-in feet. *Some protection,* he thought.

Jasper wished the last photo he'd taken of his dad was better, more poetic. He scrolled back further as Richard Ashcroft's shuddering world-weary vocals echoed in the breeze. To the photo of his dad with his arm wrapped around Millie, smiling on the boardwalk. Further back to a street view of Española Way and its cafes; further back to the bubblegum-pink and lime-green lifeguard stations with jagged geometry, standing proud on the beach at sunset the night before; his sister, long-legged and reliable, drinking from a Starbucks cup as if she were a superstar. Jasper sort of thought Millie was a superstar.

Then he saw one of *her.* He thought he'd deleted them all, but she must have slipped through the net when Jasper was too busy gazing at his dad in the foreground. He hadn't noticed *her* in it before. It was a picture of his dad, holding a comedy long 'hoagie', as they called it, pretending to take a bite from one end of a long, overly stuffed baguette, while Millie pretended to take a bite from the other end. He could hear his dad's laugh just from looking at the picture. So loud and vibrant. So solid. Who could have imagined it might be one of his last?

Jasper caressed the screen with his thumb as he remembered what happened after he took the photo: both his dad and Millie *had* taken a bite, the metre-long sandwich was so stuffed full that shredded lettuce and pink ham with funny white circles in it started to tumble onto the asphalt around their flip-flops, which only made them laugh even more.

He had been so struck by the joy within the photo in the weeks since it was taken that he had failed to notice the pinched face in the background, half concealed by an arm in the mid ground; kids around her at the food-court table. The chaos and the baby wipes and the shouting all came whooshing back to him. He hadn't noticed before: Noemie's angry gaze at Seb, jealous of the fun he was afforded while he had his back to her, posing with his daughter.

The water was so cold. I couldn't breathe.

Jasper remembered the firm hand pressing him under. The glare of the sun bursting through the surface and trying to warm his face when all he felt was an icy cold panic.

I was running out of air.

He remembered an instinct to fight and kick back as he'd never had to before.

He hovered his thumb over the delete button and felt that catastrophic temptation to do something destructive, unfixable. Like when he had the urge to jump off a bridge or swerve his mum's steering wheel into the central reservation. He'd had that urge last week when they were going to buy him a funeral outfit, and he hated himself for it.

He looked at his thumb. Tempted to erase her. Knowing he would forever lose a treasured memory of his father. His thumb was almost white with tension, as he remembered the hand on his shoulder, trying to drown him. A palm pressing him under, and the memories, the mottled sound, the struggle to breathe as he fought for his life, his white skin and skinny ribs under the water, kicking, fighting this shock attack he hadn't seen coming.

His hand started to tremble against the pressure he was putting on himself.

The strings looped and the song started to phase out.

Delete it! Get rid of her!

But he looked at his father's smile. He thought of his teacher's hug.

Mrs Foley had come to visit Jasper earlier in the week; to assure him he didn't have to come back to school until he was ready.

She gave him a workbook made of colourful sugar paper, each sheet filled with a picture and a message from his classmates, after they heard the terrible news. After their parents gasped and told them to be quiet as they watched the news.

Toby had made a collage of a camera out of newspaper cuttings that looked like a Georges Braque; Lauren had written 'I'm so sorry' in colourful bubble writing next to a drawing of a boy holding a camera. Arthur had drawn robots playing basketball and said, 'Sorry Jasper'. Nearly all of the messages had said 'sorry', or 'we're here for you'. Even Ben, who wasn't very nice to Jasper, had drawn a picture of Soren the Architect from Minecraft and said 'Thinking of you, bud' underneath.

Jasper soaked up the strength and the comfort of his friends, moved his thumb away from the delete button and turned the camera screen face down to his lap, so he could look at the casket.

24

CLAIR

December 2011, Northill, Oxfordshire

'Why would I want to go to Miami?' Clair asked, genuinely baffled, her brow creased and her chest filling with a heavy sigh from her low seat on the living-room sofa. She crossed and uncrossed her legs on the pouffe in front of her, pyjama bottoms skimming the pompom slipper boots that kept her feet warm. Seb was sitting next to her with a bottle of beer in hand, not bothered about *The X Factor* final as he scrolled his laptop.

'Why *wouldn't* you want to go to Miami? It's amazing!'

He flipped between tabs of British Airways, Virgin and Skyscanner and rubbed his eyes. It had been a long Saturday. Jasper's second birthday had started with Millie waking her brother at 4 a.m. in excitement; was punctuated by a soft-play party for a couple of Jasper's toddler-group friends and four of Millie's from school, and finished with a double meltdown in Pizza Express. Both Millie and Jasper crying into their little ice-cream sundaes in total exhaustion. Martin, Tina and SJ had joined them for dinner, and although SJ didn't hold back on her eye-rolling, even Tina finally dropped her forced smile and looked as if she had genuinely had enough.

Now the kids were in bed and Clair and Seb were slumped, as Clair kept her gaze firmly on the TV, hand gripping the cup of tea she was resting on the arm of the sofa. She couldn't believe Seb didn't understand why she was annoyed. Had he learned *nothing* since becoming a parent?

'We can't just swan off on a family holiday!'

'Why not?'

In her peripheral vision she could see Seb smiling, and it wound her up even more.

Seb felt the tension in Clair's rising shoulders and wanted to touch her, to massage them, tell her to relax, but she'd been so prickly lately. He couldn't understand why she was so offended. He thought it a great idea: in January he was going to Miami for the 'topping out' ceremony at The Elmore hotel – a celebration with the client and the construction team, of the building being watertight – his first project as lead architect for Rennie + Byrd. Usually Seb was partnered with Ken Keppel, an old-school Old Etonian with bulging eyes and floppy jowls; or, if he was lucky, he worked with Federico Rivera or Fatima Rahman, as their projects were much more dynamic and neither Federico nor Fatima said things that made Seb wince.

The Elmore – a 130-bedroom former colonial beauty with a rooftop pool in the Deco District of South Beach – was Seb's first international project with him at the helm. It was his baby, and he had poured his heart and soul into it.

Jill had suggested during Friday drinks that Seb take the whole family for the topping out; they could stay in the Rennie + Byrd rental apartment while Seb was working, then tag a holiday onto the end of it.

'Take time off so you can enjoy Florida with the kids,' Jill had almost commanded. 'Go to the Everglades. Oh, you must look at the houses on the Florida west coast.'

Clair crossed and uncrossed her legs again, pompoms balling into her ankles while Gary Barlow and Tulisa took to the stage with their singers in their Saturday night finery. She wanted to kick her slippers off in frustration; she was hot and agitated now. She turned to Seb, her eyebrows flat, her nose straight.

'Jasper's too little to do the Disney thing, and we can't take Millie out of school.'

Dermot O'Leary clutched his microphone.

'She's only Year... Two?'

'Yes, Seb. Year Two,' Clair snapped. He really ought to know for sure what year his daughter was in.

'It's not like they do much the first week of January. School won't mind.'

Clair looked back at the television. Five sassy and sparkling women crying with glee, their hands clutching their faces – but not too close to smudge their make-up.

'Anyway, I wasn't talking about Disney. There's loads more to Florida than Mickey Mouse!'

Clair was conflicted. She was happy for Little Mix – she had wanted them to win since the live rounds – but angry at Seb, still flogging this ridiculous notion.

'I have to go anyway, the apartment is massive, probably more square feet than this house – and we can have a brilliant holiday afterwards. Go to the Keys, see alligators in the Everglades. Take them to SeaWorld. The houses in Naples are unreal, Clair!'

'Yeah, and how do I get a week or two of annual leave? In a month's time?' Clair's voice was almost wobbling. 'You can go there on your little monthly visits...' Seb was startled by a bitterness in Clair's voice he hadn't noticed before. 'But I can't just take time off. The rotas are done months in advance.'

'Ask Ali or Kay for a favour. You've done plenty of swaps and covered shifts for them.'

Clair let out a puff of despair and turned the volume down on the TV. All the screaming and shouting was starting to annoy her. But not as much as the sound of Seb's fingers on the keyboard of his laptop: researching flights, looking at hotels, seeing if SeaWorld was open over New Year. As if he had no clue how tough the past six and a half years of parenthood and sleep deprivation and long shifts at the John Radcliffe had been on Clair.

As Seb gazed at a carousel of orcas, dolphins and sea lions on his laptop, he tried to pinpoint when Clair had lost her sense of adventure. She was sporty and can-do at school. Always keen to muck in and get stuck in. She would have canoed from the Channel Islands to England if she could; why didn't she want a plush holiday in Florida?

As if she could read his mind, she took a deep breath, to help make her case.

'I mean, Jasper's two!' she said, as if Seb had forgotten what day it was. 'We have to pay for a seat on a plane now.'

'Money isn't a problem – work cover me – Miami accommodation is free...'

Clair shook her head.

'It's just not worth the hassle.'

The hassle?

Seb tried to imagine a world in which a holiday would feel like a hassle and tried to think when the scales had tipped for Clair. He tried to remember when Clair had stopped drinking wine on a Saturday night and started drinking tea or Cadbury Highlights. He wondered why exactly they had swapped the Greek Islands for a rainy week in Swanage, as lovely as it was. Why they'd just been to Pizza Express for the four thousandth time when a new tapas restaurant had opened in town and their friends said it was amazing.

Kids, I suppose.

Seb softened, and tried to stroke Clair's hair but she raised a shoulder.

'What's wrong?' he asked gently. Now wasn't the time for his smile. His smile could sometimes wind her up.

'"What's wrong?"' she quoted him. 'I'm knackered, Seb! I'm working twelve-hour shifts plus bank, Millie's *still* coming into our bed every night, Jasper's only just started sleeping through, the house is a mess...'

'No, it isn't!'

Seb looked around the living room. Yes, there were unicorns, cuddly toys and Octonauts strewn in corners and on the rug, but the house looked great. After nine years of extension and renovation, his aesthetic eye had turned a stuffy pokey house with floral wallpaper and shagpile carpet into a light and bright 1930s home with navy walls, gold mirrors and a beautiful family kitchen at the back. They had finished it, got artwork up and doubled the value, all while getting married, qualifying and having two kids – which felt like some achievement to Seb. And the cleaner was coming on Monday.

'The house is fine,' he protested, a puzzled smile creeping back on his face, although he quashed it again. He didn't want to irk her even more. He really wanted them all to go on holiday over New Year.

Clair turned to him, almost in tears.

'You think we can all just jump on a plane to Miami whenever you click your fingers?'

'It's not when I click my fingers. I'm suggesting a family holiday. We haven't been abroad, the four of us.'

'I don't want to go anywhere! It's knackering enough getting from work to school to home. And you think I want to get on a plane and go to Miami to see a brick being laid?'

Seb pushed his laptop onto the pouffe and stood up.

'Fucking hell, Clair... don't worry about it.'

He went to the kitchen to get another bottle of San Miguel as Clair flicked through the channels and turned the volume back up to fill the silence.

Seb came back to the living room but stopped in the doorway.

'It's my first lead. My own hotel. It means quite a bit to me, and I thought you'd want to see it.' As Seb spoke he gesticulated with the bottle.

Clair looked up.

'Yes, and my job means quite a bit to me!'

They looked at each other, in disbelief and stalemate.

'I know...' Seb said calmly. 'It's not a competition. I thought I'd been supportive. I thought we've supported each other through everything. And you're pissed off because I want my wife and kids to come away with me. To have a holiday. Jesus, Clair.' He pushed his hands back through his hair.

'Oh, piss off, Seb.'

25

JUNE 2019, NORTHILL, OXFORDSHIRE

'This is it now, Mills, you can go to the casket if you want to...'
Millie shook her head and sobbed into her mother's shoulder as
they stood up, as if bound together. With Penelope and Peter, they
were the first to stand under Reverend Jane's gentle coaxing, and
they knew all eyes were on them. Jasper clung to his camera and
shuffled forward self-consciously. He'd been told about this part.
To touch the coffin if he wanted to. And not if he didn't. His mother
whispered to them.

'It's OK, if you want...' They stepped forwards to the plinth and
Jasper put a shaky hand out while Millie walked towards the exit
doors, sobbing into the June sunshine as Penelope followed her,
her arms open. None of them wanted any of this.

Clair glanced over her shoulder, she wished no one else were
there, and she looked at Jasper's face in profile and rubbed his
back.

'Only if you want to.'

'Bye, Dad,' he said in a small voice, barely connecting his small
fingers to the casket. He buried his head into Clair's body. He was

short for his age and only came up to her chest. She pulled him in with one hand while she pressed her other onto the bamboo and felt it crease under her palm. She thought about the last time they spoke. She was leaning on the spiky pebbledash exterior wall of the hospital, still in her blues and clogs because she'd dashed out to make a call she had been desperate to make all during her shift. Seb was standing in the sunshine on a South Beach street.

'So what's the real deal, Seb?' Clair asked, suspecting he wasn't telling her the whole story. 'Are the kids OK?'

His face on the small phone screen was handsome and playful. Sometimes she could tell he was full of shit, saying what he thought he should, rather than the reality. Always the people pleaser. But he had a reassurance in his smile now; it was almost a look of relief. The sunshine reflected off the shiny silver exterior of the Art Deco dining car behind him; his pale lilac T-shirt brought out his eyes, even on FaceTime.

He promised her that they were fine – that they had had a little trouble in paradise but he had taken Millie and Jasper to Miami for a couple of days.

'Shit, Seb. You walked out on her?'

Clair knew how that felt, and she tried not to remember the searing pain. They were so happy now, gazing at each other on their phone screens. In a better place.

She said how she missed them terribly – they had never been away from her for so long or so far, and she craved to hold them, to ask them how they were getting on, to see if they missed her too. It felt so quiet without them. She'd been going into their rooms at night, almost forgetting that she didn't need to check them, and smelling their pillows and duvets instead.

He told her how they'd been on a photowalk and how happy and relaxed they were. How much the kids loved Miami; how much he loved it. And then Clair blurted it out.

'I love you Seb.'

* * *

'I love you,' Jasper said as he stared at the coffin, and Clair cried into his hair.

PART II

PART II

26

DESIREE

September 2013, London

'The client doesn't think it's working, I don't think it's working...' said Jill, the short-haired thin-lipped Rennie of Rennie + Byrd, as she glanced at a computer-generated impression on the large screen of the Shoreditch studio meeting room. 'It's too stuffy.'

She was always the blunter of the two directors. The Scottish sharp talker to Terence Byrd's quietly thoughtful, terribly English, creative.

Terence sat looking at the drawings in front of him, twiddling his pen. Despite nine enlightening years under Jill and Terence's tutelage, Seb still couldn't tell what Terence was thinking. Or whether the drawings in front of him even pertained to the project on the screen – a hotel in Vienna that was mid renovation – his thin face impenetrable behind a short grey beard.

Seb's colleague Ken sat around the oval curve of the table, shirt button bursting at his stomach from a very boozy lunch at J

Sheekey with his favourite interior designer. Ken wasn't disconcerted by the graveness on Jill's face, which lifted a little as her mobile started to ring. She looked at the screen.

'Ah, that'll be her!'

Seb and Ken looked at each other, then both back at the artist's impression of the Vienna project on the screen, as Ken licked his lips, stained purple with red wine.

'I'll be right out...' Jill said into her phone, before ending the call and walking to the door. Terence said nothing. Seb felt as if he should speak, but he was so tired in the warm dark of the room: from the monotony, from Ken's anecdotes about who he'd bumped into at lunch, from eight years of broken nights... he couldn't help wondering if he might have lost his way a bit with this project. It could be better. Jill was right. She usually was.

Ken cleared his throat, checking his stale breath on the curl of his fist.

'Opulence was what the client wanted for The Phoenix, Terence. Grandness. Exclusivity. Power.'

Terence nodded but said nothing as he surveyed the slideshow gallery on the screen – a 3D rendering of a grandiose and gaudy hotel. The click of the opening door lifted the silence.

Jill walked in with a woman almost half her age, in a sharp white trouser suit that offset her brown skin beautifully. Her eyes were wide and glimmered gold, even in the dimly lit boardroom, and her confident smile revealed two dimples, and teeth as straight and as polished as she was.

She nodded first at Ken, then at Seb, then extended a small hand to each of them as Jill made the introductions.

'Gentlemen, this is Desiree Cruz-Campbell. Desiree, this is Sebastian Cooper and Kenneth Keppel, who have been working on The Phoenix from the pitch stage.' Seb stood quickly and extended a warm hand as Ken struggled to get out of his chair.

'Hi,' Seb said, his eyes shining in the light of the projector.

'Pleased to meet you...' Desiree replied, shaking Seb's hand vigorously and then Ken's, before nodding at Terence sitting next to her. They had clearly met before.

She pulled out the spare chair that Seb realised had had her name on it all along, and primly placed her Celine bag on the floor at its side as she sat down and pushed her soft bouncing waves off her face.

Jill handed Desiree a glass of water from the gurgling cooler, while Ken shuffled back in his seat and continued his rambling as if Desiree were only here to clear the table.

'I don't know what Bertrand thought, buying a nineteenth-century building of such grandeur – wasn't it obvious this was what we were going to capitalise on in the drawings? The history. The luxury. And Bertrand bloody well approved it!'

Ken mopped his brow; it was starting to sweat under the heat he was feeling.

Jill didn't respond to Ken's mutterings. Terence stroked his small beard thoughtfully; he was such a silent assassin, you never knew when you were being reprimanded with Terence, until the cold sweat sank in that evening. Not that Seb ever really had. There had been the odd teething issue in his early years as a fully quali-fied architect. Learnings along the way in design and progress meetings, but he'd seen other architects fall foul of Terence's silence.

'Desiree is joining Rennie + Byrd,' Jill declared. 'She's going to rescue the Vienna project with her brilliance – she's been brought up to speed already.'

Ken coughed.

'And she comes with a great portfolio,' Terence added, reading Ken's mind. 'Desiree's worked on Marriott, Sheraton, InterCon-tinental...'

'You look too young to have such experience!' Ken chortled, imagining Desiree in her gym knickers. 'I say that with the most sincerest of respect, of course...' he fumbled.

'I've had the best mentor,' Desiree said, batting Ken's micro aggression away with a sparkling smile that revealed those deep dimples again. Seb was blown away. Jill gave a modest nod. Since she had taken Desiree under her wing as a Part One BA student at UCL, both she and Desiree knew she was going to have fine career ahead of her, as long as she didn't mess up. It was going OK so far, drunk codger aside.

'Desiree is bursting with energy and ideas and has drawn up suggestions on how to save this project. If you will...?' Jill asked. Desiree made eye contact with Seb, who tried not to look in awe as he waited in anticipation.

Desiree took a memory stick out of her bag and put it into the laptop connected to the projector of the big screen. Seb was transfixed. Terence looked up. Ken sighed deeply and noisily, emitting a whiff of meat that had got stuck in his molars and red wine, which Seb was on the wrong end of.

'OK,' said Desiree purposefully, standing up and unbuttoning the single fastening on her white blazer. 'I believe the disconnect with the client is that they didn't want it to be another stuffy European heritage hotel, but, looking back at the briefing docs, I don't think they conveyed it that well by using words like "opulence", "richness" and "luxury". The assumption was that they wanted to take the Viennese heritage of the properties around them and the district, and we ran with it.'

At the point Desiree said 'we', Ken let out an involuntary burp, giving Seb another whiff of poor dental hygiene and excess.

'The takeaways and challenge I saw in this project were how to create an inviting intimate atmosphere in such a grandiose space. Nodding to its noble traditions of Arts and Crafts, art nouveau et cetera, but with modern twentieth-first-century interiors and trappings. Luxurious but relaxing; opulent but inviting. Here's how I see it...'

Jill dimmed the lights further so the room was almost dark.

Fuck, Seb marvelled internally, as he watched this goddess glide into his life.

* * *

Twenty minutes later, Ken shook himself out of his lidded stupor as Jill clapped her small hands together.

'Thank you, Desiree, that is just...' She was so pleased she was almost lost for words, and pumped her two fists in front of her. 'Just wonderful.'

Terence nodded.

'Yes, great stuff,' he agreed. 'It's going to be super-duper.'

Jill stood up to raise the lights to full.

'We'd like Desiree to present this to Bertrand in Vienna on Tuesday. He wants to do a site visit and talk through the revisions in situ.'

Ken looked surprised.

'You've been speaking to Bertrand?' he asked in shock.

Jill nodded, unapologetically.

'That's right, Ken.'

'And De—Sorry, what was your name, dear?'

'Desiree.'

'And Desiree will be leading? In Vienna?'

'Yes,' confirmed Jill.

'But Seb worked like a donkey on this,' Ken objected, his jowls getting lower as he tried harder to conceal his outrage.

'Oh, Seb will still be going,' Jill assured them. 'We'd like

Desiree and Seb to take this one. We think you'd be better used on the Battersea project, Ken.'

'I beg your pardon?'

Ken had been looking forward to another jolly in Vienna. Check in on the build before taking in the opera, the stallions, the fine dining – and taking Seb to his favourite gentleman's club in the entire world. Seb had skipped it last time, citing something about young kids and a good night's sleep. Ken wasn't going to let him get away that easily again.

Except this trip had just been taken away from him.

Jill conceded a little. She really hadn't planned on demoting Ken publicly, but he wasn't getting the point.

'We've brought Desiree on specifically to lead this project and present to Bertrand. And hopefully on many more after that, if Bertrand likes it. We feel she's the perfect architect to move this forward.'

Desiree nodded, as if she was raring to go.

Ken cleared his throat into his fist again.

'No disrespect to you... er...' Ken bumbled over Desiree's name again while flapping his hands and not looking her in the eye. 'But, I, I, I...' Ken always bumbled more when he was flustered. Presenting to Old Etonian friends about projects it was a given he would win was easy. But fighting for his place among the bright young things – the architects who had learned their trade in Lisbon, Florence and Singapore – who seemed to be popping up everywhere lately made his stutter stronger and his jowls wobble. It wasn't just the new crop of architects who were younger than his children now – most of the clients, the property magnates and hoteliers, were too, and he was struggling with the notion of his experience being seen as a negative thing.

'What have you done, Sebastian? Ten years?' Seb didn't answer, but it was almost that. 'I've done thirty-five. That's forty-five years between us. This is too big for a mentee on a graduate project.'

'Desiree isn't a new grad, Ken,' Terence said quietly. 'She's an exceptional architect.'

Seb stared at a space in the middle of the oval table, where the cables popped out of the centre. This was going from awkward to embarrassing.

'No, but with all due respect—'

'For fuck's sake, Kenneth!' Jill snapped in strong Glaswegian sternness, calling an end to the meeting.

Desiree, cool and composed, took a sip of water from the tumbler in front of her and tried not to look at Seb again.

* * *

'You know what this is, Sebastian?' Ken was charging down the corridor, through the middle open-plan part of the office, past the bank of desks, and through the other corridor towards the lift.

He knew what was coming and internally groaned.

'Positive discrimination.'

Ken pressed the button to call the lift and stopped to read Seb's face, expecting him to collude.

'She's probably a lesbian too!'

'Come on, Ken, don't be that guy...'

'If she were a white man she wouldn't have had a look-in. You'll be on your way out soon, you mark my words!'

Seb tried to keep calm, his voice measured.

'Desiree said in her presentation: she's worked for a number of big hotel projects. She led on The Gekko in Glasgow.'

'Yeah, but who was she screwing to get that?'

'What?' Seb waved his arm dismissively. 'Please, Ken, you're better than that.'

'It's to tally up the numbers, Sebastian. Get some "diversity",' Ken said, making finger speech marks as he spat out the word. 'And who's penalised for it?'

Seb sighed.

'Oh, I don't know, Ken, privileged white men who are out of fresh ideas?' he shot. Seb's tongue had bite now. 'Jill wouldn't mentor anyone she didn't rate – you know that. And she definitely wouldn't get Desiree in to rescue our shitshow in Vienna if she wasn't up to the job.'

Ken shrugged as the lift arrived, surprised that Seb had snapped.

'She has a perky arse, that's as much as I'll give. You getting in?' Ken gestured for Seb to go ahead of him.

'I'll walk, thanks,' Seb said, peeling away for the emergency exit and the six flights of stairs down to street level.

'Suit yourself.'

27

JUNE 2019, NORTHILL, OXFORDSHIRE

'Come on, Granny, we need to file out...'

Desiree stood to help her grandmother up out of her chair. Violeta wasn't as cumbersome as she looked on Desiree's arm as she was so featherlight, and Desiree had to remember to be slow so as not to sweep her away.

'Why don't you pop your order of service into your handbag?' she suggested, opening the thick gold clasp on the black bag for her. Desiree often did that to her Granny. Suggest something while she was doing it herself, like the way a mother talked her baby through her actions, a one-sided conversation to help someone who didn't have the words, or couldn't find them any more.

Federico, Fatima, Mei-Xin and Tarek from Rennie + Byrd were filing through the aisle, alongside the many mourners politely edging from the standing-room only space at the back towards the exit at the front.

Turn left at the casket.

'Hey,' Federico said slowly as he put his palm on the middle of Desiree's back, kissed her on each cheek and stopped to let her and Violeta out. 'Are you OK?' he asked. Desiree gave a grateful nod that meant no. That she was putting a brave face on it. But she squeezed his arm with her free hand and took a deep breath. She knew the last of the last goodbyes was coming. Fatima was sobbing too hard to form words but looked at Desiree with wide and lovely eyes. Mei-Xin looked too stunned to speak and Tarek, at the back of the group, kept his head down lest he show Desiree the hurt in his eyes.

'We're here for you,' Federico added, letting Desiree and Violeta out. They walked slowly behind the blockage of mourners, touching the casket one final time while Noemie stood next to it, crying with her mouth wide open, facing the congregation. Desiree approached patiently, her arm looped through Granny's. The rest of the family had filed outside into the rose garden, except for Martin, who was waiting with Jake, thanking the mourners for coming; not wanting to abandon the man they loved. Desiree had to circumnavigate Noemie, the wailing woman being held up by her mother, so she could finally reach Seb.

'Desiree...'

She carefully let go of Granny's hand, making sure Federico was still on the other side of her, so she could fall into Jake's wide embrace.

'Jake, that was beautiful, well done.'

His all-engulfing grip might have squished Granny, who stood politely as Jake and Desiree clung onto each other. Martin smiled politely at Violeta's vacant face. He had never met the famous Violeta Cruz-Campbell but he had heard lots of stories about her, and imagined that, in other circumstances, they would have many to exchange. Now wasn't the time. He couldn't think of anything except Seb, lying on his back in the box behind him.

'And this must be Granny!' said Jake, who didn't know whether to scoop her up or pat her on the head he thought she looked so cute, but fortunately he stopped himself from doing either. 'You're a bit of a legend, Mrs C-C, it's great to meet you,' he said, squeezing the bridge of his nose. Violeta looked as if she didn't understand him but smiled, a thin, wrinkled smile.

'Granny, this is Seb's best friend, Jake.'

'The crazy one?' she said out of nowhere. Violeta hadn't spoken for ages, and it took Desiree by surprise. She gave an awkward laugh through her watery eyes.

'The very one,' Jake said guiltily.

'I like you,' Violeta said as Federico smiled by her side.

'I'll just...' Desiree said nervously, asking Jake's permission to touch the casket.

'Of course.'

Federico gestured that he would start walking Granny to the door, to give Desiree some space, and Jake stepped to the side, almost onto Noemie's toes, exposed in her gold leather gladiator sandals, as she stood resolute and teary.

'Shit, sorry!' he half laughed.

Desiree tried to block out all the noise, the half laughs and the cries as she approached. She tried to ignore the burning ball of tension that was Noemie Morel, standing there like a barrier to her getting to say goodbye to her love.

She stepped forward and lowered her head as she closed her eyes and put her left palm on the casket. The weave felt rough and weak; nothing like the smooth and strong man who was inside it, who shouldn't be inside it. She felt blood run from the tip of her finger up her arm and all the way to her heart.

She inhaled the through-breeze, the scents of roses and honey-suckle rolling in on it. She remembered the moment their eyes locked in the darkened meeting room of her first day at Rennie + Byrd; the sudden urge she felt to impress the man sitting opposite her. She remembered him hanging onto her every word as their plane took the flight path over the Thames. She remembered rubbing the arch of his spine after he threw up, crying, because he was just as bad as his dad – but she loved him even more for it. She remembered the elation on his face as he swam alongside a sea turtle in the Lombok Strait. She remembered his smile the last time she saw it, handsome and conflicted, in a hotel bar on the South Bank as he said he'd get the bill and she dashed off to her meeting.

28

DESIREE

September 2013, Vienna

In a wood-panelled cafe not far from the Imperial Palace, a waiter brought coffees in glasses to a small table with a crisp white table-cloth and put a slice of *Sachertorte* in front of Desiree.

'Oh, that's for him.' She smiled at the waiter, sliding it across the table to Seb.

'Have you tried any yet?' Seb asked, eyes lighting up at the confection in front of him. He always liked to try a different pastry on his monthly progress trips to The Phoenix. Last time it was *Linzertorte*, before that *apfelstrudel*. All the *Viennoiserie* tasted incredible alongside an *einspänner* coffee – strong and black and topped with a fluffy flounce of white whipped cream. He gestured his fork to Desiree in case she wanted a bite first but she shook her hand to say *no, thanks*.

'I had a huge piece, at a brasserie over by St Stephen's at the weekend.' Desiree said it as if cake was something she didn't partake in on a weekday. Let alone just before a meeting. She looked too pristine for cake anyway; her mushroom-coloured Galaxy dress shouldn't be anywhere near greasy ganache, apricot jam or flecks of fudgy sponge.

Desiree had arrived in Vienna ahead of Seb, spending the weekend checking out Hapsburg palaces, Klimt friezes and the cafe culture, getting a better feel for the city before Seb's arrival and the meeting on Tuesday. Desiree was that sort of efficient human who didn't eat cake unless her body needed fuelling, and her leisure time always worked hard for her too: a weekend break spent researching for work, happily wandering the stately baroque streets in her colourful Boden trainers, imagining what guests staying at The Phoenix might want or need at the end of a day of meetings or sightseeing.

'It was really good,' she confirmed as her dimples sank.

Seb took a hearty bite then poured them both some water from the carafe on the table. They were sitting on curved wooden Thonet chairs, cramped in around a small table in the light and airy cafe, his leather messenger bag propped against Desiree's Samsonite carry-on at their feet.

'So, Jill kept you quiet,' he said, wiping his face inelegantly on the white cotton napkin he'd just scrunched up. 'The ace up her sleeve,' he added with a mischievous smile.

Desiree laughed.

'Yes, well... she didn't want to give me a boost I didn't deserve. Made me earn my stripes at Harper + Swan first.'

'Harper + Swan?' They were renowned for pompous projects in Mayfair and Piccadilly: heritage hotels, old-school retail and dark and stuffy restaurants. Desiree Cruz-Campbell looked a bit too cool for Harper + Swan with her bandage dress and Afro hair.

'But I was in Glasgow much of the past two years at The Gekko on the dockyard development. It was the more edgy side of their portfolio.'

'Yeah, what was that like? The whole thing looks impressive.'

'Amazing. Tough. I loved it.'

Desiree spoke purposefully and passionately. She didn't dilly-dally with her words. 'And I think Jill wanted me to make my rookie errors with Harper + Swan before she'd even consider me. I went straight there as a Part Two assistant from The Bartlett.'

Seb raised his eyebrows. He'd scraped two years at The Bartlett before transferring to Oxford Brookes. He knew that anyone who had got their Part One and Part Two across seven years at UCL's prestigious Bartlett school of architecture was going to have earned their place in any firm.

'And did you? Make your errors?'

'No.' Desiree laughed. 'But Jill deigned to get me in anyway,' she said with a raised eyebrow. For someone so ambitious she was warm and honest; for someone so polished she looked as if she could laugh at herself. Seb was fascinated as he stirred the cream into his coffee.

'So you jumped ship anyway, even though it was going well?'

'Well, I think it's always healthy to move, keep on your toes. Challenge yourself.'

Seb nodded in agreement, despite feeling a little embarrassed that he had only ever worked for his dad and Roger at Curtis + Cooper throughout his entire degree and training, and Rennie + Byrd for the past nine years. But why would he go anywhere? They were currently one of the most talked about studios in the world.

He took another bite of the cake to save himself from admitting how he feared becoming Ken. How his life had got a bit stagnant. How dull his evenings on the sofa were. How he hadn't pushed himself on The Phoenix project as he should have. How maybe it was time for him to move on. But he really didn't want to now.

'I *am* always trying to get away from the docks, I suppose,' Desiree pondered. The Gekko in Glasgow. The south coast...'

'Where are you from?'

'Portsmouth.'

'Oh, I'm a harbour boy too.'

Desiree raised an eyebrow to ask where.

'Guernsey.'

'Oh, wow.'

'But I've lived in Oxfordshire for the past god knows how long. As far away from the sea in the UK as you can get, I suppose...' Seb said it as if it had only just occurred to him.

'The sea will be in your DNA, I bet,' Desiree said sagely. 'It's hard to get away from.'

Seb nodded.

'You'll probably return to it,' she said with a smile.

'So Jill sneakily stowed you away, from the Glasgow docks down to Shoreditch – how do you feel about that?'

'Look, it's really good to be back in London. It felt right. I missed my flat. I missed my friends. And, although I'll probably return to the sea eventually too, being a stowaway is in my DNA...' Desiree said it mysteriously, before realising this was too much small talk for her liking. She needed to get back to the business they were tending to.

'Huh?'

She looked at her watch. There wasn't time.

'I'll tell you later, I do need to get one thing before the meeting...' she said, standing swiftly on sharp patent beige Roger Vivier heels. 'Be one sec.'

Seb watched Desiree walk up to the counter, where she bought a postcard from a revolving rack at the till while paying their bill, stuck a stamp to it, and returned deftly, weaving between waiters who all turned a little to watch her. He'd only met her twice but already Seb could see Desiree had that kind of effect on a room.

She slid back into her curved wooden seat.

'Postcard. I send one from everywhere I go.'

Seb wondered who she might send a postcard to and tried not to look as she swiftly and sparingly scrawled a few words. Her writing was a messy but beautiful swirl.

'The streets of Vienna are paved with... culture and Klimt!'

Seb looked away as Desiree wrote out the recipient's address. Not wanting to be nosy, hoping it wasn't a man and then feeling weird about it. He picked up the strap of his bag, pressed his inside pocket to check his passport was still there, and felt his racing heart.

* * *

In a makeshift office of the half-finished building site, Desiree delivered her vision of the final look to André Bertrand, the hotel owner, and his team of accountants, assistants and flunkies. André Bertrand was the flamboyant face of the celebrity hotel world, who always travelled with an entourage to outdo his Hollywood girl-friends. One of the entourage seemed to be tasked with checking Bertrand's Musketeer-like hair always had just the right level of bounce, preening and fluffing it before smoothing it down and picking lint off his squat shoulders.

The meeting had gone well. André loved the new projections and he clearly loved Desiree too, who Seb had watched delivering the re-imagined pitch in awe.

'Yep, do it!' André said, twirling a thin moustache as he wrote the mental cheque for the reworking of the space, the change of décor, and the final touches. He seemed very casual about it given he'd been shouting at Jill on a conference call three weeks ago.

Desiree had that sort of calming charm. The Phoenix clearly was going to rise from the ashes, and André was delighted.

He invited them both to dine with him at The Opus at The Imperial that night, although he was really only looking at Desiree when he said it. She and Seb swerved it with a polite thank you as they needed to catch their flight home. Someone like André Bertrand didn't understand the limitation of airline schedules and timetables, of having to go through security and customs like most people, but he thanked them all the same and gave two thumbs about the next phase of the project, from the construction finish to the handover, as he was whisked out by his assistants.

* * *

On the flight from Vienna to Heathrow, Seb leaned over the space of the empty seat between them, to Desiree looking out of the window.

'Tell me about the stowaway thing,' he said, surprising himself, but the sensations of the plane starting to descend also gave him a feeling of urgency. That time was running out.

'Oh!' Desiree laughed. 'My granny!' She tightened the lid on her bottle of Fiji water and put it in her bag on the seat between them. 'She came to the UK as a stowaway. On a ship. So I guess what you said about Jill stowing me away from Glasgow, me jumping ship... I suppose it's in my blood. Although I can assure you I am 100 per cent committed to The Phoenix.'

'A stowaway?' Seb marvelled, his eyes widening like Jasper's during a bedtime story.

Desiree nodded.

'On the *Windrush*,' she said coolly.

'What?'

Seb pushed his hands through his hair and gave her a look of desperation to continue.

'My granny was Cuban, living in exile in Mexico...'

Desiree could see Seb didn't follow, so she took it back a few steps. 'My great-grandfather was a cobbler, and saw himself as head of a shoe empire, but the Cuban Constitution of 1940 was somewhat... limiting, for a man of his ambition.'

Seb listened intently.

'So he left Cuba for Mexico, with his wife and daughters – my granny and her sister.'

'And did he build a shoe empire?'

'Yes! They settled in Tampico, and Zapatos Cruz became famous all over the country. I suppose that explains my shoe obsession...'

Seb didn't know that Desiree had a Rockstud, loafer or pump for every occasion or that she could go grocery shopping in skyscraper stilettos and glide through the aisles – but he had noticed how polished hers were.

'So how did your granny end up on the *Windrush*?'

'It docked in Tampico – on its way from the West Indies to Britain. And I suppose she was her father's daughter – she had a taste for adventure. She jumped on board while it was in the harbour, stowed away and fled.'

Seb thought of Millie, how he hoped the rebel-girl streak he saw inside her wouldn't cause her to flee.

'She sneaked on with a load of Polish people, who'd been granted permission to live in Britain... although how they ended up in Mexico, and how the crew didn't spot my granny among them, brown skin and cheeky face, I don't know...'

Seb widened his eyes and studied Desiree's face. He could see the Latin fire in her luminous brown eyes now.

'You know how all those palm trees and conch shells blot the

Caribbean landscape...?' she added with irony. 'She wanted to escape them! For Britain. Poor thing.'

Seb laughed.

'Although, that said, this is one of my favourite landings...' Desiree looked out of the window as the plane dropped through the lowest of the grey cloud, at the O2 and its twelve yellow poles, anchoring them to Greenwich Mean Time as it came into view beneath them. She leaned back a little so Seb could take it in too.

He ducked his head so he could see London lit by the blood-red sky of sunset. The flightpath from continental Europe to Heathrow's runways took in the most wonderful sightseeing tour of London. The O2. Canary Wharf. The river's bends and majestic bridges. The Tower of London, Big Ben. The courts of the All England Tennis Club. It was a landing Desiree never tired of.

'It is pretty cool,' Seb concurred, glancing out at the verdant rectangles and triangles of Green Park, like a jigsaw puzzle around Buckingham Palace, eager, though, to hear how this story ended before they landed. The lights in the cabin suddenly dimmed, pulling Seb closer in.

'What was the journey like? Was it awful?'

'No! It was amazing. She met my grandad on board!'

Seb smiled and rubbed his emergent stubble.

'I mean, she was obviously scared – she was only eighteen. And had left her family behind, which I can't imagine. Plus first stop was Havana, which she *wasn't* expecting. She was worried she'd be turfed off. That Batista's men were looking for her...'

'I take it she wasn't...?'

'No, she was still hiding with the Poles at that point, who kept her under blankets for a couple of days. Soon she came out of her hiding place and made friends. Met some Jamaican women who said she could sit with them as she'd stand out less. Started partying with them at night.'

Seb's blue eyes sparkled.

'The parties! My granny was an amazing dancer. She met my grandad one night, somewhere between Havana and Bermuda. At one of the calypso band nights. Grandad thought Jamaican women could dance until he saw a Cuban move...' Desiree gave Seb a wink and the tiny flutter of her lashes hit him in the stomach like a punch.

'Oh my god, that's so cool.'

Seb, enthralled, urged her to go on.

'After Bermuda my grandad and his bandmates helped keep her hidden; they shared their food with her, and, well, she and my grandad fell in love, somewhere across the Atlantic in June 1948.'

'Oh wow.'

'For real.'

Seb heard the landing gear fix into place and felt a slight despair.

'What happened when they arrived in the UK? Where did they go?'

'My grandad had been offered a room in a house and a job at the docks in Portsmouth, from a naval officer who had been stationed in Jamaica. My grandad was an architect. He had helped build the officer a house in Kingston; they were friends. But he hadn't told Grandad how hostile it was.'

'I've been on a night out in Portsmouth. It's still pretty hostile.'

'He didn't realise he would be the first black person many people had seen.'

'Shit.'

'My brother and I didn't feel all that different at school fifty years later.'

'Really?'

'Progress, eh?' she said with a wry smile.

Seb winced. But then he thought about his school days in

Guernsey, and how everyone was white to the point of pink; a ruddy-cheeked shade of windswept.

'I was always pretty close to my granny. Even before I learned what a badass she was to leave her family, her language and take that risk. My grandad said we were two peas in a pod.'

Desiree looked a little mournful.

'She sounds amazing. Is she still alive now?'

'Yes,' she's eighty-three.' Desiree looked proud. 'That's who I sent my postcard to. Violeta. She still lives in the little house she and my grandad bought after they got married in 1950, on Spice Island. Which sounds tropical, but the Solent is hardly the Caribbean.'

'Yeah, I bet.'

'I grew up around the corner in Old Portsmouth. She's going to move into an old people's home soon though, but she's OK with that. She thinks it'll be another party.'

Seb laughed.

'I don't have the heart to tell her it probably won't.'

'How about your grandad?'

Noises rumbled under the fuselage as the lights around Heathrow Airport started to twinkle. The sun had disappeared now and the last of the pink sky fizzed. Desiree, suddenly aware of her surroundings, zipped away her travel wallet with her laptop.

'Oh, he passed away, four years ago.'

'I'm sorry.'

But the conversation was over. Desiree had jumped ship again. In her head she was thinking about the journey home, the evening ahead of her. Going over her Vienna notes no doubt and an email to send to Jill and Terence to feed it all back. With a polite smile the story was over and he'd lost her.

Seb fumbled for his own bits: his phone, notebook and magazine. Putting them into his bag under the seat in front of him, thinking about all the people Desiree Cruz-Campbell might leave in her wake as she smoothed down her dress, checked her belt was definitely fastened, and prepared for the bump of the landing.

As the wheels hit the runway Seb felt a treacherous punch, the force of the brakes pulling him from wanting to know more about Desiree. What her flat looked like. Who she lived with. To see her naked. To meet Violeta. To meet her family and friends.

Ridiculous, he thought. *I'm a happily married man.*

He looked away up the aisle, to the other business people urgent for the seat-belt sign to switch off; to get out of this cramped space he had loved sharing. As the plane taxied to the terminal Seb put his jacket on and looked out of the window, following Desiree's eyeline to the terminal building, the planes coming in, the lights of the M25 and the M4 as they twinkled on the arteries out towards London in one direction, towards Clair in the other.

* * *

As they snaked straight past the baggage hall and through to Arrivals, two drivers from the same private hire taxi firm stood on the other side of a metal barrier chatting, each with a board in their hand. Seb walked to the one with Cooper on it. Desiree to the one that was meant to say Cruz-Campbell next to him, although, as often was the case, the driver had written Cruzcampo, his mind on other things.

They made themselves known to their drivers and followed them out to the short-stay parking area, where two Toyota Prius cars waited.

'Well, that went well.' Seb smiled.

Desiree nodded in agreement.

'You were brilliant. I've never seen André quite so happy and so relaxed with the direction of a project.'

Desiree gave a modest smile.

'See you tomorrow,' she said coolly as she opened the car door, then stopped as she remembered something.

'Oh, I'm not in the office tomorrow. Not for a couple of days. I'm at RIBA with Jill, and then Glasgow for the final handover of the keys on The Gekko.'

Seb felt silly that he felt so disappointed but veiled it with his smile.

'But I'm having birthday drinks on Saturday. At Aqua Shard. Do come?'

He tried not to show his demeanour lifting.

'Sounds great.'

'Great. Come from eight. Jill and Terence will be there. Bring your wife!'

29

JUNE 2019, NORTHILL, OXFORDSHIRE

'Doucement, ma chérie, doucement...'

Camille put her arms around her daughter's shoulder. 'We ought to go outside...'

Noemie shook her head. Seeing Jake embrace Desiree in a way he hadn't embraced her had only made her distress levels rise, her cries louder.

'We need to step aside,' her mother said more firmly.

'Non!' Noemie snapped.

The last of the guests were leaving the chapel and Martin was doing what he could to hold it together and preside over proceedings. Jake stood, hands in his pockets, exhaling big sighs at the ceiling. Christine had gone outside to text her mother and check on Axel but he really needed her right now. He took one hand out of his pocket and rubbed it on the bridge of his nose. Remembering to smile when he could.

Noemie watched the last of Seb's friends, family and colleagues leave as she knew her crunch time was coming.

'Who are these people?' she asked Jake.

'Huh?' he said, squeezing the bridge of his nose again, as if it powered him on, kept him functioning.

'All these people, who are they?'

Jake could barely muster up the energy to answer.

'What do you mean?'

'All these people!' Noemie's thick dark brows knitted over her pale perplexed eyes. 'Who even are they?'

Jake looked blank.

'My grief! My grief, it is more legitimate.'

'What?' Jake was genuinely gobsmacked.

'I was there! It was me he wanted to spend the rest of his life with...'

'It's not a contest, Noemie...' Jake said soberly, willing Christine to walk in; wondering if Martin could hear. He had walked around the back of the coffin, surveying it for one last time.

'Doucement doucement...' Camille said, fanning herself and Noemie, whose breathing was becoming more frantic again.

'Where are my children?' Noemie said it to both Jake and Martin, but Martin was too lost in his contemplation across the casket to register. 'I want my children!'

'T'inquiète, ma chérie, les enfants sont à l'école...' Camille shepherded her daughter to the chairs they had been sitting on for the funeral ceremony and made her take a seat again.

Just Martin, Jake and Reverend Jane remained at the altar now; chapel staff had started stacking chairs at the back. They had a smaller funeral in twenty minutes. A ninety-seven-year-old World War II veteran without many relatives.

Noemie looked at Jake, tearing at her hair with one hand and gesturing to a faraway place with the other.

'If he hadn't gone to Miami! If he hadn't messed up all our plans!' Noemie despaired, pulling and pointing. 'It was an overreaction! I really didn't do anything.'

Jake looked pointedly at Martin but didn't say anything.

Camille whispered in her ear to calm her.

'You all think it's my fault but it's his fault! He went! He made the decision, not me!'

Reverend Jane walked over to Noemie and crouched down at her side.

'He left me with no choice!'

'Would you like a glass of water, Noemie? I can get you one.'

Camille shook her head and took a bottle of water out of her bag, making her daughter drink.

The reverend needed to get this family out; to give Seb's dad a quiet moment before the conveyor belt of life continued and another family started filing in.

'Shall we go out into the sunshine?' she suggested, already half helping Noemie up. 'Get some air.' Jane's face was understanding and compassionate, but she could see perhaps Seb's father wanted a last, quiet goodbye.

Camille nodded.

'*C'est bon*, I'll take her...' she said. 'She's very upset,' she added philosophically, as if no one had noticed.

Camille and Noemie shuffled out into the rose garden while Jane got back to tidying up.

'Awesome service, Reverend. Thanks for everything.' Jake wanted to hug her but thought it wasn't appropriate.

'Not at all, you did a great job,' she said as she double-checked the lectern and returned to the back of the chapel to help with the chairs.

'I'll leave you to it, big guy,' Jake said, as he patted Martin on the back. He wanted to get out and find Christine, seek solace in her sweet smile, but Noemie and her mother were blocking the door, looking frantically out at all the people they didn't know.

30

DESIREE

September 2013, London

'Thirty? Wow!'

Seb stopped in his stride and took in the sight. Desiree was
standing in a bright green shift dress and gold skyscraper
Louboutins that complemented the foliage-filled corner of the
newly opened bar she had booked, the last of the Indian summer
sunset bursting through the floor-to-ceiling windows; making her
brown skin glow. At work for the few days he had seen her; and in
Vienna for the meeting, Desiree had looked glossy in a muted way
– all whites, creams and beige. Now her lids shimmered, her hair
was full and voluminous, and the shiny gloss of the centre of her
lower lip made Seb want to bite it.

He stepped back and admired the bronze foil 3 and bronze foil
0 bobbing on tethered ribbon, London's September sunset shimmering behind her.

'Seb! Hi!' Desiree exclaimed, extending two hands out to take his, kissing him on each cheek. The feel of her fingertips in his palms sent sparks to his heart. 'So glad you could make it!'

Desiree was flanked by a blonde middle-aged woman with short hair and a tall man in an expensive-looking suit, with possibly the most handsome face Seb had ever seen. 'My parents have just got here!' She said it as if he knew them, and they greeted him warmly.

'Seb, did she say?' asked her dad, shaking his hand enthusiastically.

'Yes, pleased to meet you.'

'Timothy.'

'Timothy,' Seb repeated politely.

Seb felt a bit flustered, looking from her dad to her mum and the gathering of gorgeous women, hipster men and cool-looking friends mingling in their cornered-off section of the atrium bar. Desiree's people were polished and Seb suddenly felt very scruffy. His dark jeans were three days dirty and his shirt probably came from the ironing pile rather than the 'done' one as he'd put it on in a hurry. He smoothed it down as soon as Desiree's dad let go of his hand.

'The view is incredible!' Seb said gratefully, stating the obvious. Desiree's parents nodded, as if it were a given their daughter would have booked the hottest ticket with the best view in London.

'This is my mum, Shirlie, and dad, Timothy. This is Seb from my new office.'

'Ahhh, you're an architect too!' Timothy jibed, now pressing Seb on the arm. 'Good to meet you.'

'Oh, are you an architect?' Seb thought about his own father.

'Hell no, I couldn't even build a decent sandcastle when Desi was a kid.'

'Dad's an actor,' Desiree said, which explained why he was so bloody good-looking. Seb thought he looked familiar.

'*My* dad was an architect though,' Timothy said proudly. 'Well, he was before he came to Britain.' He turned to Desiree. 'That's what made you want to become one, wasn't it, treasure?'

'So, you're from the new office?' Shirlie asked, appraising Seb. Desiree's mum had soft blue eyes and delicate features.

'Yes, we were just in Vienna on the project Desiree has been called in to rescue. It went really well.'

'Oh, for her birthday?' Shirlie said with some relief.

Seb looked confused, and turned to Desiree.

'It was your birthday in Vienna?'

Desiree rolled her eyes as if this were an inconvenient slip of the tongue her mother was prone to.

'Yes, Tuesday.'

'I didn't know!'

'It doesn't matter,' batted Desiree. 'I was counting today as my birthday.'

'Didn't you tell anyone, love?' Shirlie asked.

'Jeez, I was the one sitting there eating cake!' Seb put his fingers to his brow and shielded his eyes in shame.

'Oh, don't worry!' assured Desiree. It really hadn't been a big deal.

'Work is work for Desiree...' her mother said.

'And play is play...' said Timothy, burying his nose into Desiree's hair with a laugh. He raised his glass towards Seb. As he said, 'Cheers!' he realised Seb didn't have a drink. 'Oh... mate!' He looked around and beckoned one of the waiters with a tray of prosecco in flutes. 'Can we get some more?' he ordered as he gestured for Seb to take a glass. Seb wasn't really a prosecco sort of man but Timothy had an actor's diction, a presence and a command that made people listen and take note.

'Cheers,' Seb replied, as he chinked glasses and took a sip, and

Desiree looked around beyond him and realised he had arrived on his own.

'Oh, is your...?'

'Clair? No. We couldn't get a babysitter...' he lied.

* * *

The night before, as Seb and Clair had sat watching Graham Norton, polishing off the last of their takeaway curry, he had tried to persuade her to go to the party in London with him.

'It's at The Shard. It's only just opened. It'll be cool!'

He sold it as a rare night out. It *was* a rare night out.

'Seb, I've just done a full week, I have a shitload of ironing. Plus *Strictly* starts tomorrow night.'

'Catch up on iPlayer!' he despaired. As they were hitting their mid-thirties, the invitations to parties came less frequently. 'I know it feels like an effort, but you'll be all energised once we get up and out. It's the tallest building in the UK. The views are meant to be amazing!'

Much to Clair's increasing annoyance, Seb's energy never seemed to dwindle: he was always up for running around the park after Millie and Jasper when they were overtired; he was always opening bottles of wine for friends when Clair had wanted them to leave an hour ago; and no matter how late they went to bed or how tired Seb was, he was always up for sex, although he was getting more nervous about instigating it lately.

'It's a bit short notice to get a babysitter.'

'I'll ask Dad and Tina.'

'Sorry, Seb, I'm just so tired. You go. I don't mind.'

Except she did mind. And as she sat with Millie on the sofa, watching Bruce Forsyth tap-dance on set from stage left, she couldn't help having the hump about how happy Seb looked to be going out into London for the evening, wallet and train ticket in hand as he kissed the kids goodnight and sauntered out of the door towards Northill railway station.

* * *

Seb was never a good liar, but he was rescued by two glossy women excitedly bobbing into the group.

'Happy birthday!' shouted one, with a white-blonde slicked-back pony, wielding a gift bag.

'Girl, how do you look so alpha when our apartment always looks so shit?' said the other with olive skin, hair down to her waist, and a bunch of balloons in one hand. Shirlie rolled her eyes and looked unsurprised as she and Timothy kissed Desiree's friends and said it was good to see them. Seb stepped back, taking a sip from his flute as he looked around for Jill and Terence. He suddenly felt old surrounded by glamorous women and their parents. Maybe he shouldn't have come after all.

Thirty. Shit.

He thought about his own thirtieth birthday almost five years ago at The Blue Bell in Northill. He remembered being hoisted onto Jake's and Woody's shoulders while 'Mr Brightside' and 'I Predict a Riot' pumped out of the Spotify playlist. Jasper the birthday surprise, squirrelled under Clair's jersey wrap dress. It was fun and unfancy; exhausting and loving.

And here he was, thirty-one floors up at The Shard, desperately trying not to look at Desiree, her animated face and sunken dimples, greeting her friends and laughing, as Jill and Terence walked in and filled him with a sense of relief.

'Ah! You made it!' said Jill with surprise. 'Really nice of you to come...' She said it as if she were responsible for Desiree having a good time.

'Sebastian,' said Terence, shaking his hand. They never shook hands at work. Seb was thrown by Terence's leather jacket. He hadn't pictured him as an Easy Rider. But the three of them took a bottle to a table where they bumped into Desiree's former Harper + Swan colleagues, one of whom reprimanded Jill for her poaching skills.

* * *

Desiree's thirtieth birthday party was something else. She looked unreal in her apple-green dress; her friends were vibrant and interesting and had travelled from near (Hackney, Clapham, Angel) and far (Glasgow, Portsmouth, Washington DC) to celebrate her. Her family were funny and warm. Her flatmates, Gaby and Sukhi, furnished Seb with cocktails he actually liked and he even danced with Desiree's dad to 'Sing Sing Sing' by Benny Goodman. When Desiree's footballer brother, Matthew, said he'd invite Seb to a game at Stamford Bridge, Seb thought he was joking, until another friend came over and said he was up next on *Match of the Day*. Which reminded Seb, he really ought to go and get the last train home, so he hugged Desiree and said thanks for a great night.

As Seb rushed to get round the Circle Line to Paddington, he felt giddy on negroni sours and optimism, for the first time in years.

31

JUNE 2019, NORTHILL, OXFORDSHIRE

'Hi... Clair...?' A woman with soft-brown curls and a freckled face nervously approached Clair, Jasper and Millie, who were standing in the rose garden with Clair's parents Adrian and Linda, and Penelope, her arm still around Millie.

'We don't want to intrude...'

It took Clair a second to place the out-of-context face – a school mum at her ex-husband's funeral – but then there was no precedent for this.

'Oh, Helen!' she said, when she finally found her words. Relief flashed over Helen's kindly face.

'It's just... Arthur wanted to come and support Jasper.'

A ginger boy with a face as timid as Jasper's emerged from behind his mother's arm.

'Arthur!' Clair said, with an exhale, which made both women relax a little under the billowing, showy clouds that were starting to give way to patches of blue, lifting the oppression in the sky.

'Jasper, look!'

The ginger boy entered the circle, his back as straight as a ruler, as he approached his friend nervously.

'Hi,' he said quietly.

'Hi,' Jasper replied flatly. He felt a bit embarrassed that Arthur might have seen him cry, not realising from the look of Arthur's wrung-out eyes that he had been too. They looked at each other, smiled, and then looked down to their own feet. They wished they were online playing Minecraft, dismantling old cameras or on the green with the drone. Anywhere but here really, but they looked back up at each other and the sympathetic curl at one end of Arthur's mouth gave Jasper some comfort. Millie tried to smile at Helen but it was too hard.

'I'm just going to say hi to Harry and Gen,' Penelope said, unlooping her arm from Millie's, squeezing her shoulder, and walking over to see her brother and sister-in-law.

'We didn't want to intrude, really, we just wanted to pay our respects. To let Jasper and you know we're thinking of you. All of you.'

Helen wanted to touch Clair's shoulder as Penelope just had Millie's, but held back.

'Thank you.' Clair smiled. 'We appreciate it.' She pulled Jasper in, almost to shake him. 'Come to The Orchard, if you fancy. There will be plenty of food.'

Helen smiled nervously, the sunlight making her freckles burst further forward on her face. 'Ah, that's very kind of you.' Helen wasn't sure.

'Arthur and Jasper can play.'

Clair's fiancé, Dave, walked back over from the car park, having been to check whether he'd put the handbrake on. He'd been worrying about it all through the service, the thought of his Skoda Octavia careering down the hill onto the A road at the bottom of the field.

'Oh, hi, Helen, nice of you to come...' he said affably. 'You OK, mate?' he said to Arthur as he ruffled his red hair. Arthur blinked twice for yes.

'Didn't everyone do a great job?' Dave said to Clair's parents, trying to take the focus off the self-conscious kids. 'Wonderful service; Jake was very brave... Jake did very well, didn't he, Adrian?' Dave was very good at filling quiet moments with amiable chit-chat. He was also good at remembering everyone's names. He was a painter and decorator and had met Clair when he was painting the hallway, landing and main bedroom. Clair had wanted a refresh, to finally get the traces of Seb out of the bedroom and choose a colour *she* wanted (Farrow & Ball Calamine) over the one Seb had chosen (Stiffkey Blue) a decade ago, and over the course of his painting, their cups of tea and chats, Dave couldn't help noticing there wasn't any sign of a Mr Cooper in the bedroom any more, and this rather special woman might be single.

'Yes, he did very well...' Adrian concurred.

'Wonderful service,' Dave repeated again, giving Clair's back a gentle rub.

'OK,' Helen said quietly. 'Perhaps we'll see you there, hey, Arthur?' She looked at both boys' faces to gauge that it was indeed the right thing to do, before ushering him away so the family could be alone.

The wind whipped slightly, blowing the bulbous clouds further apart and making the muggy skies feel a little fresher, as people with sad faces shuffled among the roses towards conversations, reunions and cars.

'See you there.' Clair smiled, and Adrian and Linda also left, to find Clair's sisters, Elizabeth and Rachel, and drive them to the pub.

'See you shortly, darling,' Adrian said as he kissed his daughter's cheek.

'Can you just check it's clear we have the pub exclusively until five?' Clair asked her mum in panic.

'Don't worry,' she said.

'I've taken care of that,' Dave assured her.

The plans, the people, the logistics, for a party no one wanted to have, had weighed on Clair to the point of distraction. Making her worry that she wasn't focusing enough on the kids' grief. Or her own. Then she looked up, as she heard the thin heels of Desiree Cruz-Campbell approaching on the path among the roses. She was giving Millie a nervous smile, a small woman on her arm.

32

DESIREE

October 2013, London

'Was that you?'

Desiree leaned on the doorframe of Seb's office with a smile, her hair tied back tight off her face, which shimmered bare except for Dior lipstick in a popping red shade called 999. She gave an enigmatic smile before walking away, swiftly down the corridor, her soft-pink wide-leg trousers kissing her heels. She'd only been at Rennie + Byrd for a month but he could recognise the sound of her expeditious gait from the other end of the building.

'Er, yeah,' Seb called out after her as he got up and followed, through the open-plan centre of the Rennie + Byrd HQ, where the Part One and Part Two assistants on their work placements were tracing drawings, organising system libraries and playing with Photoshop, to Desiree's office at the other end. Rennie + Byrd took up the entire seventh floor of the Shoreditch building, but they were going to have to take over another if they kept growing at this rate. Desiree's office had been the last to be claimed.

Even though Desiree hadn't looked back, she knew Seb was keenly following, like a puppy chasing a ball. She breezed into her office, leaving the door open behind her.

'Well, tell me about it...' she said, stopping to appraise a painting that was propped up on her office sofa, leaning against a glass wall partition that separated Desiree's office from their colleague Federico's. Horizontal stripes of frosted glass afforded Federico and Desiree both privacy when they needed it, but emerging smiles through the glass made Desiree think she and Federico might become friends.

She folded her arms and looked briefly at Seb, frozen in the doorway, then back to the picture with shrewd eyes. Seb surveyed the room, to take it in properly, as he'd only seen it fleetingly when he'd dropped the picture off in a hurry. Desiree's office was very much like his, only on an opposite corner of the building. Plus hers had about eight coats already thrown on the coat stand, an assortment of shiny shoes at the foot of it, and hand-tied posies in short glass vases dotted about among the books, pens and rulers.

'It's a birthday present,' Seb said coolly, leaning against the doorframe. He put his hands in his pockets. 'I felt terrible that I spent your thirtieth birthday with you, in Vienna, and I didn't even know it. You even paid for my cake.'

Desiree smiled.

'Technically Jill and Terence paid for the cake. I expensed it.'

'Well, still. I feel awful.'

'Oh, you weren't to know,' Desiree said with a disarming wave of her hand.

'You had to deliver your first ever presentation to André Bertrand on your thirtieth birthday.' Seb exhaled dramatically.

'Oh, I love all that shit...' Desiree replied.

'And not one person noticed on your passport either!' Seb shrugged, although he knew he would have felt even worse to find out then, as they tore through airport security to make their flight.

'It's fine. If I'd wanted to tell people, I would have. It's no big deal.' Desiree crouched to her haunches, billowing trouser hems folding onto the floor as she leaned an elbow on each thigh and drank in the picture. 'To be honest I almost forgot myself, I was so focused on Bertrand and The Phoenix. Anyway, I had a lovely evening after we got back. Dinner with my brother on the Fulham Road.'

Seb was heartened. And wondered how she didn't have a boyfriend. Or a girlfriend. She hadn't mentioned anyone and no one seemed to look like a life partner at her party.

'Well... call it a birthday-slash-welcome present. Not that you have to hang it in here. Or anywhere even. If you don't like it, I can—'

'I love it!' Desiree interrupted.

Seb had bought the picture after seeing the real thing in a gallery in Miami when he was on his last site visit to The Elmore – which was almost ready for its big launch. The artist had painted fourteen old-fashioned rotary-dial telephones in a slight variation of style, in shades of blue, turquoise and black. On some telephones the mechanical parts were replaced and propped up by faint, genderless human figures with celestial faces. Seb had been mesmerised by it, and loved how it was one part Da Vinci, two parts Miró. After an amazing chat with the artist himself, he said he'd like to buy one of the few numbered and signed prints of it.

Clair hadn't liked it. She said it was cold and odd, and it had sat in a tube for three months before Seb got round to having it framed, since when it had been propped up on the floor of the study at home.

Since he'd got back from Vienna the gold and ochre background of the whole piece reminded him of the richness of a Klimt. It reminded him of Desiree's eyes on the aeroplane home.

Her eyes lit up again as she looked at it, rising to stand as she absorbed the artwork from the bottom up.

'I love the antiquity of it – the telephones! But the way the faces look almost robotic. Makes it look modern.'

'The artist is Cuban,' Seb said proudly, his hands still in his pockets as he watched Desiree. 'Carlos Estevez. I saw it in Miami – you're coming for the opening, aren't you?'

Desiree nodded.

'So you might see the real thing yourself. I can't remember the name of this specific picture, but I can dig it out. It just really struck me.'

Desiree picked up the coffee from her desk and smoothed down her trousers. From the way her hair was tied back and the brightness of her lips, Seb thought she looked more Cuban today, but perhaps that was the reflection of the painting lighting up her face.

'Well, I love it,' she said, leaving a red imprint on her bamboo coffee cup as she sipped. 'Thank you!' Her eyes cut through Seb in the doorway. 'Just need to decide whether to hang it here or at home...' she contemplated, taking another sip.

For a flash Seb wished he could see her home; what her flat was like; how she, Gaby and Sukhi spent their Sundays; but he pushed these obtrusive and irrelevant thoughts away and tried to focus on how touched he was that Desiree liked it enough to even consider hanging it at home.

'It's funny,' she said, putting her cup down again and repositioning the picture so it sat higher, on the back of the sofa. 'My granny worked in the telephone exchange in Portsmouth most of her life. She loved it there. The chatter. The connections. Keeping people together. She's still like that now, less and less chat though, I suppose. This is so wonderful, and so pertinent to her, I can't wait to show it to her. Thank you, Seb,' Desiree said, pulling out her chair to signal the start of work.

'No problem,' Seb said, turning to leave.

'Hey, buddy,' said Federico, slapping Seb on the back as he walked through the doors from the stairwell to his office. Seb nodded a hi. He stopped and pivoted, then poked his head around the doorway.

'Oh, Desi, are we still on for lunch?'

'Yes, I have a call with a planning officer at midday but can be all yours from half past,' she said as she lowered herself into her seat and flipped open her laptop. Seb and Federico gazed at her from the doorway.

They wouldn't know from the clean simplicity of her workspace and the crispness of her clothes that her living space was chaotic. She was surprisingly messy for someone so refined.

Her open laptop and her focused eyes signalled that it was back to business. And as much as Seb wanted to linger, he meandered to his office, his desk and his projects, leaving the otherworldly figures of the Cuban artist propped on Desiree's sofa, gazing at her while she worked.

33

JUNE 2019, NORTHILL, OXFORDSHIRE

'Come on, Granny, there's someone I'd like you to meet.'

Desiree clutched Violeta's tiny, gloved hand as they walked carefully between the rose bushes towards Clair and the kids. The family had said no flowers, that donations could be made to charities the children had chosen – Millie chose WWF; Jasper chose Oxfam – and the crematorium gardens were bursting enough with blooms at their peak, the rolling scent coming off the roses giving the air a tinge of Turkish delight.

Deep breath.

She inhaled the sweetness and strode lightly on high gunmetal heels that had been a gift from Seb, over to where Clair, Jasper and Millie were standing. Dave had started chatting to a school dad whose house exterior he'd just finished painting.

You have to face her.

Desiree had to muster every fibre of confidence, put on her best work face to approach Clair, weary arms clutching her children protectively. But Violeta was Desiree's shield. Her small felt hat and huge eyes, bewildered and befuddled by all the people around her, gave Desiree the safety net to do so; besides, she was desperate to speak to the children.

It had been almost a year since she last saw them in person, and she was struck by how little Jasper had changed and how much Millie had grown – the gap between them looked bigger suddenly.

'Look at you!' she said as she saw Millie's sad smile light up slightly. Both Desiree and Millie started to cry as Millie pressed herself into Desiree, who stroked the hair down her back and repeated, 'You're doing so well; you're doing so well.'

She pulled back to make sure Granny was OK and took her hand again.

'Jasper...'

'Hi,' he said coyly.

She was desperate to scoop him up and kiss his face, but that wasn't possible. He was never the cuddliest of souls.

Desiree could sense Clair taking a deep breath too, as she realised this exchange might be as uncomfortable for Clair as it was for her.

'It was a beautiful service, Clair. You did him proud.'

Clair smiled thankfully, before finally looking Desiree in the eye.

'We all did. Thanks for the music. And your photos.'

For the first time Desiree looked back and saw warmth. They held each other's eye for a second, then Desiree turned to the kids.

'God, it's good to see you!'

Millie gave a half-smile. Jasper looked into space, looking around to see where Arthur went. He hoped he would come to the pub but his mum hadn't said for sure that they would.

'I wanted you two to finally meet! Granny, this is Millie, remember you helped her with her school project? Guys, this is my granny, Violeta...'

Millie smiled.

'Hi,' she said shyly. 'Nice to meet you.'

Violeta, a good head shorter than Millie, looked up at her, took her hand and gave her a wizened smile.

'Clever girl,' she said.

Clair's tired face lifted a little; she was pleased to meet the famous Violeta Cruz-Campbell; grateful to talk about something other than the gaping void of Seb's disappearance from their lives.

'We've heard so much about you!' Clair looked from her daughter to Violeta, who she almost curtseyed to, a little Caribbean queen in front of her. 'It's great to meet you,' Clair said, almost on behalf of her daughter, but she had meant it too.

Last autumn, although Seb and Desiree weren't speaking, Millie interviewed Violeta over Skype for a Black History Month project, which had won her a headteacher's award at school. Through Violeta's accounts of the HMT *Empire Windrush*, of settling in the UK, starting a family in 1950s Britain, Millie was able to create a lively and vivid project encompassing Cuban communism, Caribbean calypso and photographs she had discovered through the Royal Museums at Greenwich – although alas there were no photos of Wilfred Campbell in the archives – and of course none of the stowaway Violeta Cruz, but Desiree had emailed Millie some of them as a young couple.

Violeta nodded, and took Millie's hand in hers.

'Listening looks easy, but it is not simple. Every head is a world,' she said slowly and surely. The multitude of wrinkles lining her face. She turned to Clair and peered at her through her enormous glasses.

'Your daughter is a *very* good listener.'

'Thank you,' Clair said proudly, then felt terrible for smiling so wholeheartedly as other guests approached.

'We'll get out of your way,' Desiree said to Clair as she squeezed

Jasper's shoulder. Clair's eyes were certainly less hostile than they had been at drop-offs, pick-ups, school plays and gymnastic competitions over the years. Perhaps some good could come out of this awful situation.

Don't be silly, Desiree thought. They weren't destined to be friends.

'We'll see you at the pub,' Desiree said. 'We won't stay long though,' she added, nodding to Granny, whose long blinks were magnified by her glasses.

'See you there,' Clair said, hopefulness outweighing her customary curt tone, as Desiree led Violeta to a small fountain where Jill and Terence were standing with Federico, Fatima and Mei-Xin, although Tarek seemed to have gone.

There was something Clair wanted to say to Desiree, although not in front of the children.

34

CLAIR

November 2013, London

'He was refusing to go in, Seb. It was so embarrassing! Mrs Griffiths herself had to come out and peel him off me.'

She'll be back in Havana by now.

'Well, why don't I take him in the morning? See if that makes a difference.'

'Oh, right, so you think it's me.'

Seb expelled a slow, exasperated breath towards his office window as he looked out of it. On one corner of the pavement seven floors below, students from the hairdressing institute in the building next door were on a cigarette break. On the other he could see the illuminated advertising boards of Old Street rotunda. It was 11 a.m. on a dank winter morning; it had barely got light.

'No! I don't think it's you – I just wonder, if he's playing up to you. You know, clinging to your leg – he doesn't tend to do that with me.'

'Thanks, Seb, I didn't really have time to call for a lesson in parenting, *I'm* the one doing the drop-offs so it's a bit unavoidable.'

They both knew why Clair did the drop-offs: she worked nearer Northill and started later. Seb hadn't deliberately stitched her up.

'Well, let's try it. I'll come in later tomorrow, my first meeting isn't until 11 a.m. I could just make that, or ask the structural engineer if I can put it back half an hour. See if it makes a difference. But try not to worry. Jasper's not as sociable as Millie, he's a homebody, of course he's not going to like nursery as much as she did. All the noise and chaos. I wouldn't like it.'

'Noise and chaos is exactly what you like, Seb.'

Seb didn't know why this felt like an attack, but it did. He tried to disarm her.

'He just loves his mummy and doesn't want to let her go. Who can blame him?'

'Well, it's tough, he has to go. I have to work. I just don't want to be the one to always deal with the wrench of it. It makes me Bad Cop.'

'That's why I said I would tomorrow, but I can't every day.'

'I know you can't!' Clair snapped.

Seb didn't understand why everything he said seemed to come across as a criticism, it certainly wasn't meant that way, and he really didn't think he'd changed the manner in which he spoke to Clair in the past twenty-odd years.

Maybe I have. Maybe I should try harder.

Seb touched the trackpad on his laptop to awaken the latest on The Phoenix. Since Desiree came on board in September it was going great guns and even looked as if they would meet their January opening date. They had to: bookings were looking healthy; staff were being hired; events were being scheduled and the chef was building his menu. He had a conference call with the team heading up the interiors in five minutes, which Seb had to lead as

Desiree was away. Wallpaper swatches, fabrics, colour charts and mood boards were scattered all over his desk. The finishing touches that were going to seal the reimagined look and feel of The Phoenix.

Rennie + Byrd receptionist, Ivy, who also delivered the post, was doing her rounds, ice-cream-pink pompadour quiff and pale blue blazer brightening up this dullest of mornings. She walked in and put Seb's post on his desk with a wink and walked out again as he gave her a nod and a wave.

Clair hastily moved on to dinner plans for tonight and whether they should have spag bol over lasagne as Seb flicked through the pile of stuff Ivy had just dropped on his desk. *Architectural Digest*. *Wallpaper* magazine. Invoices. Flyers. Christmas cards.

Jesus, that's organised.

He made a mental note to ask his new Part One assistant, Constantine, if he had thought about Christmas cards yet, next time he passed through the central part of the office.

At the bottom of the pile, almost mistaken for a mailer, was a postcard from Miami. On the front was a picture of a row of Deco buildings in periwinkle and pink shades, reminiscent of the hues of Ivy's hair. He turned the card over. The writing was beautiful. Unmistakeable. He remembered the artful scrawl on the postcard in the cafe in Vienna. He'd seen her notes in the margins of printouts and drawings.

'Right, I'm going into Theatre. But really, can you do tomorrow? I can't go through that again. And SJ called about Christmas, she's getting in a tizzy about a joint present for your dad and I did try to say we might do our own thing this year but she got a bit pissy. We haven't even *thought* about Christmas and it's almost December. We need to sit down and do it tonight. Shit, Seb, I really have to go, OK?'

'OK,' he said, turning the postcard over and over in his right hand while he held the phone with his left. 'See you tonight.'

'Bye.'

Clair hung up and Seb pictured her solid stride, her big heart and pinched shoulders, walking the corridors of the John Radcliffe to go and mend people, before being snapped back to South Beach. He looked at the US Postal Service stamp – a poinsettia for Christmas, which jarred with the sunny scene on the front. He put two fingers to the crease of his brow, uncrinkling it as he read the card with a half-smile.

Desiree had been away for over a week and she was going to be gone for two. Three days in Miami for the opening of The Elmore, which Seb had passed to Desiree because he needed to be at home. Millie was having gromits put in her ears, and the thought of him being on another continent while his eight-year-old daughter was being knocked out and undergoing surgery made him not want to go, despite all the blood, sweat and tears he had put into his first lead project. Plus he'd been so many times, he knew the hotel like the back of his hand, he'd seen it finished on the walk-through with the owner, Sonny Girardi, and hotel manager, Beto, on his last visit. It made more sense for Desiree to go to the party; to make the connections with Miami's finest for their plans and projects. Although the Americans always loved Seb, Desiree could win more business with her razzle-dazzle and dimples.

When Millie's operation was over and she was home recuperating, Seb didn't admit to himself in the dark corners of the night, as he sat at her bedside, that he wished he were somewhere else. But Desiree was on leave now. After Miami she went to New York for meetings with André Bertrand in Tribeca, and a potential new client in Williamsburg; then she took a week off to catch up with a friend from DC and together they were going to Havana – her grandmother's homeland she had never visited.

* * *

Seb was shocked by how much he had missed Desiree. He missed the sound of her confident stride first thing in the morning; the fig and sandalwood of her scent; her brilliant ideas and mesmeric laugh. She'd only been at Rennie + Byrd for three months and already there was a void in the office when she was absent. He'd even looked on her Instagram and was blindsided to see her friend from DC was a man – a handsome one at that.

That duplicitous and dark yearning grew every evening, as he read to Millie and Jasper, curling up next to them in their beds, kissing their cheeks and inhaling their sweet scent. He was desperately trying not to picture Desiree in the reception of The Elmore. Trying not to picture her walking the Brooklyn Bridge as he read *Curious George in the Big City*. He tried not to linger on the photo of her with a very good-looking, very tall man drinking mojitos in Floridita in Havana, and driving a 1950s Chevy convertible along the Malecón. He tried not to think about her plate of rice, beans and plantain, photographed under a colourful filter, as he ate tuna pasta bake on his lap with Clair and they watched *I'm A Celebrity Get Me Out Of Here!*.

But here just for a second, with two minutes to spare before his meeting, he was allowed to think of Desiree again. She had sent him a postcard and it lifted his heart.

He studied it and could almost smell the Peau Santal as she had leaned down to write it. He missed the energy she brought to the office and his life, which he hadn't known was missing until this godawful past week without her.

The script was beautiful. Seb drank in every cursive of every letter in those eleven words and a kiss, and it made him break out into the broadest smile he had beamed in months.

The picture is called Long Distance Relationships *and it's
wonderful! Desi x*

35

JUNE 2019, NORTHILL, OXFORDSHIRE

'Shush, Mummy, you're holding me back!'

SJ scorned Tina for suggesting that perhaps this wasn't the time or the place. Yes, there were a lot of eligible men in well-cut suits in the gardens of the Northill Crematorium, but trying to find a baby-father at your brother's funeral was a little inappropriate.

SJ's debut dating book hadn't sold well and her blog posts were having to get racier by the week to keep up the engagement and likes. What had started as musings about single-girl life and the odd shag in an alleyway had soon become content about mutual masturbation, sex parties and fetishes. Which her mother had become accustomed to, and with each week that passed she felt less and less self-conscious walking around Waitrose in Headington.

Tina blinked rapidly, nervously, in the shadow of her formidable daughter, but said nothing. She smiled through gritted teeth and searched for Roger and Dora, who were standing with their daughters, Emily and Zara, now in their forties and mourning the boy they taught the facts of life to.

'The calibre of man here is much higher than the saddos I hook up with on Tinder or Bumble, I can assure you.'

'Princess...' Tina winced, but didn't go further, for fear of upsetting her daughter.

'It's a better gene pool.'

SJ liked to taunt her mother with her desire to become a grandma *in her own right*. Tina loved Millie and Jasper dearly, and was a thoughtful grandparent to them, but she knew it would be *different* when SJ had children of her own. Whenever SJ needed a leg up the ladder, asking for help to buy a new car, put a deposit on a flat, or replace her old laptop, there was always the underlying subtext that if SJ was happy, it would bring grandchildren about faster.

Tina didn't respond, she looked nervously between the Curtis family and the chapel door she was expecting her shell of a husband to exit from at any moment. She wanted to be there for him the second he came through.

'I mean, look, Mother! Woody Whatever. I am creaming my knick-knacks for those guys over there...'

Tina followed SJ's gaze to a group of men in their late thirties in nice suits with good hair.

'Architects, surely. Hopefully no baggage...' SJ almost sang to herself.

'I think they're Curtis + Cooper,' Tina said, reluctant to get involved. She looked wanly at the door. It had been closed after the last people came out of it – Noemie and her mother, followed by Jake – and she desperately hoped Martin was OK in there. That he was holding up.

'Bingo.'

'Some might say architects all come with baggage,' Tina suggested, looking a little downbeat.

'True,' SJ scoffed. 'And I want richer. Smarter. Banker or tech billionaire. I mean, I don't need rescuing, Mummy, but I don't want to slum it either.' SJ licked her thin red lips.

'I really don't think this is the right time to be looking so...' She wanted to say *desperate*. Not today of all days. 'So... *keen*,' she concluded.

'Oh, shush, Mummy. I'm trying! I'm Daddy's last hope!'

The doors to the chapel opened and a harrowed-looking Martin came out, looking for his wife.

36

DESIREE

December 2013, London

'She's here!' squeaked Jill, as Desiree wheeled in a case and unwrapped her cream coat. She looked around the private dining room that was off to one side of the restaurant, eyes lit by golden fairy lights reflecting in the smoked mirrors and bronze glass of the opulent industrial space. Federico and Mei-Xin had spent five years remodelling an old Gothic fire station for Rennie + Byrd, so the private dining room, with its artfully distressed floral carpet and gold pendant lights, were assured for the Christmas party, despite this being the hottest celebrity dining spot in London.

'She made it!' Jill stood up and hugged Desiree, who warmly hugged her back. A waiter took her coat and case. 'Good flight?'

'So-so.' Desiree shrugged.

There weren't many people Jill squealed about when they entered a room – she must have missed Desiree too – so it was obvious to all twenty architects, IT support, accounts staff and Ivy the receptionist at the Rennie + Byrd Christmas party exactly who was teacher's pet. Especially Ken, who had piggy-backed his retirement leaving dinner onto the Christmas party, and spent most of the night scoffing about how great the industry *used* to be.

Most of the Rennie + Byrd team were happy to see the back of Ken, his everyday racism, misogyny and antiquated methodologies. He hadn't ever fit into the Rennie + Byrd ethos. Jill and Terence had only got him on board when they returned from New York because of his contacts book – his designs and thinking were nothing revolutionary – and a tiny part of Seb felt sorry for him. Washed up and repellent to the bright young things who'd trained in Beijing, Lausanne and Delft. Although judging from Ken's red-wine-ruddy cheeks and bloodshot eyes, he hadn't done too badly.

Everyone except Ken cheered Desiree's return with some kind of a welcome and a wave as Seb watched her smooth down her roll neck and fluff up her hair. She looked tanned and glorious, warming up the cold December night against the chatter of cutlery and chink of glasses. He watched her eyes brighten and tried to read her lips as she told Fatima that she'd landed just an hour ago and had had a wonderful time. He looked at the martini glass Ivy handed her, enticing her to sit down and *tell me all about it.* He saw Federico shuffle up and ask about South Beach; her meetings in New York; her adventures in Cuba, and confess he'd been following it all on Instagram. He noticed how the dimples in her cheeks deepened a little and her wide lovely eyes widened further as she waxed lyrical about *ropa vieja* stew and adventures at a waterfall. Seb, from his seat next to Terence at the quieter end of the table, saw Ken cross his arms and turn away like a petulant child, for Desiree had stolen his thunder again. He saw how Ivy, Federico and Fatima were hanging onto her every word. He heard Jill ask her about The Elmore, then he saw her briefly scan the two tables, until her eyes landed on his. And when they did, he pushed his hair back, took a deep sigh, and his heart soared.

* * *

'Come on, we're going to Annabel's!' Ivy announced, soft pink quiff buoyant despite the empty bottles and detritus on the table. Her arm was looped through Federico's as they stood clutching their jackets. Only Desiree and Seb, Mei-Xin and her friend Susana, who had been dining in the restaurant with another group, remained. Seb and Desiree had spent the evening trying to get one seat closer to each other: she so desperate to tell him about Miami, the *Long Distance Relationships* original, and what a great hotel he had built; he desperate to know if Cuba lived up to her expectations. If going back to the birthplace of her grandmother had changed how she felt about her identity. If the man she was travelling with was her boyfriend. Every move of a chair or someone going to the loo or leaving brought them one seat closer, like a chess game no one knew they were part of, until the last half-hour when Seb got back from the toilet and collapsed into the empty seat next to Desiree.

'How was it?'

'The painting? Stunning. Cuba? Unreal.' It was almost as if she could read his mind. Her economy and efficiency with words making them feel as if they could talk without speaking. 'Never have I seen so many people who *look* like me.' She rubbed the bare arm of her rolled-up sleeve. 'Never have I eaten such unfussy, basic food, made of the same four ingredients and it feel so... homely. And right. And never have I felt so close to Granny, yet been so far away from her.' Desiree had never done the 'backpacking thing', as she called it. It had only seemed like a barrier to getting to UCL and her studies. To qualifying. To her dazzling career. She knew that she would be able to travel the world with her work, so why bother?

What she didn't say was that she had wished Seb were there with her. That it didn't feel right to be at the opening of his hotel without him. That she wanted to wander under the waterfall at El Nicho and go wild swimming with him.

'Annabel's? Really?' Desiree laughed at Rennie + Byrd's most dastardly duo. Ivy lived with her poker-obsessed boyfriend in Peckham and liked to party while he was up all night playing cards; Federico was so chiselled he never left a nightclub without a posh blond guy on his arm. 'I'm good, thanks,' she said, putting out a low palm, almost looking at Seb. 'I've been travelling all day, plus I'm thirty now, I can't party like I used to.'

'Please, darling, I'm forty-fucking-two!' lamented Federico. 'Please, please, please come...' he said, making Puss In Boots eyes.

Seb felt the echo of Federico's disappointment in the pit of his stomach, but he needed to get home too.

'Nor me. Not that you were asking.'

'Seb!' Ivy looped her arms around his neck and hugged him from behind. 'We meant you too!'

'I have to get my train, I'm afraid.'

'You can stay with me...' Federico flirted.

Seb laughed.

'Oh, Sebastian!' scolded Ivy. 'You're no fun any more!'

* * *

On a prim Marylebone pavement, Desiree clutched the handle of her suitcase and lowered her face into the funnel neck of her cream coat. Even in the dark of the cold December night her skin glowed, from her trip and from the mandarin martinis. She and Seb had eked out the night to the very last point possible and stood facing each other at the moment they knew they had to part. Seb coiled his scarf around his neck, his shoulders broad in his dark peacoat. The Christmas lights of Marylebone High Street draped like glittering gold chandeliers behind them, as they looked at each other, tired and tipsy, heads edging closer.

They both spoke at the same time.

'I—'

'Who is he?'

Seb's question silenced her, and they both gasped a little and moved back half an inch.

'Who?'

'The guy from Washington. The one you went to Cuba with.'

Seb's charismatic smile tried to dampen the hideous feeling of jealousy he felt.

'Adam? Oh!' Desiree looked at the passing night bus and smiled, before looking back at Seb in the streetlight. 'He's a UCL friend, from America. We met on his gap year here – he studied politics; works in the Biden office out there. He's actually played basketball with Obama.'

'Oh.'

Seb felt woefully inadequate and was embarrassed he'd even mentioned it.

'More of a diplomat than a politician though.'

He waited for Desiree to state the obvious and ask *what business is it of yours anyway?* But again, it felt as if she could read his mind.

'We went out an age ago. He's like a brother to me now.'

Seb didn't think he looked much like a brother in the photos. They had looked like a hot couple on a photo shoot.

He raised his gaze sheepishly and was surprised to see her longing look.

'I missed you,' Desiree said honestly, almost in exhaustion as she allowed all the feelings to come flooding out: how something was missing at The Elmore, and she knew exactly who it was; how she'd wished she were watching the Knicks game with Seb, not a new client.

'I missed you too,' Seb confessed, with a flood of foreboding, as they pressed their foreheads together, scared that if they pulled them apart their lips might meet.

37

JUNE 2019, NORTHILL, OXFORDSHIRE

'Desiree, how are you, darling?' Jill hugged Desiree and Violeta together as if they were one entity.

'Awful, this is so weird.'

'I bet it is. Dreadful. Who's this, then?' she said, changing the subject, knowing exactly who Desiree's companion was.

'Oh, Granny, this is Jill Rennie and Terence Byrd, my bosses; and these are my co-workers, Federico, Mei-Xin, Fatima...'

She looked around for Tarek, who Granny already knew, but he must have gone to the toilet.

'*Encantado,*' said Federico, with his most charming smile, and Violeta's magnified eyes looked as if they had come alive again.

'*Hablas el español?*' she asked creakily.

Desiree was startled. Granny spoke less and less these days, but Desiree was shocked to hear her speak Spanish as if she had only spoken it yesterday. She had never spoken it much in England. She had always been happy for people to assume she was Jamaican like Wilfred.

'*Siii, yo soy Chileno...*' he said, taking her hand.

'*Ahh que lindo!*' Violeta exclaimed, more animated than she had looked all day.

'Violeta, what an honour!' interjected Jill. She didn't have much time for conversations she wasn't party to. 'We have heard so much about you!'

'Every office party, Desiree shows us how to dance like a Cuban...' Fatima added with a wiggle.

Violeta gave a bemused smile.

'Actually, I show you how to dance like a Cuban, then Federico takes centre stage and pushes us all out of the way...'

'Sounds about right.' Mei-Xin smiled.

'How was your journey?' Jill asked with concern. Terence's mother was almost ninety, and she knew what a mission it was to get anywhere with her, let alone a loop across southern England in one day.

'Yes, fine, we listened to lots of Bruce Springsteen, didn't we, Granny?'

Violeta didn't say anything.

'Is Tarek not about?' Desiree asked.

'No, pet, he had to get off...'

Jill gave a consolatory smile. 'He said to say goodbye though... To pass on his love.'

'Oh.'

38

DESIREE

January 2014, Vienna

A shard of winter sunshine spliced through the white toile curtain onto Desiree's restful face, making her lids flicker and open. The noise of retching and vomit didn't tally with the luxuriant scene of a long, bright window, framed by stiff cream curtains they hadn't bothered closing on a dark January night. A bottle of Laurent Perrier Blanc de Blancs 2007 rested in the deep sill of the window next to a small vase of fresh white blooms. It took Desiree a second to focus. The glistening copper bedside table between her and the window sparkled as the sun hit it, the glow of a new day jarring with the strains of betrayal coming from the bathroom beyond the doors on the other side of the kingsize bed.

The noises from the Museum Quarter started to restore her and she remembered the night before.

'Are you OK?' Desiree called as she went to push her eye mask up into her hair (it doubled up as a morning headband) but realised she had left it in London.

Seb came out of the bathroom in his boxer shorts, a white flannel wiping toothpaste and treachery from the corners of his mouth.

He nodded, a haunted look on his pallid face.

*   *   *

'This woman needs promoting!' André Bertrand had bellowed to Jill in the hotel restaurant as the launch party was in full swing.

'One step ahead of ya, André,' Jill replied as she raised her champagne glass. Desiree looked surprised, from Jill to André and then to Seb, who was standing opposite her, eyes knowing and encouraging as her heart fluttered and Jill nodded.

'Great, well, I want her back in New York the minute I sign the deeds on an exciting thing I can't tell you about yet or my lawyer will kill me...'

Jill tried to contain her glee as she looked between Seb and Desiree and they did an internal fist bump. Desiree had saved The Phoenix, taking it from Ken's haughty Hapsburg to an elegant and modern hotel that had just raised the bar in Europe for being intimate and grandiose. It had been a triumph. Not just for André's portfolio or his famous friends who had turned up to party, but for the future of European hoteliers; for the potential of more projects for Rennie + Byrd.

André went off to press hands with the press, while Jill, Seb and Desiree stood in their huddle.

'Wow,' Desiree said, blushing. 'This is cool.'

'Cheers!' said Jill, raising her champagne glass again. 'And yes, it is. And yes, André has unwittingly ruined my surprise, but, yes, I want you and Seb to be partners, so I'd like to make you a senior associate too.'

Desiree gasped, and turned to Seb.

'Really?'

Seb nodded. This was a conversation he had clearly already had with Jill and Terence. Desiree turned back to Jill in gratitude and awe.

A senior associate. At thirty.

'This is next level!' She laughed, taken aback. In five months, this was the closest Seb had seen Desiree to losing her cool.

'No, *you* are next level,' Jill said, her curt Glaswegian tones cosy now.

A woman in black passed with a tray of taleggio dumplings and calf's liver, elegantly presented among pea shoots and celeriac sliders.

'You turned this project around, you made it better than I could have done. Terence and I are astonished by your ideas and your work ethic.'

'One hundred per cent!' Seb nodded, raising his glass into the circle too.

Desiree's dimples sank into her smile as she allowed herself to relax, to soak in the moment.

'Well, thank you.'

'Not a problem,' Jill said with a wink. 'Well deserved.' And she headed off to catch her late flight back to Heathrow. Her twins were in their school performance of *The Comedy of Errors* the next lunchtime and she'd promised she'd be back for it.

As Jill left, Seb couldn't help wonder if she was setting him up for a fall; not by promoting Desiree – he was over the moon about that and couldn't wait to be equals – but by leaving them alone together, to stay in the new hotel they were christening. Was it a test? He couldn't blame Jill for his feelings. He was responsible for his own actions; he knew that much.

With Jill gone and the hands all pressed, Seb and Desiree looked at each other among the swirl of champagne, of cameras clicking and music getting louder, and they both thought the same thing without saying a word: *let's get the hell out of here.*

* * *

Laurent Perrier in hand, they gently weaved through the lobby and into the lift, where their fingers weaved into each other's and they clung on tight as the elevator rose sharply and their stomachs churned.

As her bedroom door clicked closed, the passion became feverish. Seb lifted Desiree up against it and she wrapped her legs around him, lifting her cocktail dress up so it didn't rip under the opening of her thighs, the pull of her tights.

They kissed and pulled, resisted and conceded, as if in conflict or tango, as they fought every impulse and then gave into each. Touching, exploring, frenziedly, as their clothes fell piece by piece to the parquet floor Seb had chosen.

'Oh god,' Seb said, knowing that what they were about to do could never be undone; that everything was going to change.

They explored every corner of the room, every inch of each's other's body, traversing and tasting. As the fizz of alcohol faded, they evolved to a deeper connection, moving from chair to bed and back again until they lay, shattered and naked in the room they had created, under the gaze of Klimt's *The Kiss* above the bed, and fell asleep, their bodies pressed together in love and regret.

* * *

Seb slumped on the end of the bed, his feet pressed into the cold parquet floor.

'Sick from the drink?' Desiree asked, sitting up. She pushed her curls back.

Seb shook his head but kept his gaze on the floor between his feet.

'I'm not the sort of man to do this,' he said, against the sound of a siren in the street, his voice croaky from the trauma of vomiting. 'To cheat.' As he said the word *cheat* Desiree swore the skin around his spine went a sickly shade.

'I know!' Desiree said soothingly, wrapping the crisp white sheet around her brown nipples and clambering down the bed on her knees.

'No, you don't know that. But I'm not.'

'I'm not the sort of woman to sleep with my boss.'

Seb looked back in Desiree's direction over his shoulder, but not quite at her, then back to the floor between his feet.

'I'm not your boss. We're partners now. We were always partners.'

Desiree smiled remorsefully as the noises of Vienna's imperial streets got louder, sirens and traffic and children speaking German, reminding them of a flight to catch; lives to go back to; hearts to break. But neither of them knew yet whose hearts they would be.

Seb's broad, muscular back curved in shame, making Desiree feel equally terrible, but she was always practical, so she rubbed it.

'Look...'

Seb loved the way Desiree said look. She sounded as if she had a solution for everything.

'Don't feel wretched, Seb. It was coming. We're not stupid, we're not bad people. This isn't deliberate subterfuge...'

Seb thought of Millie and Jasper, getting ready for school and nursery, of Clair putting their cereal bowls in the sink, and started to shake.

'What's the matter?'

Desiree wasn't a crier and she wasn't used to men crying on her.

'I'm as bad as him...' Seb whispered quietly at the floor.

'What?'

'My dad, I'm as bad as him. Fucking cheat.'

Desiree knew very little about Seb's family, she'd been cautious not to ask many questions about his wife, his kids, his family, lest what she thought might happen would happen. And he hadn't volunteered much. When they'd been on flights or in taxis; when they grabbed a sandwich for lunch or popped to get a coffee from Shoreditch High Street, they kept conversation to work, projects, Desiree's friends and flatmates, her brother's lavish footballer life-style, or dispatches from Violeta on Spice Island and how she was settling into her new care home. Seb held back on his family talk; she held back from asking.

She edged to the very end of the bed, sheet wrapped around her like a wedding dress, and slung her arm along Seb's shoulder.

'Don't say that.'

'I am. My dad was a dirty cheat, I am too. He did this... and I absolutely fucking hated him for it. For ages. Part of me still does, even though I love him too.'

He thought about Clair brushing Millie's hair, of the turn-ups on Jasper's little corduroy trousers as he waited by the door for a day at nursery he didn't want to go to, and felt the bile rising in his stomach again.

'Shhh, shhh,' Desiree whispered into his ear, before kissing his hot temple. 'Don't feel bad. This is so right, Seb.'

Her confidence was so powerful, he turned to her and their foreheads pressed again. This time, they both knew they had crossed a very simple line, and life would never be the same again.

39

JUNE 2019, NORTHILL, OXFORDSHIRE

Vehicles were queuing down the road to enter the shingled
driveway of the pub car park, so Desiree didn't even bother trying
to get her sleek black Smart ForFour in, or use the blue badge
permit that came with Granny and a road trip. Instead she pulled
up on the road outside and lowered her window.

'Penelope!'

Seb's mother was getting out of her car just inside the entrance,
Peter sliding a tanned arm around her waist.

'Yes!' she said as she looked back over her shoulder. Her short
silver hair wasn't wrapped in a colourful silk scarf today.

Desiree leaned out of the window slightly.

'I'm so sorry, do you mind taking Granny in for me, please? In
case I can't park nearby...'

'Of course not.' Penelope smiled, almost gratefully, to have a job
and a focus, something to think about other than her grief.

She and Peter turned around and walked on the shingle to
the car, Peter going to the passenger door to help Violeta out. He
was fifty now, and looked the same age as he did when he got
together with Penelope in his early thirties. Perhaps he had

always looked fifty. Penelope leaned her long arms onto the open window.

'Hello, darling, how are you?'

'OK,' Desiree said gingerly. 'How are you?' The way she emphasised the word *you* gave an unspoken *more importantly*.

Penelope tilted her head gently as if to say *so-so*.

'Granny, this is Seb's mum, Penelope. Do you remember, from Cirque du Soleil?'

Penelope and Desiree both looked at Violeta's face to check her recognition. Peter stood at the open door. 'And Penelope's husband, Peter?'

Three years ago, Seb and Desiree had taken Penelope and Peter, Shirlie, Timothy, and Violeta to see Cirque du Soleil at the Albert Hall as a Christmas present to their mothers.

It was the last time she had broken her out of the old people's home, although with her mum and dad in tow and Violeta spending the night at their house in Guildford, it hadn't felt so renegade. They had booked a table at an Italian bistro off High Street Kensington and chatted over fried courgette flowers and calamari, then sat mesmerised watching acrobats and athletes push their bodies to the limits.

'The acrobats,' Violeta quietly said as Penelope looked through the window. Two of the acrobats had short blonde hair, and Violeta had been tickled by the fact that, at a distance, and through her cataracts, she'd thought Penelope and Shirlie had dashed off, put on sparkling bodysuits, and pulled off the surprise of the century.

'That's right,' Penelope said with a smile as Peter held out an arm and helped Violeta out of the car.

He walked her around to Penelope, who looped her arm through Violeta's and guided her towards the orchard garden at the end of the car park, and the back entrance to the pub.

The Orchard pub was on the outskirts of Northill, on the edge of rapeseed and corn fields. The family had booked it so there was plenty of space in the garden for people to spill out. So funeral memories could be compartmentalised to the pub on the edge of town.

'I'll be as quick as I can,' Desiree called out of the window as she watched her grandmother in her floral felt hat walk away like a shrunken queen, flanked by Peter and Penelope. She lowered her aviator shades and drove off down old familiar roads, past the strip of shops, past the bakery, past the church she used to walk by on her way to the railway station.

Desiree exhaled as she drove slowly, haunted by her old haunts, and considered just driving away. She turned on the radio to reacquaint herself with the outside world. Nihal Arthanayake was digesting the news on 5 Live. The talking points. She was almost surprised *he* wasn't talking about the death of Sebastian Cooper. It was all anyone in her sphere had been talking about for the past four weeks.

Despite the rising temptation to floor it, to dodge the wake, the tense conversations and the what-ifs, she knew she couldn't leave Granny. So she did a loop of the town, just to see how different it looked from the day she came to clear the last of her things in January – and it didn't look different at all. Desiree headed back towards the outskirts, where she found a spot along the road into town, deftly parked, and grabbed her bag and wrap from the back seat, checking to see if she had everything Granny would need.

Desiree's friends, boyfriends and flatmates always marvelled how she could walk interminable distances in high heels, as if it were so effortless she could climb a mountain in them too. She joked it was that she was the heir to a Mexican shoe empire, it was in her blood; even though the shoes she walked in today were only her first pair of Zapatos Cruz. She usually bought her stilettos in Selfridges, but today she wore the gunmetal pointed heels Seb bought for her thirty-first birthday. He had had them shipped over from Mexico City and took a punt that they would fit. Desiree was so touched by the thoughtful gesture, she couldn't stop marvelling at them. And they fitted her as if they had been made to measure.

The pub car park had quietened down by the time Desiree walked back to it; most people driving from the crematorium would be in there now. She took a deep breath as she teetered on the gravel, trying not to scuff her heels, and saw Clair, grabbing something from the back seat of her car. Clair shut the door of the Skoda Octavia with a solid click and looked up to see Desiree.

'Just getting Jasper's drone,' she said curtly, as if to explain herself.

'Can't forget that!' Desiree smiled.

Clair locked the car and looked around, towards the orchard, before glancing back at Desiree.

'Erm, actually, can I have a quick word?'

40

CLAIR

'I KNEW IT! I fucking *knew* it!' Clair raged, her face ravaged red; contorted into a shape Seb had never seen before.

'Clair!' he pleaded, although he didn't know what he was pleading. He was guilty all right. He knew he had to suck it up and take every ounce of her anger on his shoulders. He had broken her trust and her heart.

Christmas had been frosty and hostile enough, Seb feeling deplorable that he was excited to be going to Vienna with Desiree in the new year; their usual traditions seemed formulaic and performative for the children. They'd barely spoken since Seb returned three days ago. He hadn't had the guts to look Clair in the eye, let alone tell her. But he knew he had to. They couldn't go on.

Clair's refusal to come and sit down with Seb on the sofa, so he could tell her as best he could, meant she knew it was coming, so she had busied herself unloading the dishwasher in her PJs. Mugs that were still too hot to touch, but the burning sensation on her fingertips took the edge off what Seb was confessing to.

He had waited until the Friday evening after Vienna, so the kids had the weekend to adjust if they were to cotton onto anything. Dinner had been tense. Seb was feeling nauseous; Clair filled with a sense of dread. Both of them kept looking at Millie and Jasper and wanting to cry as Millie talked them through her new gymnastic routine, as Jasper said he didn't like lasagne and pushed his food around his plate, even though he had eaten it happily all through his toddler years.

Now Millie and Jasper were tucked up fast asleep in their little beds and the lasagne dish was clean and burning as Clair unloaded it from the dishwasher and was overcome with a hot rage.

'I fucking knew it. You bastard!' she gasped.

She smashed the lasagne dish onto the floor at the space between her feet and Seb's, her hair wild and face crumpled, as it broke into four solid pieces and chipped some of the kitchen tiles on impact.

'Fuck!' she raged, pushing her hair back and assessing the mess at her feet.

'Come here, sit down, talk to me...' Seb pleaded again.

'Fuck you!' Clair said, finger pointing. 'You don't get to do this neatly. However you planned.'

Seb went to the long cupboard with the mop and cleaning things to get the dustpan and brush, as Clair kicked the shattered ceramic further away from her to keep him at bay. A forcefield of broken pieces. Seb didn't make it to the cupboard, instead he retreated to the wall and wrapped his arms around his ribcage.

Clair took a deep breath and leaned back against the oven.

'It's her, isn't it? From work.'

Clair had noticed how enthusiastically Seb retold the takedown of Kenneth Keppel by Jill's new bright young thing the day Desiree started. She noticed how his mind seemed elsewhere as he picked up the *Toy Story* figurines strewn all over the hard wood of the downstairs living room. She knew there was a shift in the atmosphere that she couldn't quite put down to Jasper starting nursery school or her going back to the John Radcliffe full-time. She started to feel self-conscious about her lounging pants and old T-shirts, which she'd happily worn for years once she was home and showered. She tried to tell herself she was being ridiculous. Still, her instincts told her that Desiree Cruz-Campbell was going to bring her heartache, and now she was right.

Seb nodded, face calm and cold. The warm man she had married, the boy who made her laugh in French and biology, was gone.

'You shagged her in Vienna?'

Seb nodded again, his steely, shamed eyes filling with tears.

'And that's it? You're not even telling me you made a mistake? Or that it's a midlife crisis? You're just going to walk out on me and the kids for someone you've only just met.'

'I'm not walking out on the kids,' Seb said quietly.

'Me, then! You're walking out on me. Thanks, Seb.'

Clair started to shake and sob, her breathing tortured and shallow as she put her hands to her mouth in horror. It felt so counter-intuitive Seb not going to her, to soothe her, but he knew he was the one causing the pain. He tried anyway, and she flinched as soon as he came near.

'Fuck you!'

'Mummy, I'm scared,' came a little voice from the doorway.

'Jaspy!'

Clair wiped her face and tried to smooth her hair down, so as not to alarm him.

'Hey, buddy!' Seb said cheerily, glancing at the clock above the doorframe above Jasper's head.

10.21 p.m.

'I heard a smash.'

'Oh, silly Mummy dropped the dish, that's all...' Clair said. 'Everything's fine.'

'Come here, I'll take you back up,' Seb said, his arms widening, but Clair scooped Jasper up first and buried her face in his cheeks.

'You clear up,' she said, cuttingly.

* * *

Half an hour later, with eyes red and ruined, Clair came back downstairs. Seb was on the sofa with two cups of peppermint tea, one on a little table in front of the space he was saving for Clair, who had a calmer air about her now; as if galvanised by the sacredness of her four-year-old son's cuddles as she lay with him while he fell back asleep. She was in no hurry to return to the treachery that awaited her in the kitchen; plus it wouldn't do Seb any harm to make him stew.

'Is he OK?'

Clair didn't answer. Instead she guardedly tucked herself onto the sofa and stared at the steaming Cath Kidston mug in front of her, as she wondered how she was ever going to piece together her broken heart.

'How long?'

Seb rubbed his eyes and pushed the heel of his hands up into his hair.

'Only just recently...'

Clair gasped and started to cry again, as angry with herself as she was with Seb.

'I should have trusted my instincts!'

Seb didn't say anything. It wouldn't help to tell her nothing would have changed. This was written.

'I had a bad – bad – feeling about her!' The curl in Clair's lip revealed she had already searched, googled and obsessed about the woman her husband was about to sleep with: she had seen the dimples and the smile. The brown skin and white teeth. The care-free photos of someone who didn't have children. The shimmer of her shoulders and the cool street-style poses in her expensive-looking clothes. She hoped the man in Havana was her boyfriend, they certainly made a cute couple. 'Women know. *I* knew you were sneaking around.'

She clutched her mug to stop herself from swiping it off the table in front of her; of burning Seb's black jeans and scalding his legs forever, so that every time *she* saw him naked there would be a reminder of his treachery. That he could do it to her too. But the fact that he actually wanted to leave the family was something Clair was struggling to comprehend.

'I haven't been sneaking around, honestly, Clair.'

'Don't use words like *honestly*, Seb.'

He was silenced.

'So what happened in Vienna, then? Got cosy in your posh new hotel?'

Seb looked as if he might be sick again.

'I genuinely haven't lied to you once.'

Clair knew Seb so well, she knew that when he said *genuinely*, he was telling an exasperated truth.

'Oh, right, only about your feelings, your comings and goings, the lie of the life you've been living. With me and the kids when all the time you wanted out!' She inhaled a minty scent of tea and started to cry again.

'Clair...'

'How long have you wanted out? How long have you been looking at me and wishing I were her?'

'Don't.'

'Twenty years! Everything I believed in for twenty years has just been pulled out from underneath my feet, for what?'

She looked at him, pleading for this to be a sick joke.

'I'm so sorry.'

'Are you really leaving us? Please, Seb...'

Seb looked at her and felt a tightening in his chest he knew would be nothing compared to the one in Clair's. He nodded.

'Is she pregnant?'

'No!'

'You'll have kids with her, then.'

Clair shook her head in despair.

'She doesn't want kids.'

As Seb said it, he realised how ludicrous it might sound but he didn't want to say that they had never talked about it. He wouldn't want to say if they *had* talked about it. He knew it all sounded so treacherous.

But when they talked, Desiree's future plans never featured kids. It was all about travelling. Opening her own studio. Leading the best projects in the world. He knew from the way she loved to care for her grandma that she would love Millie and Jasper, but she never gave the impression of wanting children of her own.

'How old is she?'

'Thirty.'

'She will.'

'She doesn't. And it doesn't matter. Nothing will take away from me and them. From what we've built together. From how much I will always love you and the kids.'

'Oh, fuck off, Seb. Just get out.'

41

JUNE 2019, NORTHILL, OXFORDSHIRE

'Is everything OK? Silly question.' Desiree answered it before Clair had had the chance.

'It's ghastly, obviously. I just wanted to check though...'

Desiree took her aviators off and folded them into a glasses case.

'Did you get to see him? At rest.'

Desiree shook her head.

'I couldn't get in. I think *she* was there every opportunity.'

'Jesus Christ!' Clair scowled, and Desiree felt weirdly relieved by the sudden air of solidarity. Clair had a sisterly warmth in her eyes Desiree hadn't noticed before today. Tyres on gravel startled them both and they moved out of the way of a car swerving in, looking for a parking space that didn't exist. 'I asked the funeral director to be discreetly accommodating...'

'Well, he obviously was!'

'Of everyone.'

'It's fine,' Desiree assured her, while almost touching Clair's hand.

'Also, I don't want you to think you were being edged out. Of the arrangements and such.'

'I didn't think that. You asked about photos. You asked for my song choices. I appreciated it. I know *you* weren't the barrier.'

Clair looked at her feet on the gravel driveway and then up again at Desiree.

'I know I was for a long time.'

'I totally understand that.'

The women held each other's heartbroken gazes before Desiree sought to make things better.

'Look, it was really messy and complicated and so fucking Seb! Wasn't it? The way he lived and the way he died.'

Clair's eyes filled up again.

'Anyway, too many cooks and all that. I don't think I could have contributed much more than I did, and I couldn't be here as easily as some.' Desiree looked around the car park, for no one in particular. 'But I appreciate you asking. And I think you've done a brilliant job.'

Clair smiled but could barely speak, the mixed emotions of heartache and anger pulling her apart.

'She *shouldn't* have dominated the bookings...' Clair scolded, breaking into tears that surprised Desiree, so she squeezed her arm.

'Look, I'm not actually sure if I could have handled seeing him anyway.'

'It was awful,' lamented Clair, who herself had been just the one time, with the kids, to say a final goodbye in the peace of the funeral home; without sirens and helicopters and screams.

'How are the kids?' Desiree asked candidly.

'Traumatised.'

'Do you believe her story?'

'I believe my kids.'

42

DESIREE

October 2014, Ubud, Bali

'Look at the opportunities here! I wonder if Bertrand has ever considered this place...'

Desiree walked around the pool in her white bikini, a mango margarita in each hand, and put them on the little table between the two loungers that faced the infinity pool and, beyond it, the waves of the bright green rice terraces, bending in staggered shelves like contour lines on a map.

She slinked down, dropped her sunglasses onto her nose and picked up the copy of *Vanity Fair* at the foot of her lounger. 'It just feels like this place has so much untapped potential.'

Seb put down *A Brief History of Seven Killings* and rolled to his side to face Desiree, propping his head on his hand.

'You think?'

'Yes!' She said it as if it were perfectly obvious. 'The chic city hotels are great, but he should get more into resort hotels. There are so many business cases for building here. The risks would be pretty low and there's so much money to be made from the usage. What's this, £18 a night? We would have paid twenty times that for this sort of offering in New York or Miami.' Desiree surveyed the view as Seb smiled and gazed up adoringly, watching her as she continued. 'It might not have Michelin-star dining or Acqua di Parma in the bathroom, but I would say it's one of the best hotels *I've* ever stayed in anyway.' Desiree put down her drink, squeezed suncream onto her forearms and continued keenly. 'The restaurants down the road have the best food we've ever eaten. The talent in this town is insane. There's just so-o-o-o much potential.'

Seb kept smiling like a puppy.

'I'm going to talk to Jill about it.' She shot him a look. 'Not now, don't worry. But as soon as we get back.'

Desiree continued to rub suncream in expeditiously while Seb continued to smile at her.

'What?' She eyed him suspiciously.

'Nothing!' Seb smiled. 'I'm happy you're happy. But forget about work for a second, will you? This is a holiday. Enjoy the view.' She looked at his blue eyes gleaming up at her – even through her sunglasses they pierced through – and laughed at herself, a big punch of a laugh. Desiree was good at laughing at herself.

'OK, OK, you big humbug,' she conceded with some irony. 'Cheers!' She swapped her suncream for her cocktail again and tilted it towards his on the table.

Seb toasted her back as they both soaked in the view. The green terraces; the swaying palms; the pesky macaques jumping from rooftop to rooftop – one had already nicked off with a pair of Seb's swim shorts he'd foolishly left on the balcony two nights ago. The verdant Ayung valley stretched out before them and Desiree tried to take a snapshot in her mind's eye. So she could forever appreciate the beauty of her surrounds – not just for the potential it offered future projects, but so she could appreciate how fortunate she was to be here with Seb.

She had flitted from relationship to relationship since her mid-teens: Joey at school; Adam the American at UCL; Tristan the chef in Glasgow; peppered with Sam the out-of-work Aussie actor between most of them – but she had always been the one to jump ship. None of her previous relationships had been as consuming or made her feel as deeply all-in and in love as the relationship she'd never thought was an option. Until that night in Vienna when suddenly he was.

'If only we could transport *this* and plonk it in the middle of Northill...' Desiree said dreamily as she drank in the view.

'Yeah, the shoddy play park at the end of the road would look nicer for some rice terraces and palm trees.'

The last phone call Seb and Desiree had made before flying out to Bali was to put an offer on a small Victorian end-of-terrace house three streets away from Clair and the kids in Northill. It didn't have the deco charm of the family home on Priory Green, nor did it have the high ceilings of the grander Victorian houses at the other end of the street near the pub, but it had three bedrooms, a little garden with a patio terrace, and it was near school, a park – even if it was a shoddy one – and, most importantly, Millie and Jasper. For months they had to-ed and fro-ed from Desiree's flat in Clapham, to a six-month rental in Northill while they searched for houses at weekends, living like guilty love migrants.

Desiree couldn't quite commit to selling her flat, but the money she made renting it out would cover half the mortgage on the new house so Seb could keep paying for the one on the green.

Desiree smiled, buoying herself. She loved Seb and she loved his children. She could forgo the dream house for now. Contemporary clean raw-concrete lines teamed with rustic-chic Balinese furniture wouldn't look right in Northill anyway.

'I know Rowan Road isn't your dream home,' Seb said, carefully putting his drink down. 'But we'll make it so.'

Seb was already imagining festoon lights in the small garden and ways to wallpaper Jasper's room. Jasper had recently started Reception but didn't follow the binary options of dinosaurs or cars that little boys were expected to like. He seemed obsessed with mechanics and mechanisms – taking things apart and examining the insides. He loved the Big Apple Viewfinder Penelope and Peter had brought back from New York and was fascinated with how it worked. Seb had managed to source a wallpaper with cool mechanical robots that looked like Fritz Lang figures from an interior designer he worked with, and was excited about sorting out rooms for him and Millie.

'My dream home is wherever you are, Seb,' Desiree said with certainty as she held out the bottle of SPF 30 for him to do the honours on her back, and he moved onto her lounger and sat behind her. As he rubbed cream into her shoulders and felt the soothing salve of her skin, they looked at the world in front of them and Seb thought about the torment. The anguished phone calls from Clair's parents, Adrian and Linda, asking him to reconsider. The angry texts from her sisters, Elizabeth and Rachel, who called him all manner of things he hadn't known were in their vocabulary. He thought about the filthy looks from the Year Four mums, whose children played with Millie and who all knew what an utter shit Seb Cooper had been. He thought of all the terse exchanges with Clair when he picked up the kids and handed them back.

And he realised, nine months after he did it, as he put his lips to Desiree's shoulder and inhaled the smell of suncream and her skin: this was what he was craving when he crawled St Peter Port absentmindedly, getting drunk with Jake, Leo and Woody. Desiree was the inspiration he was looking for when he felt lost and friendless at The Bartlett. She just hadn't got there yet. Desiree and her ideas and her energy and her enthusiasm and her beauty, she was everything he had been searching for his whole life, without even knowing it.

43

JUNE 2019, NORTHILL, OXFORDSHIRE

As guests made their sober entrance into the beautiful wooden pub, they tended to peer into the side room on their way to the bar. It was the room usually reserved for quiz nights and group dinners, that had fairy lights draping the fireplace year-round. Now it had a bounteous spread of sandwiches, pastries and carafes of juice on the table, that people peeped at as they walked past, tummies rumbling as they headed to the bar to reconnect with family and old friends; wondering if it would be rude to be the first person to help themselves to sandwiches at a wake.

'Someone has to,' said Roger, selflessly, as he walked into the room and grabbed a triangle of bread bursting with egg and watercress.

At one end of the bar, Elise and Lucia were catching up: on Elise's life in London, where she worked in publishing and had two young boys; on Lucia's – after swimming at three Olympics, she was making a name for herself in punditry, such was her TV-friendly look. In a nearby corner, Woody was lamenting to Leo how he regretted not getting the boys together at his hotel in Cumbria before Seb died. Standing up in another, Federico was furnishing

Martin with details of his next project in Dubai. At the bar, Jake was ordering drinks for whoever was in his vicinity; at a table by the toilets, Roger's daughters, Emily and Zara, were chastising their dad for taking the first sandwich.

At a rectangular table at the far end of the bar, Penelope sat with Peter and Violeta, who had been joined by Desiree, and were catching up on Penelope's latest art direction. She had recently moved into pottery and her eyes lit up for the first time that day as she told Desiree about the intricate floral creations she was firing in her kiln. Millie nestled into her grandmother but felt a bit torn by all the people she wanted to hold it together for, so she flitted between that table and the one by the door to the orchard, where Clair, Dave, Jasper, and their other Guernsey grandparents sat deconstructing the day, explaining to the kids who people were in the jigsaw of their lives.

'Remember Aunty Valerie's husband's nephew?' said Adrian cryptically. 'That's him there.' And, 'You remember your mum's friend who competed in the Olympics? That's her there. She's married to a woman, you know...' Millie tried not to roll her eyes at the clumsiness of everyone, and kept moving tables as the music and the chatter all seemed to get a little louder, a little less sombre.

At another table, SJ, dressed to the nines, and her mother sat side by side in silence, eating crisps from a small bowl. Tina nibbling nervously while she watched Martin like a hawk talking to Federico, Fatima and Mei-Xin; SJ shovelling crisps into her mouth and sucking the salt off her fingers.

The pub was fit to bursting, and guests were already spilling into the orchard garden through the back door when the front doors opened and Jasper gasped as the music stopped.

Noemie entered, black mascara tracks now cleansed from her cheeks; her unkempt hair now brushed. She looked as if she might have had a power nap in order to reconvene, and had changed into a paisley, floaty dress with beading on it. Everything seemed to stop for a second. The music, the chatter, Jasper's heart.

'What are you all looking at?' her mother asked.

Millie hastily returned to her brother's table while the barman managed to reconnect the Wi-Fi and put the Spotify playlist back on. 'Tryin' to Throw Your Arms Around the World' by U2.

'Come on,' Millie said, putting a protective arm around Jasper. 'Let's see if Arthur's in the garden...'

44

CLAIR

November 2014, Northill

'You're all moved in, then?'

'Yeah, it's looking nice.'

Clair didn't say she'd walked past Seb and Desiree's new house on Rowan Road three times on her day off – just on her way to Sainsbury's – when she knew they would be at work in London.

It didn't look anything special.

'The kids seem to like it,' she conceded, through terse teeth.

'Well, not as much as they love it here, by the looks of things,' Seb said. He was dropping Millie and Jasper back home after the weekend spent in their new, second bedrooms, and stood on the doorstep, rubbing his hands together to warm up. It was clear Clair wasn't going to invite him in.

'Anything I need to know?' she asked brusquely.

'No, they've seemed fine and happy. Took them swimming yesterday and I only remembered the costumes tonight, so they're in the wash back...' Seb pointed his thumb over his shoulder while Clair frowned.

'Great. They have swim lesson after school on Mondays. I need them back.'

'No problem, I'll drop them on my way to the station tomorrow.'

Clair imagined the sick-making vision of Desiree and Seb skipping through the park to the railway station, giddy for a day in London, while she had packed lunches, reading records, and everything else to sort for school and then work and then the childminder.

She gave a sarcastic smile. It was just too much. She hated the handovers. The relief at having the kids back dampened by the anger that he had caused all this. That he had chosen to live apart from them. It all too upsetting and she wanted to shut the door on his smug and happy face. Except it was the face she loved.

Seb looked as if he was lingering.

'Yes?'

'We need to talk about Christmas... and Jasper's birthday.'

Jasper's fifth birthday was going to be his first since the separation, and although Millie's ninth birthday in May was a bouncing bonanza at the local trampoline park, Clair had got through the day without even looking at Seb. He didn't want this to be as awful.

'What do you want, Seb?'

He wanted to go in, see the kids settle in, have a conversation in the warm, but he knew he'd blown that when he left.

'I just want to know what you want, Clair – I'll work around you.' It was going to be the first Christmas apart too, and he knew it wasn't going to be easy. He remembered the one when he was eighteen back in Guernsey.

Clair gave another sarcastic thanks, her arms folded across her gilet, as she looked out onto the dark green beyond Seb's shoulder, hoping that staring into the darkness would stop her eyes from stinging.

I have to be strong.

'Well, I don't want any of this,' she said sadly, softening.

Seb felt the blow to the stomach. He had hurt the person he had been closest to on the planet, and he felt wretched about it.

'So I don't know, I guess you tell me what you want. I can't face Guernsey at New Year. Too many explanations. My parents said they might come here. We might all go to the Wirral. Rachel's bought a puppy, that might cheer the kids up.'

Whoosh.

'That sounds nice.'

Clair shot Seb a look as if to say *fuck off*.

'Well, I'll work around you – maybe you do Christmas and I can take the kids to Guernsey for New Year. See my mum – I could take them to see Adrian and Linda too, if they don't come over...'

Clair smiled sadly. The thought of it terrified her, but maybe New Year's Eve on her own, or with her nurse friends or her mum mates, might be a healthier way to say *fuck you* to the worst year of her life.

'Think about it.'

Clair nodded.

'And Jasper's birthday?'

'I'm doing a party here.'

Seb was surprised – Jasper seemed to hate parties, so Seb was going to suggest a day out to one of the London museums.

'I've invited some of his new friends from Reception. On the day, after school. You're welcome... if you want.'

Perhaps he could do that too. His spirits lifted a bit.

'Yeah, OK, shall I sort a cake?'

'If you want.'

A chilly wind blew across the green, making some of the

Christmas lights that had started to go up in trees and bushes jiggle in the wind. Making Clair's watery vision distort even more.

Hold it together, she thought.

They both knew this first festive season apart in twenty years was going to be brutal, and Clair begrudged the optimism Seb would be starting 2015 with.

'OK, cool. I'll see if I can get a cake with a robot or something Jaspy on it.' Seb looked galvanised, grateful to have a role. 'I'll keep you posted about what I sort.'

He turned around to walk back down the path. The deco houses on the green all looked cosy with their lights and wreaths. Sunday night was in full swing. *Strictly* results. Smells of roast dinners and spiced bakes. The world closed.

'Oh, and, Seb,' Clair called as he reached the end of the path. He stopped and turned around. His face still tanned and handsome from his autumn holiday to Bali.

'Don't bring her.'

'No, of course.'

45

JUNE 2019, NORTHILL, OXFORDSHIRE

'Look! There he is!'

Jasper went straight to Arthur and his mum, Helen, who were sitting at a bench table, each drinking a half pint of lemonade, bubbles bursting and leaping from the bottom of the glass. Millie gave a downbeat smile and walked straight to the swing at the bottom of the pub garden and sat on it, her legs slightly too long for it now, half wishing she had a friend there too. It hadn't even crossed Millie's mind to invite Lottie or Daisy, and she didn't want to text anyone and put them under pressure to come to her dad's funeral now. They had sent her texts this morning. She knew they cared. She didn't want to make them panic about whether to come or what to wear.

Dave opened the back door of the pub with his elbow; Jasper's drone in one hand, pint in the other.

'You want this, buddy?' he asked, holding up the toy.

A happy flash dashed across Jasper's face for a second. He'd been wanting to show Arthur his new drone but hadn't been in school to even tell him about it.

'Just watch the apple trees, eh?' Dave advised as he turned it on, placed it on the grass, and handed the control to Jasper. 'You don't want to get it caught in them.'

'Cool!' Arthur blurted, springing off the bench as a light buzz hummed. Both boys marvelled as the drone rose between them, neon lights of the rotators reflecting colour in the whites of their eyes.

Dave perched on the next bench to Helen and they watched the boys follow the drone around the garden, carefree. He raised a thumb to Millie on the swing, who couldn't bring herself to raise her thumb back but fleetingly nodded as she launched herself higher into orbit, wondering if the swing might take off and she fly away from here.

'How are they doing?' Helen asked candidly, when the boys were out of earshot by the field with two horses, who were looking a little disconcerted by the drone. She tucked a light brown curl behind her ear.

'Not bad, considering...' Dave replied, as his eyes too followed the drone before looking at Helen. 'Nice of you to come today. Some normality helps. They're still in shock, I think...'

'It's just so awful.'

Dave nodded.

'Poor things. It must have been so horrific out there. And poor you and Clair here.'

Dave nodded and took a laboured sip from his pint.

Helen spoke with caution.

'Are the police going to press charges?'

Dave sighed and shrugged.

'We don't know, it's all such a mess. Obviously no matter what happens with that, it doesn't take away the fact he's gone. Our focus has to be on the kids...'

Helen nodded.

'*Ooh la la!*' said a sudden sing-song voice behind them. 'So hot in there!'

Dave and Helen turned sharply to see Noemie's mother, Camille, wafting a fan frantically in front of her face as she stood on the step outside the back door of the pub.

She surveyed the garden as she walked grandly down the short steps to it. The apple trees looked green and blousy, with no signs of autumn's bounty budding yet. Between the two horses in the field next door, and the buttercups and daisies dotting the lawn, it looked like such a typical English country garden, Camille thought it slightly amusing. She fanned herself as she watched the boys follow the drone.

'Afternoon,' Dave said, agreeably.

Camille said nothing as her gaze continued to follow the boys following the drone.

'Why are my grandchildren not here?' she responded after a long pause. There was a jovial defiance in her voice that threw Dave. Helen shot him a look and neither answered. 'It's so pretty out here. How England should be but how I never see it. My grandchildren should be playing here.'

'It has turned out beautifully...' Dave responded, tactfully.

Camille couldn't stand how English people always turned the conversation back to the weather; how they couldn't just address the real issues.

'Is nicer out here than in there anyway.' Camille shrugged philosophically.

'Would you like a seat?' Dave asked, as he moved along to the very end of the bench in case she might, but Camille didn't take him up on his offer. Instead she walked around the garden, examining its apple trees, rose bushes and lilacs. Looking at the horses in the adjacent field. Barely acknowledging Millie on the swing, who ignored her, before Camille's imperious eyes landed on Dave and Helen.

'She didn't kill him, you know,' she said casually.

Helen's pale face flushed a russet shade of red. She'd not come here for any trouble and already felt guilty for having brought it up with Dave. She just wanted to keep out of the way and for Arthur to be there for Jasper. Dave cleared his throat awkwardly. Another thing Camille didn't like about the English.

'Who's saying she did?' Dave asked.

'Ahh, no one.' Camille shrugged. 'But I see how people look at her.' She tapped a rounded forefinger to her temple.

Dave looked down at his feet.

'Anyway, my grandchildren, they should have been here. It's been hard for them too.'

Before Camille had even finished saying it, she was halfway to the fence, hands clasped behind her back, to examine the horses chewing hay in the field. One black, one white, both majestic, and she continued to fan herself as she stood in the shade of an apple tree.

46

DESIREE

August 2015, London

'What, this came from the actual moon? In the sky?' Even when Jasper was marvelling with excitement, his face was sweet and measured.

He pressed his nose to the glass. A huge case for a small rock called the Great Scott.

'Yep, 1971, even before *I* was born,' Seb noted. 'Can you read what it says?' he asked enthusiastically, although he read it for him. 'It was brought back on the Apollo 15 mission by an astronaut called David Scott.'

'Wow...' Jasper gasped.

'And actually that little rock formed three billion years ago!' Desiree said, bending down on her haunches, her eyes level with Jasper's in the dark of the space gallery at the Science Museum. 'Before humans became human!'

Jasper sighed in awe, while Millie walked around the glass case to see if she could see her little brother from the other side of it.

* * *

It was Seb and Desiree's turn to have the kids this weekend, and the day had taken a surprise turn. Over porridge at breakfast, Desiree asked the kids what they wanted to do today. Swimming was getting tired, Millie had outgrown soft play – Jasper never really seemed to enjoy it anyway.

'How about the Science Museum?' Seb asked, rubbing his hands together. He'd been meaning to take them for ages.

A flash of suppressed excitement crossed Jasper's face and Millie liked the idea of going on a train.

'We can go to Covent Garden afterwards, see what's going on in the Piazza,' Desiree added.

The train ride was exciting; they saw the statue of Paddington at Paddington Station. The moon rock and flying machines in the Science Museum were out of this world, plus they nipped next door to the Natural History Museum to see the animatronic T-rex, which the kids were surprisingly unfazed by. Over spaghetti in Covent Garden, Millie mentioned Mummy's new friend, Dave, and how he was always up a ladder, which piqued Seb's interest and he asked subtle questions. Millie said he was funny and that he always wore a white onesie like the Ghostbusters; Jasper said he made them hot marshmallows on a bonfire. Seb said he sounded like a nice man. After lunch they watched a street artist dressed as Mr Bean entertain tourists from a little pedestal in the Piazza, although Millie found him creepy so Desiree took her off to Oasis and bought her a bag and a hairband in a matching print. Seb took Jasper to the Tintin shop on Floral Street to buy him his first comic now he could read, and by the time they were back in Northill, watching *Big Hero 6* on DVD, Jasper and Millie had fallen asleep.

'"Dave", eh?' Desiree said to Seb, once the kids had been transferred to bed.

'I know!'

'How do you feel?'

Seb loved Desiree's honesty. Her ability to not shy away from any subject. He didn't feel upset or weird about it, but knew that if he did, he could admit that to her.

'Well, I just hope he's a nice guy and doesn't break her heart,' Seb said with a guilty flash.

'He sounds like a nice guy. "Up a ladder", eh? Maybe he can build me that walk-in wardrobe...' Desiree said with a wink.

Both hoped it would make life easier.

47

DESIREE

June 2019, Northill, Oxfordshire

'Hey you!'

Christine was a Valley Girl with glossy brown hair tinged gold at the tips, ridiculously straight teeth and a soft sweet voice. She hadn't seen Desiree at the service, so when she saw her go to the bar at the pub she jumped up from her padded banquette seat and weaved through on skyscraper heels.

'Hi!'

They hugged.

'Want a drink?' Desiree asked. 'The barman's just doing my round...'

'Oh, no, I'm great, thanks, I have a water over there and Jake has enough lined up for, well, I don't even want to think about that...' Christine waved a hand dismissively and winced, half jokingly. The noise of chatter, reminiscence and laughter meant that the playlist

Clair and the kids had made was barely audible and Christine needed to raise her voice.

'How are you doing?' Her eyebrows knitted in concern halfway up her loveheart-shaped face.

'Oh, you know,' Desiree conceded, with a stabbing pain in her chest. 'Broken-hearted. But isn't everyone?'

'It's just awful. Jake... he's been in pieces.'

'He did so well though! Seb would have been so proud of him, and what he said to the kids was just...' Desiree choked.

Christine nodded.

'Seb said *you* were doing great though – when we last saw him.' Christine suddenly looked ashen. 'Said you were moving to New York!'

Desiree shrugged it off, and tried not to think about how Seb might have relayed the news to Jake and Christine. Would he have been relieved and glad to be rid of her? Or was he sad? She wondered when the conversation would have been? January after she collected her things, or May when they bumped into each other in London – that would have changed a lot – but there was no point dwelling on it.

'Yeah, it's all a bit up in the air at the moment, with Granny and everything, I don't know...'

'Oh, well, you know I'm a California girl but I spent my happiest years on the East Coast. Before I met Jake anyway...' They paused, both aware of Noemie's back moving towards them, tattoos of a lotus flower and Sanskrit words and symbols trickling down her spine as she edged nearer, in intense conversation with Martin and Roger.

'Anyway, how are you? How's Axel?' Desiree asked excitedly.

Desiree was always deft at changing the conversation; taking the focus off her and onto where she wanted it to be; managing everything so it was cool and composed and perfect. It had worked. Christine's face lit up.

'Oh, he's just the cutest. Into everything at the moment. Talking and jabbering lots. He's loving bumbling about in the garden... he's just a dream.'

Noemie's conversation was getting louder now, her French accent stronger, her arms more animated, about whatever it was she was deep in conversation with Martin and Roger about, yet acutely aware of the women behind her back.

'God, you've got to show me some photos. He was tiny when I last saw him!'

'Yeah, I don't really do the Instagram thing,' said Christine, although she had already considered how she was going to artfully announce the secret she was guarding in her womb when it was safe to. Baby scan photo, all going well? Or perhaps Axel in a T-shirt saying 'big brother'. She tried not to think about it too much. She knew it was a conversation best left unsaid.

'I've got a ton on my camera roll,' she said, getting her phone out of her bag. Desiree smiled to see how happy Christine was. Despite the secret *she* was guarding, but there was no point disclosing to anyone.

48

DESIREE

October 2016, Spice Island, Hampshire

'When are you going to have a baby, then, *cariña*?'

The question came from wrinkled lips that ran in a thin line under the huge glasses Violeta needed now. Every year at her eye appointment, the glasses got bigger, thicker and rounder, making her delicate head shrink behind them. Every year in the seven since her husband Wilfred had died, her accent had become more affected, less Hispanic and more Caribbean, as if emulating her husband might keep him close to her.

Despite almost seventy years living under the grey sideways rain of England's south coast and staring out to sea, Violeta had never sounded English. Her eighteen years in Cuba and Mexico were a strong cement and years living alongside Wilfred's beautiful Jamaican lilt meant she was never going to sound as if she was from Hampshire. Her accent had always been uniquely Violeta.

'Oh, Granny!' Desiree laughed, as she placed a blousy bloom of blush pink tea roses in a vase on the windowsill. 'Even Mum and Dad don't ask me that. It's rude to ask anyway, you know.'

'Well, I'm eighty-six, I can ask and say what I want.'

Desiree nodded as if to say *true*.

Seb brought in a tray of biscuits and three cups of tea he'd made in the communal kitchen of the Georgian seafront care home that might have been mistaken for a hotel, it was so pretty. Prim flowerpots led down the steps of it to the cobbled streets of Spice Island, the curved walls of 'the Battery' and the Solent out to sea. Violeta had moved in there a couple of years ago, from the terraced house she had first lived in with Wilfred one street behind. A few streets from the house near the cathedral, where Timothy and Shirlie had raised Desiree and Matthew, although they had since moved halfway to London for Timothy's work and to be nearer their children. For someone who had crossed an ocean so young, Violeta's turning circle soon became a small and blissful bubble she didn't like to stray from.

'I don't even care that you're not married.'

Seb laughed. He was fond of Violeta's bluntness. Her stories. Her colourful hats. He loved their visits to see her; her occasional visits to London, or meeting halfway at Desiree's parents' house in Guildford.

'Granny, *no one* cares that we're not married!' Desiree laughed, widening the net curtains to extend Violeta's panoramic view. The net curtains – and some of the matronly staff – were the only downsides of the place: why open a care home somewhere so stunning, and make the décor so stuffy? Desiree had wanted to overhaul the room – paint it in cool hues and get some mid-century modern furniture that would suit Violeta's vibe, but apparently that wasn't allowed.

'What's this?' Seb asked cheekily, trying to disarm Violeta with his charm. Violeta had loved Seb from the first day she met him. He was much nicer than the footballer Matthew had tried to set Desiree up with, or the Australian actor, or the uptight American boy who still occasionally sent her postcards from Washington.

'Just Granny being Granny,' Desiree said fondly, propping the pillow behind Violeta's head in the armchair that swamped her.

Violeta turned gingerly and looked up at Seb, who sat close on a pouffe near the window and placed her cup of tea on the side table next to her.

'I was asking when you two are going to have a baby.' Violeta smiled mischievously.

Seb laughed and rubbed the Sunday stubble on his chin.

'You can't mess around with these things, you know... you never know what hand God might deal you.'

'Oh, look at that bird trying to land!' Desiree said, pointing to the black and white Arctic tern battling the wind.

'Your grandfather, he said to me on the *Windrush*, before we even docked. He said, "Violeta: I love you, I need you. I want to make some beautiful babies with you, *if* you would do me the honour... if you would care to join me when this ship docks..." He was always so honourable! Not that I'm saying you aren't, Sebastian.' She blinked slowly at him and picked up her tea with a shaky hand.

'I didn't know Grandad proposed to you on board,' Desiree said, hands in her pockets, head turning quizzically at Violeta.

'Technically he didn't. And I didn't care that he actually hadn't at that point. I knew I was going wherever Wilfred was going, that we were going to become husband and wife. He was an architect, like Desiree!' Violeta said proudly. Seb nodded and smiled as he handed Violeta a plate of malted milk biscuits and she shook her head.

'Desi?' Seb said, proffering the plate. She didn't take one either,

her gaze back and fixed on the tern trying to land on the unforgiving and moody waterline.

Seb took one for himself and studied Violeta's face as she continued. It was a story he'd heard before: how the bright dashing architect wooed the Cuban girl on the HMT *Empire Windrush*; how they fell in love over the Atlantic; how Wilfred Campbell was promised a job cleaning on the naval base in Portsmouth. It made him sad, he preferred the stories of heady nights over the Atlantic. Card games with the Trinidadians. Violeta teaching the Polish women to dance the Cuban *son*. Wilfred falling in love with a twirl of her skirt.

'He didn't even have to ask. I knew I was going to marry him and have lots of babies...'

Desiree turned around more sharply this time, an eyebrow raised.

'Of course, we were only blessed with Timothy, but, gosh, he was a pudding. The bonniest baby either of us had ever seen. Although parents of ugly babies say the same.'

Seb laughed.

'But Timothy really was born beautiful...'

Desiree rolled her eyes. Her father's good looks had been his currency, acting in a soap opera and on stage for all the time she could remember. It was why she was so determined to become a successful architect. Finish the job Wilfred Campbell had trained to do, the job he *should* have had. Build the Campbell name into architectural notoriety.

Seb looked at the photo on the table behind Violeta. A black man in a sharp double-breasted suit with a carnation in the lapel. A woman in a fitted cream jacket cinched in at the waist and a full black skirt, as if she had meticulously copied Dior's New Look – and added felt flowers to her hat.

He wondered how soon after Timothy was born that they gave

up hoping. Why no other children came along. For the first time, Seb considered Desiree's dad was an only child, like him. Or at least, as Seb had been before he found out about SJ. If he was honest, he still felt like an only child.

Violeta looked beautiful in the wedding photo on the sideboard – the girl from the telephone exchange standing next to the guy from the naval base, from places no one really bothered to ask about. She looked beautiful sitting in the chair in her room. Seb thought she must be the oldest woman in the care home with the most marbles and the brightest spark behind those cloudy eyes.

'Well, I'm too busy to have a baby, Granny!'

'Too busy! Too busy! Always too busy! Your brother is always too busy to visit me!' Desiree ignored the jibe about Matthew. Yes, he was away a lot with work – this week he'd been in Lisbon and Liverpool playing football, and weekends were mostly out – but he could have whizzed down to see his grandmother around training, she didn't like that he left it all to her. But Desiree wasn't thinking about Matthew as she looked out around the coastline.

'See Spinnaker Tower?' Desiree pointed westward to the development beyond Old Portsmouth.

The tower was a Millennium Commission project announced when Desiree was at school: a landmark to take Portsmouth into a new era, thwarted by financial and political wranglings and delayed by six years before it finally opened – a sail-like structure tourists could climb and see all the way to the Isle of Wight from the top.

'I would have made it better. And on time,' Desiree said with assured aplomb.

Seb laughed. He knew that much was true.

'Well, I like it,' Violeta declared.

Seb looked out towards it, to the children looking for crabs over the edge of the hot walls; to Gunwharf Quays and the tower, jutting like a metal sail in the America's Cup.

'I would have made it better. I would have built something more spectacular. It was such a waste. And I have so many ideas and so much to do, Granny – and Seb and I are going to do it all together.'

He looked up at Desiree as she raised an eyebrow at him and smiled.

'We just don't have time to have a baby, Granny. And we've got Millie and Jasper – we will bring them down to meet you, Granny. They're adorable.'

Violeta widened her eyes mournfully, as wide as they would go anyway, under the weight of thin folds and wrinkles.

'But you can't let the Cruz line stop.'

Desiree thought this romanticism was nonsense. There were enough Cruzes in Spain and Latin America for the name not to die out. She wasn't sentimental about bloodlines when the whole planet was going tits up and the best thing for it was to *not* have children.

Violeta continued.

'Matthew won't have children at this rate – none he'll know about anyway...' She gave Seb a sage look.

'Oh. Granny!' Desiree said in exasperation as she clasped her hand.

'*You're* a rule breaker! Maybe this is just me breaking the rules.'

But as she said it, she glanced at Seb's face to check he was reassured by her indifference; to see if his reassurance would reassure her. To ignore the deep and nagging feeling inside that was so disappointing that its emergence was starting to make her feel sick. She had just turned thirty-three. She'd read the scare stories. She knew the science. She had the life, the income, the boyfriend. She could have it all if she really wanted to. If *they* wanted to.

49

JUNE 2019, NORTHILL, OXFORDSHIRE

The barman placed Desiree's drinks in a line in front of her on the shiny wooden bar as she took her bank card out of her wallet.

'Oh, no, you're all good,' he said with a smile. 'Tab's still open.'

'Oh, thanks,' Desiree said sadly. She didn't want the free drinks. She just wanted Seb back, alive and well.

'Here, let me help you with those....' Christine said, straightening her dress. Desiree had taken off her jacket and Christine couldn't bear the thought of Desiree spilling even a drop of Peter's pint, Penelope's gin and tonic or Violeta's rum and Coke on that beautiful cream silk top, capped perfectly at her shoulders.

'Oh, it's OK, I'll get a tray. Can I get a tray?' Desiree asked the barman. 'Anyway, I want to see a photo of Lord Scrumptious before I take these over. I bet he's grown so much!'

While Desiree put her wallet in her bag Christine scrolled through the photos on her phone. At a glance it looked as though her entire camera roll was full of photos of Axel. Her eyes lit up as she scrolled through moments and milestones.

'Oh my god, wait... no, hang on... oh, he kills me...' she said as she landed on a favourite and held it up for Desiree. A boy with beautiful brown eyes, cheeks wider than Desiree had ever seen on a baby, and a mop of curly hair, wrapped up in a fluffy towel.

'Awwww!' she cooed.

'I know, right. All wrinkled like a puppy after a bath, that was a couple months ago, he's a bit less chubby now, but... ooh, I love the wrinkles.'

'He's gorgeous! And all that curly hair! Where does he get it from?'

Christine pulled a look of mock guilt as she ran a hand down her billowing mane.

'Oh, that'll be me. I look the same without a blowout...' She giggled.

With that Desiree pondered that at every brunch, lunch or dinner they had shared, whether Christine was hungover, pregnant or nursing a new baby, she must *always* have had a blowout, as she called it.

Both women were aware of the rather unsettling om tattoo edging nearer, giving them a foreboding feeling that their conversation was being listened to, but neither acknowledged it as they kept their eyes firmly on the phone.

'Oh, my goodness, Christine, he's edible.'

Noemie turned around, hastily. Martin had gone to talk to someone else and she wasn't interested in Roger's chit-chat. She'd never met him before and had no interest in meeting him again. His speech was nice, but he wasn't Noemie's style. Plus she was always more interested in baby talk. It was her forte, having had four. Her sea-green eyes penetrated the screen Christine was holding up for Desiree.

'He's grown so much!' Noemie interjected, asserting that she, too, had met baby Axel.

Christine looked a bit confused, and conflicted, running through the Rolodex timeline in her mind.

'Oh, I think this was taken around the time you saw him... Must have been Easter. He's even bigger now.'

'Well, he's very sweet and fat,' Noemie stated, erecting an invisible ice sheet between her and Desiree as she looked straight at Christine and her phone.

'He certainly is very sweet, Christine, you must be so smitten,' Desiree said coolly. She was not going to be rattled.

Noemie continued, again as if Desiree were not there.

'People who don't have their own baby... they don't understand those fat thighs and wrists, how you just want to eat them up...' She gave a ravenous look as she licked her lips and made a nibbling sound like *num num num*. Christine smiled diplomatically but looked cautiously at Desiree.

'Erm, yeah... so sweet. Actually, I might need to call my mom and check he's OK. She's got him today.' Christine tucked her phone into her bag, still surprised by how light it was without all of Axel's paraphernalia. 'Sure you don't want a hand with those drinks?' she asked sweetly, looking at the tray.

'No, I've got it,' Desiree said with an assured smile, and the three women dispersed into three different directions.

50

DESIREE

October 2017, Northill, Oxfordshire

'How was it?'

'Rubbish!'

Desiree walked in and slumped her gym bag on the table next to the Sunday papers before pulling off her long, sport-luxe puffa jacket and slinging it over the door. Her cheeks were tinged pink, her hair pulled back to highlight the gentle glimmer of a sweaty brow.

For someone so efficient and so well put together, Desiree was a nightmare with mess. Piles of box files, magazines and post dominated the dining table; expensive make-up littered every bathroom shelf. Millie's and Jasper's bedrooms were strewn with clothes until half an hour before they arrived (and then Desiree would do a whip round and pile cashmere, merino and leather onto her and Seb's bed for the weekend).

She took off her sweater and stood in her matching crop top

and leggings, drinking from her water bottle while she admired Seb at the hob as he got cracking with dinner.

'Pauline was away and the replacement couldn't dance for shit. She's the gym's yoga teacher or something. Qualified in Zumba too apparently, but the class would have been better with me running it.'

'Oh. That's a shame,' Seb said as he kissed her nose.

Desiree grabbed an apple from the fruit bowl.

'That's what you get when a Frenchwoman without an ass dances mambo.' Desiree didn't mention the other most notable thing about the Zumba teacher, as she took a bite out of the juicy, deep red apple, forgetting she didn't have much of an arse herself, but she was a quarter Cuban and a quarter Jamaican – that counted for a lot when it came to Zumba.

'Dinner will be about an hour,' Seb said, taking the chicken he'd been prepping since he dropped the kids back at Clair's out of the oven and onto the hob. It had been a landmark day. He had finally met the mysterious Dave, who it had been stop-start with for a while as Clair came to terms with that small matter of *trust* again.

'Yum, thanks. Did you meet him? What was he like? Are they official?'

Seb moved oil around the tin as he swayed to 6 Music, contemplating his answers.

'Yeah, I did.'

'And?'

'Seems like a nice guy. Clean. Normal-looking. Two eyes, a nose and a mouth...'

Desiree wanted more details, but she didn't know why. 'Looked happy to see the kids and they looked happy to see him. Obviously I didn't ask if they were official, it's not my place, but I guess the fact that he was there, and I met him, and Clair was acting like it was normal, means it will be the new normal. They've taken their time, I suppose.'

Seb looked as if the weight of four thousand lies had lifted off his shoulder, even though he had only ever told Clair one. That everything in Vienna had been 'fine'.

'Great!' Desiree said, launching herself on the kitchen side as she watched Seb pour wine, stock and saffron over the chicken and chorizo, sizzling in the tin. She and Clair still didn't exchange much more than short smiles and practical texts about the kids, but perhaps the introduction of Dave would help things.

'He doesn't look like you, does he? Like Ross and Russ in *Friends*?'

'Desi!' Seb shook his head and gave her a reprimanding look.

'Sorry! I just want to know!'

'No, he's mousier. Bit shorter maybe. Quite normcore. Painter and decorator. He's got a nice van with Dave Drinkwater down the side of it.'

'Oh, that's him?' said Desiree, taking another bite. 'Handy!'

'No, he's cool. Well, not cool. But he seems nice, the kids like him, and Clair looks happier than...'

Seb tried to think back to when he could remember her as happy as he saw her today, but could only picture her holding Millie as a newborn. The decade plus between had flown by in a furrowed blur.

'Well, good. I love a happy-ever-after!' Desiree smiled as she threw her apple core in the compost bucket next to her. 'Hmmm, that smells amazing,' she said, inhaling the paprika aromas as she rubbed her tummy.

She appraised Seb as she watched him cook, thinking about all the ways she loved him. His strong shoulders. His bright eyes and disarming smile. His patience and warmth. His thinking face when he was working through a hump on a project. The way he shook the roasting tin. The way he wrapped his arms around his children.

She suddenly remembered the Zumba class. The petite, French instructor with yoga-lean arms, a tanned face and slim, muscular calves, who proudly displayed a large, distended stomach under her Lycra vest. It wasn't her heaving baby bump stopping her from being a dancer. It was that she had stiff joints, no hip rotation, no sway. She wouldn't have known what a Cuban *son*, *casino* or *timbre* even looked like, let alone heard of them. But as Desiree duly followed the teacher's jagged steps to Jennifer Lopez, she realised, like a slap around the face, that she didn't like her because the instructor had something Desiree wanted, and it gave her a searing, jealous pain, like a needle poking through her belly button.

'I'm going to shower,' she said, sadly, as she jumped down from the kitchen counter and went to wash the sweat and the tears away.

51

JUNE 2019, NORTHILL, OXFORDSHIRE

'Granny, do you want to have a little snooze in one of the deckchairs in the shade?' Desiree asked as she came out of the pub holding two glasses of water. Violeta had drunk two Cuba libres in the past hour and Desiree was worried she might feel poorly.

'It's fine, *cariña*,' she replied shaking her head, not wanting a fuss. Violeta was too intent on eavesdropping on all the exciting conversations around her; too tickled watching the shenanigans of the young people in full swing.

The late afternoon sun brought a glow to the pub orchard, its lilac trees and smells of cut grass and cider making it feel like more like an English country festival than a funeral wake. Which was fitting for a man like Seb. He would have been the last person to want solemnity and misery at his funeral; Seb was always the first person to get up and dance badly at a family gathering – the last thing he would have wanted was po-faced misery.

Elise and Lucia were drinking Pimm's talking with Clair about The Good Old Days while they watched Woody orchestrate a game they used to play back in Guernsey. *A magic trick*, as he sold it to Millie, Jasper and Arthur while the rest of the Guernsey friends stood in formation, so they could demonstrate what they would do in home room when they were waiting for their form tutor at the end of the day, when spirits were high. They would stand in a circle around a comrade sitting on a chair in the middle of it, in turn placing their flat palms above the head of a person on the chair.

'One potato... two potato... three potato... four...' Woody chimed as the stack of hands rose. Until, on his command, all the people around would suddenly remove their hands, bend their knees and lift the chair, featherlight for a few seconds as they thrust it into the air. Leo was the only one foolish enough to volunteer to sit down first, Elise rolled her eyes and Jasper and Arthur looked on in awe.

Elsewhere in the garden, Clair's sisters sat with their parents and Dave at a picnic bench, trying not to discuss the elephant in the garden of Dave and Clair's upcoming wedding; Camille and Noemie were talking quietly as they looked at the horses in the field; Martin was at a table with Tina, Dora and Roger, whose daughters had already left to get trains back to their kids; and SJ was pressing against Federico, laughing while she prodded him with her elbow as she stood with the Rennie + Byrd architects near Desiree and Violeta.

'How did I not know about *you*?' she said as she placed her palm on Federico's chest and sloshed an Aperol spritz in her other hand.

Fatima tried not to catch his eye.

'You worked with my brother and he kept you hidden away?'

'Yeh, we all worked with him,' Mei-Xin said helpfully. 'He was a brilliant architect. It hasn't been the same since he left...' She meant to move jobs, almost forgetting for a second that it was his funeral they were at.

'Are you single?' SJ asked straight up.

'Always!' Federico said with a flirtatious smile, while Fatima implored with him not to be silly.

'Seb told us you were bringing out a book,' Mei-Xin interjected, trying to divert the conversation.

'Yes, came out last Christmas. I'm brainstorming ideas for my next one right now. My fans *loved* it, so I want to give them more...'

'What was it about?' Mei-Xin asked. She liked crime dramas and domestic noir.

'Oh, it's a dating book, but I'm thinking about pivoting into fiction. A bonkbuster!' She looked at Federico and licked her lips as she said it, while Fatima tried not to choke on her pink lemonade.

Mei-Xin was a serious soul and didn't know what a bonkbuster was, but nodded as if to say it sounded interesting.

Desiree and Violeta exchanged a knowing look in their deckchairs next to them. Desiree laughed inside about how polar opposite SJ and Mei-Xin were.

'Or I can ask the landlord if there's a quiet corner and an armchair inside for you, Granny. If you'd like forty winks?'

'Forty winks?' Violeta scoffed with a chuckle. 'Don't give me that!'

Her laugh was so infrequent now, it made Desiree chuckle too.

'What?' Desiree laughed, sucking on an ice cube, wondering if Granny was drunk on rum.

'I'm not having a nap now! This is all too interesting.'

'What is?' She looked around the garden.

She nodded conspiratorially to SJ standing next to her. 'When is someone going to tell her that Federico is gay?'

'Oh, right.'

52

DESIREE

December 2017, The Cotswolds

'What's the matter?'

Seb walked out onto the terrace overlooking a field and inhaled the dark chill. The dry-stone walls that divided and carved out the lines between *mine* and *yours* were fading away into the background on a cold New Year's Eve where the stars were sparkling overhead. The kissing gate in the corner of the field shut for the night, all of 2017's kisses filed away into the field's archives.

'Nothing,' Desiree said, too quickly for it to be true. She wrapped herself in the huge cream and grey checked blanket shawl she had packed, and was looking into the darkness to try to make out shapes of the small hills she had walked earlier in the day.

The light of the modern house behind them, designed by Seb as a favour to his friend, illuminated Jake and Christine, rushing about with a bedtime routine for Axel they didn't yet have nailed given they had only been parents for four weeks. Jake had prepared a long slow stew in the kitchen Aga that they hadn't got round to eating yet, and smells of red wine, mushrooms and heartiness permeated into the countryside.

'Well, come in, you'll freeze out here,' Seb pleaded. 'Dinner should be any minute...'

They'd spent New Year's Eve day walking the woodlands and wildflower fields of the Cotswolds, following dry-stone walls and climbing stiles, accompanied by the little coos of baby Axel in the sling strapped to his parents' chests. Christine and Desiree talked animatedly about architectural projects and big make-up jobs Christine had done working on film sets – despite both of them feeling hideous on the inside. Christine from the fatigue of being a new mother; Desiree from the uncomfortable feelings brewing inside her, growing month by month to a rage she had never felt. On the outside their conversation was jovial and sisterly. Christine had been the friendliest of Seb's female friends, she and Jake were the quickest to welcome her into the fold four years ago, when Seb confessed he was in love with another woman he had left Clair for. Jake had been conflicted – he adored Clair – but knew that he would have Seb's back. It helped that Christine had no emotional tie to the group – she didn't have to justify her new friendship to Guernsey friends or school mums – as she was the newcomer before Desiree. And although Desiree went to the baby shower at The Berkeley with Christine's make-up-artist colleagues, and ate afternoon tea with biscuits shaped like handbags, although she loved Christine's sweetness and her loyalty to Jake, they'd never got that close. New motherhood meant they wouldn't get closer. A physical barrier of baby in a sling between them; an emotional one when Desiree tried to smile at talk of meconium, night feeds and vaccinations, when she was crying on the inside.

On the walk Seb had noted a growing quietness in Desiree, a lack of interest to talk about anything other than Jake's tech sphere or projects of their own. When they stopped for a pint and to sink into the Chesterfields at a Cotswolds country pub, Desiree spent most of the time talking to the old couple who ran it, about who owned which property on the estates around them, and all the potential for projects, while Seb and Jake watched Christine coo over Axel kicking his legs on the sofa.

Now they were hungry, for dinner and for a new year, and Seb stood on the flagstone patio terrace behind Desiree and wrapped his arms around hers to provide warmth. Her body felt jagged, her shoulder rose.

'Hey... what's wrong?'

She spun around, her usually serene face anguished.

'This is torture, Seb.'

'Huh?'

'Look... all weekend, I've had to ooh and ahh at them in their perfect bubble and pretend I don't care.'

'What do you mean? You do care, they're our friends.'

'I do care – I'm happy they're happy... but...' Desiree's voice started to rise. A cow mooed in the darkness as if to respond to her. 'It just highlights how miserable we are!'

Seb was flabbergasted, so much so he almost laughed, which wasn't welcomed.

'We're not unhappy!'

'I am.'

'Since when?' Seb asked, pushing his hair back and retreating half a step. 'We've got everything we wanted.'

'No, we haven't.'

Seb was baffled. They finally had a more harmonious relationship with Clair. The kids were happy. The house was decorated and felt like home. He'd even mentioned putting the Clapham flat on the market so they could sell both and design and build something bigger in Northill.

'I want her life, Seb.' Desiree jabbed a hand towards the light of the house. Disappointed and disgusted in herself for the feelings burning inside her. 'I didn't expect it, but I want it. To grow something that isn't a building. To have *our* baby strapped to *me*. The chaos and the bullshit and the wittering about feed schedules. I want it. As well as my work...' she said quietly, almost as if not to offend her projects.

'I thought you were *bored* by all that baby chat.'

Seb wondered how he could have missed it.

'I'm jealous. And I hate myself for feeling something so... nasty.'

'Desi!'

She looked back out to the hills, to stop herself from crying.

'Please. We're so happy. Christine probably wants the freedom we have. The sleep. The lie-ins. Our travels. She was saying how she wished *they* could go to Costa Rica at Easter but can't...'

Desiree shot Seb a look to say *don't be ridiculous*. Who would wish their baby away?

The mooing cows in the dark seemed to get louder, more pained and strained, as if to echo the tension on the patio; or perhaps one was giving birth, as if out of spite.

'Look, I can't do this.' Seb always loved the way Desiree said 'Look' at the start of a sentence. It was so purposeful. He didn't like it now though. It rendered him speechless in a different way.

'I've wasted nearly four years, Seb...' She said it mournfully.

'Wasted?' Desiree couldn't see how hurt Seb looked. 'Please, Desi...' He held out a hand to her, to turn her to face him. From the light of the moon he could see a quiet tear tumble down her cheek. 'Is that how you see it – *wasted*? I love you.'

'You'll be forty next year.'

'Hang on, it's not 2018 yet...' he tried to joke, looking at his watch.

'Millie will be off to uni before we know it.'

'Uni? She's thirteen in May!'

'The time will fly, trust me.'

'What do you mean?'

'You won't want to go back to that. You don't want a baby.'

'I don't want a baby,' he concurred, which stabbed at Desiree in a way he couldn't know. As casually as he said it, he knew it only sounded cruel, so he desperately tried to back-pedal.

'Desi... my love. You knew that! I never said... *you* never said.'

She nodded, coldly.

He had a horrid sick feeling inside. This really wasn't anything he could fix with an arm around her or an amazing hike through a cloud forest in Costa Rica. This was fundamentally and inextricably inside the core of Desiree, a yearning he hadn't even known about, and now it was hanging in the air between them, he didn't know how to make it OK.

Desiree sighed.

'We've just been so in synch on everything, Seb, I feel totally floored.'

'So do I!' he almost gasped, while he rubbed the small of her back.

'When we knew, we knew. On projects, on trips. On holidays. With Millie and Jasper... We've always been in step and worked so well together.'

'We do!' said Seb, his warm smile and thick jumper pulling her in.

'I just rather hoped that you would feel what I feel now. But...' Desiree looked down at her feet, warm in her fleece-lined Le Chameau wellies. 'It's taken me by surprise so I know it will you.'

Seb studied her face with his thoughtful one.

'Let's go inside, you're freezing.' He rubbed her back more vigorously now. 'I love you so much.'

He leaned in to kiss her, but Desiree pulled back and studied his face. Was he not going to even consider it? Disappointment wrung out her already dejected heart.

'Look, I'm thinking maybe it's best I don't come to Guernsey. You go with the kids.'

'Oh, man! Mum's so looking forward to seeing you.'

'She's more looking forward to seeing Millie and Jasper, I'm sure. You go. I need to get my shit together. Take a closer look at the Kew project. Recalibrate. Tell Penelope I had loads of work on. I *do* have loads of work on.'

Seb looked hurt again, but knew that when Desiree decided something, it was pretty much set.

Inside the house Jake and Christine had finally got Axel down and were laying the table, pretending they hadn't noticed a heated and hurt-looking exchange outside.

'He sleeps!' Christine said in sweet relief as they walked back in, dusted down their feet and took off their boots.

'Great,' said Seb.

'Cards Against Humanity before dinner?' suggested Jake.

'After! I'm starving!' Seb said, trying to make light of the rumbling in his tummy and the discord in his heart.

53

JUNE 2019, NORTHILL, OXFORDSHIRE

'We're going to have to make a move,' Christine said as she walked into the orchard, clutching her phone and searching for her husband. She stopped at the picnic table where Desiree and Jasper were playing Dobble, watched by Violeta, who couldn't keep up. Arthur and his mum had gone home for tea, where Arthur awaited his own father's return from work in London and cried when he walked through the door.

Desiree held fire on the game.

'Oh, is that the time?'

'Yeah, I wanna get Axel down and my mom will be shattered. Have you seen...?'

Desiree smiled and pointed to the commotion on the lawn by the horse field. Jake was now sitting in the chair – his Paul Smith tie knotted around his forehead as if he were about to go into battle with the Karate Kid.

'Jakey, honey!' she called.

Millie had bet Woody and Leo that they couldn't lift Jake, the most strapping of the adults, into the air as light as a feather with his witchcraft, and Jake was happy to test them – to make Millie smile if nothing else. The playlist had got a little louder through the speakers in the garden, a little more raucous than the easy listening they had started with, and Jake roared like a feral beast while the circle took turns to stack their palms in a pile over his head, building momentum before the big lift.

Christine rolled her eyes affectionately.

'Three... two... one... rocket launch!' Leo cried as they removed their hands into the air at once and effortlessly lifted Jake up. Woody claimed that in the right conditions he might be able to do it with his little finger.

'Yeah right!' Millie scoffed, too shy to smile.

'Come on, baby...' Christine implored, while her sweaty and dishevelled husband hugged his friends.

Noemie stepped into the garden with a face like thunder, wondering why people were being so cheery and what she had just missed. Her gaze was looking increasingly drunken and combative as her eyes landed on Desiree and she tutted as she headed down the garden.

'Not sure what her problem is,' Christine tried to say under her breath, so Jasper wouldn't notice. He was quietly trying to explain the symbols on the Harry Potter Dobble to Violeta, who still had no idea what a Marauder's Map was despite the explanation. 'She seems real angry with you.'

'Yeah, I noticed.'

'What's her issue? He was with her. You're not giving her grief. Are you?'

'No!'

'And you could have...' Christine said with a nervousness.

It was the first time Desiree had ever heard Christine say anything controversial, and she wondered what she might know.

'No, I'm just giving her a wide berth...' Desiree said diplomatically, relieved to see Noemie land on SJ at the bottom of the garden – her gestures getting wilder, her voice more animated.

'Looks like it might be a good time to leave. I didn't realise it was almost six. We'll probably not be much longer.' Desiree looked down at Granny, pointing to a picture of a chocolate frog and laughing.

'Yeah, I want to catch those bedtime cuddles,' Christine oozed.

'I have to get Violeta back to Portsmouth before midnight. If I can tear you away, hey, Granny?'

'Jakey! Come on!' Christine called, while Jake went around the garden hugging everyone. His big exit. As he gripped Leo he told him he loved him; as he fist-bumped Millie and pulled her in he told her to stay gold; and as he hugged Martin, he lifted him off the ground and sad feet dangled.

'Bye!' He waved to SJ, who had wanted a squeeze of Jake herself, but he was too quick to move round to Jasper at the table with Violeta, Desiree and Christine.

'Buddy, get your mum to text me about a fishing trip, yeah?' he said as he slumped his head onto Christine's shoulder, tie still knotted around it. Clair came out of the pub; even from the inside she could hear Jake's enormous presence departing. 'Or better still, get your mum to get you a phone and we can sort it out. Yeah, yeah, you're only nine or whatever but we need to send each other silly gifs...'

Jasper's eyes widened. He'd been pestering Clair for a phone for months, and didn't know she was going to concede now anyway. He needed to stay as connected as possible with his family and the few close friends he had.

'All right, all right, leave that with me...' Clair said as she stood on tiptoes and hugged Jake, then Christine, who she had only met a couple of times before, when Jake and Christine were visiting

Northill, but thought she seemed lovely. Desiree got up and followed suit.

'Come on,' Christine said, taking her car keys out of her purse. 'I don't know who needs putting to bed first, you or Axel...'

'Oh, Axel!' Jake almost sobbed, an enormous relief enveloping him. He had got through the hardest day of his life. And he had managed to swerve Noemie for most of it. In his drunken state he just couldn't pretend any more. He didn't have to.

54

DESIREE

July 2018, Northill, Oxfordshire

'My dad's offered me a job.'

The longest day had been and gone, but still the sky glowed at almost ten o'clock as Seb and Desiree finished the last of their dinner in the garden. It had taken him this long to pluck up the courage to tell her.

'What?'

Seb had been distant all day. On the train into London, in the office – he didn't join Desiree for their meeting at Kew Gardens either, and now he almost had his back to her as he told her this monumental piece of news as if it were a tidbit. The detritus of an epic chicken salad lay on the oilcloth-covered table, Moroccan tealights almost reached their stumps. Seb stared into the fire of the chimenea that kept the chill away and didn't answer as quickly and efficiently as Desiree wanted.

'At his place?'

'He wants me to take it over. His clients. His projects. He and Tina want to retire to Spain by the autumn.'

'What?'

'Yeah, he wants to hand the studio to me...'

'What about SJ?' Desiree asked, when really she was thinking *what about me?*

Seb shuffled a little in his seat as he swirled his glass of wine around from its stem on his knee. SJ had never warmed to Desiree. She followed the Other Woman narrative because she didn't like how accomplished and polished Desiree was when they were almost the same age, although she did invite her to be on a podcast with her when a blogger friend suggested she needed more diversity on her grid. Desiree politely turned her down. She'd read the terrible dating blogs, watched the vlogs and listened to the podcast: she apologised and said she wasn't very good at the whole social media thing. Which only infuriated SJ more. She had stalked Desiree's Instagram and she *did* update it fairly regularly.

'SJ can't take over Curtis + Cooper.'

'No! Of course not! But how will she cope with Mummy and Daddy living in Spain?'

SJ was thirty-three and thrilled to be writing her debut book – *The Superlatively Single Girl's Guide To Dating* – but despite her big social media following, she was barely scraping a living and still hugely dependent on her parents, financially and emotionally.

Seb shrugged as if to say it wasn't his problem.

'And what about Roger?'

'Roger barely does anything now. Dad wants me to head up his team. There are five of them. Out of the studio on the Cowley Road.'

Desiree picked up her wine glass and hugged her knees into her ribs on the uncomfortable wrought-iron chair. She was wearing her post-work uniform of cigarette pants and a thin cashmere jumper.

'You said no, surely? Why would you drop Kew Gardens and Williamsburg New York for housing projects in Blackbird Leys?'

Seb looked at Desiree and said nothing, as the pit in her belly grew.

'What did your dad say?'

'I'm taking it.'

'You're what?'

Desiree's mouth hung open in shock.

'I told Jill and Terence today.'

'You did what?'

Desiree's stomach hollowed in, as she pictured her on a site meeting at Kew while Seb stayed behind to talk to Jill and Terence; as if she were being pulled back from something she was running towards. She gasped for breath.

Seb looked from the crackling flames back to Desiree. His bright eyes full of fire and guilt.

'You didn't think you should discuss it with me first? This is our life, our work, our mortgage we're talking about here...'

She was astute enough to know what was happening and it made her rage. She stood up, scraped her chair back and walked to the end of the garden to catch her breath.

'Desi!' Seb said exasperatedly. These exchanges had increased in the past six months. The rows, the smashed plates, the hideous disappointment. She paced the end of the small garden, her hand to her brow.

'Jesus, Seb!'

'Desi, come on...'

'But what about Kew?'

She clutched at the only space she felt confident in right now: work.

'I haven't really worked on Kew for months, have I?'

Suddenly the treachery started to sink in. He'd been planning it. Her eyes burned as she walked back to the chimenea and looked at him, seeing his plot laid out.

'You're flying with it,' Seb said. 'You, Fatima and Constantine are flying with it. You won the bloody Young Architect of the Year award. Jill wants you to lead on Williamsburg too, surely?'

Desiree nodded, but she was starting to see through him now, and a rising mix of resentment and rejection was building.

'Your trajectory is fine, whether I'm at Rennie + Byrd or not. If anything, I'm holding you back.'

Desiree knew that. But she also knew what this meant.

'You bastard,' she said in sing-song disbelief, her eyes wide and angry. 'This is your exit strategy. All the time we were sleeping and shagging and rowing and crying, you were plotting this?'

Seb shook his head and stared into the fire. His face was pale and his brow sweaty.

'You bastard.'

'Desi—'

'This isn't about Curtis + Cooper, or Rennie + Byrd, is it? This is about us! And you've been discussing it, behind my back, with your dad and Jill and Terence and—'

A look of horror washed over her face. 'Fucking hell, Seb, have you been planning this with Clair even? For the kids?'

'Clair doesn't know anything about this! I'd never tell her before you!'

Desiree bit her lip before speaking.

'What about *discussing* it with me? You're just *telling* me this!'

Seb ignored the question, tried to package it as beneficial for the future.

'I'll be closer to home, closer to the kids... Millie is wanting to stay here some school nights, Clair's so much more relaxed about it and where they stay. They can't just do that if I'm in New York or Dubai. I can't go to their plays and parents' evenings easily.'

'You did it yesterday for Millie's summer show.'

'I had to take the afternoon off and work from home. My time with them is running out.'

They both knew Seb's argument was convenient, and Desiree's face started to crumple as she shook her head, still pacing, her hands on her hips.

'Is this how you break up with me?' she said, stopping under a string of festoon lights. She wavered between calm and cool and utterly crushed every few seconds. Seb felt sick.

'Get all your ducks in order?'

'No!' Seb was starting to wobble; he beckoned Desiree to come curl on his lap. She shook her head defiantly. 'But it might be best for us to have some distance – at work, I mean. Maybe it'll help with everything else if I take this job.'

'What do you mean "if", Seb? You already did!'

Seb stood to approach her, and held out his hand, which she flicked away.

'I'm sorry, we just can't go on going round in circles. I'm trying to do something to shift things.'

'You shit.' She shook her head. 'You've been planning and plotting this with everyone else, without even discussing it with me. After everything we went through! Every hurdle we jumped! Everything we did to make this house feel like home. You've been sneakily planning this behind my back!' Her voice got louder.

'Desi...' He held out a hand again but this time she swiped it away with a roar.

'FIVE YEARS! I've wasted five fucking years of my life with you! My best years!'

The fact he wasn't fighting it made Desiree realise her worst fears were true.

'No!' he said weakly, as she walked around the table to go inside.

She had to get out. Jump ship, before she was pushed. 'And *you're* a fucking coward.' She pointed at him now. 'Taking over Daddy's practice on the sly because you don't have the balls to just end it?'

'That's not true. I love you! But we can't go on like this. It's breaking both of us!'

'Oh, really?' Desiree looked at him with derision.

'Yes! I feel sick every fucking day, Desiree, because I can't make you happy.'

'But you're not willing to try.'

'This is not a surprise, Desiree. I can't give you what you want.'

She wanted to scream *why*.

'I'm doing—'

'Doing me a favour?' she said caustically, an eyebrow raised, goading him to say it.

'Doing *us* a favour. *If* we can't move through this. Which it doesn't look like we can.'

'Oh, fuck off!'

And with a swish of her arm Desiree smashed the crockery clean off the table onto the patio floor and went inside to pack.

55

JUNE 2019, NORTHILL, OXFORDSHIRE

'Adrian, Linda! Mind if I join you?' Penelope asked the assorted Armitages while Peter hit Swingball with Millie and Jasper. The early summer evening was still light, and the yellow tennis ball of the game orbited the orchard like a small second sun.

'Do...' said Linda, extending a hand to the opposite side of the picnic bench, while Dave stood up to shuffle along and make way for her.

Penelope slid in and perched on the end of the bench.

She, Martin, Adrian and Linda had been friends of sorts – united in the nineties when their children started to date; Adrian and Linda offered support and strength when Seb was going through turmoil about his dad in his teens; they were united in the noughties through their children's marriage and shared grandchildren; they shared childcare handovers when Millie and Jasper were visiting the island. They offered to help out in these most terrible of weeks. Other than that, their paths didn't cross much, although Linda did always look longingly at Penelope's artwork in the galleries and boutiques of St Peter Port and wish she were so talented.

'How are you?' Linda asked. Her face had a stern yet caring sheen, like her eldest daughter's.

'Bereft,' Penelope said, tired of answering that question because she hated not being able to say *fine*. Penelope had always been a calming people pleaser, but today she couldn't be. 'But tell me about you two,' she said keenly to Dave and Clair, sitting alongside her on her side of the picnic table. 'How's the planning going?'

Clair looked a little sheepish as Adrian and Linda encouraged her to answer, much as they would have when she was a child.

Penelope saw the conflict in Clair's brown eyes.

'Oh, sweetheart, it's OK for you to enjoy it. It's your future!'

Dave nodded and breathed a sigh of relief while Penelope put her hand on Clair's. 'Goodness knows the children need something joyful to look forward to.'

'I know...' Clair said, as if she was still trying to convince herself. 'It just feels a bit weird, today.'

'Sebastian would have been nothing but happy for you, in fact I know he was happy for you.'

'Yeah, he was...' Clair said gingerly.

'And the kids were so excited when they told me, practically doing cartwheels. Well, Millie did some sort of Arab spring thingamabob.'

Everyone laughed a little.

Dave helped Clair.

'They've been keen to talk about it, haven't they?' he said, turning to Clair. 'Even since—'

'Yes, they have...' Clair cut in, buoyed by Dave's encouragement; by Penelope's concern for her.

'Dave's mum and dad own a barn in Derbyshire, he's from up there...'

Dave nodded again – he was good at nodding, like an obedient dog – as he stared lovingly at the pint in front of him.

'It's just going to be a quiet thing. My nurse friends; a few of the school mums. Dave doesn't have many workmates to speak of as he works alone...'

'I'm a painter and decorator,' he said, as if to explain. 'My Roberts radio and whoever is on Radio 2 are my colleagues really...' He chuckled to himself. 'But all my rabble will be there. A few aunts and uncles.'

'Have you chosen a dress?' Penelope rubbed her hands together.

'Yes – it's quite different from the first one.'

Penelope tried to picture Clair on her wedding day but didn't want to think of Seb right now. How handsome he looked in his suit. How proud she was of him. How he wasn't here.

'Sort of a 1950s shape. In and out a bit.'

'Don't give too much away...' Adrian joked, tapping the side of his nose twice and then pointing to Dave.

'Oh, Dad, he's seen it!' Clair said, rolling her eyes.

'And lovely she looks too,' Dave said proudly, stroking Clair's hair.

Clair wasn't one for all that so wafted a hand and leaned forward to look along the bench at Penelope.

'Actually... Dave and I were chatting about this... and wondering... Would you like to come? It's September. Near Matlock. You and Peter. It would be great if you could make it.'

Linda watched eagerly.

'Clair, that would be lovely. Thank you.'

PART III

56

_____

NOEMIE

December 2018, Northill, Oxfordshire

Seb twisted his gin and tonic on a square beer mat from his perch on the stool at the bar. Through the clear fizzing liquid and ice, he could see the distorted yet familiar image of a peanut brand he didn't ever buy. An animated nut wearing a top hat looked up through an ice cube infused with a rosemary sprig, challenging Seb to buy a bag of peanuts to accompany his drink. *Fuck off,* Seb thought as he caught the peanut's eye, then he laughed to himself for telling an animated character to fuck off.

He took a sip of his drink to ease the unfamiliar sensation of nerves in a familiar place. The Blue Bell was *his* local. The pub halfway to town at the end of *his* street. It was where he'd had his thirtieth in the little barn in the pub garden; where he'd had drunken nights with friends; and it was where he and Desiree enjoyed Sunday lunches, dirty burgers and Christmas dinners. But the discombobulating sensation made him feel weirdly alive. He almost wanted to give a maniacal laugh while his stomach fizzed and he looked at his phone.

7.50 p.m.

Ten minutes.

'I'll have another, please, mate,' Seb said, raising his almost empty glass at Jim, the barman with the bushy beard. 'How's the baby?'

'Yeah, not bad, thanks. Shits, feeds and sleeps. But I think she's pretty cool,' Jim said with a wry smile as he pressed a fresh glass to an optic.

Seb had never been on a first date with a stranger. He wasn't sure if he'd been on a first date with anyone, now he thought about it. Not since he went to see *The Lion King* with Clair, but even then they were already mates. After that they hung out by the Martello tower or outside the Beau Séjour cinema drinking Schnapps and smoking cigarettes awkwardly – their fumbles cheap and unsophisticated.

First dates with Desiree had been stolen: lunchtime sandwiches at Pret followed by guilty dinners on Clapham High Street after he'd moved out. He'd never done it like this before. The old-fashioned way of app dating.

But five months after Desiree had left, Seb looked at the wall, thought *fuck it* and downloaded the Bumble app SJ was always shagging men from. And the instant Noemie's face flashed through the roll of matches, he was hooked. Her eyes were sea green and sexy, her brows dark and thick in a straight line across them, and her hair was beach blonde and wavy, as if she had just walked off the shore into a cabana. It didn't look as though the photo was taken in Northill. Her crop top, spray-on leggings and prana pose confirmed she probably *was* a fitness professional, like her profile said. Kids. She had kids. This was a relief as Seb didn't want to go over the heartache of the past five years again.

'Noemie' stared at the lens, oozing vitality, and Seb wondered who took the photo; how many men would fancy a woman as hot as she was. From her washboard stomach it didn't look as if she had grown and birthed kids, so perhaps that wasn't true. Perhaps that wasn't even her photo – he was about to find out. Either way, Seb was looking for a distraction. Someone to lift him out of the doldrums, and her photos certainly suggested she might.

The photo can't be her, Seb feared – surely he would have noticed a bombshell like this in the supermarket or at the gym.

Jim placed a new gin and rosemary tonic on a new beer mat, peanut face down, as the couple sitting at the small round table by the door waved goodbye.

'Thanks, mate, actually, I'll take it over there...' Seb said, tapping his debit card on the reader and walking off. Jim gave Seb another of his enigmatic smiles as he ripped off the receipt. He could tell from Seb's smart shirt and nervous demeanour that something was amiss tonight.

7.55 p.m.

Seb sat on the chair by the door just as the woman from the photo entered next to it, so his bottom bounced back up.

It is her!

'Noemie?' Seb asked, a bit too keenly. 'Hi!'

Noemie took off her mittens and scarf and unwrapped her large sheepskin coat as the warmth of the pub hit her and her eyes lit up.

'Sebastian!' she said in a heavy accent, his name sounding more beautiful than the way anyone else said it.

'Seb, please...'

She gave him a kiss on each cheek and removed layer upon layer like a Matryoshka doll, piling them up on a spare chair.

She's French! he thought, wondering why she hadn't said so on her profile, yet knowing it was inconsequential. From her photo he wouldn't have guessed she was French. She oozed such vitality and small power, he'd thought she had looked Australian.

'Great to meet you!' Seb said, taken aback. With the removal of each layer Noemie became more and more beautiful. More and more strong, as he could see the hardness of her body under her tight black wrap dress and tights. 'What can I get you?' he asked, almost laughing. Her picture really was real. Surely this never happened.

'Burgundy, please!' she said, gazing at the bar beyond him. The lights of the gold Christmas fairy lights trimming the bar illuminated her pale eyes beautifully as she sat on the chair opposite and watched Seb walk the short distance to the bar.

'Burgundy, was that?' Jim asked with a knowing smile. 'Rouge or blanc?'

Seb turned to Noemie.

'Red, please.'

'Size?' Jim asked.

'Large,' she said, sticking her tongue out cheekily.

Jim and Seb blushed in unison before Jim went about sourcing the wine. 'And a pint for me, please.'

*　*　*

'You know, I've not done this before,' Seb confessed, nerves already gone.

'Nor me,' admitted Noemie as she sipped her drink. 'But I think we got lucky already,' she declared. 'We're both good-looking people, I like your style...'

Seb laughed, not sure if she was joking. He had never thought of himself as stylish, even though he had made an effort in a shirt and his darkest, smartest jeans tonight. 'But I just knew when I saw your picture that we would have... chemistry. You know?'

Seb held Noemie's gaze and already pictured them naked, entwined.

'Where are you from?' he asked, trying to conceal his thoughts.

'France. Marseille, then my family moved to Paris. But I lived here six years, most people can't tell I'm French any more...'

Seb definitely thought she was joking now, her accent was so thick, but he didn't know her well enough to laugh about it, lest she think he was taking the piss.

'I had my kids here and everything. Well, two of them.'

Seb nearly choked on his Camden Pale Ale.

'Two of them? How many do you have? Surely you're not old enough to have had more than two kids...?'

'Well, thank you very much but I have. I'm thirty-two, and I have four kids.'

Seb felt a slight panic rise in his throat. He wanted to date someone who was already a mother – he didn't want to go through the turmoil he and Desiree had come through – ideally their kids would be the same age and would all play happily ever after – or better still, they'd never need to meet each other's kids because he and Noemie would become really excellent fuck buddies and she would help him get over the emptiness he'd felt since Desiree had gone. But *four*.

Seb looked at Noemie across the small table from him and thought of her taut stomach and imagined the face she might make when she came; when she was asleep next to him.

'How old are they?'

'Nine, seven, three... and my baby just turned one.'

'Wow, you have a baby?'

'The older two have a different dad to the younger two,' she said, as if explaining a four-year gap in procreating.

'Oh, right.'

'Yeah he was a fucking asshole. Brought me to this shitty country with his job.'

Seb loved how her foul mouth jarred with her sexy face; how dirty words sounded clean and comedic with a French accent. 'Then he fuck around and left me.'

Seb made a sad face.

'Oh, I'm sorry about that.'

'Yeah, shit happens.'

'And your younger children... their father?' As Seb asked it, he thought he didn't really want to know.

'Oh, he wasn't for me. I just wanted more kids at the time. And he was... here. You know how stars align?'

Seb didn't really.

'He's moved back in with his parents now.' Noemie waved her hand as if she were flicking a bug off her shoulder. 'Quite far away, in the north. So it's good he doesn't see the kids that much.'

Fuck!

Seb was so shocked, the thought of Clair saying such a thing – knowing she could have taken the kids back to the Channel Islands at any point and got a nursing job at the King Edward VII or Princess Elizabeth hospitals and brought the kids up without him – pummelled his heart a little, yet his eyes marvelled at Noemie's beauty and her bluntness.

Seb felt as if he ought to change the subject but kept being pulled back to it. Four kids under ten – and she looked so amazing! He struggled to keep up with a thirteen-year-old and a just nine-year-old, and he only saw them for half of every week.

'Where are they now – do all your kids live with you?'

Noemie looked at her phone with a slight mania in her eye.

'Of course! They're at home with the au pair...'

But Noemie didn't want to talk about the kids either. She didn't want to remember that actually Layla, the au pair – her seventh in almost ten years – had walked out on her this afternoon and she had had to leave the kids home alone.

* * *

'This is my number. Only call it if it's *really* important,' she had told her oldest, a boy called Samuel. He looked terrified – Layla had never asked him to be in charge; Layla had never popped out.

'Is OK!' Noemie protested with a wave of the hand. 'You know how to give Gabriel milk, and if your sisters wake up, just tell them I'm popping to the shop. The best thing is you all go to sleep and I be back before you know it. My big boy, huh?'

As she had walked out of the house, grabbing her purse and mittens, Samuel had curled up in a ball under his blanket, hoping and repeating that his siblings wouldn't wake up, that his mummy would be home soon, that a creepy cackling goblin wouldn't come and kidnap them all.

Noemie wasn't going to miss out on this date – not when she had known just from Seb's picture that she was going to be with him until the very end.

* * *

'So, you're in the fitness industry...?' Seb segued, off the subject of babies for both of them. He had lost himself in the gym, CrossFit and running since Desiree left. He'd got quite into it and was in the best shape of his life.

'Yeah, I'm a yoga teacher. I trained in Zumba too, so sometimes I teach that. But yoga is my passion and keeps me zen, you know...'

She said it with energetic eyes. Seb nodded as the door opened and the winter chill swept in. A group of friends were arriving for quiz night, and looked around the pub for a table, and suddenly Seb felt a surge of pride to be in this thrilling new corner of a familiar world, on a date with a gorgeous powerhouse of a woman.

57

JUNE 2019, NORTHILL, OXFORDSHIRE

As the evening air started to nip at goosebump-bare arms outside, most of the guests had taken their drinks back into the pub, which had now reopened to the public, lifting the funereal feeling and making life feel a bit more *normal* again.

Desiree and Violeta were comfortably ensconced with Federico, Fatima and Mei-Xin, joined by Desiree's old flatmate Gaby, who couldn't get the day off work but had whizzed down the M4 for the latter stages of the wake. Desiree had been grateful for another ally. The group were rapt, listening to Federico's family stories about life under a dictator in Chile, which Violeta listened to quietly and intently.

'We're gonnae make a move, Desi,' Jill said, as she came back from the bathroom with her jacket slung over her arm. Terence was standing behind her.

'God, is that the time?' Desiree looked at the thin gold watch on her wrist.

'Sorry, we have to get back to London.'

'Oh, let me get out...'

Federico, Fatima and Mei-Xin all waved goodbye to their bosses while Desiree shuffled out of the banquette she was sitting on.

'I'd really better get you home soon, Granny,' Desiree said as she got up. 'I feel like I've bust her out of jail,' she confided to Jill.

'Don't worry, pet, it'll be good for her,' Jill said as she hugged Desiree emphatically. 'You've done brilliantly. I'm so, so proud of you.'

Jill was always hard in her manner but generous in her praise, especially of Desiree.

Terence nodded in agreement and sighed a *what a day* kind of sigh.

'I don't want to put you under pressure, but the offer is still there, you know...'

Now Jill had met Violeta, now she had seen this pull keeping Desiree anchored, she could understand Desiree's change of heart a bit more.

'I know...' Desiree smiled gratefully.

'Do think about it, won't you?'

Desiree nodded.

'Take your time,' Terence added tacitly.

Jill squeezed her hand.

'I know it's been awful for you... but you've done so, so well.'

'Hmmm,' Terence agreed.

'It's been awful for all of us,' Desiree said candidly. 'We all lost him, Jill...'

With that, Desiree saw the creases on Jill's small forehead crack and her eyes fill with tears, for the first time in knowing her. Terence squeezed Desiree's arm and the two left, to drive back to London.

Desiree looked at Violeta squished up among her workmates and Gaby. She must have been tired but she seemed more animated than she had in years. She thrived on energy and beauty. And Desiree felt utter conflict, about the life that had been on offer to her, the life that had been cruelly taken away, and confused about what the hell she was going to do, because she couldn't leave Granny and take away her only real energy source.

58

NOEMIE

December 2018, Northill, Oxfordshire

'What you do for Christmas?' Noemie asked, pressing the bones of her bare pelvis into Seb's bottom as she ran a fingertip along his arm.

It was the morning after their second date. The first one had ended abruptly at 10.45 p.m. when Noemie had a call from 'the au pair', who was apparently throwing up, and with regret she had to get back to her kids.

Noemie's mother had arrived in England just in time for Christmas and for their second date, which was more relaxed, even though they were going out for dinner so it could have felt more formal. Seb's nerves had dissipated, and they met in the best tapas restaurant in Northill, ate padrón peppers, drank copious amounts of sherry, and were back at Seb's house by 9.30 p.m., where she demonstrated her cat and cow poses – naked – and Seb watched the spectacle in awe before they had sex on the living-room rug.

'Oh, I'm spending it at Clair's. My ex. With the kids...' Seb said. He rolled over to face Noemie. He wasn't sure if this was going to be a problem, but knew it would be ridiculous if it was. He gazed into her eyes and stroked the bridge of her nose with his thumb. It was the most beautiful nose he had ever stroked, small and straight with a refined tip.

'It's the first Christmas Day we've done together since we split...' he said, excited that he would be spending pretty much the whole day with Millie and Jasper. 'All together with Clair and her boyfriend. Her fiancé!' As he said it, he wondered why he was explaining himself; why he was so keen not to upset the applecart.

After four fraught and fragile Christmas handovers, they wouldn't have to carve up this year. It had been increasingly easier in recent years, but he knew the Christmas dinner invitation wouldn't have come if Desiree hadn't moved out, if Clair weren't now engaged.

'Ah, nice,' Noemie said, unconvincingly. 'Where does she live?'

'Here, in Northill. On Priory Green. Her fiancé, Dave, is a nice bloke.'

'Oh, cool, it sound very Gwyneth and that guy...'

Seb smiled. How far they had come. He couldn't pretend it wasn't going to be weird, but he knew it was going to be harmonious. Dave was a really nice guy and he'd not seen Clair look so happy in a long time.

'Well, it's taken a while...'

Seb gazed into Noemie's eyes and could almost hear the ocean. He wasn't sure if, in their short encounter in The Blue Bell and last night in the tapas bar before they'd got down to the important business of making each other come, he had explained that it *wasn't* his wife he had recently split from. But he must have told her he was with Desiree in between otherwise her sharp eyes would have picked up on it.

'What about your parents?' she asked. She didn't want to talk about any exes. 'When do you see them? Are you close to your mother?'

Noemie's questions were direct and beguiling.

'Well, my dad and stepmum are coming to Northill on Christmas Eve, with my half-sister; then I'll take the kids to Guernsey for New Year, you know, where I grew up.'

'Ah *oui, les Iles Anglo-Normandes*,' Noemie said, her head leaning on closed palms beneath her cheek as she stared into Seb's eyes. Their gazes felt intense and heady for having been on just two dates.

'It gives Clair and Dave some space and a break, I get to see my mum... Clair's parents have them for a couple of nights...'.

'And your mother? How is your relationship with your mother?'

Seb didn't really want to talk about his mum while his cock was pressed up to Noemie's pubic bone.

'Er, yeah, it's great. She's lovely.'

'And you have a sister? I didn't imagine that.'

Seb thought of Sara-Jayne. It was hard to imagine they were siblings either. He hadn't known she existed for half his life, and despite seeing her more regularly for the past eighteen years, he didn't really think of her as his sister.

'Yeah, we do the presents thing with my dad, Tina and SJ on Christmas Eve, before I drop the kids at Clair's. My half-sister isn't married and doesn't have kids, so she kind of spoils mine.'

When she isn't competing with them for attention, he thought, but didn't want to be bitchy and say that out loud.

Noemie gave a half-hearted smile. She didn't understand women who didn't have kids.

'How about you? Is your mum staying for all of Christmas?' Seb wondered if they would get to have a night like this again since Layla the au pair had apparently left shortly after their first date.

Noemie didn't feel bad that within an hour of her mother stepping off the Eurostar at St Pancras, she was out of the door to meet Seb. They had all of Christmas to fall out anyway.

'Yeah, she usually goes to my sister's but she rudely went to Cape Verde this year, so my mum have to come here. At least she can look after the kids – so you and I, we can go out!'

Seb felt a bit sorry for Noemie's mum but didn't say it. He liked the idea of the sleepovers, but the brightness of the alarm clock behind Noemie's head reminded him this one needed to end.

'Shit,' he said, sitting up. 'I've got to go to work.'

It was 8 a.m. and still dark outside, but even now he knew the traffic into Oxford would be disastrous.

'Oh, no-o-o-o-o-o, this is too nice. I don't have any classes until the afternoon. Why don't you fill me up again?'

'I wish,' he said, kissing her smooth forehead. 'But I have a meeting at ten; then the Christmas lunch...'

Seb thought about his first Christmas lunch as head of Curtis + Cooper. He'd booked the tasting menu for everyone at Le Manoir and was hoping for it to be a belter. Martin was back from Spain so said he'd pop in for a bit, but didn't want to tread on Seb's toes. He thought of Rennie + Byrd parties and pictured Desiree at The Ivy or Bocca Di Lupo. How different this year would be. He felt a strange concoction of relief and sadness: last night was the first time he had slept with anyone since Desiree – Noemie was the third woman he had slept with in his life. It was an odd sensation. Different but wonderful. The Christmas party would be the same.

Seb jumped out of bed and walked into the bathroom.

'You don't have to rush,' he said, as steam started to rise in the small white-tiled room. Seb was the sort of person to trust someone he didn't know in his house. He would go out and leave a key in Jasper's welly next to the door so he didn't have to carry it, and forget it was there for days. 'Take your time if you don't have to get back for the kids.' Seb figured that Noemie must have already missed the school run and assumed her mum was doing it. 'Have some breakfast.'

'I want to eat you for breakfast!' Noemie said cheekily, poking her tongue out between her teeth as she did a long and naked yoga stretch on his bed.

Seb lingered longingly at the bathroom door.

'Man!' he said, as he walked into the shower, where Noemie joined him and he made her come one more time before going to work.

* * *

After Seb had left for Oxford, Noemie padded around the house, towel drying her hair and exploring the new man in her life. She looked at the kids' rooms: interested to see what a thirteen-year-old girl was into (Billie Eilish, Simone Biles, Dua Lipa and Harry Styles, seemingly); glad to know he had a Millie while she had a Mila; glad to see that his nine-year-old son was into some of the same things as her nine-year-old son: books, robots, cameras, Minecraft. Samuel and Jasper were bound to be best friends.

She was pleased to see Seb stocked food she liked in his kitchen cupboards and fresh fruit and vegetables in the fridge. That he was clean, healthy and solvent. That he had weights by the kitchen door and a skipping rope hanging from the garden trellis. As she rubbed her hair and looked in the mirror in the living room, she saw photos on the mantelpiece. Old and recent school photos of the children in frames: they were cute and had nice faces, and she could see Seb clearly in both of them.

She flipped through a little stack of loose photos, party invitations and thank you cards propped above the small Victorian fireplace. Then it caught her eye. On a low shelf behind the TV sat a thick black frame holding a photo of Seb with his ex. Noemie stopped rubbing her hair and picked the frame up. In it was a beautiful woman with brown skin and bare shoulders in a halter-neck dress, one arm at her side and the other slung around Seb's waist, clinging onto him in a bow tie and tux. Seb's face was nestled into the woman's soft curls as she looked at the camera, bronze eyes sparkling, pretty dimples and neat features laughing as she flaunted their relationship. Noemie felt a rising anger.

Judging from her skin and the colour of the kids, this was not the children's mother. This must be The Inbetween. The Stopgap. The one she wanted to ask lots of questions about but, equally, didn't want to know anything about.

Noemie finished drying her hair, brushed through it with a comb she found in Millie's bedroom, then closed the front door behind her as she headed out into the cold December morning, launching the photo frame and Desiree's smiling face into the bin on the corner as she headed home.

59

JUNE 2019, NORTHILL, OXFORDSHIRE

Millie sat squished between Clair and Linda, three generations of strong sporting women who felt weaker than they ever had. Linda had been part of the British Showjumping club in Guernsey as a teenager in the 1960s and broke the Bailiwick records for her age category in the Puissance. Clair was a keen rower, although motherhood had stopped her after-work jaunts along the Thames under Oxford's bridges. And Millie held county records in her gymnastics competitions, although the thought of competing without her dad there felt a little pointless.

'You're a pioneer,' he'd say to her. 'Like Millicent Fawcett. You're named after her, you know...'

Millie would always eye him suspiciously. 'I thought I was named after Great-Granny Guilbert? Granny said Millicent was her middle name.'

Her father would wink at her.

As she looked around the bar she saw Noemie walk past eyeing her suspiciously, as she carried a fresh vodka and tonic from the bar to the garden, even though most people were coming inside now.

Millie saw the flash of acrimony in her eye and didn't like the way the mask had slipped. As if she were angry with her. As if she, a girl who had just turned fourteen and had lost her father, was a foe. It made her feel on guard, it made adrenaline course through her body again. It took her back to Florida and she felt sick.

The look was as quick as a flash and menacing. Millie didn't think Clair had noticed – and she didn't want to make a scene by telling her.

'Mum, can I go to Daisy's, just for an hour...?'

Clair looked at her watch. Jasper was pale and tired, reading a comic on the other side of her, and she looked hesitantly across the table at Dave. She wasn't sure what the etiquette was about letting your daughter leave her own dad's funeral wake.

'What do you think?' she asked. Dave gave an *I don't see why not* face.

'Her mum says it's OK, she's home too...' Millie said, making her case. She thrust her phone screen at her mother to prove it.

'We can drop her,' Adrian said, shaking his car key. 'We were going to head back to the hotel soon anyway, weren't we, love?'

Clair's mother nodded.

'If that's OK with you?' Linda asked.

'Of course!' Clair said.

'So can I?' Millie pleaded.

Jasper rubbed his eyes and looked forlorn. He didn't want his sister to leave him, and Clair sensed it.

'Pleeeeeease?' she begged.

Clair looked around the pub. There was hardly anyone left from the funeral now. Penelope and Peter were sitting nearby with Elise, talking with tinges of sadness about being mothers of boys; and although she couldn't see Martin, Tina was sitting next to Roger and Dora, looking twitchy without him. And just the Rennie

+ Byrd lot remained, with Desiree and Violeta, on a table near the toilets.

'OK, but just an hour,' Clair conceded. 'We all need to get home soon. Jaspy's shattered. You must be too.' Jasper was looking back at the graphic novel laid out across his lap. He'd run out of things to say to old relatives or people he'd never met.

'If Grandad and Grandma can take you, I'll pick you up in an hour, yeah?' Dave said, standing up to let her out.

Millie nodded, feeling a sweep of relief as Adrian and Linda stood up to shuffle out with her. If that was the only way she could break out of here, fine, she just needed some air, a distraction. To see Daisy and talk about something else. She needed to be away from Noemie's menace, and to not be thinking about her dad, if only for an hour.

60

NOEMIE

December 2018, Northill, Oxfordshire

'So-o-o-o!' SJ said theatrically. 'When Sebby told me he was seeing someone, I was just so thrilled for him – it was a *such* a tragic split...' She cocked her head to one side and emphasised the word *such* as if she didn't mean it, yet it handily affirmed her status of Family. Of having known what went before. 'So much so that I wanted to bring you a gift.'

'A gift?' Noemie looked embarrassed, sitting squashed into SJ on the sofa of the large Pitcher & Piano on Northill's town square.

SJ handed her a beautiful-looking rectangular present, wrapped in tissue paper, a bow, and a handwritten card, as if a calligrapher had artfully penned the name Noemie across it.

Noemie was flustered. She hated being given presents, they made her feel uncomfortable and self-conscious, and she hadn't brought anything for the half-sister she hadn't even known was joining them for Christmas Eve drinks. SJ wasn't anything like Seb:

she was loud, wore crazy clothes, and was a little bit... well, embarrassing.

Noemie looked around the busy pub filled with revellers, hoping she wouldn't bump into any of her yoga clients from the gym. It wouldn't be good for her reputation to be seen with a fat person. Her face went hot as she tugged at the ribbon, not noticing the card fall to the floor.

She could feel it was a book. She didn't read books.

She pulled it open with caution, and was startled to see SJ's face, mouth open in a knowing smile, on the cover. Heavy eyebrow arching up suggestively under a bubble font that read *The Superlatively Single Girl's Guide To Dating*. The strapline underneath said: *How To Date Men, Women & Yourself As A Balls-To-The-Wall Millennial.*

'I mean, obviously you don't need this now you're dating my brother, but there is a chapter on threesomes should that be your thing,' SJ said conspiratorially.

Seb got up to go to the bar. He was a bit embarrassed by his sister's book too. He didn't like to think about her penchant for anal play, let alone his mates ever reading about it.

'One more?' he politely asked, hoping SJ would say no.

She looked at her Apple watch.

'Oh, I don't know – what time did Daddy say he wanted to leave by?'

Martin, Tina and SJ had come over from The Baldons to Northill to see the grandkids and give them their Christmas presents, and when Seb took Millie and Jasper back to Clair's for bed, SJ begged her parents to stick around for a couple of hours so she could meet Seb's new flame.

'I dunno.' Seb shrugged. Embarrassed that, at thirty-nine and thirty-three, he and his sister were talking as if there were a curfew on them. 'Half nine?' he said, knowing it must be past that. He hadn't wanted SJ to crash his date, but he hadn't had the heart to say so.

'I'd better not, then. I want to be foxy and fresh faced for when Santa fills my stocking tonight...' SJ let out a loud guffaw as Slade played on the pub music system and Seb looked at Noemie. 'Wine?' he asked expectantly.

Noemie nodded, clutching the book and wishing Seb wouldn't leave her.

'I'll text Daddy to come now.'

Seb walked over to the bar.

Noemie held SJ's book in both palms without having opened it and rearranged herself in her seat.

'Thank you, but it's not my style,' she said, handing it back to her.

SJ's face, eyes wide and theatrical, went through a whole gamut of emotions in 0.8 seconds, from rejected and hurt to fuming and outraged, before settling on shocked.

Noemie had no idea what she was about to say as she tipped her head back and roared.

'FUCKING YES!' she belted.

'Fuckin' what?'

Noemie was taken aback and a bit embarrassed as one of the Zumba mums had walked in just as SJ was roaring and clapping.

'THIS IS EVERYTHING!' she howled at the high ceiling of the pub, as she clapped her hands.

'Huh?'

'I just love love love your honesty, girlfriennnnnd,' she said, holding up a chubby bejewelled hand for a high five that wasn't met. Noemie looked back to the bar to see where Seb was.

That wasn't the usual reaction Noemie met when she was honest with British people.

'Oh,' she said with a gentle smile.

'You know what, can I be candid with you? I feel I can be really candid with you, Naomi...'

'Noemie. Yes.'

'When I met you earlier I thought you were going to be a right cunt—'

'What?' Noemie laughed.

'Look at you! You're tiny, you're gorgeous, and you're French. But WOW, I am so empowered by you and your honesty – no one ever says they *don't* want my book, but this is everything. It's so damn refreshing that I just want to give you a hug. Can I give you a hug?'

Noemie winced as SJ opened her arms and pulled her into her heaving bosom, as if she were the mother of four.

Noemie wanted the exchange to end as quickly as possible so she patted SJ's back briefly but powerfully and promptly released herself. She definitely didn't want any of her clients to see them hugging.

'Obviously I'm not taking it back and you have to keep it,' SJ commanded. 'I've written a personalised note on the inside, I can't give it to anyone else. And you might change your mind and need it, if things don't work out with my brother...'

Seb returned from the bar as Noemie stood up promptly to go to the toilet.

'Everything all right?' he asked as he tried not to spill the drinks.

'Yes, wonderful,' SJ said, looking at her phone. As a blogger and dating columnist, she rarely let her phone out of her hands. 'Daddy's outside. I'll just find my coat.'

'Fairytale of New York' came on as the school dads and the gym mums and the groups of old school friends who had all come home to Northill for the holidays all raised the Christmas cheer, while SJ rummaged in the pile of coats thrown on an old decorative piano.

Noemie slinked back from the toilet and Seb stood up to let her back in.

'That's from my pussy,' she whispered in his ear as she wiped a moist finger across his cheek, leaving an invisible stripe.

'What?' Seb laughed, hooked.

'You're mine now,' she added with a flirty smile.

'Got it!' shouted SJ as she pulled a leopard-print faux-fur box coat out of the pile. 'Happy Christmas, lovebirds,' she said, putting it on and grabbing her orange clutch bag. 'Noemie: it was *such* an honour to meet you, you're adorable,' she said patronisingly. Noemie smiled. SJ turned to Seb. 'Have the most *wonderful* day tomorrow, won't you? And say hi to Clair...' she added cautiously, looking to Noemie's face as she said it.

'Yep, will do. You too. Happy Christmas.'

SJ gave Noemie a kiss on each cheek, feeling chic while she kissed an *actual French person* the way she liked to greet her friends; then she kissed Seb twice while Noemie smiled to herself at the thought of her scent on SJ's nose and her not even knowing it.

'I'll tell Daddy you said bye,' she hollered, waving behind her, clutching her bag as she teetered out of the grand former bank on stilettos. 'Happy Christmas!'

'Happy Christmas!'

'Joyeux Noël!'

As they watched SJ walk out, Noemie slid her hand into the back pocket of Seb's jeans and gave his right buttock a squeeze.

'You're really naughty, you know...' Seb said, feeling slightly bad for SJ.

'I know,' Noemie almost sang.

61

JUNE 2019, NORTHILL, OXFORDSHIRE

The last of the light had dipped beyond the horizon and the stars were starting to sparkle over the sky above the orchard; even the hardy stragglers were heading inside while a barmaid briskly went around the garden with a crate, picking up the empties from the picnic benches.

'That done with?' she asked Martin, who was hovering over an empty pint glass. He nodded, while Noemie downed the rest of her vodka and handed the barmaid her empty vessel.

'I'd better check on Tina and SJ, get back inside...' Martin said as he looked blearily around the garden, slightly disconcerted to see they were the last ones in it, save for a smoker, hovering by the back door.

Noemie put her hand, shaky from a cocktail of tranquillisers, alcohol and sleep deprivation, onto Martin's thigh and squeezed it briefly.

'I wanted to say thank you, Martin, you are a good man.'

Martin felt uncomfortable.

'Not at all,' he said, unsure of what he was thanking him for.

'I knew it the first time I met you, on Christmas Eve, remember?'

'Ah, yes.'

'After that, well... sometimes I thought it was *you* I was making love to when it was Seb. Does that make sense?'

Martin was so thrown, it didn't make sense at all.

'Not really,' he said politely. 'Shall we...?' He thought about standing up – Tina would definitely be getting worried now, she got nervous if she couldn't see him in the room – but something stopped him. Something more than Noemie's delicate hand keeping him pressed in place on the bench.

'You don't judge me. You were so kind to me in America, such a good man. Honest. I see Seb's kindness and his truth and beauty in you. He get it from you!'

They were startled by a sudden creak by the swing at the back of the garden, and looked over towards it like startled deer.

'Must be a rabbit or a hedgehog,' Martin said. Either way, it was his cue to get up. This was going from weird to weirder.

'You and he are just... such real men. You are what I need, I crave you right now, you know...' She pressed her hand into his groin.

Martin – with his strong hands and sparkling eyes – had been hit on a few times by younger women in his seventy-two years, but never like this. And he was completely and utterly baffled. He hadn't drunk *that* much.

What the hell is going on?

'Look, you're a wonderful girl, Noemie, I'm very flattered...' He rubbed the crown of his head the way Seb did. Used to. 'But I think perhaps it's best we go inside and find your mum, yes?'

'You don't want me?'

She looked at him more intently now.

'I want you to be OK.'

'Am I not good enough for you?'

Martin ignored the question. It was so ludicrous.

'I want you to find your mother, get some sleep, and be there for your kids in the morning. You can do it too, I know you can.'

As he said it his eyes gleamed in the moonlight, and Noemie looked down at her dress and nodded.

'Let's go inside,' he said, standing and collecting glasses the barmaid had missed in the dark.

Martin was always a diplomat: with tricky clients in his career; a go-between between friends who had fallen out; with friends on the golf courses of Spain. Always good at holding court, leading not following, making people feel comfortable and saying the right thing. Perhaps if he'd known the whole story, he might not be so diplomatic.

62

NOEMIE

January 2019, Northill, Oxfordshire

The frenzied knock at the door didn't sound like Desiree's hand, but then she used to have a key so Seb would rarely have heard it.

Rat a tat tat.

He tried to think of her rapping on the door of the flat in Clapham when she'd been for a run around the common without her key; when she'd popped to Sainsbury's in Northill and only taken a bank card.

Rat a tat tat.

No, this definitely wasn't her knock.

It was even more feverish a second time, and Seb, rushing to tidy up the house, leaped down the stairs, three at a time.

'Coming!' he hollered cheerfully.

He looked at the clock on the wall as he walked past the open door to the living room. It was 12.45 p.m. on a Saturday lunchtime in a cold January.

She's early.

He ran his hands through his hair and straightened his burgundy sweatshirt before opening the front door with a nervous anticipation in his stomach.

'Oh.'

It wasn't Desiree.

'Why you take so long?' Noemie admonished, her accent thick and her voice soft, jarring with the snappiness of the words that came out of her mouth. 'I got you a coffee, it's goin fuckin' cold me standing here!' Noemie walked in, thrusting a hot lidded cup in Seb's hand.

'Oh, thanks,' he said, a bit befuddled. The cup made him feel even hotter after he'd been zipping around the house. 'Everything OK?'

'*Oui*, why?'

'I just wasn't expecting you.'

Noemie pressed Seb up against the wall and kissed him, hot coffee burning in each of their hands; the smell permeating the tips of their touching noses as they kissed.

'My class is cancelled. A toilet flooded at the gym and there's shit everywhere, apparently.'

'Nice.'

'Aurelie has the kids... I hoped you'd be in!'

Noemie had managed to secure another shy French girl through her mum's friend network, which meant Noemie could date Seb freely. She started to rub his groin as his cheeks flushed red.

'Oh, man, I can't. I've got loads of stuff to sort out...'

'Oh, are your kids coming?' Noemie looked excited, keen to meet them. She kicked off her UGG boots and walked through to the kitchen in her bamboo yoga wear.

'No, they're coming tomorrow,' Seb said, following her in. 'But my, er, my ex is coming over, to get the rest of her stuff.'

'Why don't you just give it to the kids?'

'Not my ex ex. Desiree.' Seb mumbled slightly. 'She's coming from London, to get the rest of her things.' Seb tried not to look at the clock on the oven behind Noemie, nervous that Desiree would be here in a few minutes.

'Oh.'

Her face dropped. Seb had mentioned Desiree a couple of times – only when he had to explain who he'd been to Costa Rica with or why there were prints from the McQueen Savage Beauty exhibition at the V&A on the wall. She hadn't liked the way the letters formed and came out of his mouth. He carried a world of emotion in two simple syllables.

Des-ray.

The name sounded too exotic, even though it was French.

Des-ray.

She was sure he lingered over the word.

Des-ray.

The way he said it hurt her.

Noemie could just about stomach the sound of Clair – as mothers they had something in common, plus she was getting married again so she must be over Seb. But surely this other woman – *Des-ray* – Noemie knew she wouldn't be over a man like Seb.

'Actually, she'll be here quite soon.' Seb winced.

'You're kidding!' Noemie half laughed in a half whisper, her beautiful nose scrunching in disappointment as she tried to conceal her anger. 'You have to be in?'

'She doesn't have a key any more, and I can't just leave her stuff on the doorstep.'

'Yes, you can. Anyway, it's OK, I got rid of some of it when you went to work. Made it easier for you.'

'What?'

'Her suits were ugly anyway.' Noemie smiled at him as if she was expecting praise for a good deed done, so Seb concluded she must be joking. Still, a redness crept up his face and his smile faltered. Nothing about Desiree had been ugly, and he didn't like hearing it, even in jest.

'You are joking... right?'

Noemie looked unrepentant and shook her head from side to side as if it were the perfectly normal thing to do.

'Shit, man, she's going to go mad! She'll think I threw them out!'

Desiree wasn't a throwaway sort of person. She was messy as hell, but she treasured those piles of clothes scattered around – the cashmere, silk and luxuriant leathers; all of her clothes were investment pieces.

'Well, if she notices, I'll tell her it was me.' Noemie shrugged helpfully.

'What?' Seb still couldn't believe she wasn't joking.

'It was just a couple of things, Seb! Honestly! You make more fuss than Mila! Tell her you gave them to the charity.'

Seb's red rash crept higher to his cheeks, and Noemie realised to her surprise that he was actually annoyed with her.

'Hey hey, don't worry. She obviously wasn't that bothered about her clothes if it's taken this long to get them, huh? How long since you split? Ages, *non*?'

'Six months.'

'Well, come on—' Noemie walked around the kitchen table to put her arms around Seb's neck.

'No, no...' he said pulling back and rubbing his temples. 'I don't think you should be here.'

You're not *going to be here.*

Seb knew that would be a disaster.

Noemie pouted and her eyes welled up.

'You don't want me?'

Seb felt terrible. She had just brought him a coffee and he really did want to get naked with her.

'I do, but not right now. That wouldn't help anything.'

Noemie stalked nearer, like a compact big cat, sea-green eyes glistening.

'You don't want to fuck me? Give your ex a nice little show through the window?' She stuck her tongue out flirtily from between her white teeth.

12.58 p.m.

'Shi-i-i-it, Noemie.' Seb blushed. 'You'd really better go.'

* * *

Desiree

'Well, obviously it's gone to shit since I left...' Desiree joked apprehensively as she looked around the neat living room. Without her mess of expensive bags, shiny shoes, impeccable clothes; without her piles of papers and box files; without her copies of *Red*, *Vogue* and *Wallpaper* she didn't ever get round to reading, the living room felt light and airy, as if the house were about to be photographed to go on the market.

Except it wasn't going on the market. Seb had bought Desiree out of her half of the house and she had moved back into her Clapham flat, this time on her own, after spending two months in her brother's flat in Chelsea while the tenants served their notice.

Seb laughed. He didn't say out loud that he didn't miss her shit lying everywhere, even though he had missed her. He wanted to kiss her neck and hold her tight but thought of how he had been kissing Noemie only minutes earlier, before he had to bundle her out of the back door. He felt a guilty pang towards both women.

Desiree perched on one end of the sofa and looked at the storage boxes and Ziploc bags Seb had carefully packaged up, lined up on the geometric tiles of the hearth. Bin bags would have felt too brutal, her stuff too nice to stuff away in sacks, so he'd bought a load of boxes and clothing storage bags from Ikea and duly packed everything up, trying not to think about how Desiree filled each item of clothing, how they smelled of her, as he'd carefully folded her things into them the night before.

'Sorry to do it here,' she said, businesslike and friendly. 'It's just too embarrassing to chuck a load of bags into the boot outside The Blue Bell. Not that you put it in bags...' Desiree gave Seb a grateful, dimpled smile.

'Of course. That would have been horrid. And it's... it's nice to see you.' Seb lingered in the doorway.

'It's nice to see the house,' Desiree countered. 'And you.'

'Do you want a cup of tea?'

'No, thanks. Well, maybe yes. Hang on, I'll get these out of your way and in the car first,' she replied, scouring the boxes with eager eyes.

'I'll help—'

'Is that all of it?' she asked, looking at the assortment of belongings she'd left behind. 'I thought there'd be more.'

Seb rubbed the back of his head while he tried to push Noemie to the outer echelons of his brain.

'Yeah, I got a new cleaner – I think she might have taken a couple of things. I thought there had been more too.'

Desiree frowned.

'Oh.'

'Have a look through it and let me know if there's anything missing. It might be in the loft...'

Desiree crouched down and peered through semi-opaque plastic.

'As long as she didn't take my cream Reiss coat; I've missed it this winter...' she said, rubbing her arms. 'But that's a bit shit.'

'Yeah, I know. Check through it and I'll have a word...'

'It's not really the clothes I was missing anyway.' Desiree looked surprisingly relaxed. Seb had thought she might go mental, but, her favourite coat aside, her bronze eyes were glowing and her dimples were sunken. 'It's the irreplaceable things I was worried about. Stuff from Granny and my parents. The postcards you sent me.'

You.

Seb was taken aback as Desiree looked disappointed in herself, as if she'd let herself down. She'd made such good progress at healing her broken heart. She'd been running again; she'd started boxing; she was loving her work, and she'd started dating, feeling positive that she might fall in love again one day.

'Oh, yeah, everything's there. Obviously I didn't go through all your personal stuff, but anything that didn't look like it was mine or the kids'... I bubble-wrapped the McQueens and *Long Distance Relationships*... Thought you would want that.' He pointed to the cardboard-covered rectangles propped under the sash windows.

Desiree nodded and smiled.

'Shall we?'

Politely passing each other up and down the short path they quickly loaded Desiree's belongings into the boot of her black Smart car parked at the kerb and closed it, lingering in the road as Saturday afternoon shoppers passed in the winter chill, not taking any notice of this major thing that was happening because it looked so innocuous. They both spoke at once.

'Are they kids O—?'

'How's Rennie—?'

They laughed nervously.

'Hey, shall we go to The Blue Bell?' Seb asked, hands in his pockets, his *fuck it* shoulders dropping.

Desiree looked conflicted, as if it might not be the best idea.

'One for old times' sake...?' Seb smiled hopefully.

'That would be lovely.'

* * *

Sipping hot winter Pimm's by the fireplace, Desiree brought Seb up to speed on all the Rennie + Byrd projects, the office gossip (omitting the recent development between her and Tarek), Shirlie and Timothy's news, and how Granny was doing at the old people's home on Spice Island.

Seb told Desiree about architectural life in Oxford – he'd just recruited a sixth architect and had started a project in the grounds of Magdalen College, and he was about to pitch for some work back in London on the South Bank, his Rennie + Byrd credentials helping Curtis + Cooper get an invitation to pitch.

By talking about work and the kids, they conveniently avoided the elephant in the room: that they were both dating.

'Millie won an award for her Black History Month project – the one Violeta helped her with,' Seb said keenly.

'Yes! She told me. I was over the moon for her.'

Seb looked heartened. He was worried the kids wouldn't stay in contact with Desiree, but he knew Jasper wanted to post her some photos he had developed in the dark room at school, and Millie had her own phone, so Seb hoped they would text each other from time to time.

'Thanks so much for that. You didn't need to.'

'Oh, it was a pleasure! You know how Granny likes to talk.' Desiree took a sip of her hot syrupy drink and licked her lips.

'Although less so now. And it was gorgeous to see Millie on Face-Time. We've had a couple of calls. I've missed them.'

'They miss you.'

There was a pause as they both stared into the flickering flames of the fireplace. Desiree had an idea, but stopped herself from hitting Seb on the arm as she thought it.

'You know, you should bring them to Kew! It's so cool, not just for little kids with the play park, there's so much there. And – inside scoop – there's a Dale Chihuly exhibition coming in spring. Stunning installations. Jasper would take amazing pictures of them, I'm sure.'

'Wow. Yeah, I'll bring them. I miss the cafe we had breakfast meetings in.'

'The Orangery?'

'Ah, the sausage rolls!' Seb said dreamily.

'It's still a bit of a schlep from Clapham, not as much as Northill though.'

'Well, there you go,' Seb said, as if splitting up was a good idea. Desiree laughed, then looked cautiously across at Seb for a second as he smiled at the flames.

'I might be moving a bit further though...'

'Oh, right,' Seb said, finishing his glass. 'Where?'

'Jill wants me to go to New York, to open an office there. Head up the Williamsburg project, lead a few more.'

'Wow, they're going back to New York?'

'Well, *they're* not. They still want to be London based, they just want fingers in both pies and thought I would be best to lead it.'

Seb beamed from ear to ear, a smile of pride and panic as the realisation set in.

'You would be,' he said, trying to veil any mournful tone. 'And it sounds great!' he forced.

'You think?'

'Yeah,' he enthused. 'Do you not?'

'I do... I'm just a bit, torn. Do I jump ship *again*? Williamsburg is going to be amazing, and the projects beyond that look so exciting. And I think I can head up a team—'

'I know you can.'

'But it's a big leap. I'd worry about Granny. I'm just starting to get everything back together. The flat is looking great. I've started to—'

'I'm sorry,' Seb burst, shaking his head.

'Huh?' Desiree frowned, her voice quiet, her bronze eyes calm.

As Seb looked at her he felt awash with grief and sadness and wasted opportunities.

'I'm really fucking sorry.'

'What for?' She said it in a breathless whisper, the collar of her dusky pink roll neck making her feel hot in front of the fire.

'For this,' Seb said, nodding to the bar, where Jim was talking to two old-timer regulars. 'That it came to this. Chatting like friends in a pub.'

'We *are* friends in a pub.'

'But that we're not planning these things together. That I wasn't the guy you needed me to be.'

Desiree wrapped her fingers around her glass and gently shook her head, her soft curls bouncing on her shoulders.

'Don't be sorry, Seb.' As much as she wanted him to beg her not to go, she knew it was right that he didn't. 'What we had was wonderful. Five amazing years I wouldn't change for the world.'

Seb smiled.

'OK, maybe four I wouldn't change, and one shit one at the end...' They both gave a little laugh but the dimples in Desiree's cheeks didn't quite sink in this time. 'Look, as angry as I was six months ago – as angry as I was deep down a year ago, if I'm honest

– perhaps I wasn't the woman you needed me to be either. Maybe I didn't have both feet in the relationship.'

Desiree thought of the flat in Clapham she never sold. Her hesitancy to compromise and buy the house at the other end of Rowan Road when really she wanted something more memorable. Her reluctance to fully embrace life away from art and inspiration; living in the suburbs, away from the hotels and bars she had helped fashion.

Her constant urge to always want to jump ship. To look towards the next project. She had had a lot of time to reflect on it since their split, and she wondered if the yearning in her belly of the past couple of years, what she'd thought was a desire to have a family, was in fact a twisted way of jumping ship. Of getting out. Except as she looked at Seb in profile, facing the fire, something was pulling her back in.

* * *

When it was time for Desiree to jump ship one last time, they walked back to the house they had bought and renovated together, and lingered on the pavement by her packed car. The teasing prospect of a Saturday afternoon turning into dinner and a Sunday morning full of regrets flashed through both their minds, but neither said it. Desiree knew she had to go. Seb hadn't begged her not to go to New York and she knew she could be happy and feel alive there. Still, as they faced each other on the pavement, she had an urge to wrap her arms around Seb's neck; her legs around his waist.

'Look...'

Seb's heart pounded in his chest. He was in her command.

'... this really hurts.'

'I know,' Seb said, rising and falling on the balls of his New

Balance. 'It hurts me too.'

She didn't need to say that she wouldn't be coming back to Northill; they both knew it. They pulled their heads in together, foreheads touching as they had that night on the pavement after the Rennie + Byrd Christmas party, just weeks before they'd got together. Their eyes longing and their lips, sweet and spiced with one glass that had turned into three, drew together as they went to bid their last goodbye with a final kiss.

The loud ring and buzz of Seb's phone in his jeans pocket made him jump, which in turn made Desiree, and they pulled apart abruptly.

'Shit.'

'Argh.'

They laughed. As Seb slid his hand into his pocket to silence his phone, he already knew it was Noemie – perhaps it was the timely jolt he needed.

Seb opened his arms into a huge inviting embrace and pulled Desiree in. She slipped her hands under his arms and pressed them into his back. His strong and solid spine she would never kiss again.

As she pressed her forehead to his chest and took in his smell for one last time, Seb looked up and down the road with slight panic in his stomach, wondering if the timing of the interruption was more than a coincidence.

'Take care, hey?' Desiree pleaded.

'You too,' he said, kissing her head. 'Send me postcards from New York?'

Desiree nodded, eyes filled and face crumpling as she pulled away from his embrace and walked round to the car door, too cut up to say another word.

'And pick Violeta up and give her a little twirl around for me?' Seb called, trying to make light of everything, as he always did.

63

JUNE 2019, NORTHILL, OXFORDSHIRE

'Give me your seed!' SJ whispered into Woody's ear as she humped him on the swing. Her thighs pressing through the cold metal triangles of the swing's side structure; her cream faux-fur stole now in the earth, being infiltrated by ants and worms. Her red lipstick had smeared all over their faces, like his 'n' hers strawberry goatees. 'Plant yourself in me and grow grow grow!'

Woody groaned.

She tried to move faster now, the swing creaking under her girth on Woody's wiry body; his thighs burned with the effort of trying to support her. He didn't want to put their combined weight on the swing, which he thought might give at any point.

Creak.

He grunted and groaned and tried to move faster, just so this whole episode could end more than anything because his thighs couldn't take it.

SJ's groans got louder as she checked to see the garden was empty now, and she tried to eke it out of him.

SJ and Woody had danced a dance no one else was aware of all afternoon. From a stolen glance in the crematorium to a quiet hello in the rose garden. Getting closer and closer at every hurdle, SJ fell: with Federico; with Jim the barman, who had a night off from The Blue Bell to pay his respects; with the new (married) architect from the Oxford office. As she had watched Woody buffooning about with Millie and Jasper and his magic trick, she thought perhaps the life of a hotelier's wife might be grand. Perhaps she didn't need a City boy or banker. All those moody winter lakescapes and water-falls would be Instagrammable. It could be her follow-up book: the Beatrix-Potter-inspired posts with their toddler. The summer days and cream teas. Perhaps the Superlatively Single Girl could pivot happily to life in the Lakes.

'Faster, you dirty beast, faster!'

'Huh?'

'Fill me with our future!' SJ whispered into Woody's ear as she bit it.

'Ow!'

He thrust forward with a growing creak, pain on his lobe as well as the burning in his rectus femoris.

Clunk.

'Fuck!' SJ hollered.

'Argh!' Woody whimpered. And at the point he came, the whole swing structure came crashing down on them.

64

CLAIR

March 2019, Northill, Oxfordshire

'So, is she your girlfriend?'

'Er...'

'If you're introducing her to the kids, she must be...'.

Clair, wielding a pan of spaghetti and a stainless-steel claw, paused in anticipation at the kitchen island over five dinner plates.

Seb leaned on his elbows at the other end of the island and looked between Clair and Dave, who was grating cheese with gusto.

'Sounds exciting!' Dave said with a flourish of Parmigiano Reggiano.

Seb laughed nervously.

'Want some?' Dave asked, hovering over a generously piled bowl.

'Please, mate...'

Seb watched Clair and Dave's teamwork, a production line of

spaghetti, sauce, parmesan and garlic bread, as he deliberated how to answer the question. He had called round to collect the kids for the weekend, but after-school drinks had turned into them having dinner together, before he would take Millie and Jasper back to Rowan Road for the weekend. On Sunday they were going to meet Noemie's kids for the first time.

Millie and Jasper had already met Noemie in February when she joined them for smashed avo on toast in a cafe by the square, but this felt more formal; more daunting.

Six kids!

'I just don't think it's avoidable, is it?'

Clair froze, saucepan in one hand, spaghetti claw in the other; only the steam rising from it moved. Her face had a look of astonishment.

'What's not avoidable? Her being your girlfriend?'

'No, the kids. Introducing them.'

'Oh.'

'She has four. We're going to London Zoo on Sunday.'

Dave looked terrified and Clair's eyes widened as if to say *wow*.

'Good luck, mate, sounds eventful!' Dave said. 'Feeding time and all that...'

Clair was stuck for words.

'They're sweet. Really good kids,' Seb insisted.

Despite all the progress they had made recently, how friendly they had become – especially in the months since Seb and Desiree had split up – Clair felt irked to hear Seb say that about another woman's children, which she knew was ridiculous.

'How old are they?' Clair asked, trying not to look as if it mattered.

'Nine – almost ten – seven almost eight, three and, er, one.'

'A baby! She has a baby?'

A thickness stood in the air above their dinner. Clair desperately tried not to look at Dave.

'Hands full!' Dave said, trying to change tack. Clair wanted to ask what happened to the dad, but didn't want to show too much interest. More children? It sounded like a disaster given what Seb had told her about why he and Desiree had split.

It was the obvious point no one made.

'Yeah...' Seb agreed. 'I just don't think I can avoid them meeting each other if Noemie and I are going to be seeing each other.'

Clair's eyebrows knitted into an astonished frown. Noemie wasn't the woman Seb left her for, so she could get on board with it, even though she did feel sad for the kids about Desiree – they missed her – but the thought of the upheaval for Millie and Jasper, the threat that four children might usurp their own children in Seb's life, didn't sit well, especially if this wasn't going to go anywhere. Surely it couldn't. It was a flash in the pan.

'Yes, but is she your girlfriend, Seb? If she's not ever going to be, then there is little point introducing the kids to her and her kids, and vice versa, no?'

Practical Clair. Always sensible.

Seb looked unsure. He wanted to say *whoa, hang on* and felt a little hot in the face – or perhaps that was the steam from the dinner – but he didn't want to upset this new, harmonious, normal.

'It's just a fun day trip, it's not like we're getting married.' He winked.

Clair blushed.

'Well, you can do what you want, but just think about Millie and Jasper. Six kids will be intense, Seb. However sweet they are.'

'I know that.'

Millie's timely entrance into the kitchen felt like a relief to Seb. 'Hey, princess, what you been doing up there?'

'Is dinner ready? I'm starving...'

65

JUNE 2019, NORTHILL, OXFORDSHIRE

Most of the family hadn't noticed the seamless transition from funeral wake to Friday-night punters, walking into their local for a pint. It had happened gradually, which helped wind things down and eased the general trickle of departures back to their homes, where the shock would sink in and the real mourning would start.

It also helped water down Noemie's rising hostility: her slurred speech and accusatory eyes. With other people entering the fray, the ascending agitation of her prowl was diluted slightly.

Desiree could still feel her circling though.

'Hey, Granny, I'm going to the toilet now and then we'll head home, yes?' Desiree said loudly, so Violeta could hear over the music that had been turned up another notch. She nodded like a well-behaved child. 'Do you need a wee?'

'No, *cariña*.'

'Fatima will sit with you, yes?' Fatima nodded reassuringly and Violeta smiled.

She'd been such easy and good company, listening more and talking less than she used to when she held court at the telephone exchange or family parties.

But she loved hearing the stories of the bright young architects and their travels. Their dreams reminded her of Wilfred's as a young man.

She'd attempted to play Harry Potter Dobble with Jasper but had been so exhausted by it, even though Jasper had let her win some of the cards, she'd had a little snooze in an armchair in the corner of the pub to give her a second wind before eating some left-over sandwiches before they were cleared away.

But it was 10 p.m. and this was the latest Violeta had been out in years. She was starting to wane now. Desiree worried about reproachful comments from her parents if she told them; she wondered whether she should stop at their house in Guildford for the night, even though they were away. Whether she could make it back to the south coast for Violeta's midnight curfew.

'I won't be long,' Desiree said, as Gaby let her out. Gaby had met Federico, Fatima and Mei-Xin a few times, when she used to flatshare with Desiree, and they'd decided to all get the train back to Paddington together.

In the toilet Desiree used the free cubicle, washed her hands and examined her eyes in the mirror. Her mascara had held out, but she gave a cursory swipe with her finger underneath each eye anyway, before adding a quick slick of nude gloss on her pink lips.

The door to the Ladies opened with more force than was intended as the woman entering gasped as the handle on the back of the door smashed into brickwork, where a little dent already sat. This obviously happened regularly. Still, Desiree was startled. More so to see Noemie, who must have known Desiree had gone to the loo, given the close eye she was keeping on her.

'Oh. It's you,' Noemie said, without any effort to hide her disdain.

Desiree gave a polite smile before putting her gloss back into her bag.

'Why you not look at me, huh?' Noemie asked Desiree's reflection.

'Pardon me?' Desiree swung round.

'You think *I'm* the piece of shit?'

Desiree looked back at her bag as she zipped her make-up away and took another hand tissue from the dispenser. This was the last thing she wanted right now or ever. Noemie slipped slightly on her gold gladiator sandals down a small hidden step where the door had closed behind her. She edged closer, much smaller than Desiree in heels, but her face defiant, knotted in anger.

'You think you're better than me, huh? You try to humiliate me...'

'Look, I don't know what your problem is—'

'*My* problem?' Noemie spat, examining Desiree with utter revulsion, hovering as if she was on the precipice of a decision that could shape her life.

'You think you're Miss 'igh and Mighty—'

'No, I don't,' Desiree said coolly.

'But Seb, he was with *me*!' She almost spat it as she said it.

Desiree paused and looked at Noemie with a coolness that only enraged her more. Then she snapped back.

'I know what you did...' Desiree cautioned. 'Good luck sleeping at night.' She slung her bag on her arm and walked out, calling on everything in her fibre to keep cool, not cry, and walk around Noemie without shoving her out of her way, which was what she wanted to do. She couldn't help whispering, 'Fucking psycho,' quietly under her breath though.

Noemie followed her out hurriedly, a painful stab of a cry coming out of her mouth as she wailed and clutched her hair. A flush from the other cubicle went unnoticed at the now-empty sinks.

'Granny, we're going to go. Now,' Desiree said, in her calmest of keep-calm voices, as she stood at the table where Violeta was sandwiched.

'SHE HURT ME!' Noemie bellowed, to the last funeral-goers and Friday-night drinkers. 'SHE PULL MY HAIR!' People stopped their conversations and turned around.

'What?' Desiree scoffed. This was not going to happen. It was definitely not going to happen in front of Seb's parents; in front of Jasper; in front of Violeta.

Noemie scoured the pub, there were fewer and fewer people she recognised now, and there hadn't been many to start with, as she sought her mother or Martin among the stragglers, pulling at her dishevelled hair on one side of her head as if it had just been ravaged. Her mother stood up from where she'd been sitting with Tina and Dora, speaking frantically in French.

Noemie was sobbing, bent over double clutching her hair, telling her mother what had happened, except she did it in English so everyone could understand.

'She hit me, scratched me, pulled my hair!' Camille put her arm around Noemie and looked at Desiree with horror.

'You are having a fucking laugh,' Desiree replied calmly. It was embarrassing enough that Noemie had even approached her, let alone deliberately caused a scene and told grotesque lies. Desiree felt an anger rise in her like never before, but she didn't want any of this near Granny. Gaby, Federico, Fatima and Mei-Xin looked on in absolute shock while Desiree searched for Violeta's coat.

'She did!' Noemie wailed. 'She assault me!'

'Bullshit,' Desiree said, looking at Federico for backup.

'Of course!' he professed.

'Granny, do you have your bag?'

Desiree's busyness, her rush to leave, did make her look slightly guilty as Martin walked over and put his arm around Camille and Noemie.

'Are you OK, love?'

'That monster! She pulled me by my hair! Dragged me around the toilets!' Noemie clutched her forehead too now. 'Hit my head on the sink!'

The pub had gone quiet; the music stopped. People looked on in astonishment. Jasper curled into Penelope. Tina was on turbo twitch mode, shaking her head. Roger and Dora looking aghast.

The landlord came from the other side of the bar to see what the commotion was about. The air thick with accusation and grief.

'Absolutely not!' said Clair, coming out of the Ladies, her voice shaking in fury. 'That 100 per cent *didn't* happen, I'm not having it!' Jasper was shocked. His mother was using her worst telling-off voice, and he was glad it wasn't aimed at him.

Thank god, Desiree thought, standing up with the coats, mortified to be embroiled in such a scene. *At Seb's funeral.*

'I was in the toilet, I heard it all.' She pointed a finger at Noemie. 'You were spoiling for a fight and she didn't take your bait. Outrageous!'

Jasper looked at his mother, the lioness, in awe.

Martin looked between Clair, Desiree, and the women in his arms, baffled, but knowing he had to do something. He had felt this building all day and evening too. All eyes looked to him to sort this out and be the man Seb needed him to be right now.

'Let's see if there's a taxi outside, yes?'

Noemie was sobbing to the point she couldn't speak, her confused mother smoothing down her hair. 'Have you got your things?' Martin asked, keenly.

Camille muttered in French as Martin shepherded them out, turning back to Desiree with a reassuring glance. Noemie sobbed like an overtired child who hadn't got their way, wittering about her broken heart and how much she loved Seb.

Desiree breathed a sigh of relief, the landlord got back to business, and the music restarted as the back door to the garden burst open, and SJ stood there, hair in disarray, faux-fur stole matted with leaves and thighs pressed together so she could keep as much of Woody inside her as she could.

'What did I miss?' she asked her gobsmacked mother.

66

NOEMIE

March 2019, Northill, Oxfordshire

'Your daughter, she really look like you...'

Noemie's fascination with which parent which child looked like was intense. She talked about it a lot with her children and she had been so excited about their family day out together, so she could properly meet Seb's kids and study their faces.

Seb hadn't given it much thought. It was hard to tell with your own kids – he knew their faces too well to be able to see anything other than the beauty in them. But everyone said Millie was the spit of him: her mischief, her sparkle. And that Jasper had Clair's serious face and kind eyes. But he couldn't really see it.

Noemie was annoyed that both of her daughters looked like their different fathers; but again, Seb couldn't tell. Especially as he'd never seen the fathers. Maybe he just wasn't good at that sort of thing.

'You think?' he said croakily. It was Monday morning – not

ideal to start the week with a hangover, but they had been cele-brating the end of an exhausting introduction of their children to each other. The blended family trip to the zoo had been a success.

Millie thought Gabriel was super cute and spent much of the day pushing his buggy around Regent's Park; Jasper and Samuel discovered they had Minecraft in common, although Samuel was even more morose than Jasper and they didn't speak much about it; and the middle girls, Alice and Mila, mostly played with each other, skipping around looking for the red pandas that wouldn't come out of their box.

Seeing Jasper and Samuel side by side made Seb think that maybe Jasper was OK: perhaps he had coped better than Seb feared with his parents' split; with the upheaval of losing Desiree in his daily life. He had worried about his quietness, his seriousness. But Samuel was even quieter, and together they seemed content to co-exist with the odd amenable exchange about Creepers and Iron Ore.

The day had gone well, even if they hadn't seen the red pandas, and the eight of them had stopped for dinner at Wagamama on Wigmore Street before getting the train back to Northill. After Seb had dropped Millie and Jasper back at Clair's and given her two tired thumbs ups, he'd gone back to Noemie's for a glass of red to celebrate.

'Yeah, the shape of the back of her head, it's just like yours.'

Seb laughed and rolled over in bed to look at her gazing at him, his eyes tired and his mouth parched. 'The back of the head? That's a new one,' he said with a husky throat.

Noemie had woken Seb early so they could have sex before the kids woke up and his body felt blissful and listless. The new au pair, Aurelie, had selfishly gone to Paris for the weekend to see friends and wasn't back until this afternoon, which Noemie wasn't happy about: not only had she had to cancel her classes on Saturday, but she'd also had to entertain her own kids while Seb had taken his shopping for Easter eggs and clothes. At least Seb had shared the load at London Zoo.

'I wonder who our daughter will look like,' Noemie reflected as she contorted her body into what looked like a sit-up and stayed there, in a V-shape, her six-pack crunching. 'Me, finally?' She raised her legs a little higher. 'Although probably you – first kids are genetically meant to look like the father, so the man stays around and provides. I would like a girl to look like you.'

Seb didn't quite hear as he drifted in and out of sleep, the lines of dream and reality blurring.

'Huh?' he mumbled.

Noemie stared at him peacefully and stroked the gentle arc of his strong nose, which had caught the sun at the zoo. Then her face lit up as she remembered something.

'I know!' Noemie got up, repositioning the tiny thong and see-through bra that had gone askew during sex, and padded over to the dressing table. She pulled a piece of paper from the mirror she had pinned it to, walked back to the bed softly so as not to wake the kids, and thrust the paper under Seb's nose. His eyes were half closed again.

'See!' Her voice was both dreamy yet manic.

He opened his eyes to focus: it looked like a page from a Boden catalogue or a magazine. A photo of a small tanned girl with brown-gold hair, bright eyes and saltwater curls wearing a summer dress.

'It's what our little girl will look like. I see it!'

Seb sat up and rubbed his face.

'Oh, oh, no, I really don't think...'

'You can't see it?' Noemie's voice was soft and sweet. Seb wondered if something had been lost in translation. Was she hypothesising or predicting?

No no no.

He was waking up fast.

No no no.

Seb had been through this, for five years. He loved Millie and Jasper so much. He had loved Desiree – and lost her – because of this.

No no no.

He couldn't go through it again. His heart couldn't take it.

He rubbed his eyes and looked cautiously at Noemie's beautiful smile.

'You're joking, right...?' He searched her face for clues.

Noemie looked even more alert than usual.

'I thought that!' she gushed, as if it were funny. 'What a coincidence! But she could be our daughter, *non*?'

Seb took the piece of paper jabbed into his hand. Even after rubbing his eyes again, and focusing on the photo, he couldn't see it at all. She was just a child model in a nice shoot for some pretty clothes.

'I mean, she's cute, but are you being seri—?'

Seb was saved by a thunderous knock at the door that made them both jolt.

Noemie let out a gasp. Seb turned his head, startled and unsure of whether the alarm was internal or external. Alice padded into the room clutching a comfort cloth, looking dishevelled and confused.

'Is it school already, *Maman*?' she asked with a frown.

Gabriel cried from his cot in the room he shared with Samuel next door.

The door rattled again.

'Fuck!' hissed Noemie. 'Who the fuck...?'

Seb looked at the clock.

5.47 a.m.

It was earlier than he'd realised. What time had she woken him for sex? Today was going to be awful, he already knew it.

'*Retourne te coucher, Alice, ce n'est pas encore l'heure de te lever.*'

Alice turned around and the bang escalated, in volume and relentlessness, as Seb jumped out of bed and threw on his jeans from the night before.

'*Maman!*' called Mila from her bed.

BANG BANG BANG.

'Hang on!' shouted Seb as he fled the bedroom and flew down the stairs both as fast and as quietly as he could before another thump pounded.

The rapping was more urgent now, more aggressive. The glass shaking in the panel of the front door.

'Arghhhhh!' shouted Seb as he trod on a piece of Lego on the stairs and nearly lost his balance. 'For fuck's sake!'

'*Maman*, what's going on?' Samuel grizzled flatly as he rubbed his eyes and slunk into his mother's bedroom.

Seb gave up on being quiet now he could hear a fourth child awake.

This is fucking crazy.

He jumped down, three steps at a time, as much upended by what Noemie had just said as he was by the thud at the door.

On the other side of the mottled glass Seb could see the distorted silhouettes of two figures and laughed to himself that, while they looked like two bald and burly men, it might be his tired mind playing tricks on him: it could be Aurelie, home early from Paris with her backpack; it could be Noemie's elderly neighbours in need of help. He imagined them later laughing at how scary and foreboding their shadows looked in first whispers of a dark March dawn.

As Seb opened the door his heart sank when he saw two bald and burly men, with surly horizontal grimaces between the folds of their faces. One was taller than the other. His worst-case scenario was in fact true and Seb knew their visit wasn't going to be cordial.

'Everything OK?' he asked as he rubbed the back of his head, trying to make his arms look bigger. 'What's all the noise about?' He tried to sound firm but friendly, as unrattled as possible as his heart raced.

But Seb was a talker, an amenable guy. He thought of all the times he'd got Jake out of a tight spot, the skirmishes he'd talked them out of in curry houses, or the architectural pitches he'd won. He could get through this one.

The taller of the two men shouldered past Seb, almost knocking him into the hallway wall as he lumbered into the living room.

'What the fu—?'

'Where's our client's money?' asked the stouter man, still standing on the doorstep, a hollow grin in his wide face.

'What? What money?'

Seb kept looking between the man at the door and over his shoulder in panic, to check the burlier one hadn't gone upstairs to Noemie and the kids.

When the shorter man didn't get a satisfactory answer, he too shouldered past, into the kitchen at the back of the house. Thick metal-toed boots clanking on the Middle Eastern runner that dampened down the floorboards.

Seb followed the man into the kitchen.

'This is the residence of one Naomi Morel, is that not correct?' said the man, surveying the kitchen as if he were appreciating the décor.

'Yeah, but—'

'BUT what?' he asked, as he pivoted with a grimace; a challenge. Seb took half a step back. 'If your little lady friend ain't not gonna pay our client, we'd better get some of this gear, as a little deposit.' He surveyed the laptop and iPhone on the kitchen table, while the taller man exited the living room holding a PS4 and controller cables.

'Come on, mate. That belongs to her kids. There are four kids upstairs trying to sleep. This is their stuff. Is this really fucking—?'

As he said it, the shorter man pushed Seb up against the kitchen wall, stubby, badly tattooed fingers firmly around his neck. Seb was taken aback and tried to keep his breath steady while he choked, as Gabriel's cries got louder from his cot upstairs.

'I don't give a *fuck* how many men have blown their beans up Ms Morel, nor do I care for how many kids there are upstairs. We're here to make it clear that she needs to pay her debts, or those four kids are gonna have bigger problems than having fuck all to watch and fuck all to play on. Do you hear me... "mate"?'

Seb nodded, gasped, and slid down the wall a little as the man released him, his heart beating out of his bare chest.

Resigned, Seb stepped aside and stood guard at the bottom of the stairs as he watched the men walk out of the house with the TV, the PlayStation, a phone and the Nespresso machine – plus a croissant the stout one tore from a packet on the kitchen table – slamming the door behind them.

* * *

Three minutes later, Seb leaned, palms splayed on the table, head hung, examining the knots in the wood as he stood in just his jeans. His breathing was heavy but he tried to regulate it with deep breaths through his nose as he heard Noemie scramble down the stairs.

'Jesus fuckin' Christ, are you OK, Seb?' she asked, pushing her bedhead back and tying her short Liberty robe.

Deep breaths.

'What the hell's going on?' Seb asked calmly as he stared at a swirl in the wood near his left palm; a glimmer of a torn croissant packet in his peripheral vision near his right hand.

'Oh,' she said flatly, noticing the coffee machine wasn't there.

Noemie filled the whistleblower kettle from the tap over the butler sink and put it on the stove.

'*Maman!*' called Alice from the top of the stairs.

Gabriel was still crying.

'*Maman!*'

Noemie shouted something fast and angry in French but Seb couldn't focus on it; all he could think was how frightening that had been.

This is not my problem to fix. This is not my problem to solve.

Seb looked up, to Noemie by the hob, her hair frantic and dressing gown half open as she looked at him with defiance.

'How much do you owe?'

'I'm sorry, Seb. I'm a proud woman, I don't want any help.' Noemie's glacial eyes welled up and Seb softened a little, his shoulders dropping. She was so beautiful, even amid all the craziness.

'How much do you owe?' he repeated.

Noemie didn't answer, instead she walked over to him and teased her fingers up the curve of his spine. Seb stood up and turned around, resting his bottom on the kitchen table as he rubbed his arms to warm himself.

'Does your mum know?'

'No!' Noemie replied in a flash. 'She would only humiliate me about it.'

'Humiliate you? She's your mum! I'm sure she'd want to help if she had any inkling that guys like that were around her grandkids.'

'Yeah, she'd pay it off, but then I'd never be able to forget it.'

'Isn't that just...?'

Seb was thinking *gratitude*.

'Is OK, is not happening.' Noemie drew a line under the conversation but Seb couldn't let it go.

'Look, we all fuck up...'

Seb couldn't help thinking about Sam, Alice, Mila and Gabriel, that Noemie going cap in hand to her mother and clearing her debt was surely worth the embarrassment if thugs weren't going to smash on the doors, terrify the kids and take their things.

'Maman!' Samuel called now; Alice had started dressing Mila.

'Just get ready for school!' she shouted. 'I have to take you today!'

'Gabriel's crying!'

Noemie looked flummoxed as the kettle started to whistle and floorboards creaked above them.

Damn the men for revealing her secrets to Seb!

Damn Aurelie for going away for the weekend!

Damn the kids' fathers for getting her in this shit!

Seb looked at her, exasperatedly, longingly, then nodded to the whistling kettle behind her. She turned and flicked the gas off, then looked back at Seb, almost pleadingly.

'It's just one little food shop... it goes on the credit card, then another... And with Samuel now eating big-boy portions the food bill is more. Then they need school clothes... then school trips, then trips to the zoo and fun stuff I don't want to deprive them of just because their dads are fuckfaces.'

Seb was pretty sure he'd paid for everything for their trip to London Zoo yesterday – the trains, the dinner, and he'd spent £140 in the gift shop making sure everyone had a keepsake. But he didn't say it.

Noemie must have been scared. She looked scared. Scared of the men or scared Seb might walk out, he wasn't sure, but he opened his arms and pulled her into his chest. As she started to kiss his neck ferociously he looked at the room around them: the

Eames chair with a luxuriant sheepskin thrown over it. The butler sink she'd had put into the ex-council house. The £1,000 spice rack he himself had coveted in The Conran Shop but always thought he couldn't justify. The Agent Provocateur underwear he'd enjoyed peeling off her, wrapped in an expensive Liberty dressing gown. It was no wonder Noemie racked up so much debt on a yoga teacher's salary.

'I'll speak to my sister,' she said vaguely, pressing her hips into his. 'It's not a problem, I can sort it out, or work more classes.'

Seb knew she'd have to teach a lot of yoga to cover whatever it was she owed. He pulled away.

'How much are we talking?'

Noemie released herself and retied her dressing gown defensively.

'I'll sort it.'

'How much? Are we talking thousands?'

She looked away.

'Tens of thousands? Hundreds of thousands?'

'No!' Noemie snapped, horrified. 'Just ten thousand pounds.'

'Fuck.'

'OK, fourteen. But it happen so easily, Seb, I—'

Samuel walked in with a rosy, teething Gabriel, sweaty in a romper suit and grizzling on his big brother's hip.

'He's hungry, *Maman*,' the boy said sombrely.

Noemie looked beleaguered. She did *not* want to lose Seb over this, so soon.

'Fuck!' she cursed as the baby cried.

'Come here...' Seb said as he lifted Gabriel out of Samuel's arms and offered him some croissant from the packet on the table. The reminder of the man left a nasty taste in his mouth.

'You hungry, little man? Want some breakfast?'

Gabriel took the croissant and gripped it in his fist, pastry flakes tumbling like snowflakes onto Seb's chest. Samuel padded away to get his school uniform on.

Noemie made a peppermint tea and looked on fondly at the beautiful man embracing her son.

'I promise I'll sort it, OK?' she reassured. 'You want a peppermint tea? I'd make you your coffee but...'

'No, I've gotta go.'

Seb kissed Gabriel's cheek and handed him over to his mother, and kissed her on the nose.

'I need to be in Oxford for 8.30 a.m. Aurelie's back this afternoon, yes?'

'Tonight, yes.'

Seb ran upstairs to get his T-shirt, his wallet, his watch, and to check in on Samuel, Alice and Mila. As he peered around the door to the boys' bedroom, he grabbed the baseball bat he had noticed in the corner, then jumped down the stairs, two at a time, before resting the bat by the front door as he put his trainers on.

Noemie walked from the kitchen to the hallway, jigging Gabriel on her hip.

'Leave that there for now, while I think of something,' Seb said. Noemie looked shocked as Seb put his jacket on and kissed her on the cheek, checking his phone was in his pocket. 'OK, see you.'

'Tonight?' Noemie asked hopefully. 'I can go out if Aurelie is back in time.'

'No, I have a shitload of work I need to do. I should have done it yesterday.'

Noemie looked disappointed.

'Ah, OK.'

'But I'll call you,' Seb said as he kissed her again and opened the door. 'Oh, actually, they took your phone...'

'FUCK!' Noemie shouted, startling Gabriel.

'Do you have a spare? An old one?'

'How am I meant to sort this shit out without a phone? It had all my pictures from yesterday!' Noemie shook her head.

'I'll see if I've got my old work one, will drop it round, you'll have to get a SIM...'

'OK, love you,' Noemie called out after him, as if it weren't the first time she had said it. He stopped on the pathway beyond the door and looked back at her, baffled, more surprised by her timing than her feelings. He had felt it coming.

Samuel walked past her, gripping the newel post of the stairs, so he could get to the kitchen and get all the breakfast stuff out for his siblings. The girls came chasing down after each other, arguing over a wand that one of them was clutching triumphantly. Gabriel gurgled, dribbling with his croissant.

Seb paused. Watching the chaos pass Noemie by.

'Catch up later, eh?' he said. She nodded, and closed the door in disappointment.

As Seb walked down the path and back towards his house, as he walked under a railway bridge and through the park, past the early-morning commuters heading into London and Oxford, back to his serene and still house, he wondered what the hell he was getting into.

Love?

Heavies?

Six kids?

Maybe a seventh after what she was going on about in bed.

How the hell was he going to find fourteen grand to bail her out without Clair knowing? Without a reminder that it would be money better spent on his own kids. Noemie clearly wasn't going to ask her sister for help.

The hangover, the banging in his head, from last night's wine or the door knocking, he couldn't work out which, sloshed around his stomach and he ran to a bush on the other side of the path so he could throw up.

He didn't have an 8.30 a.m. meeting in Oxford. He had just wanted to get out of there, so he could have a bath, soak his neck, still sore from the bald man's grip on his Adam's apple, and work from home.

He retched. Vomiting up tension and stress and the fear of not being able to breathe. As he stared at his meagre pile of puke and bile in the bushes beneath him, a woman in a navy skirt suit looked disapprovingly as she hurried past to catch her train, and Seb wondered how the hell he was going to extract himself from all of this.

67

JUNE 2019, NORTHILL, OXFORDSHIRE

'Thank you for that. I'm so glad you were there,' Desiree said, coats slung over her shaking arm.

Clair looked livid – as if she were carrying all the indignation in the world as she stared at the pub door closing behind them. She wished Dave were here to rub her back right now but he had gone to get Millie.

'I can't believe I let my kids go away with her,' she said, shaking her head. 'I can't believe I let Seb...'

SJ walked over, rubbing her smeared red lipstick from her jawline with the back of her hand. Putting on her best compassionate face.

'Are you OK, darling?' she questioned in the most insincere of kindly voices. Desiree wasn't sure if she was talking to Clair or to her, but she nodded a yes anyway.

'What a cunt.'

Clair looked startled at SJ for using such language near Jasper.

'I always knew it,' she said as she patted them both on the arm on her way to the toilet to clean herself up.

With SJ gone, Clair and Desiree gave each other a look of relief.

'It's not your fault,' Desiree said, one eye on Granny, who was rummaging in her handbag, looking for the glasses that were on her nose. 'Neither of us could have stopped him going. It's not our fault. It's not even her fault.' Desiree nodded to the door. 'Not really.'

Clair looked surprised. But then Desiree hadn't heard the kids' account of the holiday. She hadn't seen their terrified and grief-stricken faces when they were reunited in Florida.

'Well, I don't know why she did that... she's insane. I was in the cubicle. I didn't know you'd been in the one next to me until I heard her talking to you. Jeez.'

She shook her head.

'It was coming,' Desiree said coolly. 'I'd felt it brewing for hours.'

'What was her problem? She was the one who was with Seb! You were moving on. You were moving to New York!'

'I don't know,' said Desiree with a sigh, although she thought she might have an idea.

68

NOEMIE

April 2019, Northill, Oxfordshire

In the tapas bar where they had enjoyed their second date four months ago, Seb tried to act as if he were hungry. In front of him was a delicious array of heritage tomato salad in sherry vinegar, herby spatchcock chicken surrounded by garlicky chorizo, and juicy albondigas on chickpeas. But he just didn't fancy any of it. He didn't want to upset Noemie by letting on, so he judiciously pushed and picked at the offering between them.

He had wanted to see Clair and the kids after school and popped round with a box of Krispy Kremes, only to be presented in return with a beautiful (if wonky) rainbow cake Millie had lovingly made her father for his fortieth birthday. Clair had put up balloons and banners. Dave cued up 'Happy Birthday' by Stevie Wonder on Spotify.

One doughnut, two slices of cake, three glasses of champagne and a group FaceTime call with Penelope and Peter in Guernsey later, Seb looked at his watch and panicked.

'Shit, sorry,' he said. 'I'm meant to be picking up Noemie, our table is booked in fifteen minutes...'

* * *

As Clair saw Seb to the door and the kids hugged him and went back inside, she looked at him framed by the green behind. The nights were definitely getting lighter. Cowslips and dandelions were blooming. There was a feeling of excitement in the air, but perhaps that was the bubbles of the fizz they had popped.

'Happy fortieth, Seb,' Clair said, with a sincere smile.

Seb stood with his hands in his pockets and looked back.

My birthday.

Seb had always liked his birthday. The revelry and hoopla. He remembered how he and Clair had first had sex on his sixteenth birthday. How she had nursed his hangover after his eighteenth in the glass house overlooking the sea. The curry crawl in Brick Lane for his twenty-first and the surprise party that wasn't a surprise for his thirtieth in the barn at The Blue Bell. He had loved them all, and today had been great too. He felt a pull towards Clair he hadn't felt in a long time, and he wanted to stay with her and the kids, here in the house on the green. But perhaps that was because he was full on cake and really didn't fancy the dinner.

An hour later and it was all laid out in front of him. Delicious food he loved; a beautiful woman he wanted to get naked with. But his busy mind couldn't focus on what was in front of him. Instead he thought about Clair, Dave and the kids – whether they had continued the game of Trivial Pursuit he'd had to abandon. He thought about the fig tree Desiree had sent by courier to his desk at Curtis + Cooper with a simple card signed:

Happy 40th, old man! Dx

He thought about what Desiree might be doing today, and who she might be doing it with. Was she thinking about him, or was she in New York by now? He'd sent her a WhatsApp to say thanks for the fig tree but hadn't heard back from her.

'You don't want any of the *pois chiche*?'

Noemie proffered her fork with an energy and a mania that was perking him up despite his fatigue. He opened his mouth to be fed as his phone lit up and rang on the table. It was probably his dad and Tina calling from their hot tub in Marbella; or perhaps SJ, phoning from an ashram in India where she was researching sexual silence for her latest dating column. Seb looked at the screen. Jake. If he spoke to Jake, Jake would hear the conflict in his voice, so he rejected the call and took the bite from Noemie's fork.

'Yummy, huh?' she enthused.

Seb nodded, dreamily.

'OK, I think my birthday boy needs a little pick-me-up, *non*?'

Noemie rummaged in her suede fringed bag and pulled out a large envelope. 'Sebastian' was written on the front in the cursives of a foreign hand. 'Here, 'appy birthday!' she simpered, leaning over and licking chickpea purée from Seb's top lip. He lingered on the kiss.

'What is it?'

'A card! Open it!'

Seb felt the spotlight of the restaurant light on his face as he opened the envelope and pulled out a large card. On the front was an illustration of a bear clutching a loveheart.

'HAPPY BIRTHDAY TO MY BOYFRIEND' it read on the front, with a rudimentary 4 and 0 added to the bear's tummy in Sharpie. 'Look! Inside!' Noemie clapped her hands together in delight as

Seb slowly opened the card and a folded piece of A4 fell out, which he caught just before it landed on the floor.

'Oops,' he said to himself. He opened the card first, slowly and thoughtfully.

A twee Hallmark message he would read later separated 'Dear Seb' from 'I love you, Noemie' with a loveheart drawn underneath it.

'Ahhh, thank you...' he said, with a smile.

'Open the paper!' she demanded. Seb felt as nervous as he was intrigued.

He carefully unfolded the A4 sheet to reveal the relentlessly happy face of Mickey Mouse – or at least a human in a Mickey Mouse costume – waving at the camera from his spot in front of a manicured garden in front of the Magic Kingdom.

Noemie had printed in a rainbow font:

Happy 40th birthday Seb. Florida baby! You, me and the kids!
Love you, Noemie xxxxx

What?

Seb smiled, his face hot.

Florida.

'Shit, Noemie, that's too...'

'May 'alf term 'olidays. All of us!'

'*All* of us?'

His face burned red and his mouth went dry. Noemie raised her glass of Bordeaux and gave a self-congratulatory smile. Cutlery clattered at the next table as Seb tried to gather his thoughts. Noemie had mentioned spending a week in Provence, at her mother's holiday home this August, but Seb had been non-committal; he didn't know where his head would be at in August; he had wanted to see what Clair's summer plans were first.

Florida?

'Yes! Virgin flights, all the best. A nice suite in a BIIIIIIG 'otel in Orlando, park passes for a week. VIP speed entry so the kids don't have to queue...'

'*All* the kids...? Mine too?'

Noemie nodded proudly.

'And Gabriel?'

Seb was struggling to process this while also maintaining his smile of gratitude and surprise.

'Yes, OK he too young for most of the rides but we take it in turns with the kids holding him. Millie was very good with him at the zoo. She can take him a lot of the time. Train her up to be an au pair already!' Noemie laughed.

Seb felt sick.

'Disney?' It was all he could say.

'Yes!'

Noemie looked so proud of herself while Seb felt terribly guilty. He'd had no idea this was her thing.

'But it must have cost a bomb. We just paid off—'

'Please, Seb, don't insult me, I know what I'm doing. I've been working hard.'

A month ago, Noemie had been £14,000 in debt. A debt Seb had borrowed on the business to clear so thugs wouldn't go knocking on her door again. Surely this holiday would cost that again. And then some.

'What about Clair? Have *you* spoken to Clair about this?'

Seb couldn't conceive that Clair would let the kids go to another continent without a lot of thought and consideration. He knew Clair and Noemie had never met.

'Me? No! Of course I haven't. You can do that, *non?*'

Seb was gobsmacked.

'But the holiday is paid... without checking if we can go?'

Noemie looked deflated.

'It's quite a big deal,' Seb said gently, his smile belying the severity of what he was saying, the panic he was feeling. 'Clair might not want the kids to go so far. She might already have half-term plans – we haven't discussed it yet. Millie has end-of-year exams and Jasper has his play – I don't know if they'll be done by then.'

'Well, now you're pissing me off.'

Noemie slumped back in her chair, hurt and angry.

'No, no, no, I'm sorry, it's incredibly generous of you. Thank you!'

Seb grabbed Noemie's fingers and entwined them in his.

'I'm just not very impulsive, am I?' Seb lied. Clair had often accused him of being too impulsive in the past. But this was next level.

Noemie shrugged and pouted.

'Really, this is so kind of you. Thank you. There's just a lot to sort out, logistically I mean...' Seb clasped his palms together in gratitude and Noemie's frown started to lift. 'But I'm incredibly grateful. Thank you. What a lovely, generous present. What an amazing woman.'

A smile started to creep to the corners of Noemie's full lips.

'You're welcome! Now shush, and kiss me with those sexy *pois chiche* lips of yours.'

69

JUNE 2019, NORTHILL, OXFORDSHIRE

Martin tapped the roof of the taxi twice as a farewell salute, sending Noemie and her mother back to Noemie's house on the other side of the town centre. He knew Noemie hadn't meant any harm – grief and lack of sleep had just brought out the worst in her. It must have been awful for her too.

He put his hands in his pockets and made a mental note to check in with her in a few weeks, just to see if she was OK. He took a deep breath and walked across the pebbles of the car park, back to the pub that had been taken over by people in a happier frame of mind. People who deserved their optimism.

Time to head home, he thought as he slowly walked, looking at his feet. He was tired and wanted to sleep. He closed his eyes briefly and thought of the glass house on the cliff. The home Seb had torn through as a toddler on his little wooden horse on wheels. The house they had held parties in for their island friends, where Seb genially mixed drinks for their guests. 'Coke, wine and beer anyone?' he had said with a cheeky grin. He called it 'kedgeree' for some reason. As a cocktail it never took off. Martin smiled as he remembered.

He thought about the serenity of the top-floor studio and its views across the channel. The stormy nights out at sea, which were as beautiful as the sunny days without a cloud in the sky.

His heart felt clogged as he opened his eyes and examined his shoes.

Time to go.

Back to the chocolate-box cottage in The Baldons, where the roses were now in full bloom. His summer house, as opposed to the winter one in Andalucia, which sat among the white houses and Moorish *azulejos* tiles; where he used to showboat about his son and his achievements on the golf course with his friends.

Bed.

He needed his bed, the one in the room with the peach décor. The house SJ often went back to and looked after, even though it didn't suit her life either. The cottage where Seb had stood on the doorstep and stared him down with such shock and hatred, the day he'd learned the truth Martin had been trying to hide.

And then he saw her on the steps, waiting with a jacket over her shoulders. The person he'd wanted to hold all day.

70

CLAIR

April 2019, Northill, Oxfordshire

'Are you fucking kidding? America? At half-term? No!'

'They'd love it, Clair.'

Dave watched from his corner of the kitchen as he, Clair and Seb stood, like three pieces on a chessboard, all poised for what Seb had said was a weird chat he needed to have with them after work. Dave had a look of concern too – he wasn't sure how Clair would cope with the kids so far away – but he kept a respectful silence. He knew his place.

Seb slumped onto the sofa by the bifold doors to the garden and put an elbow on each thigh. Clair walked over to the dining table, sat at a chair and pushed her sleeves up.

'I know it's a bit left-field, but hear me out—'

'No.'

'It could be brilliant for them – just what they need right now.'

'What they need right now? You talk as if they're super troubled, or it's a last wish or something... They're OK.'

Seb looked diffident, while Clair continued.

'If this is about us getting married... we talked about it, Seb, they're absolutely cool with it.'

Dave nodded gently from his perch against the island.

'No, I know that!' Seb waved a hand, before leaning back and rubbing his eyes with his palms. He knew he had to fess up. He couldn't put this on the kids and pretend it was all for them. 'But... erm... she's booked it already.' Seb did the thing he did when he was feeling awkward: smile. His biggest, most charming and sparkly eyed grin, which Clair wanted to slap.

'What?'

Dave grimaced.

'It was her surprise present, for my fortieth.'

'What? What's wrong with a jacket or a hot-air balloon ride, for fuck's sake?'

Clair put her hand to her brow. 'Well, she'll just have to lose the deposit. Amend the booking. Take Millie and Jasper off. I don't care what you do with her and her kids, but she might have thought to check with me what she does with *my* kids. I'm their mother! She's barely met them!'

Seb winced.

'It's all paid, their flights are locked in. It's only five weeks away.'

'Well, then, she's fucking mad.'

'Hey hey...' Dave tried to calm the tension. He wouldn't like his ex-partner calling Clair mad, but then Clair didn't give her any reason to. 'How about a cup of tea? Anyone want one?' Dave asked chirpily.

Seb had deliberately called round late, hoping the kids would be asleep; he wanted something stronger.

'Got a beer, mate?'

Dave nodded and went to the fridge.

'Look, I know it's a bit weird, but it's also incredibly generous of her.'

Seb didn't want to think about the credit-card debt she was about to rack straight up again. He pictured the burly man's grimace as he gripped his hands around his throat, and rubbed his neck. 'Just have a think about it. They will *love* it. I'll look after them so well, I promise. And Noemie has such a good heart – she wanted to treat us all.'

Clair glanced at Seb. She didn't want to tell him that Millie had described the new girlfriend as 'weird'; she could tell he was in a tight spot so tried not to go too hard on him.

'Remember how they always used to talk about wanting to go?'

'I don't remember them ever mentioning it...' Clair said defensively, as Dave handed Seb a beer and offered another to Clair. She shook her head so Dave took it and went to get Clair a fresh cup of Earl Grey. 'Millie wouldn't be bothered about Disney now, I'm sure, she's almost fourteen.' She slowed down and tried to be diplomatic. 'And not like this anyway. With Naomi—'

'Noemie.'

'Noemie – *sorry*,' Clair said without meaning it. 'And her kids. Plus they've never travelled without me!'

'They've flown to Guernsey without you loads of times. They're fine with me.'

'Yes, but that's the Aurigny! It takes an hour. They have family there. Their dad's full attention. Grandparents spoiling them. This is another bloody country. Another continent. They've never been that far before, and without me!'

They sat in deadlock while Seb contemplated paying Noemie for Millie and Jasper *not* to go and Dave made the tea. He handed her the hot mug before sitting down on the sofa with Seb.

'I just don't know what to do, then!' Seb shook his head and looked despairing. Clair was furious with him – but she felt sorry for him too.

'Maybe they'd love Disney,' she conceded. 'But they'd love it with you and me!' Clair looked to Dave quick as a flash. 'Me and Dave,' she corrected. 'But not with four kids they barely know, vying for their dad's attention. It's just so rude, Seb, that she didn't even think to run it past me before booking!'

'Six kids in a theme park!' Dave almost chuckled. 'Isn't one of them a baby?'

'He's almost one and a half.'

Clair snorted.

'Well, that doesn't sound fun! Or safe!'

'They're really easy kids.' Seb knew this was a half-truth. They were easy in that they barely spoke, they were solemn and disengaged – so they didn't run away or cause a ruckus in a restaurant, but that also made them hard work. 'It'll be fun!'

Seb had no choice but to fight for this.

'You and Dave can have a week to yourselves. Plan the wedding. Look at venues and stuff. Have some downtime.'

'We were going to take the kids to see Rach.' Clair laughed bitterly. The Wirral was probably going to be a harder sell to the kids than Florida.

Seb looked at Dave apologetically, who gave him a sympathetic half-smile as Clair started welling up into her tea.

'Oh, sweetheart...' Dave went over to her. He hated it when Clair welled up, and he pulled up the dining chair next to hers.

'They *will* love it – it might loosen Jasper up a bit – and it's not like they're on their own. They'll be with Seb; Millie will have done her exams by half-term – it sounds like a great opportunity for both of them to let off some steam...'

Seb gave his unlikely ally a thankful look.

'It's just so... far!' Clair said with a whimper. 'And dangerous.

The flight and the roller coasters.' Clair the homebody had become scared of going anywhere. She had become so straight and serious, but Seb noticed that Dave could bring out a more vulnerable side to her as he rubbed the back of her head and she leaned her forehead on his shoulder for a second. Dave and Seb looked at each other, hopefully.

'For fuck's sake, I guess I have no choice!' Clair said, raising her hands to the ceiling. Despairing in defeat.

'Thank you.' Seb pressed his hands together. 'You're the best. And they're going to LOVE it.'

'They will,' Dave concurred.

Clair sniffed and smiled.

'And we'll bring you back a Mickey fridge magnet.'

'No, really, Seb, don't.'

Dave laughed.

'Just make sure you call me, every day. I want to see them on FaceTime; know they're OK.'

'Of course!'

'They'll be fine.' Dave smiled.

Clair blew her nose into a tissue that was always in her sleeve and rearranged her ponytail.

'Jesus, Seb,' she said, shaking her head. 'She must be the best-paid yoga teacher in the world...'

71

JUNE 2019, NORTHILL, OXFORDSHIRE

'Peter's just settling up the tab...' Penelope said, forlornly, standing on the steps of the pub with her jacket slung across her elegant shoulders. Her hands, too, were in her pockets, mirroring Martin in front of her. 'I just couldn't face going round the pub, saying all the goodbyes again. I'm just so...' She looked at Martin, his blue eyes brightening in the passing lights of the car park.

'Empty?' he offered.

She nodded.

He nodded back.

They looked at each other, knowing that they were perhaps the only people on the planet who could understand the void, and held the gaze that had first made them fall in love.

'What will we do?' Penelope finally said, hopelessly, quietly. And then it came. Martin finally crumbled.

'Oh, Penny...' he said, his face cracking, his shoulders wilting. She walked quickly down the steps and they fell into each other's arms and clung, as they both held each other tight and cried into the other's neck. Crying for their son; crying for everything they had lost.

'What will we do?' Penelope repeated, searching for help in the comfort of Martin. He always used to have a solution. He didn't answer. He couldn't answer, so he squeezed Penelope's back and cried and tried to reassure her everything would be OK, even though they both knew it wouldn't. Nothing would ever be the same again. The one thing that held them together; the thing they both loved more than anything else in the world, was gone. And they didn't want to let each other go now.

Headlights illuminated and dimmed as cars entered and exited the car park.

'I'm so so sorry...' Martin sobbed, into the shoulder pad of her jacket. She was almost as tall as him in heels.

'What?' Penelope whispered, clutching Martin's back with her palms, wishing her grasp could bring their son back.

'For everything I did. For treating you badly. I'm a fool.'

Penelope hugged him tighter, giving a gentle nod with closed eyes.

Martin pulled back and opened his, forcing her to as he squeezed her shoulders and looked into her eyes.

'I always – *always* – loved you. It was always you...'

Penelope inhaled. The cracks in Martin's armour always galvanised her. She had to be stronger now. She pulled back.

'I just wish we could go back and—'

'Shhhhh...' She put a finger to his lips. 'Don't say anything.'

'But—'

'It won't bring him back.'

'But it's true, Pen. I love you and miss you and deeply regret everything I did to hurt you...'

'Oh, Martin.' She smiled serenely as she put a palm on his cheek. 'I know you do.'

Penelope always had a warmth, a gentle reassurance about her. Even now, he could see it. It was the way she used to calm Seb when he had fallen over as a child; or when he was heartbroken to have found out the truth about his father's other family.

'I love you too,' she said simply as she looked over her shoulder at the pub door, then turned back to him, and pushed a lick of hair off his forehead.

* * *

The Skoda Octavia that had swung into the car park seconds ago parked up and the front doors clicked open.

'Oh my god, it *is* Grandma Guilbert with Grandad. Weird!' Millie said as Dave busied himself by clearing the back seat. He'd noticed when his headlights lit a lovers' embrace, and was as puzzled as Millie was.

'Let's just get inside, eh?' he said diplomatically, picking up some Starburst wrappers from the back seat before locking the car.

They passed Peter in the doorway of the pub, jumper slung over his shoulders and tied at his sternum.

'Oh, Millie, you're back!'

'Erm, yeah...' Millie replied slightly awkwardly, worried about what Peter might see behind her.

'We're just off, but we'll pop round before our flight tomorrow.'

'Are you off now, Peter?' Dave said, unnecessarily loudly as he tried to make himself as big as possible in the doorway.

'Yes,' Peter said, puzzled because he'd just said that.

'Yeah, come round for breakfast, mate, if the hotel one isn't up to scratch, yeah? Adrian and Linda will be here still. Actually, you might be on the same flight back come to think of it. Oh, no, they're going to see Elizabeth for a few days, aren't they?'

'Will do,' Peter said, bemused by the wittering as he lightly bumped Dave on the arm with his fist and shuffled past him.

'All done!' Peter said, tapping his pocket as he walked down the steps and saw Penelope standing alone under the shard of a streetlight.

72

DESIREE

May 2019, London

Seb ran up the steps, two at a time, to the platform at Blackfriars station, as he heard the train doors beep and close.

'Shit...' he muttered to himself, almost punching the air in defeat. As he reached the top of the flight of stairs, thin tie pulling around his neck, he saw the train gently pull out of the station. 'Fuck!' he groaned, louder than he intended as the afternoon sun shone through the glass walls of the bridge station, making Seb feel even hotter under the collar.

He wanted to get back to Northill: to pick up the kids from Clair's and finish packing. Begin packing even. He hadn't even got his suitcase out of the loft and they had a super-early start the next morning.

Seb watched the train snake out of the station northbound, towards King's Cross where he would get the circle line to Paddington. Just not yet. As it gathered speed and the carriage windows started to blur, Seb looked across to the southbound side of Blackfriars station and the curving river. Behind it St Paul's, the Cheesegrater, the Walkie-Talkie and Tower Bridge. It was a tourist's dream, only few tourists knew about this secret window to the Thames. The sight of the buildings sparkling in the sunshine lifted Seb as he exhaled in defeat.

And then like a dream he saw her, standing on the other side of the platform, framed by Tower Bridge. She was looking up at the information tickertape to check how many minutes until her next train.

'Desi!' Seb shouted across the tracks.

One minute.

She looked over and laughed.

'What are you doing here?'

'Heading home, just missed one!'

Desiree knew that home. The cosy corners. The bed they used to lie tangled on.

'You?'

'Cocktails with a client,' she called. 'London Bridge!'

Seb surveyed her standing on the opposite platform. Cream, billowing trousers and a bright red capped-sleeved top that hugged her lean and muscular arms.

'Got time for one?' Seb asked, thinking, fuck it. Early starts were painful no matter how prepared you were.

Desiree looked at her watch, and then disappeared behind her train as it arrived out of nowhere into the station.

Shit.

Seb wasn't sure if it had been a yes or not, but it was too serendipitous to have seen her not to go and check, so he flew back down the steps he'd just run up, a different kind of panic in his chest now, to go under the tracks and up to her platform and see. When he got to the bottom of the stairs he was surprised to see Desiree already there.

'I can do a quick one. Sea Containers?' she suggested. 'I have forty-five minutes.'

'Perfect!'

* * *

Sitting on a teal velvet sofa at a low gold table, Desiree smiled at the waiter who brought cocktails and a jug of water.

'Two Rosebuds, madam,' he said.

Desiree rubbed her hands together and looked at the confection in front of her. At Seb, handsome in his suit.

'So how's Magdalen?'

'Yeah, it's going well. We're just at spatial coordination. Planning is obviously a bit of a nightmare but we're getting through it.'

'Oh, great. And how did you get on with the South Bank pitch?'

'We won it! I was just meeting the client now, before I missed the train.'

'Awesome! Tell me about it.'

'It's a community library by the undercroft – you know the skate park along the river?'

'Yes!'

'Yeah, it's going to be super cool: like this hip library for all the kids who hang out there. "Books and boards" kinda thing... People assume the kids skating are playing hooky from school but most of them are super bright – why can't the two go together?'

'Wow...' Desiree gasped, clasping her hands together. 'I'm so jealous. I want to work on books and boards!'

Seb looked proud.

'Yeah, it's the first project won entirely organically through me and not through Dad or Roger, and I think it's going to be great.'

'It sounds amazing, Seb. What's the client like?'

'Really cool. A guy from Lambeth council, and a woman from Southbank Centre. No issues about using an Oxford firm. Liked my international credentials. Both totally on board and forward-thinking. It's really cool.'

'That's brilliant, Seb. Cheers to you,' Desiree said as she raised her pale pink drink. A caramelised marshmallow languished across it on an ornamental toothpick.

Seb lifted his and met her toast. Floral cocktails weren't really to his taste, but if Desiree said it was a good pick, he knew it would be.

'Not bad,' he said, taking a sip. 'You even got me looking elegant drinking it,' he said as he pressed his sticky lips together. Desiree had to agree. He looked very sharp in his suit. 'So how about you? What are you up to? Is New York on the horizon?'

Desiree nodded.

'Not until late summer/early "fall" though now – as Williamsburg took a hit with the technicals. The legals out there are just so-o-o long winded. I blame Trump entirely, of course.'

'Of course.'

'That's OK, it gives me time to get my head around it. Finish up on Kew. Tie things up.'

'What things?'

Seb didn't really want to ask, and Desiree didn't really want to tell him.

'Oh, you know, the flat and stuff. How are the kids?'

'Good. We're off to Disney World tomorrow, for half-term.'

'Oh, wow! They must be super excited. If that's their thing...' Desiree looked puzzled. She couldn't really imagine either Millie or Jasper getting excited about the Magic Kingdom. Her parents had taken her and Matthew when they were in their early teens and they'd loved it, but they were different kinds of kids.

'Yeah...' He looked quiet and thoughtful, and drank some more of his sickly cocktail to hide that it really wasn't their thing. He was glad she wasn't asking who else he was going with, then sad that maybe she wouldn't care. He looked up. The sparkle in his eye had a chaotic edge; a heartbreaking hue.

'They really miss you.'

'I miss them, Seb. It's hard.'

'*I* miss you,' Seb confessed, surprising himself.

Desiree paused.

'Oh, Seb. I miss you too.' She squeezed his leg with one hand and put her cocktail down with the other. 'But... I'm moving on, I'm dating...'

Seb nodded enthusiastically, even though the news he'd expected felt like a punch in the gut.

'Who is he? I'll kill him...' he joked.

Desiree laughed, ignoring the question.

'Hence why New York has gotten a bit more complicated, you know? Working out whether to plough forward and move there together. Or not. It's early days.'

'No, really, who is he?' The joke in Seb's eyes had faded.

'You know Tarek?'

Seb nodded. He knew Tarek. He had guessed Tarek always had a thing for Desiree. He'd seen the puppy-dog eyes in the kitchen and the longing in the boardroom.

Dammit.

Tarek was ten years younger than him, handsome as hell, and a brilliant architect: studied in Singapore, trained at MIT and joined Rennie + Byrd two years ago.

They'll be the toast of New York.

'Look, there's a lot to work out. It's a tough one.'

Seb nodded.

'Hey, in fact I'm meeting him, with Jill and the client – you remember Lukas from DHP? They'd all love to see you.' Desiree looked at her watch and shuffled with her bag. 'Fancy it?'

Seb felt his heart pounding out of his chest. Then sighed as he twisted the fancy stick his marshmallow had been threaded on.

'No. I really have to get back. Pick the kids up. Pack. I'd better get going.' Seb nodded to the window out onto the South Bank, love and regret reflecting in his eyes in the early evening sunshine.

'OK, well, it really was great to bump into you,' Desiree said as she gathered her bag and the sharp cream blazer that had been threaded through its strap.

She looked in a hurry.

'You go, I'll get this...'

'You sure?'

Seb looked around for someone to pay as Desiree stood.

'Course!' He pressed his hands on his thighs and stood up as she kissed him on both cheeks, lingering at the second. To his surprise, he kissed her briefly on the lips and she returned it, sweet, and full of yearning. She sensed the optimism in him and didn't want to dampen it. They both laughed.

'OK, have a brilliant holiday, huh? Give Mickey my best and I'll give Jill yours.'

'Yeah, do. Not Tarek though...' Seb pulled back and gave a mock scowl.

Desiree laughed again, smoothed his forehead out with her thumb and hugged him tight. She knew he was joking. There was a playfulness about him that she wanted to ride; she didn't want to get heavy. She couldn't get heavy. She couldn't ask all the questions she wanted to.

'Let's catch up before I go to New York, yeah?'

Seb nodded. He wanted to tell her he loved her but knew that would be inappropriate.

Let her move on.

'That would be great.'

73

JUNE 2019, NORTHILL, OXFORDSHIRE

'God, it's almost ten-thirty! I really ought to get you home, Granny...'

'Before I turn into a pumpkin!' Violeta giggled mischievously.

Desiree smiled but didn't find it that funny. She'd kept her eighty-nine-year-old grandmother out way too long already and it would be at least an hour and a half to the south coast.

'And we have a train to catch!' Federico declared, half in panic. 'Come on, girls!'

He ushered Fatima, Mei-Xin and Gaby up out of the banquette as he straightened his suit.

'Do you need the loo, Granny? You've had enough rum...' Desiree gave Federico a guilty look while Violeta shook her wrinkled head.

'No, mija, todo bien...'

Federico smiled and held out a chivalrous hand to help Violeta up out of her seat. *'Gracias, señor,'* she said with a dainty nod.

'Encantado, mi reina,' he replied with a smile, almost curtseying as he said it.

'Shit, will we make it?' Fatima panicked.

'When was the last one?' Mei-Xin gasped.

'It's OK, we have time,' Gaby asserted. 'And we all have tickets, right?'

Desiree broke from putting Violeta's coat around her to hug her friends goodbye. She thanked them profusely for coming and said she'd see them back in London after the weekend. Federico hung back and looked at her as if it were more final than that.

'Look after yourself, will you?' he said, slightly dramatically.

'Of course!'

He hugged and squeezed her.

'And whatever you decide will be right. Tarek will be OK. He's made of strong stuff, you know.'

'I know...'

'Fede!' shouted Fatima from the door.

'Shit, better go. Violeta, *usted es la bomba*!' he said as he bowed, and Desiree went back to putting her coat and hat on her grandmother.

Clair, Dave, Millie and Jasper were making their move too, as Clair caught Desiree's eye and both women felt a strange unease that they might never actually see each other again.

'Are you heading off?' Clair asked, formally again.

'We should have left hours ago; couldn't tear you away, could I, Granny?' Desiree laughed, as she spruced up the felt flowers on Violeta's hat.

'Where are you parked? Would you like me to wait with Violeta?' Clair offered. 'Or, Dave, will we all fit in the car?'

'I had to park outside that little row of shops on York Road.'

'That's all right, we'll drop you there,' Dave said helpfully. 'Can't have either of you walking at this time of night...'

Dave's keys were already jangling in his hand.

'That'll be great, thanks,' Desiree said, looping her arm through Violeta's and checking she hadn't left anything behind.

74

NOEMIE

May 2019, Florida

In the hotdog queue just off Main Street, the smells of old frying oil
permeated Seb's nostrils under a large Goofy baseball cap with
droopy ears, making him feel slightly nauseous as well as ridiculous. Millie sighed next to him, lungs shrinking under her strappy
green vest, long legs golden in her denim hotpants that Seb
worried were too short for a theme park. He'd noticed teen boys
and flustered dads looking at his daughter, and it had added to his
general sense of ill ease walking around the park.

The magic of the Magic Kingdom was starting to wane, and as
Seb glanced from the queue over his shoulder to see Noemie
remonstrating with her daughters and a vacant looking Jasper and
Samuel not speaking to each other, he wondered if perhaps it
wasn't just him.

He exhaled forcibly, lest the chip-fat aromas weaken his addled
brain.

Reading his mind, Millie shuffled forward at his shoulder.

'Erm, Dad...'

Seb looked at her from under his cap.

'Do you mind if I hang by the pool tomorrow, if that's OK?' Millie seemed almost nervous to ask, which made Seb feel terrible.

'What's up, princess?'

'The others love it – and I love it – but I'm just a bit... Disney'd out. Do you mind if I just chill? I won't leave the complex, I'll just read and sunbathe...'

Millie leaned her head on her father's hot shoulder. His cream tee already dirty from roller-coaster seat belts, splashes and cotton candy.

Seb nodded as he pressed his palm to her cheek, bringing her head closer in.

The holiday *had* been exhausting so far. On the packed flight from London they were the family no one wanted to sit near: Gabriel screamed all the way over the Atlantic, hammering his ears with his fists, and after they settled into their capacious apartment just outside the theme parks, Noemie panicked and called Reception to call for a doctor. The duty doctor said it was just pressure from the flight and probably wasn't worth antibiotics, but prescribed a course anyway and some American equivalent of Calpol, which they already had in Gabriel's change bag. Before the doctor left, he handed Seb a bill for $950, which Seb put on his credit card as he felt bad enough that Noemie had paid for the trip.

Gabriel improved and the blended family hit Disney World the next morning with vigour. Three full days in and they were all feeling somewhat shattered – and that was without throwing the shouting into the mix.

Seb and Noemie had argued every night of the trip so far: on the first it had been about the doctor's bill – Seb hadn't told her how much the half-hour visit cost, so she rummaged through his wallet and when she saw the receipt she was angry.

On the second night, Seb said he was too tired for sex because Space Mountain had stolen his mojo – which he thought was funny, but Noemie threw a glass of iced water on his face after he fell asleep on the sofa watching *Mary Poppins Returns* with the kids, and they went to bed on bad terms.

On the third night, Noemie flipped after Seb asked her at dinner, in front of the kids, why she was so angry.

'We're on holiday! Don't sweat it!' he said, and she shouted at him in French and stormed out. Six pairs of eyes looked around the table at each other in silence.

But Seb was flummoxed. They were on holiday and he just couldn't understand why Noemie was so unhappy.

And last night they argued while the kids were having a swim and Seb and Noemie cooked dinner with Gabriel watching TV. Seb made an offhand comment about six children being plenty enough as it was.

'You don't want me?' Noemie had raged, while Seb was laying the table. A giant saucepan of corn on the cobs had been on a rolling boil, which Noemie had wanted to throw at his idiot face.

* * *

In the queue for hotdogs, as Seb pressed his palm to Millie's cheek, he felt so tired and drained, he thought he might fall asleep standing up. He could see where she was coming from.

'You too, huh?'

He ran his palm down Millie's golden-brown hair as she raised her head and looked into her dad's eyes. Her face was symmetrical and serious, her eyes world-weary. Seb marvelled at her beauty and smiled reassuringly.

'I'll go no further than the pool and I'll keep my phone on me all day so you'll know I'm OK. I promise I won't leave the complex or talk to any freaks.'

Millie was fighting a battle she didn't need to.

Seb nodded.

'My Millicent Fawcett, eh? My trailblazer, flipping Mickey the middle finger?'

'It's not that I'm not grateful—'

'Shhhh, I know. It's cool.'

Millie was bright and trustworthy – Seb thought he could probably leave her at the apartment complex for a day, if he asked the concierge to keep an eye out for her. But a seed of a thought had been brewing in his mind: it started over the Atlantic and grew as they landed. Now it was awakening with his rising fatigue.

'How do you fancy going to South Beach for a couple of days?'

Millie's gasp gave her a sense of renewal.

'Miami?' she asked, her eyes widening as the couple behind them urged them to shuffle one step nearer to the front of the queue.

'Remember how you loved *Iggy Peck, Architect* and *Rosie Revere, Engineer* when you were a kid?'

Millie's face lit up at the memory of her favourite childhood books.

'Yes! They were so cute – so... American!'

'Well, I don't know if you remember, I used to go to Miami a lot because of a hotel there...'

'The Elmore?' Millie asked, surprising herself that she did.

'Yes! It's where I bought those books actually, in a bookshop on Lincoln.' Seb was starting to wake up now too. 'Whenever I went I would think how much you and Jasper would love it. More and more as you've got older – and given we're so near.'

'*Is* it near?' Millie just assumed America was so big everywhere was far away.

'Only a few hours down the Turnpike...'

'Oh my god, I'd *love* that, Dad!' Millie had suddenly got her zing back.

'I can take you on an architectural tour. Jasper can photograph it. Stop for a shake at my favourite diner, if it's still there...'

'Yes!' Millie almost punched the air, before looking over at the hungry family, getting increasingly agitated waiting for hotdogs in the sunshine.

Millie's shoulders dropped a little.

'What, all of us?'

'No, just you and your brother. He wanted to do a photo project this holiday – there's no better place than South Beach.'

Millie curled her nose at the crowd around her.

'Beats taking photos of hicks in bad clothes or paedos dressed as Mickey...' she said flatly.

'Millie!' Seb cautioned.

'Well, it does.'

Seb nodded; she had a point.

'Just a day and a night. I can see if I can get us a suite at The Elmore. I think Beto is still general manager. I'll give him a call.'

As they neared the front of the queue Seb tried to remember the family order: three plain beef foot-longs with chips for Jasper, Samuel and Mila; a Hawaiian Island dog for Millie, a plant-based Bratwurst with sauerkraut for Noemie; 'Three Little Pigs' for Alice and a plain dog for Gabriel... and him? Seb didn't fancy any of it, but went with the Texas chilli cheese dog because it sounded so bad he hoped it would be good.

Millie wrapped her arms around her father's neck and leaned on his shoulder again, only this time with more vigour.

'Wow, Dad, that would be amazing,' she said gratefully as she squeezed him tight. It was nice to have a quiet moment to hug him. He put his arms around her waist and pulled her in. She inhaled his scent and appreciated the moment. Millie didn't feel she could hug her dad with Noemie around. 'But, erm, what about... you know...?'

'Leave that with me, she'll be cool.'

Millie released her hands from his neck and looked down at her flip-flops.

'I heard you arguing again last night. Before dinner.'

Seb looked embarrassed. He hadn't thought they could hear by the pool.

'Did you?'

'Yeah, she was raging, Dad.'

'Oh, princess, I'm sorry.'

He squeezed her again.

'I nearly came in but didn't want to be shouted at myself... sorry.'

'Hey, you have nothing to be sorry about!' Seb said, lowering his head to meet her eyes. He took off his Goofy hat and could see Millie's bottom lip starting to shake. 'Oh, Mills! Don't worry. I'll deal with that part. I think she's just tired...' He spun the hat on his free finger and they both watched ears fly around like helicopter blades. 'From Gabriel and the excitement of everything, it is full-on. Maybe we *all* need a pool day.'

* * *

Back at the apartment suite, as they got changed and Seb and Noemie considered their dinner options, he stood in the bedroom doorway clutching a bunch of restaurant leaflets and flyers, shower fresh in a lilac T-shirt and trousers. Noemie sat on the bed, putting make-up on in a hurry. Millie was helping Mila through the shower while the other kids sat almost on top of each other, sucking thumbs and staring at *Spongebob Squarepants* on the TV.

'Hey, er, do you mind if I take Millie and Jasper off for a night – tomorrow – show them the hotel I built in Miami?'

Noemie froze, shimmer shadow on one finger, compact mirror held at her face. Her body didn't move but her eyes looked at Seb. Wide and bewildered.

Seb carried on talking in an unusually wittery, jittery, English way.

'It's just they've heard me talk about it so much – it was such a pivotal part of my work when they were younger and I did all these trips; brought back all this stuff; it would be great to show them the hotel for real...'

Noemie lowered her mirror and knitted her eyebrows, a look of hurt and befuddlement on her pretty face.

'What?' she almost whispered. 'We're on 'oliday!'

'Yeah, but... you know, I think my two could do with a day off Disney. I'd just take them overnight. Go tomorrow afternoon maybe. Look around Miami, stay one night and come back in the morning. If we leave early enough we can be back by the time the park opens on Thursday.'

'Is it not really far to Miami?' Noemie dropped her eyeshadow pot back into her make-up bag with a clunk.

'My phone says four hours.'

Noemie looked utterly confused.

'You don't like it here?'

'No, I do... it's just...'

'Everything I thought about and planned for your birthday?'

'No, I know, I'm grateful, I just—'

'What about the paddleboarding and inflatables? I booked it all. For you!'

'That's Friday. We'll be back in plenty of time for that.'

Noemie looked blindsided, and Seb felt an increasingly familiar pit of dread in his stomach. She threw down her compact mirror and got up from the bed. Her hair was wet and slicked back, her short cropped halter top revealed her tight six-pack over a floaty skirt.

'I can't believe you're doing this,' she said quietly. 'You're so cruel!' She almost smiled as she said it, a manic smile that looked as if it could turn to tears.

Seb inhaled deeply in the doorway but said nothing. He looked over his shoulder, at the kids on the sofa, mesmerised by mindless television.

'Is this about last night?' Noemie asked.

Seb didn't know exactly what she meant – it could have been about any night, to be honest. But he didn't say that – her hurt face was so beautiful.

'No, no... it's about my kids. This is their half-term too, and I think a day doing something different would be good for them. They're not as into the whole Disney thing as your kids,' he said, although now he thought about it, none of them had seemed all that into it. Maybe Alice and Mila.

Noemie untied and readjusted the neck on her top, her small biceps flexing behind her head as if she were about to go into battle.

'Ungrateful brats.'

Seb dropped the restaurant and takeaway leaflets on the sideboard by the door.

'What did you say?'

'It just seem a bit ungrateful, Seb. I bring them to the most fun place in the world and they want to take their daddy away from me.'

Seb, still gobsmacked that she had called his children brats, rubbed his chin and tried to think. 'They're in a foreign country without their mother; I need to consider their needs too.'

'Oh, right, that's how it is...' Noemie nodded, furiously.

'With all respect, they didn't ask to come here. They've had a brilliant few days, but they're exhausted. We could all do with a day off. Why don't you spend the day by the pool when we're in Miami?'

'Oh, yeah, fat lot of fun that will be with the kids, thanks, Seb!'

The sun-kissed rash at the base of his neck was creeping up to his throat. His need to get away rising with it.

'Samuel will help you. There's a crèche here, for fuck's sake!' He tried to say it as gently as he could.

'Why are you being like this with me?' Noemie begged. 'You break my heart! I do something nice for you that nearly kills me and you treat me like dog shit. You humiliate me! This was meant to be fun!'

Seb bit his lip. He didn't want to say that without her – causing friction, shouting at the kids, stressing about every minute thing, her mania racing a million miles per hour – the holiday *would* be fun. But it wasn't. They were all miserable in the Magic Kingdom, and she seemed to be the most miserable and angry of all of them.

Noemie started pacing the large bedroom, with its dark mahogany furniture, as oppressive as the atmosphere, as she looked for her bag and all the kids' paraphernalia she crammed it with. Her breath started to become shallow as she furiously stuffed baby wipes, playing cards and packets of Le Petit Beurre biscuits into it.

Seb could feel it coming. He pushed the door to a little behind him.

'I did this for you, and this is how you treat me?' Her soft voice started to harden, to get louder, until she bellowed: 'Happy fucking birthday, Seb! You use me and go off with your kids. Have fun! You piece of shit.'

As she shouted, she dropped her bag and picked up an unused marble ashtray, sitting on the shelf below the large television unit, and threw it, with two raging hands, right in Seb's direction.

'Fuck!' he shouted, ducking out of the way so the ashtray struck the doorframe behind his head, chipping and splintering part of the architrave away. The ashtray smashed into sharp shards and chipped the tiled floor.

Seb froze. Shell-shocked and scared, a hand on each temple. Noemie, horrified at what she had just done, clasped her shaking hands to her face and started to cry.

Jasper opened the bedroom door and saw the mess. His meek face looked forlorn.

'Dad?' he asked cautiously. 'Are you OK?'

Millie followed closely, looked over Jasper's shoulder and gasped.

'Dad?' she asked, more sternly but still nervous and unsure. Looking from a paralysed Noemie shaking and whining, to the ashtray on the floor at their father's feet. 'Daddy, are you OK?'

'Yeah, we're all good,' he said, nodding at Noemie. 'Pack an overnight bag, each of you, we're going to Miami,' Seb said gently, not taking his eyes off Noemie, still standing at the foot of the bed shaking.

'Tonight?' Millie frowned. 'I thought you said tomorrow...'

Noemie put her hand to her heart and tried to speak through her open crying mouth.

'You plan this with her?' she implored. 'You plan this all along? You piece of fucking dog shit.'

Jasper looked startled.

'Change of plan, princess,' Seb said to Millie without turning around. 'We'll head off in half an hour. Go get some things.'

* * *

The dusk ride was sombre and sedate, but the car was filled with an air of relief. For most of the journey down the I-95 highway in their massive rental car, they sat in silence. Jasper looking at the photos he'd taken on his digital SLR screen, Millie entrusted with Spotify, as she looked between her playlist and views out of the window. The highway was palm-tree lined in places; pelicans flew past the windows as they approached West Palm Beach and continued into the evening, the lights of the city's skyscrapers illuminating their path. Seb paused Ed Sheeran to put a call in to Beto, hoping he'd remember him.

'Hey, man!' he said over the car speakers. 'Of course! Come right on over, I'll get you the best suite we have! It'll be great to see you again my friend...'

Millie and Jasper giggled at the man's enthusiasm for their dad, and they carried on for the rest of the way, handing the keys over to the valet outside The Elmore an hour later.

At 9 p.m. they were in the penthouse, Millie and Jasper gasping and running the length of it, before they called room service, ordered club sandwiches and watched *Black Panther* on the enormous screen on a wall between two windows that looked out to the Atlantic beyond it. They didn't mention Noemie once, and as Seb climbed in the huge double bed, his son and daughter eschewing their own palatial bedrooms to lie either side of their dad, he watched them sleep, safe and secure. Millie, her ombre hair like a curtain over her sweeping eyelashes. Jasper, his birdlike features tense even in his most relaxed state. As Seb watched CNN on low volume with subtitles, he sent Noemie a late-night text saying he hoped she and the kids were OK – he was more worried for the kids than he was for her – and that he'd be back on Thursday morning. She didn't reply. But the relief he felt of being away from her helped him drift into the best night's sleep he'd had in ages.

* * *

In the morning Noemie sent Seb a text saying:

I'm sorry. I love you.

Seb replied:

Sorry I took the car – use the shuttle bus if you're going to the park – it leaves from the front desk every 15 minutes.

That was it. Functional and practical. The emotions needed putting aside for a few days.

At breakfast on the street, as vintage convertible cars whizzed up Collins, Millie called Clair on FaceTime while she was on her lunchbreak at the John Radcliffe.

'Miami! How? Why?'

Clair knew there was more to the story than the kids were letting on, but she could see they were happy and healthy – and they didn't want to worry her so they kept it light and protected their dad – but she looked at Seb pointedly and said she'd call him after her shift.

After filling up on pancakes with bacon and French toast, they headed to the Wolfsonian for opening time, where Millie got lost in an exhibition of Cuban magazine covers and Jasper started taking pictures. But it was too sunny to stay indoors, so Seb led the kids on a walking tour around the Art Deco district between 10th and 15th streets, zigzagging between Washington, Collins and Ocean Drive, past Essex House, The Carlyle, the Clevelander and the Breakwater, the kids marvelling when Seb told them that the ground beneath them used to be a tropical swamp.

Millie loved the Versace mansion and the Miami Modern buildings, Jasper particularly loved Española Way, although most of the time he spent looking through his lens.

At lunch they sat in the 11th Street Diner, a former Art Deco railroad dining car, restored and polished to shiny silver perfection, as they scrolled through the photos on Jasper's camera.

'You've got some great pictures there, buddy,' Seb said proudly as a waitress brought buffalo wings, a pulled pork melt and a waffle fried chicken sandwich, with three gargantuan milkshakes in three different colours. They spent a minute working out which milkshake was which, until Millie had blood orange, Jasper had peanut butter and Seb had French vanilla.

'The food's way better here than at Disney,' Millie enthused, pulling apart a chicken wing.

'I know right.' Seb shrugged. 'Best diner in the world huh? I knew you'd love it.'

For a few minutes more they sat in fast-food bliss. Then Jasper broke the happy silence, his mouth straightening into an anxious line.

'Are we going back to her, Dad?'

Seb finished his mouthful and wiped ketchup from the corner of his lips onto a tissue napkin.

'Yes, we are. Tomorrow. Noemie brought us here. We'll go back, we'll have a brilliant last couple of days. We still haven't seen the light parade and we've got all the lakeside fun on Friday. It'll be great!'

'I kind of want to stay here,' Millie said, looking guiltily between her brother and her dad.

'Well, we're not going back yet. We'll go in the morning. And when we do we'll have a great time. We've got one more day at Disney, so let's make the most of it. We've hired paddleboards – apparently there's the best ice cream in the world at the lake. You'll have so many cool stories to tell your friends.'

Neither seemed that excited, but they focused on the here and now, the best food in the best diner with the best dad in the world.

* * *

When Clair called back on Seb's phone, he took it out of his pocket guardedly and told the kids it was a work call.

'Order me the most ridiculous dessert you can,' he said as he excused himself from the booth and stepped outside into the hot sunshine, finding a strip of shade against the diner exterior wall so he could see Clair on his phone.

'So what's the real deal, Seb? Are the kids OK?'

She was still in her scrubs, leaning against the spiky exterior wall of the hospital, pebble-dashed and grey, and he could see smokers outside the hospital doors beyond her. 'I've been worried all afternoon.'

'Nothing to worry about, really.'

Seb told Clair that there had been a little trouble in paradise, but the kids were fine – better than ever. And they'd rejoin Noemie in a day or two.

'Shit, Seb. You walked out on her?'

Clair shook her head; she knew how heartbreaking that felt. But part of her was immensely relieved that this time it wasn't her. That maybe he wasn't as into this new woman as she had feared. Anyone who would try to take her children out of the country without their mother's permission, or spend god knew how much on a holiday with a new boyfriend, was clearly unhinged. She could tell from Millie's texts that she was holding something back. Clair didn't really want the kids around unhinged, but had tried not to say so.

He didn't tell her about the marble ashtray – she would have told him to come home immediately.

'Really, it's fine. We just needed a breather – it was pretty intense. She was fine about it.'

Clair knew Seb was lying and gave him a doubtful look.

'As long as the kids are OK.'

'They are – god, you should see how into the Deco stuff Millie is! And Jaspy has been taking loads of pictures. He wants to make a photobook when we get home. They love it here, Clair. *I* love it here.'

'I love you Seb,' Clair blurted. Before she leaned her head back on the hospital wall and put the back of her hand to her forehead. She rubbed her tired eyes.

'Hey?' Seb laughed.

Clair paused, her face flushed red, her hair dishevelled after a long shift. Then she lifted her head and looked straight into the screen.

'I love you, Seb. I mean, I hated you for a few years, but I love you. I love how good a father you are. They're OK?'

'They're OK.'

Seb smiled, appreciatively. He then saw his smile reflected in the shiny exterior of the diner, on the face of a man in shorts and a lilac T-shirt clutching a phone. The man looked so happy his heart swelled. It was all he wanted. To be a constant, solid, honest father. No curveballs, like his dad had thrown him. That was why he was so adamant he would take Millie and Jasper out of the toxic situation, the anger in Orlando.

'I love you too,' Seb said. There was a pause while they looked at each other and tried to understand what that meant. An ocean between them had opened up and subsided again. But all they felt was gratitude and friendship.

A neon-pink sign saying COCKTAILS & DINNERS buzzed in the diner window, an illumination in the bright daylight, bringing Seb back to where he was.

'I'll make sure the kids FaceTime this afternoon, before you go to bed, yeah?'

* * *

Millie and Jasper overruled their dad on the pudding as they were all so full from lunch (and had spotted a cool yogurt parlour further up Ocean Drive that morning), so they spent the afternoon ambling in the sunshine, taking pictures, walking the boardwalk, dodging the tourists clumsily riding segues, laughing at the beefcakes working out, marvelling at the magazine photo shoots, until they all stopped at the same time, outside an art gallery with a large glass window and a familiar-looking painting on the wall inside it.

'Oh my god!' Millie said. 'I so recognise that! Didn't you...?'

Seb nodded.

'It's still there!' he said to himself. 'Let's go in.'

He opened the door and let Millie and Jasper pass through it as a gallery worker nodded and said, 'Hi, how are ya?' while the three of them scattered around the light and airy space, taking in all the pictures. Except they couldn't help the pull of the painting they recognised. Jasper raised his lens.

'Oh, I'm sorry, no pictures,' said a woman in an origami-style dress. 'But there are postcards in the gallery shop through there...' She pointed. Seb and Jasper gave each other a knowing look – the officious gallery manager couldn't know Seb had already bought a large, numbered, limited-edition print of it anyway.

Millie sidled up behind them.

'It's bigger, more colourful, more... impressive in real life.'

They all tilted their heads gently in unison.

'Where's your one, Daddy? I don't remember it going, but it's not there any more, is it?' Jasper asked.

'Desiree has it. And she might have even given it to Violeta, I don't know.'

'It's cool,' Millie said. 'So old-fashioned.'

Millie and Jasper had never even had a modern landline in their home. All they knew was mobiles. These archaic dial phones looked like something from another era, a lifetime ago.

'Yeah,' Seb said, fixated in awe. Hands in his shorts pockets. He had seen the original here before, six years ago, but only now, as he got lost in the mechanical cables, wires, communication, as he got lost in cogs and conversations, it made his heart actually hurt. He pictured her. Her dimples. The way her eyes lit up, the same rich gilded glimmer as much of the painting. The same glimmering ochre as Klimt's kiss. And he took a deep breath.

'I miss her...' Jasper mused.

Seb looked at him in surprise.

'Huh?'

'Desiree, I miss her,' he said.

'Me too,' Seb said as he rubbed Jasper's back.

* * *

Seb bought a postcard of *Long Distance Relationships* from the gift shop, and late afternoon, as the kids called Clair and gave her a grand tour of the penthouse, Seb sat at the suite's desk, looking out to the ships harboured on Dodge Island with the sun setting behind them. The enormous cruise liners heading to the Caribbean, the Panama Canal, or Europe. The Disney Cruise ship, identifiable by the huge black silhouette of Mickey's head and ears atop it. Under its foreboding gaze, Seb wrote the postcard, and put it in his jacket pocket for the concierge.

'Right, let your mama get to bed. We're going to a fish shack for dinner...'

75

JUNE 2019, NORTHILL, OXFORDSHIRE

'Thank you, Dave,' Desiree said as she edged out of the back seat and stepped onto the dark pavement behind her car. Clair breathed a sigh of relief, easing Jasper off her lap as she followed. It had felt a bit weird to be sitting thigh-to-thigh to the woman who had ruined her life.

Desiree opened the passenger seat at the front to help Violeta out.

'No problem. Where are you stopping tonight?' Dave asked as he mirrored Desiree in case Violeta needed more help. Dave was a man who was interested in logistics.

'Oh, there's a little hotel along the seafront from Granny's care home, that'll do me. I'll take her out for breakfast, then head home in the morning.'

She looked at Violeta's subdued face. That was if they made it that far. It was getting so late she thought she might have to stop halfway at her parents'.

Clair ushered the kids out so they could say a proper goodbye to Desiree, and they stood side by side waiting in the night while Desiree helped Violeta into the Smart car and buckled her in, laying a blanket snugly around her. Millie and Jasper wanted to laugh – she looked like a little caterpillar in a cocoon. One wearing enormous glasses and a floral hat.

Desiree turned around, straightened herself out, then said, 'Come here...' to Millie and Jasper, feeling free to hug them now, as Clair watched on smiling. She put an arm around each of them and squeezed them in.

'You guys stay in touch, yes? I want to hear all about what you're up to.'

'Sure.' They both nodded.

'Message me any time you need anything,' she said to Millie. 'In London... or if I do ever make it to New York, you're always welcome to visit.'

Millie gasped quietly as Desiree gave Clair a look of *that means you too*.

Jasper seemed too tired to contemplate anything except curling up under his rocking robots bedding and sleeping for the whole weekend. Perhaps his dad might even visit him in his dreams.

'Sounds excellent.' Clair smiled as the kids got back into the Skoda.

'Come on, you, bed...' Dave said to the collective.

Desiree and Clair stood on the pavement, the row of shops – a bakery, a paper shop, a small post office and a hairdresser – all closed behind them.

'Good luck, yes?' Clair said, formally. This was when they knew the hard work really started.

'Yes, you too,' Desiree replied. 'Can't wait to see the wedding pictures – I hope it all goes well and you just... enjoy it.' They looked at each other as Clair nodded.

'Thank you.'

To Desiree's utter surprise Clair threw her arms around her, squeezing her swiftly, the woman who had broken her heart; the woman her husband had left her for; the woman who had made her feel sick and broken and inadequate. The woman who was standing alone with nothing except a long journey into the night ahead of her.

Desiree squeezed her back.

'Drive safely, yes?'

Desiree smiled, before getting into the car.

She looked over at Violeta, who was already asleep, as Dave, Clair and the kids pulled off from behind her, back to the house on Priory Green.

'Come on, then, Granny,' Desiree said to the silence. 'Let's get you home.'

76

NOEMIE

May 2019, Florida

'Stop it, girls! *Arrêtez ça!*'

The shout made Millie jump, but she calmed herself by focusing on Gabriel and the breadstick house of cards she was building for him on the checked picnic blanket. He was so transfixed at the tower he didn't notice his mother get up and slap his older sisters each on the back of the head. They had been bickering over a cheese triangle until it was crushed in Alice's hand. Spiteful eyes taking pleasure as Mila failed in her efforts to grab it, until worms of processed cheese oozed out of tears in the broken foil.

Noemie continued to shout at her daughters in French: things Millie didn't understand but she got the gist of, as she entertained Gabriel and stole glances at his mother. Millie couldn't help thinking how ridiculous Noemie looked, standing on the banks of a beautiful lake, watermelon slice in one hand, shouting at her daughters while wearing a white bikini so small Millie could almost see her entire bottom.

'*Arrêtez de vous battez maintenant!*' Noemie shouted, as she dragged Mila away, almost by her hair, and pulled her onto the rug where Millie was sitting with Gabriel.

'*Assieds-toi et tais-toi!*' she commanded, before wafting her brow with an *ooh la la*.

As Mila complained about the cheese in her hair, Millie scanned the lake side for Samuel, waiting in the queue for one of the famous ice creams that just looked like a Mr. Whippy to her, from a hut by the water's edge. His face was melancholy, not that of a child about to buy an ice cream. Beyond him Millie tried to make out the figures of her dad and Jasper on the lake, to see what fun they were having, but she couldn't see them, there were too many paddleboarders, windsurfers, jet-skiers and waterskiers between them and her. Still, she imagined how they might be laughing and wished she were with them. It felt safer than being on the bank of the lake with Noemie and her kids.

'We'll take it in turns,' her dad had said. 'Jasper first, then you, that OK?' Millie had nodded OK and the minutes dragged while she waited. She decided to build another breadstick level, hoping Gabriel would smash it down so she would have something else to do.

Start again.

Noemie peeled the triangle of her bikini top down and rubbed Piz Buin into her nipples.

'You 'ad some lunch, Millie? Help yourself...' She gestured.

Millie looked at the cool box and rug, the spread Noemie had gathered from the breakfast buffet in the resort's restaurant, and didn't fancy any of it. She had a sick feeling in her stomach.

'Thanks, I'm not hungry.' She smiled politely, with a slight shake of her head.

'Is Samuel getting you an ice?'

'No, I really don't fancy anything.'

Noemie studied Millie's face and tried to guess what she was thinking. She rubbed cream on the small moles under her boobs and Millie tried not to look.

'What you get up to with your dad in Miami, huh?'

'Oh, nothing,' Millie answered nervously, turning back to the breadstick tower. She didn't want to say what a cool time they'd had. How they had pleaded with their dad to spend longer there – Beto, the hotel manager, had said at breakfast on Thursday morning, *'Mi casa su casa...'* and invited Seb and the kids to stay longer. But Seb had said they had to get back to Orlando; they had a flight to catch.

On the drive back north Jasper asked his dad why he had lied and he said he didn't really know: they sort of did in a few days. After a silence Seb admitted he was worried about Samuel, Alice, Mila and Gabriel. He needed to help them all get home. But there was fun to be had on the lake first.

'It couldn't have been nothing. Nothing sounds boring!' Noemie said, her half-smile veiling her deep-rooted anger.

'Oh, you know, we just hung out...'

Noemie didn't like the teenager's frugality with words. She didn't like not knowing what Millie knew. She didn't like the fact that Seb would choose Millie over her if push came to shove. She dropped her sunglasses from her head to her nose to obscure her ire, and slicked back her oiled blonde hair as she slumped onto the picnic blanket and angled her pert boobs at the sun.

* * *

'Squeeze your stomach muscles, Jaspy, that'll give you more control...'

Jasper stood gingerly and tried to balance his puny frame on the paddleboard as small waves created by a passing jet-ski made it wobble.

'Dad!' he gasped.

'Arghhh!' Seb wanted to berate the driver for making his boy more nervous, but he knew he was long gone and wouldn't hear, so he suppressed his swear words and shook his head from his own board bobbing on the water.

'It's OK, just stand firm – strong legs – engage your tummy muscles, like you're trying to squeeze a six-pack. It'll help centre you.'

'Can I just sit down, Dad? Until the waves go?'

'Of course you can, buddy. Stay there...'

Jasper hesitantly lowered himself and sat cross-legged on the board. Clutching his paddle tensely, his knuckles white.

Seb paddled over and held onto Jasper's board so they could ride the waves caused by the jet-ski together. He reached it, steadied the board and kissed Jasper's head, noticing how long his wet lashes looked; how his light freckles sparkled in the sunshine. He thought Jasper must have the sweetest face in the world.

'What...?' Jasper asked self-consciously.

'You're beautiful, you are,' Seb declared. 'So handsome... you must get it from me.' Jasper gave a scowl and looked back at the water.

'Samuel said I looked like a gimp in my life jacket.'

'A gimp, did he?' Seb tried not to laugh, although he was half outraged that anyone would insult his son. It had just sounded funny the way Jasper said it.

'And that I'm a dork for doing paddleboarding.'

'You're neither a gimp nor a dork. You're my hero!'

Jasper looked quietly pleased with himself.

'No other bugger was coming out with me on the lake. Except

you and Millie. Samuel was probably scared and trying to deflect from his fear.'

Jasper didn't look convinced.

'Samuel's not been very nice to me since we got back. He called me a traitor and said his mum hates me.'

Jasper looked hopeless and Seb felt terrible. He pulled their boards closer, so they practically overlapped.

Jasper felt comfort in the cool water.

'Hey-y-y... Sam's probably jealous, buddy. He probably wanted to get away to Miami too. I'm sure he doesn't mean it.' They sat in silence, looking at the water return to its shimmering, stiller state. 'It can't be that easy for him. He has a lot on his shoulders. Looking after his little sisters and brother.'

'I'm glad I don't have any little sisters or brothers.'

Seb laughed to himself and looked around.

'Come on, want to try again?'

Jasper nodded, unravelled his legs and stood up carefully, while Seb tried to hold his board steady.

'That's it, strong stomach,' he said, looking at Jasper's skinny frame. Seb heard what felt like the hum of a wasp irritating his ear, except it came with a whoosh and a wave; a speedboat that was so close, the waves knocked Jasper off and he fell into the lake with a scream.

'Dad!'

'FUCKING IDIOT!' Seb shouted, as he saw the back end of a silver-haired man, whizzing off, legs akimbo on waterskis and totally out of control. 'Jasper!'

Jasper had fallen off the other side of the board and was flailing in his red life jacket, his jagged, panicked moves and the sharp waves putting distance between the two boards. Seb clamoured to reach the edge of Jasper's, to steady it for his son on the other side, but the act of trying only pushed his board further away.

'It's OK, Jaspy! You have a life jacket on! You're OK!'

Jasper's limbs were thrashing, his face pale and panicked as he searched around for his paddle.

'Just lie on your back, Jasper!' Seb commanded. 'Don't worry about the paddle, just lie there and I'll come round and get it!'

'I feel seasick!' Jasper said weakly as he tried to tread water furiously.

'You don't need to panic, you will float if you lie on your back and do nothing. I'm coming.'

As the distance between Seb and his son grew, he climbed up on his board, picked up his paddle and started to glide through the choppy water. 'Just do nothing!' he called. From the board he could see the speedboat turn in a large circle and start to head back round to them again.

Surely he saw us.

'HEY!' Seb bellowed. He waved his oar in the air so the driver would definitely see them. 'THERE ARE PEOPLE HERE!'

He made his arms and body big, like a goalkeeper about to save a penalty, but it looked as if the boat was actually approaching and he had to get Jasper out of the water and up on his board at least.

'HEY!'

The boat was heading closer, so Seb paddled faster. Ferocity in his biceps.

Surely he will see Jasper.

Surely he will see me.

'Dad!' Jasper cried, in a panic seeing the fear on his father's face.

Seb narrowed his eyes to focus on the driver in the sunshine. Then waved his paddle again as the boat continued to approach.

'PEOPLE HERE, TURN!' Seb bellowed so hard his throat was rasping, but the boat was still heading in their direction. 'STOP!'

As the boat got nearer Seb could see the driver: a younger man with a baseball cap on backwards, can of drink in his hand. He wasn't even looking forwards towards them. He was laughing at the man on waterskis at the back of the boat.

'HEY! NO! STOP!'

Seb felt as if he was shouting underwater, his voice drowned out by the sound of the speedboat's motor, by the music playing from a ghetto blaster on top of it – and he could see it heading straight in Jasper's direction.

'JASPER! GET ON YOUR BOARD! STAND TALL!'

Jasper felt seasick. The nausea and the panic and the taste of the water making him retch on the surface of the lake.

'Dad!'

'STOP!' Seb roared. 'MY SON!'

Seb looked between the speedboat and Jasper, pale and helpless floating and kicking in the water, and could see the two were about to collide. He unzipped his life jacket and cast it away as he dived off his board and swam, as strong and as fast as he could, fighting the ripples and the waves as the boat got closer on its collision course.

'Dad!' Jasper shouted with a smile in relief as Seb reached him.

'NO!' he yelled back as he pushed Jasper's head under the water, impinged by his life vest, plunging him as low as his arm could manage so he didn't rise to the surface with his flotation jacket. Jasper was confused and terrified, limbs flailing and fighting his father as he wondered what the hell was going on. Why the person he trusted most in the world was seemingly trying to kill him. Jasper's lungs weren't full – he hadn't had time to gasp for air before being thrust under – so he fought and kicked and tore at his dad. As Seb plunged his son as deep as he could, he was struck by the boat – the tussle suddenly over and Jasper free to float to the top.

77

JUNE 2019, NORTHILL, OXFORDSHIRE

Desiree blinked to refresh her eyesight as the green road signs, lit by dull spotlights in the night, started to merge into each other on the repetitive lines of the A34. Was it fatigue or sorrow blurring her vision? Neither was conducive to getting Granny home safely.

She had decided to plough on through – a detour to Guildford would take almost as long as getting straight to the care home – so she turned on the radio and flicked from 5 Live to 6 Music. She listened to an electronica artist from Morocco singing in Amazigh-Berber. The music was like nothing she'd heard before: emotive, eerie and haunting, all to a rousing beat, and as Desiree zoomed down the country in a near-trance, she turned the volume down, so as not to disturb Granny, who kept emitting little puffs of air from her thin mouth in her sleep.

As the miles and the motorway peeled away behind her, and rabbits nibbled and hopped on grass verges in the headlights, Desiree dreamily remembered the phone call that came when she least expected it. When her world came crashing down. Shattering an epiphany.

It was a sunny Saturday morning last month and she was

running, her first long run to the river. She had been building up to it. Coming out of her heartache from the split with Seb last summer, she'd taken up running again. Starting out tentatively around Clapham Common. Running and healing and building it up through winter, gaining the strength to leave Clapham Common and extend her route to Battersea Park. That day she was planning to cross the river and run to Hyde Park. Perhaps stop at the Serpentine and dip her toes before running back – or getting a cab if she couldn't, but that would be OK too. Her target was to cross the river.

She had so much to think about. Seb. Tarek. New York. Everything was clear now, everything made sense. Through bandstands, refreshed by fountains, past a peace pagoda, feeling music and joy in her heart as she weaved. Even when she had to cross the noisy busy roads, she felt an elation in her heels.

As Desiree approached the majestic red and white steel suspension bridge and the Thames, she felt proud of herself. It was there, laid out ahead of her. The final stretch to the other side, all she had to do was leap.

She was over halfway across Chelsea Bridge when her phone rang, and the spark in her heart was extinguished.

It was Penelope.

They'd only spoken twice on the phone since the split. She was intrigued.

She stopped and leaned against the blue-grey railings.

'Penelope!' she said, her voice brimming full of hope.

There was no sound at the other end.

'Hello? Hello?' She looked at her phone screen. 'Penelope...? I think you might have mis-dialled.'

'He's gone.'

'What?'

Penelope could barely speak.

'There's been a terrible accident. On the water. In America. My baby is gone. I'm so, so sorry, Desiree.'

Desiree's legs buckled underneath her, her knees slamming onto the concrete, her face hitting one of the railings.

'What? NO!'

Penelope told Desiree what had happened. That Martin, Jake and Clair were on a flight right now. That she was helpless and stuck in Guernsey, and the two women cried down the phone at each other until a passer-by asked Desiree if she was OK. Until her brother Matthew came to rescue her and took her back to his apartment. Until Shirlie and Timothy stroked her to sleep.

As she drove into the night and this most harrowing day came to an end, Desiree realised the bruises on her knees had faded, but the pain of Seb's loss would always be there.

'Nearly home, Granny,' she whispered as they curved around the Solent and onto Portsea Island.

78

CLAIR

May 2019, Florida

'Oh my god!' Clair cried as she walked into the complex manager's office less than twenty-four hours later. A shell-shocked pair, huddled together on a bench seat, jumped up and into their mother's arms in sobs. Martin and Jake stood outside the office and heard the roars of grief from the children. Martin shook as he looked to the pool, empty because all the guests were having fun at the theme parks. An inflatable flamingo bobbed in the afternoon sun.

The complex manager, a man named Mr Edwards, but he said everyone could call him Earl, and a police liaison officer who told the kids they could call her Betsy, welcomed Clair in, and stepped outside so Clair could have a private moment with her children. Meanwhile they explained to Sebastian Cooper's father and best friend what had happened on the lake: that the boy was unharmed but his father was in the hospital morgue and needed identification.

'His girlfriend...' the manager with Hollywood teeth and bright skin said. 'His girlfriend has been sedated; my colleague Marissa is in the suite with her, checking that her little ones are OK.'

'Are her kids OK?' Jake asked, bewildered to be asking after children he had never met. When they'd come to a BBQ in the Cotswolds at Easter, she had left the kids at home with the au pair. He couldn't even remember their names.

The officer nodded.

'Yes, sir. They've all been looking after each other. And those two in there have done a great job,' she said, nodding towards the room. 'Ms Morel was completely beside herself, a doctor at the scene administered Valium and the house doctor here has been keeping everything calm while we waited for their mother and you.'

'Really, your grandkids in there,' Earl said with a small smile, pointing through the glass. 'They've been wonderful. Holding everyone together while their world falls apart.'

'Christ,' Martin said, looking up to the sky, before putting his hand over his mouth.

'And the driver? Of the speedboat?' Jake asked the police officer.

Betsy gave a reassuring nod.

'He's in police custody, sir, over at the county sheriff's office. His blood alcohol concentration was above legal limits and he's being transferred over to Orlando.'

'Is it a crime to be—?'

'It is, sir, it's a federal crime to be under the influence at the helm of a boat.' She nodded.

'And do we know if anyone is coming out for Noemie? For the kids?' Martin asked Earl and Betsy.

'Ms Morel's mother is on a flight now,' Betsy answered, looking at her watch. 'She lands in about two hours... Mr Edwards has arranged for a driver to collect her and bring her here. We assume she will be taking her daughter and grandchildren home, and that these guys will be going with their mother. Is that correct?'

Jake looked at Martin, who nodded.

'Thank you, Officer,' Martin said formally.

'Not at all,' said Betsy. 'I'm sorry for your loss, sir.'

79

DESIREE

June 2019, Spice Island, Hampshire

'She really shouldn't have been out for so long, Miss Campbell. Her routine is going to be all over the shop tomorrow.'

Sue, the night manager of the Spice Island Causeway Care Home, had curly hair in the shape of a helmet and the appearance of an angry headteacher from the 1970s.

'Well, she had a great day!' Desiree countered. 'Made loads of friends. Ate well. Had a nap. And, look, she's fine!'

Violeta smiled in her nightie as she folded her enormous glasses onto the bedside table and swung her little legs up for Desiree to tuck in.

Desiree was glad she hadn't stopped for the night at her parents'. It would have been as much hassle to find the key under the secret stone, turn off the alarms and get Granny into the spare room as it had been just to power on through. It was the right choice. She looked like a content old woman, in her own plump bed as Desiree released the pins that kept her plaits twisted in a bun, and they came tumbling down to her shoulders. Violeta gave a little hiccup and giggled; Desiree hoped Sue wouldn't smell the rum.

She'll sleep well.

'OK, well, visitors shouldn't be here at this hour... if you don't mind.'

Oh, fuck off!

'Look, just give me a second to say goodnight, yes?'

Desiree's tone was now as short as Sue's, and Sue knew not to mess.

'I'll wait by the front door to let you out.'

Desiree watched Sue leave, trying not to mutter 'For fuck's sake' as the door closed behind her, and turned back to Violeta. She cupped her grandmother's wrinkled hands in her smooth ones. She kissed the wedding ring on her left hand. Violeta Cruz hadn't taken it off in sixty-nine years and one hundred and seventeen days. Since the day she married Wilfred Campbell.

'Thank you for today, Granny.'

'No problem, *mija*...' She gave a drunk smile. 'Thank you for helping me get there.'

'You don't know how much you helped me, you know?'

Violeta peered. She could hardly see her granddaughter's face without her glasses on, but she knew every curve and contour of it.

'It was a nice send-off,' she said quietly.

'It was a nice send-off,' Desiree repeated.

'Do me a favour, will you, *cariña*?' Violeta asked.

'Anything, what do you need?'

Desiree looked around the room to see what she'd forgotten to put within Granny's reach on her bedside table. She had her thick glasses, the old tiny iPod Nano and the huge headphones to listen to her favourite Latin artists at night. She had her Ikea glass of fresh water. Her call button.

Desiree looked at her expectantly

'*Vete,*' Violeta said gently.

'Oh, right, yes, I'm going, Granny...'

'No, *vete*. Go.'

'Huh?'

'*A Nueva York...*'

'Oh.'

'*En serio*. Don't stay for me, *cariña*.'

Violeta's eyes were almost closed now.

'It will kill me, you not living your life, more than it will kill me the ache in my heart of missing you.'

Desiree's eyes welled up.

'Plus I have all these gadgets,' she said, nodding to the iPod Nano. 'I can see you every day.'

Desiree laughed to herself at the prospect of Granny trying to make a video call through a half-broken Nano, then cried at the thought of not being able to see her, to hug her, to smell her sweet shea-butter skin. She wouldn't be able to get back in a hurry if the worst happened.

'But what if you need me, Granny?'

'You were going to go and I was going to be fine. Nothing has changed, *mija*. I have Timothy and Shirlie, and Matthew. I have Wilfred in my memories.'

'Everything has changed for me.'

'More reason for you to go. *Disfrutate*. Have an adventure.'

A tear rolled down Desiree's cheek and even though Violeta couldn't see it, she wiped it away with her frail thumb.

'I would rather you were busy living there than waiting for me to die here.'

Desiree shook her head.

'Don't say that, Granny!'

'Well, it's true. Besides, I will come and visit you. You can take me to all those Cuban bars in Hell's Kitchen.'

She gave a gummy chuckle.

'Or the Jamaican ones in the East Village!' Desiree said, her eyes lighting up, knowing that this would never happen. They dulled again.

'I'm scared, Granny.'

'I know.'

'I lost him.'

'*Cariña*... We both lost the love of our lives, but you have time to find another.'

'I'm scared I'll never fall in love like that again.'

Violeta's face relaxed and lit up.

'You will.'

80

NOEMIE

May 2019, Florida

In the departures hall of Orlando International Airport, Noemie sat on a row of seats alongside three of her children playing on devices, while Camille walked up and down through the terminal with Gabriel. She sat staring at the shimmer on the shiny floor, waiting for reality to hit. For the sounds of her children to stop being so echoey. For the girls to stop bickering. For the time when she had to board the plane. At least her mother had stopped talking at her as she toddled Gabriel up and down the vast expanse of tiles, to tire him out ahead of their night flight.

Clair, Millie and Jasper had returned to the UK ahead of them. Martin and Jake were staying behind to deal with paperwork and repatriation. As Noemie stared into space somewhere in the middle of an airport, she wondered how she was going to get up and out of the chair. How she would physically get herself home, let alone anyone else.

Noemie had spent five days on the vast bed, staring at the ceiling fan, the folds in the curtains, the chipped architrave; drifting in and out of states of sleep and consciousness before her mother told her they were flying tomorrow.

'No! I'm waiting for Seb!' Noemie had slurred. *Je ne pars pas sans son corps!*

'We have to go, *mon amour*. Get the children home; they need their home. Plus we have to vacate the apartment. The goodwill of Mr Edwards is wearing thin.'

'But Seb!'

'Seb's father is taking care of him now, Noa.'

Camille had packed all the things strewn across the apartment and somehow they had made it to the airport. She'd shepherded her four grandchildren and catatonic daughter through Check-In, Security and the departures hall. There was no concierge to help them through, no French ambassador to clear their path. Camille was outraged, but still, she sat Noemie, Samuel, Alice and Mila in a row of seats while she walked Gabriel up and down, up and down.

Noemie blinked and turned her head slowly, to the line of children next to her. Samuel plugged into headphones, playing Minecraft on the cracked iPad. Alice and Mila tussling, pushing and pulling whatever game they were playing. Noemie stared at them. Did they not understand what had just happened? Noemie felt irritated, lost. The one person she needed right now wasn't here. She looked around the hall for a toilet sign. She needed the toilet. It would be a small test.

Je vais aux toilettes,' she said, lifting one of Samuel's headphone ears. Samuel blinked his acknowledgment. 'Watch your sisters.' Samuel blinked twice as Noemie pulled herself up, the effort hurting her bony frame after almost a week of barely eating; her muscles and strength starting to gnaw away, as she almost waded through treacle, to the toilet at the other end of the terminal. Far away from her children and her mother, without looking back.

In the ladies' bathroom Noemie stopped to examine her sallow reflection in the horizontal strip of mirror above the sinks: her cheekbones were haunting and her bright eyes dulled, as she pulled the skin down under one of them to examine what was there. To check that she was still alive.

'*À peine...*' she mumbled to herself. '*Mort.*'

She ran her fingers across her lips and remembered the last time Seb touched them, as he kissed her on the lake's edge, giddy because he and Jasper were about to do something fun. She didn't know from the touch of her cracked lips that he was happy to be going far from her, for some peace out on the water. She smiled at him, a little nervously, hoping that the break – space between the hurtling ashtray and the fun on the lake – had been a chance to draw a line under everything. To start afresh. But still, something made her feel weakened, something irked her as he winked at Millie and said, 'Love you,' as he and Jasper clipped on their red life jackets and jumped onto their paddleboards.

Noemie's lips were no longer plump. They no longer tasted of watermelon. They were now dry and barren, so she felt in her pocket for lip balm. Perhaps it wasn't too late to embalm that kiss and preserve it forever. Then she realised this wasn't her jacket. She was wearing Seb's, as she had worn his jumper, his socks. As she had slept clutching his T-shirt so she could smell him and imagine he were there. The lip balm wasn't in the left pocket as it usually was. She put her hand in the right, sniffing the ribbed neck of his light grey bomber jacket at her collarbone, as she felt a stiff corner of card dig into her ribs. She slipped her hand inside the right pocket, to see if it concealed a keepsake she could cling to.

It was a postcard. Of a weird painting. Scary figures and telephones. She flipped it over.

It's him!

Although Noemie wasn't very familiar with Seb's writing – they dated in the age of swiping and texts – she knew it was his.

She gasped.

Something he had touched.

Something she could hold onto.

So she took it with her into the toilet cubicle, lest anyone try to take this memory away from her too.

Noemie locked the door, pulled down her harem trousers, slid down her knickers and sat on the toilet, turning the postcard over and over before she dared focus on the script long enough to read it:

I love you, I need you. I want to make beautiful babies with you, if you'd do me the honour... If you'd join me, when this ship docks? Sx

It was addressed to Desiree Cruz-Campbell of Clapham, London.

Noemie let out a little howl from the confined walls of her cubicle, then stood up swiftly, spun around, and vomited. Her breathing started to race again as the room started to spin and a trickle of sweat ran down her spine.

This must be a hallucination.

'No!'

All the drugs! I'm seeing things!

'Are you OK in there, miss?' came a kindly American voice from the other side. Noemie stifled her sob.

My heart can't take this.

'*Oui*, yes!' Noemie called quietly, between the racing breaths. 'Fine...'

She flushed the toilet to let the concerned woman know she

was OK, to send her away. 'Nervous about flying!' she lied, before placing her hand over her mouth like the silencer on a gun.

'OK, miss, godspeed...'

Noemie leaned her head against the cubicle door as she heard the footsteps disappear in the distance and tears dropped onto the postcard still clutched in her hand, smudging the letters of Seb's plea.

'No!' she said to herself, standing tall. Firmly, decisively. *'Non.'*

She tore the postcard four times, into sixteen fragments, then lifted the blood-smeared lid of the sanitary bin and threw the pieces into it.

'No,' she said finally, before exiting the cubicle, glancing at her reflection in the mirror, and going to find her mother and children, who were waiting to board the plane.

EPILOGUE
JUNE 2019, SPICE ISLAND, HAMPSHIRE

As Desiree stepped onto the cobbled streets and started walking a loop towards her small hotel, she heard Sue pointedly double lock the front door of the care home behind her.

Misery.

The shackle of the door and the noise of her Zapatos Cruz heels scraping the empty street reminded her that she didn't *have* to wear them. She was on the final stretch. The cool cobbles were dry, so she took her shoes off and walked in stockinged feet, clutching her heels in her hand.

She walked elegantly, daringly, as if she were on a tightrope, past the tiny terraced house Wilfred and Violeta had first lived in as new Brits and newly-weds; round the bend of the Spice Island Inn and along the seafront wall, towards the family home she and Matthew had grown up in by the grammar school. Desiree inhaled the salty air and walked along the arches of the Hotwalls – once barracks but now galleries, all closed. As she looked at the starry sky above Battery Row she thought of another Battery, near where she stayed in New York. Another tip of another city island, where a battery of cannons also lined up to protect territories and hearts.

She thought of Seb, and looked up to the sky, wondering what he would want her to do. She looked out to the glittering ferry coming into the Solent, and thought of the lives and loves of all the people on board, coming into dock. She wondered if perhaps she could jump ship. Make a new life for herself in New York.

She thought about the phone call, four weeks and one day ago. The call *before* the call from Penelope to tell her that her love had died. The phone call that changed everything, yet nothing at all.

She was at her desk at Rennie + Byrd in Shoreditch, putting the finishing touches to a pitch. It was after midnight and the office was empty and quiet, punctuated by the occasional whirr of the sleeping photocopier; the buzz of the elevator in the lift shaft going up to the top-floor bar. Ivy's reception phone clicking to say there were messages. Desiree rubbed her eyes and weighed up whether to plough on, refining the pitch, or whether to walk away, get the car that was waiting downstairs for her, and go home. With every minute that ticked by tinkering with the presentation she knew her sparkle would fade a little for the crucial pitch tomorrow.

The light and sudden vibration of her mobile on her desk made Desiree jump. She assumed it was the driver downstairs, checking to see if she was coming, and did a double take when Seb's name flashed up. Her phone screen softly lit her face in the dark office and she answered the call with a smile.

'Seb!'

There was noise in the background. Trumpets and trombones, cheers and laughter. It sounded as if he were walking the Yellow Brick Road to Oz. He was leaning into a call booth no one used on Main Street in Disney World, talking into his mobile, the light parade passing slowly through the crowds.

'Hey.'

'How's it going?' Desiree asked, perplexed by the call but happy to hear his voice.

'Terribly!' He laughed.

'Oh.'

'But it's good, it's all good. I've had an epiphany. I've seen the light.'

He rubbed his temples as a gaudy illuminated float passed, carrying actors dressed up as characters from *Frozen* wearing itchy-looking wigs and waving at the crowds. The bizarreness of the balmy evening added to the febrile madness of his heart.

'*Long Distance Relationships*, Desi. I saw it again. In Miami.'

'Oh, cool!'

There was something hurried about his call, as if he knew he were on borrowed time.

'I bought you a postcard of it, but I haven't mailed it yet. It's still in my jacket pocket.'

'Oh, right. Well, that's OK, I have our print, don't I?'

Desiree looked around her office in the dark, even though the picture was on the wall back in her flat.

'I couldn't wait for the postcard to reach you, to tell you how I feel.'

'What?'

'So I thought, fuck it, Desiree. I just had to call you.'

'What?'

'I love you.'

Desiree put her free hand to her cheek in disbelief.

'Like Wilfred loved Violeta.'

She wanted to tell him not to mess with her.

'I know that ship might have sailed, and you might want all this with Tarek, not me...'

Seb couldn't see Desiree, smiling into her phone. 'But I want it with you, Desi. I want to be with you. Have babies with you, if we're lucky. I would love it. Millie and Jasper would love it, I know it. If you would do me the honour.'

'Seb, oh my God, what are you doing?'

She slumped back in her chair and rubbed her eyes.

'Are you out of your mind?'

'No!' He laughed. 'This is the most clear I have ever been about anything in my life. I *love* you. I want to be with you. I'm in this crazy place in a fucking crazy situation and I couldn't wait a second longer to tell you that, OK?'

Desiree heard a brass horn honk somewhere near Seb, adding to the feeling that this was all a big joke. She sat in total shock.

'I just couldn't wait to get home; or wait for the postcard to get there. I had to tell you, Desi, I love you. What do you say?'

* * *

'Yes,' Desiree whispered to the sea, as she walked along the smooth stone wall, to the sound of the lapping water.

ACKNOWLEDGMENTS

This is my first book with Boldwood and I'm so excited for the journey ahead and to be reunited with the Axis of Awesomeness that is my editor Sarah Ritherdon, alongside my brilliant agent Becky Ritchie. You are both gems and I feel that, together, the world is our oyster. Thank you so much for everything you both do, it's great to have the band back together.

The wider Boldwood team are just wonderful and I'm so grateful for all the energy you put into making books fly: Nia Beynon, Claire Fenby-Warren, Jenna Houston, Megan Townsend, Emily Ruston, Tara Loder, Caroline Ridding, Laura Kingston, Emily Yau and Amanda Ridout – you publishing queens.

Thank you to Alice Moore for the brilliant cover design, and Sue Smith, Sue Lamprell and Sandra Ferguson for the eagle eyes and super-slick copy-editing and proof-reading. Who knew it was 'just deserts' and not 'just desserts'? I didn't!

Research wise, thank you Alison Start for sharing years of dedicated nursing experience and the vernacular with me, and to Elise Armitage, Queen of Guernsey, for reminding me of our fun times on the island. Thanks also to Louise Massie for enlightening me on the world of architecture, how you got to where you are, and what it's like to be a female architect. Thanks to Bekah Nicolas, library service goddess who is a fount of knowledge, a cheerleader and a treasured friend. Paige and Greg Toon, thank you for your bookish wisdom, generosity and friendship; Francesca Brown, thank you for your immense support – you are lovely; and thank you beta readers Ian Critchley, Kathleen Whyman, Guro Eide and Anna Black. Thank you too Kendra Okereke for being my friend, my millennial sense checker and my inspiration in more ways than you could possibly know.

This book is the first published since my beautiful dad passed away suddenly. I had no idea while I was writing it that grief was about to hit me like a truck – although perhaps that helped me better understand my characters during the edits. Usually my dad devoured my paperbacks, shortly after being released, and would send me long and enthusiastic emails telling me what he loved, what tickled him, what he thought was clever – and occasionally what he didn't like so much – with humour and kindness. His feedback was always full of generosity and pride and I am grateful to have had such a warm and loving dad.

I am grateful too to my mum Judi and stepmum Gerlinde for their strength and support, and my siblings and stepsiblings who came together as we stood shoulder to shoulder in heartbreak.

Final thanks to the rocks that kept me going while writing about love and loss; and soon after when we faced it together: Mark, Felix and Max. Thanks to your love, hugs and support, along with my dad's spirit, I still believe like he did, that every day is a gift.

@zoefolbigg

MORE FROM ZOË FOLBIGG

We hope you enjoyed reading *The Three Loves Of Sebastian Cooper.* If you did, please leave a review.

If you'd like to gift a copy, this book is also available as an ebook, digital audio download and audiobook CD.

Sign up to Zoë Folbigg's mailing list for news, competitions and updates on future books.

https://bit.ly/ZoeFolbiggNews

ABOUT THE AUTHOR

Zoë Folbigg is the bestselling author of four novels including the chart-topping The Note. She had a broad career in journalism writing for magazines and newspapers from Cosmopolitan to The Guardian and Sunday Times Style, plus a weekly column in Fabulous magazine. She married Train Man (star of The Note) and lives with him and their children in Hertfordshire.

Visit Zoë Folbigg's website: https://www.zoefolbigg.com/

Follow Zoë on social media:

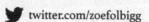

twitter.com/zoefolbigg

facebook.com/zoefolbiggauthor

instagram.com/zoefolbigg

bookbub.com/authors/zoe-folbigg

tiktok.com/@zoefolbigg

Boldwood

Boldwood Books is an award-winning fiction publishing company seeking out the best stories from around the world.

Find out more at www.boldwoodbooks.com

Join our reader community for brilliant books, competitions and offers!

Follow us
@BoldwoodBooks
@BookandTonic

Sign up to our weekly deals newsletter

https://bit.ly/BoldwoodBNewsletter